The Basel Exodus

Being Part 2 of The Basel Trilogy

Ian H. Lane

This is a work of fiction. Names, characters, organisations, places, events and incidents are either products of the author's imagination or are used fictitiously.

ISBN-13: 978-1530396184
ISBN-10: 1530396182

Printed by CreateSpace. An Amazon.com Company

Dedication

For Benjamin, Daniel, James, Matthew and Toby (in alphabetical order) my lively and sporty grandsons in the UK and Australia

Contents

Acknowledgements	Page i
A Word of Explanation - False Memory Syndrome	Page ii
The Story So Far	Page 1
The Turning Point	Page 3
Chapters 1 to 41	Pages 7 to 497
Glossary of Terms	Page 498
And what next?	Page 502
About the Author	Page 503

Acknowledgements

With grateful thanks to:

Herr Kurt H Freiermuth, Direktor, Untersuchungsgefängnis, Basel-Stadt (the remand prison) for providing information and the opportunity to visit the women's wing of the prison.

Dr Jeremy Stephenson, a President of the Strafgericht Basel-Stadt (Basel criminal court) for a detailed account of how a murder trial would proceed. What is correct in this novel is due to Dr Stephenson, any errors are those of the author.

Herr Christian Anderegg of Airport Helicopter Basel for guidance on hiring one of their helicopters.

Sonia Dell, a friend of long standing, who with her husband Dr Dennis Dell made us most welcome as their guests during their twenty years in Basel. Sonia was most helpful as a translator and in negotiating fact-finding visits in Basel including those to the helicopters, the remand prison and the criminal court.

A word of explanation regarding false memory syndrome.

At a time when many accusations of historic sexual abuse are being made and many perpetrators punished, it is worth remembering that not all such accusations are factually based. There are those who jump on the bandwagon making false accusations for a variety of reasons and also irresponsible therapists who create false "memories" in the minds of their patients. All accusations must, of course, be taken very seriously but they must also be tested no less critically than accusations of wrongdoing of any other nature.

Sam's "big book" is *"Victims of Memory - Sex Abuse Accusations and Shattered Lives"* by Mark Pendergrast, Second Edition 1996, Upper Access inc, Hinesberg, Vermont: ISBN 0942679180 and on Kindle.
This is a highly regarded work on the subject and gives a salutary warning of the harm that can be done by therapists planting false memories.

Sam also refers to a study by the British academic, Professor Jean La Fontaine for the Department of Health for England and Wales, published by HMSO in 1994 as *"The Extent and Nature of Organised and Ritual Abuse"*
ISBN 0113217978 9780113217977
She has said of this publication, "In 1994 I reported to the Department of Health that in the 84 cases in England and Wales that were the basis of my research, I could find no supporting evidence for the existence of such a satanic cult."

The Story So Far

As told in The Basel Formula, Part 1 of The Basel Trilogy

Elizabeth Fielder, born Lizaveta Feldman, Moscow, 12th June 1964, an agent of the SVR the successor to Russia's KGB, is in prison in Basel, Switzerland. She is charged with the murder, on the night before the city's annual *Fasnacht* carnival, of a colleague Eugene Preston, also known as Vladimir. She had come to Basel with Peter Lewis her boss, the director of a small north-London scientific glassware company, to make a delivery to a research laboratory there. The company had been targeted by the SVR, who had been led to think that it provided the *entrée* to the laboratory which they believed was developing a drug which they planned to steal. Elizabeth and Peter are lovers but the affair is fast unravelling as Peter's son is suffering psychologically from the absence of his father, for which situation the boy blames Elizabeth.

Keeping the Russians under surveillance both in London and in Basel was Israel's Mossad in the person of Sam Charles. The SVR had been set up by Mossad but the project had taken a turn that affronted Sam who resigned at the debriefing in Tel Aviv. He had fallen for Elizabeth almost from his first sight of her and he is determined to secure her liberty, though how he will do so is very far from clear to him.

Now read on!

The Turning Point

Tuesday 8th July 1997, 10.55 p.m.

Henryk Pankiewitz stood at the window of his apartment in Zamenhofa in northern Warsaw. It was nearly 11 o'clock and once he had finished his night-cap of Zubrowka he would be making his way to bed. He looked down from the fifth floor at the memorial which stood on the edge of the gardens across the road from the apartment - the Memorial to the Warsaw Ghetto Uprising which had been there since 1948 and which he had lived opposite for the last 23 years. They said it was built from stone intended by Hitler for the construction of a triumphal arch. That always appealed to him, it seemed an appropriate judgment on the man's arrogance and overweening pride. Henryk kept a proprietorial eye on the memorial, its presence somehow reassured him - there *was* justice in this world even though it didn't always seem to catch up with those who deserved it.

Visitors came to the memorial day in, day out. Some came in parties, some in small groups and others on their own. Some came to it as "one of the sights to be done", clicked away with their cameras and went. Others were less hurried, spending time to take in the figures on either side and to give time to reflection or prayer. They came, both Jew and Gentile, to this memorial which was but one of a great number that crowded the city. There were many reminders of the violence that had engulfed Warsaw and from which the city had emerged as surely, though not always as attractively attired, as the phoenix.

Henryk was about to draw the curtains when a taxi

pulled up across the road and a solitary man climbed out, paid the driver and set off for the far side of the memorial. Henryk's eyes were sharp and he took in the beard and thought he detected a scull cap. He guessed that the man might be in his thirties, he certainly moved energetically. He wasn't going to see much of the memorial in the dark. Weren't there enough hours of light in the day? Still, perhaps he was passing through town and this was his only opportunity for making a visit. Henryk waited for him to reappear and in a few minutes he did so. He seemed intent on the relief panel on the near side, at any rate it was illuminated by the street lights. Henryk knew it well: a panel carved in the gray granite depicting a rabbi and his people being marched to the death camps. Some visitors didn't see it, their attention taken up with the heroic bronze statues on the other side. This man hadn't missed it and he continued to stand there, evidently gripped by what he saw. And then, to Henryk's surprise, he seemed to take a few steps of dance before checking himself. Had he danced or was he merely unsteady on his feet? After a pause to take another look at the panel he set off southwards at a brisk pace. 'A drunk or some sort of religious nut I expect,' muttered Henryk Pankiewitz. He downed the last of the vodka, drew the curtains and headed for his bedroom. But, as it happened, the sightseer was neither drunk nor a religious nut and the impression made on him that evening was to prove the turning point in his life.

Chapter 1

Monday 10th March 1997

The door of the interview room closed behind Elizabeth Fielder and the prison officer as they returned to the women's wing of the *Untersuchungsgefängnis Basel-Stadt* - the Basel Remand Prison. There was a moment's silence before her Swiss interrogators spoke.

'So, what now Erik? What do you make of the woman? How much wiser are we after our two hours with her than we were when we left Bern this morning?'

'Somewhat wiser, though I confess there's a lot more I'd like to know, Uri.'

'She certainly didn't confess, did she?'

'Not to spying, no. About the killing she's confused, though whether that's genuine or put on I don't know.'

Lieutenant Erik Blum and Captain Uri Spiegel stood at the window of a large room of the Basel Public Prosecutor's Office which was conveniently placed next to the remand prison. They weren't local officers but members of the Federal Prosecutor's staff from Bern, the Swiss capital. Their concern was with matters of State Security rather than with commonplace crime. Beside the security aspects of the case it had been necessary for them to deal with the investigation into the killing of which she was accused, a matter that would normally have been dealt with by the Basel-Stadt Public Prosecutor and which might well be passed back to him to bring to court if they decided that there were no security offences with which to charge her.

They were a contrasting pair. Blum tall dark, clean-shaven and a shade morose, Spiegel short and round with a goatee beard, a healthy extrovert. Blum in sports coat and navy trousers, Spiegel in an expensive dark gray lightweight suit, probably of Italian origin. Blum with a dark tie that was never quite in place, Spiegel with a yellow bow tie patterned with small blue dots. Two men in their thirties, used to working together effectively, but who would never be close friends. Blum cared little about what others thought of him, Spiegel always had an eye to the impression he was making, particularly with attractive women.

They were looking at the suspect's photograph and the summary of particulars from her passport.

'Elizabeth Fielder's certainly a good looking woman, Uri. The photograph is a good likeness but it doesn't really do her justice. When you see her in the flesh, her personality makes a powerful impression even in a place like this. A lively, warm and very intelligent woman. A pretty woman. No, she's a beauty without a doubt. And a good team player, I suspect. If I were still doing recruiting for our Service I'd certainly offer her a job.'

'They call it the "halo effect", Erik. A pretty woman - sorry, a beautiful woman - sways your judgment, I'm afraid. It's just as well you're not still doing the rounds of our universities selling careers in secret work to the boys and girls.' He was amused at Blum's response to the woman. It was unlike him to speak in this way, if he'd had such thoughts in the past he'd kept them to himself.

'Well the Russians seem to have selected her for intelligence work - so I'm not alone in my assessment, am I? Besides an encouragingly high proportion of my recruits are still with us and they're doing good work.'

'I'll give you that, Erik. OK, go through what we know

and what we have been able to discover.'

'Fine, Uri, there's a good deal more that we would like to know but the score at the moment is this. Her name is Elizabeth Fielder but her real name appears to be Lizaveta Feldman. Born 12th June 1964 in Moscow - making her age 32. That's if we believe what she says, although I can't see any good reason for her to have invented it. She entered Switzerland on a false Canadian passport but she admits to being Russian. The passport particulars tally perfectly, of course: brunette hair, greenish-brown eyes and height 5 feet 9 inches, that's 175 centimetres in proper units. I'll come back to the passports in a moment. She was formally arrested in hospital, the Basel *Kantonsspital*, on Tuesday 18th February, the second day of the Fasnacht Carnival. The killing took place late on the Sunday evening, around 11 p.m. - five hours before *Moorgestraich*, the 4.00 a.m. start of the carnival. It's not a time that the Basel police would have chosen for a murder investigation but then crime isn't generally carried out with the convenience of the police in mind! There doesn't seem to be any doubt that she was the killer.

'The victim's name was Eugene Preston, though the real first name was Vladimir. Family name isn't known. Another Russian passing himself off as a Canadian – again the Canadian passport was obtained irregularly. She was found on the Monday morning on the floor of her room at the Hotel International in Basel, lying unconscious beside his corpse with a small pistol beside her. The bullet that the pathologist removed from his brain had come from the same handgun, which had her fingerprints on it and those of nobody else. The bullet had entered the back of the victim's head, so he was probably attempting to flee from her when he was killed. We've got enough evidence against her for the murder charge. Short of having a witness to testify that they saw the shooting take place, the evidence is as compelling as you can imagine. Elizabeth Fielder herself claims not to be able to remember what happened. The medical people have suggested she's possibly suffering from trauma induced amnesia. No doubt the shrinks will be able to encourage her to work at remembering!

'The victim had been no stranger to her, she had known him in London where they claimed to be cousins. He did business with an Englishman who ran a company in London. Preston introduced her as his cousin to the Englishman, Peter Lewis. Lewis gave her a job as his secretary and she later extended the scope of her duties by becoming his mistress. More of that later. They certainly were not strangers - Elizabeth and Eugene or, in reality, Lizaveta and Vladimir - but then murder by a stranger is less common than murder by a relation or an acquaintance.

'Their Canadian passports were checked out with Ottawa and found to have been obtained irregularly. Suspicion about her Canadian nationality was aroused when she came to in hospital on the Monday afternoon. Fortunately the police officer guarding her had the presence of mind to record her first words which turned out to be in Russian. Basel acted promptly and called us in.

'At first she wasn't very anxious to talk. But that was probably as much due to her shocked reaction to being charged with murder, as to the unwillingness to come clean that you would expect a foreign agent to show when caught. We've been very gentle, eventually coaxing information out of her without having recourse to threats. This is, let me see, yes my fourth meeting with her. She's told us something about her activities here and in London but the problem facing us now is whether she's been completely honest about what she was up to here in Switzerland.

'You remember, Uri, there were a couple of happenings around the beginning of the Fasnacht carnival that are still on the file as unsolved mysteries. One of them certainly involved the Russians - you remember the Ambassador having to come here to collect his Second Secretary after he was caught at the SBB Station with a pile of bank statements for members of the Council of State and some other highly respected members of our upper echelons in his briefcase.'

'I could hardly forget it, Erik.'

'And then there was what the young boy - the *legitimate* son of our young woman's employer and lover - called the beginning of World War III. That took place on the Monday afternoon as the main carnival procession was on its way around the city, an entirely separate show.'

'Yes, the kidnapping *and rescue* of the boy, his mother and a Swiss woman, Frau Gold.'

'It seemed too much of a coincidence that all those things were going on at the same time as our young woman was waiting to be charged with killing a colleague from the Russian Foreign Intelligence Service. And her assistance this afternoon has suggested that the kidnapping wasn't just a coincidence: it was part of the operation that had brought Vladimir to Basel, though she says she knows nothing about the business of the bank statements.'

'She was quick enough to admit to being a Russian but her membership of the Russian Foreign Intelligence Service took a litlle longer to uncover, didn't it?'

'Well, put yourself in her shoes, Uri, she is in enough trouble without having to add to it. But then, I think, perhaps she began to worry about her safety, about whether she was in danger - not from us but from her former SVR employers in Moscow - either that or she realised that she would be better off coming clean with us, getting it all off her pretty chest, making a clean breast of it so to speak.' He smiled. 'And in any case it wouldn't have been easy for her to deny Russian origins after saying quite a lot in that tongue as she came to in hospital.'

The two men laughed, Spiegel as much at the impression she had made on his colleague as at any humour in Blum's comment.

'You have a point there, Eric, she may well be scared of her SVR paymasters – we'll have to make sure that there's an armed protection unit around when she attends the maternity unit at the hospital and if she goes to court for the remand hearings.'

Blum continued, 'She's admitted that poor Vladimir was involved in a larger enterprise but she denies being directly involved.'

'Do you believe her, Erik?'

'On balance, yes I do. Let's go over what she said about her involvement. She won't go back any further than early last year when she got the job with Lewis, at his scientific glassware business in some unfashionable part of London, but it's likely that she was up to something in Canada or the USA before that.'

'Probably that's far enough back for our purposes but we can think about trying to get her to go back to her USA days later, might produce something for us to pass on to the CIA, build up some credit with them in return for future favours.'

'More like getting you a trip to Langley, Uri. Give you time with their Liaison Officer - Sarah Williams isn't it? - the one who brings a whole new depth of meaning to the word "liaison"!'

Spiegel flushed, 'You shouldn't pay attention to office rumours, Eric.'

'Of course not Uri, but you should take more care - it attracts attention when you give so much more time and attention to her visits than you do when Liaison Officers from other agencies call on us in Bern.'

'The attraction is the CIA and the clout it carries - not its emissary, Eric.'

'I don't doubt you, not at all. I was just warning you against small minded people who put a more interesting and human construction on the evidence before them!'

'Coffee?'

They moved back to the table and poured themselves a couple of cups from the vacuum pitcher. They took seats facing one another across the table. Blum suspected that his superior was returning the discussion to a more formal basis, his comments about the cool blonde from Langley had probably been too accurate for Uri's comfort.

Spiegel took charge of the review, 'Forget her probable activities in the New World for the time being. If our masters agree, we might leave the Americans to do their own interrogation, rather than take up our time with it. So let's look at what may concern us directly. It's March 1996 and she steps into the shoes of a dead woman when she takes over as Lewis' secretary. She knew that her predecessor was going to be got out of the way but she had no idea just how thoroughly, or so she says. Persons unknown, but in touch with her late lamented friend Vladimir, drive a car into a Mrs Ash and kill her.'

'Mrs Nash, Uri. It wasn't until her funeral that she was reduced to ash.'

'The pun may work in both English and German, Erik, with ash and *Asche* - well it almost works in German, but it's not in particularly good taste.' Blum knew that the comment was more on his earlier introduction of the Langley woman than on his reference to the disposal of the mortal remains of Lewis' secretary. Spiegel continued, 'Our Elizabeth took the vacant job and her task was to get news of Lewis coming here, to Basel, with a delivery of glass to the business of his friend Jakob Gold. And the visit took nearly a year to come off, so she had plenty of time to get to know Lewis, become his lover and have a child by him.'

'A child that's not due until August and that she says is Lewis'.'

'So why all this Russian messing around with Lewis and his business?'

'You've just said that there was to be a delivery to Gold's business here. Seemingly their security is very tight and Vladimir was after some drug they were developing, wanting the product and the research and development paperwork.'

'Just so, Erik, and what might have been the Russian plan of action?'

'Our young woman insists that she wasn't told by Vladimir, but she links it with the kidnapping of the boy and the two women. Though she claims that the first she heard of the events of World War III, as the boy called them, was when Lewis told her about them here after she had been arrested. We can check that from our tape of their meeting, at any rate we can find out what Lewis had to tell her on the topic. Anyway she links the kidnapping of Frau Gold with an attempt to get the drug.'

'That gives us the identity of one of the combatants, the Russians. But the other side, the rescuers? Everything points to the Americans, doesn't it?'

'It does, all right. But just think for a moment, if you were responsible for an operation by the CIA or some other outfit from the USA would you make sure it was doing all but fly the Stars and Stripes to attract attention? They were almost shouting, "We're Yanks having a post-Cold War spat with the Ruskies!" '

'So, if not the Yanks, who was it? Who were the others Erik? Our masters would be much happier and would sleep more soundly at night if we could tell them. If only we could get hold of the mystery American - Sam Charles wasn't it? - the man who spent the whole of Sunday with her until a little more than an hour before the killing? An American. Planned or coincidental? Which was it, I wonder?'

Blum had his suspicions but kept them to himself, 'You're probably right about the Americans, perhaps some band of irregulars rather than Langley's troops. Perhaps we could offer her to the CIA for questioning about her earlier history provided they come clean about fighting their wars on our soil? Bern would rap them over the knuckles and tell them not to do it again, but it would be a relief to have them own up and let us put our file away. And the Brits, they've still to interview Peter Lewis and I assume that they will wish to speak with our woman about what she was up to in London as well as about the murder of her predecessor as Lewis' secretary. That's if they're not too busy pursuing their ex-employees who so admire their old service that they can't help telling all in books about it! Anyway, if they've got time for it, I can't see any objection to letting them see her, though she doesn't seem to be admitting to anything very untoward in

London either. As I said, the Brits have yet to see Lewis. We've seen him, of course, and let him go back home afterwards, though he has returned here once since then. He seems genuinely bemused by all that's happened. In fact he seems in a pretty shaky state. The consequences of his fathering her child have come as a shock to him. He feels a responsibility for her and their child, I think. And he can't be too happy at the thought of his child spending its first few years in jail with the mother. He's been separated from his wife for a while but now he's returned to the nest – and their son is very disturbed by it all – so Peter Lewis has a plate-full of problems!'

'So, Erik, she was part of a team involved in commercial espionage against a Swiss company - Gold's outfit - she was placed with Lewis to find out when he was going to Basel and to facilitate their use of his van to get into Gold's premises. But, Erik, can we show that she in fact did anything that we could charge her with and have a reasonable hope of success in the Courts? You've just as good as admitted that she doesn't seem to have been involved with active espionage either here or possibly in London. And do we really want to publicise what happened? After all a conviction on the murder charge will put her behind bars for quite a long time. There's also the passport offence. We don't really want more difficulties with Russia ... '

'You mean let their money flow in, give their liberated businessmen the facilities they need for keeping their money out of harm's way ... '

'Precisely, Eric, though of course we wouldn't wish to put it quite that way on paper. The recorders are off, I hope.'

'Yes, to the best of my knowledge and belief, though I'm not sure I'd trust these Baslers not to be listening in on us.' He had raised his voice as he finished the sentence as a gesture of defiance against anyone who might have the impertinence to be listening to their conversation. He returned to Spiegel's question, 'On the present evidence there's no mileage in it. None at all, we'd have no success whatsoever with a prosecution for espionage.'

The idea of being overheard by their Basel colleagues was not an attractive one for Captain Spiegel, particularly with the comments that Blum had made about him and Langley's Liaison Officer. 'Right, Erik, let's wind this up. Collect our tapes - and any others you find - from the sound engineers and we'll get back onto the *Autobahn* to Bern. I'm taking my wife to the theatre tonight and don't want to be late.' Blum didn't let on that his niece was attending a committee meeting of a women's organisation at which Mrs Spiegel was due to preside. If Spiegel wished to live dangerously ... that was his problem. He collected the tapes, watching the engineer closely as he sought his confirmation that there weren't any other recordings. The engineer gave the required assurance, but nevertheless Blum wondered.

As they put their briefcases with the tapes into the boot of the car a thought occurred to Blum, 'One final point, Uri, the drug and the paperwork - they were safe, no one got their hands on them?'

'Completely safe, Erik. At any rate the Russians are not believed to have made off with any Swiss property, either tangible or intellectual. But I have my suspicions as to whether the drug ever existed, I won't explain why, I've no wish to compromise my source of information. And if there were no drug in the first place it looks as though Vladimir and his team were set up by someone else. But who?'

'The other combatants in World War III is the most straightforward guess.'

'I'd like to hope so, otherwise it becomes even more convoluted and impenetrable and there's enough fog about already, surrounding this case as well as on the *Autobahn*. Don't take too long to get back but do drive carefully, Erik. I don't want to disappoint my wife this evening.'

Blum smiled to himself and wondered who it really was that would be disappointed if he were late in getting Spiegel back to Bern.

Chapter 2

Monday 17th March 1997

"This secret fire goes out when you use the bellows ... turn your back on it and attend to your duties, and then it will blaze."

C S Lewis, The Problem of Pain.

'Another day in captivity'. She looked at her watch, making her eyes focus in the morning light. 'Only 6.25', she told herself. It would be fifty minutes before they unlocked the door of her cell and she could join the other women for breakfast. She would give herself another twenty minutes in bed and then spend a leisurely half hour getting herself ready for the day ahead. She was glad to have a cell to herself and that, for the thirteen and a half hours from being locked in at 5.45 each evening until being let out for breakfast, she was not being held in close proximity to another woman. Even with someone of acceptable personality and habits, being caged together would have been hard to bear for Elizabeth. Not perhaps the proximity but more the inability to withdraw to be on your own *if* you wished, the knowledge that an authoritarian organisation had imposed its will on you and said, 'From now on the two of you will be together whether you like it or not.' That hadn't happened and she was grateful. She had a lively inner life and solitude was no problem to her. She was using the time to the full and varying each day so as to head off the advent of *ennui*.

Today would see her first monthly visit to the *Strafgericht*, the court, in the afternoon. To keep her in custody they had to get renewed permission at intervals from the

Hoftrichter, the remand judge, and this involved visits to the court. Her lawyer had told her that there was no need for her to attend as there was no possibility, with the nature of the murder charge against her, of being given bail. But a visit to the court was a chance to be out of this prison, for a moment to set foot elsewhere, to breathe other air, even if it were polluted city air, to see the sky through the branches and leaves of any trees which might grow there. Not much was likely to happen but it was an outing she would not miss.

At 6.45 she got out of bed and made for the toilet facilities near the door and screened from the rest of the cell by the cupboard behind her bed head. Her own lavatory and wash basin, quite civilised really when you compared it with what you might face in some countries, even if the lavatory pan was without seat or lid. She took her time to wash and spent a while brushing her hair. She dressed in her own underwear and then pulled on a sloppy jumper and jeans, she liked to be comfortable in the prison and remand prisoners were allowed to wear their own clothes. After lunch she would change for the visit to court, she was always concerned about how she looked when she saw her lawyer or other visitors and now even more so when she went to court - she wanted to declare that she was herself and not beaten down by circumstances and events, though she was careful not to appear arrogant and over assertive. She applied a light makeup and lipstick carefully. Once again she regretted their refusal to let her have perfume - nothing containing alcohol was permitted. Still it was better to have the cell to herself and do without perfume than to have it and be forced to share. Elizabeth tidied her bed, pulling the undersheet tight over the mattress, shaking and folding the striped duvet and placing the small pillow on top of it.

Then she picked up the book she had been reading the previous evening, a life of the composer Franz Liszt. She knew why she had chosen that book. How long ago was it now? Only six months! In September she had been in Southern France with Peter and they had spent an idyllic day at *Fontaine du Vaucluse* where the poet Petrarch had once lived. She had done some research on Petrarch and his unfulfilled love for Laura, a chaste and married woman. Liszt had taken some of Petrarch's sonnets about his love for Laura and set them to music, later producing versions without the words for piano. Elizabeth's enforced stay in the Basel *Untersuchungsgefängnis*, the remand prison which was also known as the *Waaghof*, gave her time for research and she was keen to find out the significance that these sometimes tormented sonnets had for Liszt.

Her thoughts, which had turned to Peter, the father of the child she was carrying, were broken by the sound of the key in the door. She greeted the woman officer and went out into the common room area to have breakfast with her fellow inmates. They were a mixed bunch but she got on well enough with them. A few were into drugs and prostitution, some were there for theft, one was charged with wounding her husband, and made it clear that her only regret was that she hadn't killed him, another, Andrea, had killed her lover and, regretting it bitterly, had retreated into her shell, hardly communicating with anybody. Generally they were from the lower orders of Swiss society, casualties of the system and the cycle of deprivation as well as of their own selfishness and fecklessness. None to her were wholly bad and she had made it her task to befriend them, applying herself to learning the local *Basler Deutsch* as well as polishing up her *Hoch Deutsch*. She had discovered that the local dialect was not some bastard German of which the natives were ashamed, rather it was the language that they used daily for their important business as well as for private conversation, indeed to her surprise she had been told that the court used *Basler Deutsch*. The other women liked her for trying to speak to them in the local tongue. She nodded to the four or five companions at the table, '*Grüezi*'. The greeting was returned and she got a couple of smiles, though Andrea remained silent, wrapped up in her thoughts and remorse. Breakfast was much the same day by day but you could always vary the cereals and there was no objection to daily toast. The coffee was institutional but drinkable, at first you wondered why you bothered with the stuff but then you became accustomed to the beverage.

Generally their breakfasts were quiet affairs without a lot of talk unless there was some startling news on the TV, not world shattering political news of course - in Switzerland there was a feeling of being insulated from anything going on 'out there', they had even avoided joining the United Nations in case it should compromise their neutrality, a neutrality that had at times paid off handsomely - rather the supposedly interesting things that happened to film stars and other celebrities. The German TV and magazines usually had something of that sort to offer, some said that they invented it if there was no hard news! There was no lack of an audience or readership and, of course, such a need ought to be satisfied, especially when there were good Deutsch Marks and Swiss Francs to be made by the media tycoons. Today was one of the quiet days with the women none too enthusiastic at the prospect of another day inside. Towards the end of the meal Trudi, who was awaiting trial on a charge of supplying heroin, looked up from the other side of the table, 'Elizabeth more English lessons, please, this afternoon if you are able.'

'Once I'm back from my outing to the court I'll be free to see how you are progressing.'

'You like the idea of meeting with the judge don't you, Elizabeth - it won't do any good, he's not the one who's going to hear your case.'

'I know that, Trudi, but it just might make me feel better to look good for the occasion and get out of here for a short while.'

'It's not worth going, there's no hope of getting out of here before the trial. The Public Prosecutor tells him that we will re-offend or beat it if we're let out and the old judge believes him. I went once after the first time but I haven't bothered since then.'

'I need to get out even if it's only a ride in a prison van and a few minutes in the court. I need a few seconds out in the open air - I know we have exercise here out on the roof in the open air but you can't see anything but prison walls and that wire over the top to keep the helicopter taxi service away.'

They laughed.

'If a helicopter taxi called I'd give you all a lift and we'd go to some nice tropical island where we could do what we want, eat what we like and take what we like.' It was Greta who was being weaned off drugs by the prison doctor and the psychiatrist and who was not enjoying the experience.

'I miss trees and things that grow,' Elizabeth was wistful.

Greta responded, 'Is that all you miss? Would you be happy locked up in a prison in the forest with plenty of trees to keep you company?'

Elisabeth shook her head, 'No there's plenty else I miss ... '

'Like your man?'

'Like my man. Yes, like my man for a start.' But she knew that circumstances had taken Peter back to his family. She had memories – that was all – memories of those wonderful months with Peter ... and also of a day in the Alps with Sam Charles, that day when, later on, her whole world had come crashing down.

Andrea got up without a word and went off to her cell. The death of her lover at her hands was something she couldn't live with. The pills they gave did little to ease the guilt and grief she felt. In a few minutes one of the other women would take her a cup of coffee and stay for a while trying to ease the pain. She would be grateful but it wouldn't lessen the anguish. She had one wish and that was to kill herself. The prison staff knew that or at any rate suspected it and kept a close watch on her.

There was silence at the table until Greta spoke. 'I'm sorry I hurt her but it's so difficult having to avoid speaking about men, it's so unnatural and in that respect I'm very natural.' The others smiled, they were very natural too, but they did not laugh out loud as they had no wish to be heard by Andrea and hurt her further.

Trudi patted Elizabeth's stomach, 'With that growing in there you ought to be with your man so he can give you both some care and tenderness.'

Elizabeth nodded and sighed. If she did get out would Peter be in any state to help? He was still suffering from the breakdown that had overtaken him not long after her arrest. And she had no wish to further complicate his life or that of his family. In any case Andrea wasn't the only one suffering from remorse - Elizabeth bitterly regretted killing Vladimir, if only she had let him go when he tried to flee her room - that is what they had told her he was doing when she had fired the gun. Her mind went back to the events of that night but she still couldn't understand them, there was something there but try as she might she couldn't retrieve the memory. It was like being confronted by a locked cupboard holding things you needed but whose lock would not yield to any of the keys you had. If only she could get at the memory in all its detail she might begin to understand - she had dark suspicions about what had happened but she could not be sure. It was like waking from a nightmare and knowing that you had been disturbed, deeply disturbed, by things in your subconscious and at the same time being unable to identify them, to give shape or name to the spectre in your dreams.

And she too suffered from remorse, for Vladimir had been her friend and lover as well as a colleague, at any rate he had once been these things and, although he had afterwards done much to offend her, she still treasured the memory of their time in the USA. When they first worked together he had been an experienced KGB agent and she had been fresh from training school, on her first assignment in the West and enjoying the freedom and the lifestyle, or rather parts of that lifestyle. She had been selected as an agent on account of her good looks as much as for her linguistic and computer skills. She had been trained to use those good looks and her sexuality to get and keep employment and access to commercial secrets. The way to the secrets was often by way of the boss' bed and although it had been fun at first she had quickly come to loath the techniques she had been trained to employ and to despise the men who used her for their temporary pleasure. She understood something of the life of the women who were for the time being her companions, women forced to sell their bodies to buy their drugs. Women who had started foolishly and were now captives of the low life of this Swiss city. They would never have guessed that her sympathy was based on her personal experience, though they were aware of her real concern for them and their welfare.

She thought of Vladimir and sighed. In her heart of hearts she was aware of her guilt and of a growing conviction that, whatever the sentence that would be handed down for her crime, she would view it as a necessary expiation of her guilt. She was beginning to feel that if she were given the key of the *Waaghof* and told to go she would refuse and stay to take the punishment she deserved. No she wasn't suicidal like Andrea but she felt amidst the anguish that, if she were ever to be reconciled to herself and her conscience, she would first have to suffer the consequences of having killed a fellow human being and one who had once been her friend and lover. And then there was Peter. She had delivered one lover into the hands of the morticians and the other into the hands of the shrinks!

Someone was speaking to her, 'Are you all right Elizabeth?' She looked around and found that the others had left the table and that Greta was the only one left. 'You don't look too happy Elizabeth. Don't let it get you down, we need you to keep us going!'

'Sorry, I was lost in my thoughts. Life's a mess for all of us, isn't it, Greta.'

'For all of us and for some it's worse than for others. It can't be easy for a nice girl like you in here.'

'Killers aren't nice girls!'

'But you were pushed into doing it weren't you? You didn't set out to kill him did you?'

'No, but the horrible thing is that I can't remember

exactly what happened. There's something there that I just can't dig out of my memory.'

'Try the shrinks, they might be able to help.'

'I might even do that, Greta. Thanks for the idea.'

They piled their dishes up, took them off for washing and made for their cells to get ready before the morning's work making jigsaw puzzles. For most of them life was a puzzle and they had yet to find a satisfactory solution and quite likely they never would. 'Poor child,' she mused as she sat on the edge of her bed and felt it kicking, 'his father's had a breakdown and is in the hands of the shrinks and now his mother is also thinking about undergoing therapy!' And she knew that she would only be able to keep the child with her in prison until it was three. She wondered how they would both be able to cope with separation after that. Would Peter be able or willing to take responsibility for the child he had fathered in happier days?

***

'... And how did you have enjoyment with your visit to the court this afternoon?' There was an hour left before the evening meal and Trudi had come to Elizabeth's cell for her English lesson.

' “How did you enjoy”, is what you should say Trudi. But don't worry you're doing OK. By the way do you want to learn English English or the American variety?'

'The sort the Americans use, I would like to entertain American bankers and businessmen - you know, the upper end of the market.'

Elizabeth knew but she simply nodded, 'OK American English it will be if that's more useful.'

'How did you enjoy the trees at the court?'

'A lot. The police were in no hurry and they let me stand there outside the court, under the trees for a few minutes before we went in. It was a lovely afternoon, a blue sky, small cotton wool clouds, a warm breeze and the sun streaming through the fresh green leaves of the trees. I stood there and enjoyed the sun and the breeze, watching people go by. Some stop to look at you coming out of the prison van and you wonder what they are thinking about you, but that doesn't matter.' She paused and sighed. 'And it will be another month before I go there again. The visits to the maternity clinic at the *Frauenspital* aren't as good, you don't get any time outside. The doctors and nurses are kind enough but I'm sure that they think of me as a creature from another planet!'

'I've been there for abortions, I could not bring a kid up in my kind of business. And I wonder if I could have one after a couple abortions.' She was wistful, 'I'd like a kid sometime but not if I've got to give it the sort of childhood that I had got. Sometime I'm hoping that I'll get off drugs and off the streets, marry a husband and be a good wife and mother. But I think it's all a dream and I'm stuck with my way of life - what decent man, and I suppose there are some, would want me?'

'Don't despair Trudi! What about learning computer skills while you're in jail so you're set up for a job when you get out. If you can kick the drugs habit while you're here it will give you a good start and you could be using your American English for secretarial instead of sexual purposes.'

'The two things are different?'

'It helps if they are - unless you work for your husband!'

They laughed and there was understanding and comradeship.

'Thank you Elizabeth, you encourage me. You make better things seem possible - other people don't do that.'

She gave Elizabeth a hug and Elizabeth's eyes filled with tears. 'Never lose hope Trudi. Never lose hope.'

'I'm glad you enjoyed your trees. And how was the judge, I hope you didn't seduce him!'

'I doubt if I could have done that even if we had been locked up together in the cell at the court for the rest of the day. Still I think I looked my best and he won't forget me. Perhaps he'll even begin to look forward to our monthly meetings though he seemed pretty satisfied with life. But it was odd seeing life going on outside the railings, seeing people go by, oblivious of your real plight, with their own small concerns. It would have been nice to have been invited out to dinner by one or two of the men!'

'It's being in here Elizabeth, your imagination is playing tricks on you. Seeing any half decent man is going to convince you that you would like a date with him. I can tell you - I could do with a half decent man at the moment - even a quarter decent one would do!'

It was half an hour before their meal and Trudi left to do some laundry while Elizabeth went to take a shower. She would change back into her sloppy jumper and jeans for the evening. She would write up her diary for the day and continue putting her memories of childhood onto paper, being here was an opportunity to find out whether she had any ability as a writer and working through your memories was a way of using the solitude that this place gave in large quantities. Her long term memory surprised her with it's accuracy and detail, she found that she was able to recall just how she had felt at significant times in her life. It was the short or medium term memory that troubled her: Just what had gone on between her and Vladimir that night at the Hotel International? If only she could find out. Perhaps the shrink might be able to dredge the memory to the surface. She took her towel and made for the shower. The menu announced that they would be feasting on two fried eggs - *Zwei Spiegeleier* it said - spinach and boiled potatoes. She made the most of the opportunities for exercise as she wished to remain trim and attractive. She was glad that she had been able to remain concerned about herself and her appearance, unlike Andrea who had just let herself go and wandered around like a lost soul, and an unkempt one at that, but she was also glad not to be obsessed with herself. Tomorrow she would give Andrea some of her time - the Swiss girl had come to realise that Elizabeth also felt the pain of remorse and this meant that Elizabeth could get through to her in a way that the others couldn't. In just over one hour's time she would be locked in her cell once again and begin a time of rich recollection, taxing her memory and writing powers to the full. This time alone somehow helped her to be at the disposal of the others and perhaps of some help to them.

***

As she lay on her bed, locked into her cell for the night, Trudi's words came back to her:

'You make better things seem possible - other people don't do that.'

But for herself better things seemed suddenly so remote. For the moment her optimism had gone, drained away, leaving a sense of hopelessness. She knew she had to work at it to drive away this feeling. Remorse was one thing and to her it seemed appropriate and right. But despair and depression were foreign to her. She had to convince herself that for her too "better things were possible" - the encourager needed to be encouraged. She had to be buoyant to be of any use to the others, she owed it to them to sort herself out.

Her thoughts turned to Peter, the father of her child. She had begun the day with memories of a time of happiness together in southern France. She wondered how he was getting on and felt desperately sad for him. Sylvia, her lawyer, had passed on information on Peter's treatment: he was recovering from the breakdown but progress was slow. The tension from his teenage son's own psychiatric problems, caused by the break up of his marriage to Ruth, had nagged at him for months and the arrest of Elizabeth and her identification as a Russian agent had proved more than he could take. His sense of betrayal had been acute. It had hurt him badly to find that someone so close, so loved had deceived him as to her identity and purposes. But the attention of British Security had been the last straw for poor old Peter. Would better things be possible for him?

She remembered the night in January when they had celebrated Russian Christmas without Peter knowing the significance of it for her. She remembered his gift of the Steinway piano that evening. The melody of the Chopin Nocturne she had played came back to her. She wept for the memory of happiness past. Her memories of life with Peter were good ones. She knew him to be an upright, selfless man, caring for the employees of his small business and respected by them.

He had been separated from Ruth for some time and satisfied that his marriage was over before he and Elizabeth had fallen in love. He was certainly not a man who cheated on his wife or his lover. Her thoughts went to the first time they had slept together, to the delight they had found in one another that night at the Casterbridge

Hotel in Dorchester. A place quintessentially English. She remembered the Hardy novel she had finished while Peter was on his way to her from London. Was Hardy's desperate pessimism right? Was life as bad as he depicted? Some words from the final chapter of *The Mayor of Casterbridge*, the earlier thoughts of Elizabeth-Jane, came back to her:

> ".... happiness was but the occasional episode in a general drama of pain."

'Not so', she had said when she read it. Now she wondered. But then, that wonderful evening, she had been filled with such overwhelming happiness, not simply with that of sexual anticipation but with something far deeper that had permeated her whole being.

And the memory came to her of the visit earlier that day to the old Dorset hill fortress of Maiden Castle, the name a corruption of the Anglo Saxon *Mai Dun*, Hill of Strength. She pictured herself there, under the warm sun and blue sky, as she lay on the grassy summit of the hill. The pictorial detail had an incredible vividness, and it seemed to her she could again smell the warm, moist earth of the hilltop. Above all it was the memory of the skylark's song that held her. But beyond that song and its beauty was the memory of the experience of joy and longing that had so overwhelmed her there on the ancient hilltop. And as she remembered, the joy and longing returned, once again unbidden, unexpected and utterly transforming, taking possession of her. She abandoned herself to it and had no idea how long the experience lasted. She was grateful that it had come while she was locked in her cell, without anyone or anything to disturb her. As on the first occasion she heard herself say,

"Thank You", again wondering at the inadequacy of the words, and, as she had done on the Dorset hilltop, she crossed herself. A totally inadequate response, she knew, but it was better than none.

She had begun to wonder about her Dorset experience once things had started to go wrong for her, first with the gradual disintegration of her relationship with Peter and even more so when she had found herself in custody here in Basel. The experience had seemed to be summoning her to a genuine and settled life, to a union with a man she respected and who really cared for her. Instead she had found herself in a cul de sac, with her hopes turned to ashes. But now the experience of joy and longing had come to her once again but this time in the midst of her tribulations. It certainly didn't do away with her questions, and she would keep on asking them, but she was more certain that there was a pattern behind it all that would appear in its own good time. She renewed her determination to be of assistance to the other women in the wing, they were all in the same boat and that made quite a difference to the way in which her help was received by the other women. She was incarcerated in the *Waaghof*, well she would make the most of her time here! And as she sorted her papers she picked up a postcard that had come a few days before with its view from the Rigi mountain and the message:

> "Elizabeth, you are not forgotten. Don't lose hope. Sam."

No, she would not lose hope. But where was Sam Charles? - back in the USA she supposed.

***

Later that evening she once again found that the written record of the experience paled into insignificance beside the thing itself. And she rejoiced that her optimism had returned, not simply for her future but also for that of others. Ruth, after all, was caring for Peter, supporting him and keeping his business afloat. They would make a go of repairing their marriage and supporting their son, Michael. And she was glad that they should, even though she was carrying Peter's child. Bolstered up by hope she would do her best for the other girls in the women's wing of the prison - Trudi had to be given self respect and a way out of her present life, Andrea had to be helped out of her depressed state and made to feel hope for the future. Elizabeth wondered whether she wasn't being foolishly optimistic in her plans for the two girls but she knew that without the experience of hope and joy that had come to her it would be an even more difficult task. She would work and do all she could to give them hope. Yes, she would see a therapist, as much to get some idea of how to give better help to the two other girls as for her own benefit, though she would take whatever personal support they had to offer. And it would be no small benefit if they could help her to remember more clearly what had gone on between herself and Vladimir that fateful night.

As she drifted into a deep sleep she thought of the open air and trees she had enjoyed that afternoon, standing outside the court with the world going by.

Chapter 3

Friday 21st March 1997

'Don't you ever stop working, Sam?'

He looked up from the tractor engine, or at any rate from as much of it as he had managed to reassemble that afternoon.

'You're becoming more and more like your father, Sam. You do remember that you're eating with Rachel and me this evening? It's eight o'clock already and you look as though you've been bathing in oil or something really mucky.'

'Eight ... I'd no idea, Jon. I was intent on getting this thing back together. You know that they're short of machinery at the moment?'

'I'm well aware of that. When you're as strapped for cash as this kibbutz is, shortage is something you come to live with. Management becomes non-stop crisis management and you end up like a juggler keeping all the balls in the air at once, or as many of them as you can. Gone are the days when the kibbutznik was the aristocrat of our country and the elite of the IDF. When we had our backs against the wall people were happy to live a communal existence, to work together, eat together and if need be die together. But now, even with suicide bombers and car bombs from Hamas, people have gone soft and selfish - not you of course, and I'm not just saying that to butter you up, people admire you and your dedication but they aren't queuing up to copy your attitudes! We're heavily in debt as a kibbutz and the youngsters aren't coming back in the numbers they once did after their time in the military and their visits to the USA and the other parts of the *Diaspora*. The communal life is having less and less attraction for people, and that is so even for the older folk.' He looked at Sam, examining his face with care now that he had moved back from the engine and stood in the pool of light shed by the safety lamp that dangled over the tractor. 'You've been quiet since you came back and you haven't stopped working. Like I said just now, you *are* like your father or like he was now and then. There's something troubling you, isn't there Sam?'

Sam fetched a tarpaulin and covered the engine, 'Keep any muck out, there's no point in making the job harder, is there?' They made their way to the wash room and there was silence as Sam worked the hand cleaner into his hands and arms. He smiled as he held his hands under the hot tap and the oil washed away. 'That's the sort of invention I'm always grateful for, something basic, simple, effective, harmless and with no side effects.'

'And invented for a totally different purpose, I understand.'

'Really?'

'I've heard it was developed for treating women's silk stockings and when it wasn't needed for that anymore someone found it was valuable as a cleaner.'

'You're always a repository of useless knowledge, Jon. But it's interesting, I agree - without the women and their stockings I might be having a hard time to clean up and I certainly would be very late for dinner with you and Rachel.'

'And without women, or at any rate a woman, you would not be as driven and withdrawn as you are at the moment. Am I on target, Sam?'

'On target as usual, Jon. You didn't study psychology for nothing, did you?'

'No, it's been useful in managing this place and

understanding people and where they're coming from.'

'I know where I'm coming from, Jon. It's where I'm going to that's the problem.'

'If you want to talk, you know I'll always lend you an attentive ear. Rachel's got to do some work on the kibbutz accounts and stats after we've eaten, it's for tomorro w's management meeting. Don't let me pressure you, I know I couldn't anyway, but if you want to think out loud I'll be happy to be your sounding board.'

Sam finished drying his hands and arms, 'I think I'll take you up on that.'

'Good, I've opened a couple of bottles of red Gamla wine from the Golan. By the way, we're thinking about diversifying into wine production and I'd like your ideas on the subject. I don't know whether you have any expertise in growing grapes and making wine - though I do know that you have a discriminating palate! It'll be good to eat together and then chat afterwards, like old times.'

They made their way from the workshops towards the living area and then to their separate houses.

'I'll see you in ten minutes looking rather more respectable and do give my apologies to Rachel for the delay won't you Jon.'

'She'll probably give you the job of washing up afterwards as a punishment, the dishwasher's broken down.'

'Who's getting a bit soft down on the kibbutz now? What would the pioneers have made of your dishwasher? OK, I'll be your *plongeur* tonight, and tomorrow I'll have a go at repairing the machine - once the tractor's working, that is!'

***

'There's just over a bottle to keep us company through what remains of the evening, It ought to be enough!'

'Perfectly adequate, Jon, especially as you have a management meeting tomorrow and I have the mechanical malfunctions of the kibbutz to put right.'

'Well what do you think of the brew? Is it to your liking?'

'A pretty decent Cabernet Sauvignon, we're coming on with our wines, aren't we? Another reason, besides the strategic one, for not giving the Golan back to the Syrians! They wouldn't be allowed to drink the stuff if they did get the place back, think what a waste that would be - all those years spent bringing on the vineyards totally wasted! They'd probably drive their tanks all over the vines.'

'I don't have very fond memories of the Syrians from my time as a child back in the early 1960's at Ein Gev on Kinneret. They lobbed shells down on us whenever they felt like it, hardly a neighbourly way to proceed! We should never have to live with that again.'

'Nor with Katyushas finding their way over this part of the border! The Security Zone hasn't put a stop to their attacks has it, as the people of Kiryat Shmona know full well! And there seems no end to the IDF's losses in the Zone from Hamas bombs and our own mistakes like the helicopters that collided. I'd like out but it would most likely increase the attacks on you and the other folk in the Upper Galilee, so we seem to be stuck with staying in Southern Lebanon unless we can persuade someone reliable to come in and demilitarise the area and keep it that way.'

'You have personal reasons for loathing their rockets. Does the memory still drive you?'

'It did, you're right about that, but not so much now.

The pain's still there, of course. The sense of unfairness about it all. The old man survived the horrors of the camps and the loss of all his family, made a new life in Brooklyn and then brought us here to this kibbutz. Then suddenly, at the end of a day in the workshops, a rocket sails over the border and snuffs him out. Five minutes and he would have been back home and out of the way - but none of that, we can't live in a world of "if only", can we? No, I've worked my way through it and I'm no longer hate driven. As a rabbi I never should have been. You know, I thought that I was good at pastoral care until I had to deal with my own response to sudden and violent death in the family and I found that words that once satisfied my mind didn't satisfy the heart and its pain. Oh, I'm reconciled to what happened, though it did take a while, and the words do console me now, it was just that the pain was so great at the time.'

'You're not hate driven you say and I wouldn't dispute that but you are driven by something and you've already identified a woman as the cause. Do you want to chat about her?'

'Why not, I respect your judgement and wisdom, Jon, not to mention your discretion. I can't tell you all the details for security reasons but I can tell you enough without compromising the Institute. It began about a year ago, I had been assigned to keep an eye and ear on a woman in London - not a Brit but a Russian, though you would never have guessed her origins, she gave every impression of being from North America and her passport was a Canadian one. They had planted her on a Brit, a small businessman and he fell for her and, surprise to tell, she for him.'

'And you for her?'

'And me for her, and that was early on.'

There was a break in the conversation and Jon refilled their glasses.

Sam pondered what to say and what to leave out. He began again, 'She was - no, she is a striking woman with a tremendous sense of life and energy. I won't forget the first time I saw her at close quarters. It was on a London railway station, I was making sure that she got on her train so that we could bug her apartment undisturbed. She stood there, elegance itself, and then with a shake of her head which sent her hair bouncing she had me wanting her and wanting her badly.' He paused again. 'Meeting her was out because of her employers and mine.'

'Hers were the KGB, I assume.'

'The SVR, the same thing but with a new name or set of initials - Moscow likes to window dress from time to time. I expect that they've some fine sounding mission statement but behind it all it's the same grubby crew doing the same grubby work!'

'And of course Mossad is whiter than white?'

'I never said that, Jon.' He paused. 'I won't go into details, that would be a breach of trust, but there were things about the operation that I didn't like, that stuck in the gullet. So much so that my Mossad days are over. I told them I'd had enough and that's why I'm here, working things out of my system and trying to see a way forward.'

'You've got several problems running together, then?'

'Not really. Mossad is no problem. I had no difficulty in reaching my decision - gut and intellect were in agreement so I had no doubts about going - I've got an adequate pension for my efforts. I've still got many friends there and an invitation from the top to lecture the new recruits. I may well take that up, it's a chance to influence them for the good and give them some decent standards to live by.'

'Standards that weren't applied to your last operation by your masters in Tel Aviv?'

'No comment on that, Jon. Still, you know the sort of problems they're having with botched assassination attempts and superannuated agents seeming to feed in fictitious reports of Syrian plans - whether or not that's true the story doesn't do Mossad any credit does it?'

'Sadly it doesn't? It's a pity you're not back there cleaning up the show. Still if you can have some formative influence on the new blood they recruit it will be for the benefit of all of us. We're heavily reliant on Mossad and the GSS and we're likely to stay that way - until the Messiah comes at any rate!'

'Into theology now then, Jon?'

'No. I said it without thinking. Last week I paid a visit to a religious kibbutz and I must have picked it up from them. You'll have to tell me what's the current Lubavitcher view on the matter, but leave that for the moment, you're supposed to be using me as a sounding board as you sort out your relationship or non-relationship with the Russian/Canadian lady with the bouncing coiffure.'

'Call her Elizabeth. It's the name on her Canadian passport and it simplifies things.'

Sam picked up the glass of wine and held it to the light and then savoured the bouquet. He paused and then took a generous mouthful. After a minute or so he smiled, 'They've got it right, I think. It would be hard to better this. It's not just the wine, of course, it's your company as well. Wine and food, wine and friends. It needs a companion to keep it company.'

'And that's the subject of our conversation - you need a companion and her name is Elizabeth. But she's spoken for isn't she. You mentioned a Brit, a businessman I think.'

'He was separated from his wife when Elizabeth came along, so you would expect him to realise his luck, complete his divorce formalities and marry her. But, as usual life is a bit more complicated than that. He has a son of thirteen. Now, whether the cause was his parents splitting up or whether it was a germ the SVR put in his drink in an effort to make him sufficiently ill to worry his parents and get them back together for the child's sake, whatever the cause was the boy began to have psychiatric problems. Then, to move the story on to its conclusion, Elizabeth shot and killed one of the other Russian agents. The Brit found out that she wasn't the person he thought she was and besides she had attracted the attention of the Swiss authorities and they accommodated her in the Basel *Untersuchungsgefängnis* … '

'Which is?'

'The remand prison. Ultra modern, about three years old, and on a prime city centre site but very much a prison. Her Brit can only see her through a glass screen and in any case he's had a breakdown and gone back to the wife of his youth.'

'So the way is clear for you but … '

'But, and it's a very big *but*, she's in a Swiss prison and on a murder charge!'

'Well Sam, with your professional training and expertise that should only be a small problem. As a Mossad agent you could blow a hole in the wall and get her out. As a rabbi you could argue her case in court and they'd be so confused when you'd finished that they'd be glad to let her go!'

'And many thanks for your invaluable practical advice, Jon! Unfortunately it's a real world and not a fantasy one.

And the Swiss are highly efficient, except that is when one of their banks needs to find records from before World War II ! The prison is brand new and there's no easy access to the prisoners. The Public Prosecutor is in the same building so there are no outings from the prison to meet him - it's all indoors apart from visits to the ante-natal unit at the hospital but under escort, of course.'

'So she's pregnant? By her English boss?'

'Just so, yet another complication! Also there's a monthly trip to the *Strafgericht*.'

'Which is?'

'The criminal court. The Prosecutor has to renew his permission to keep her locked up month by month, so she has an outing to the court one afternoon a month. The proceedings are in private and in any case I don't think that I would risk being in the same room with Elizabeth.'

'Your emotions?'

'No, not that. She would recognise me and that would cause all manner of problems.'

'You were keeping her under surveillance but she rumbled you?'

Sam took another sip of wine, savoured it and once again paused. He looked at Jon and resumed the story, 'No she didn't rumble me. I spent a day with her in the Swiss Alps. I was just a stranger who happened to sit at her table in the hotel restaurant at dinner the night before and she invited me to come with her to the mountains the next day. Which I did. It was a day we both enjoyed. But it was contrary to rules and common sense.' He paused, reflected and continued. 'That evening, after we had dined and I had set off, so she thought, for Hamburg, she put a bullet through the skull of a colleague called Eugene, an SVR thug who had drugged her and tried to rape her. She passed out and came to in hospital with the

Basel police taking care of her. They looked for the man who had spent the day with her but without success. The attention of the Swiss police is something I can happily do without.'

'Your conduct was unprofessional then.'

'Yes, that has been made very clear to me - not that I needed telling. That's not why I left, they didn't throw me out! The operation was a success, not that they will ever tell the world at large about it. But there were things done with the approval of my bosses which offended me and so I'm in retirement and with unlimited time to think about Elizabeth and think - fantasise to be honest - about ways of getting her out of jail.'

'You said she worked for the KGB or whatever it calls itself now ... '

'The SVR, Jon.'

'OK, the SVR. Aren't they likely to be pondering the same problem and with far greater resources at their disposal than you have at yours?'

'All I can say to you on that is that she wouldn't want to go back to Moscow and I wouldn't want her to end up in their hands. But I believe the SVR would be wary of offending the Swiss at the moment – I won't say why, but I'm pretty sure that's the case.'

'Another wilful agent, then, Sam?'

'Something like that. What was a success for us, in my masters' eyes at any rate, was a fiasco for them and they wouldn't be too gentle with her but, as I've said, the SVR are likely to be wary of further offending the Swiss. None of her colleagues who got back to Moscow survived the experience.'

'Is she completely safe then? Presumably she's secure from outsiders in prison but what about her trips to court and the hospital - surely the SVR could take a pot shot at her.'

'OK I'll tell you this much, as part of our operation I planted some papers that led to an official of the Russian embassy in Bern being arrested with them in a briefcase. The Russians are sufficiently embarrassed by that not to want to draw attention to themselves by murdering a woman who is known by the Swiss to be one of their agents. That's so for the moment but whether it will continue to be so does worry me at times.'

'And adds to your drive to lose yourself in work, repairing tractors and washing machines?'

'Something like that, I suppose. But this is only for the moment. I'm planning to head off to Basel next week. Perhaps once I'm there something will suggest itself.'

'Well Sam, the only thing that occurs to me is mitigation. You said that Elizabeth was drugged and threatened with rape? Then surely a court will take that into account?' John picked up the bottle, 'One more before you head off to bed? Good!' He filled their glasses. '*L' chaim* – to life – and to liberty!'

'Yes, to liberty! Thanks for your help, Jon. There's a lot in the mitigation point and I'm sure Elizabeth's lawyers will press it on the court. But I've got to go back to Basel to see what I can do.'

***

He had told Jon more than he should have done but he knew that with Jon it would go no further. He had told him of the emotional hold that Elizabeth had over him but not spoken of the other force driving him to seek her release – his guilt at having built up Eugene's sexual desire by tempting him with a little blonde who had then failed to turn up for an assignation that day. The sexual frustration engineered by Sam had provoked Eugene's attempt to rape Elizabeth. Any involvement by Sam in the recovery of Elizabeth's freedom would go some way towards expiating the guilt that gripped him.

Chapter 4

Monday 31st March 1997

Jakob Gold faced Elizabeth through a glass screen in the visiting room of the *Untersuchungsgefängsnis*. It was a solid sheet of glass with communication by means of microphones and loudspeakers, a system guaranteed to remove any vestige of intimacy or privacy from conversation.

'I'm grateful to you Jakob for coming – you're my link with the outside world and with the past. My link with Peter, no don't worry, it's as the father of my, our, child that I regard him – my lover and future husband no longer. I've accepted that he's going to remain with Ruth and Michael and I don't see that he could do anything else. No, I'm reconciled to that, I know I've lost him but I do hope that he will have a rôle as our child's father. But how is Peter, any sign of a recovery?'

Jakob paused for a moment before replying, 'Well, Elizabeth, I'm relieved that you see it that way. As you know we nearly lost him after the Security people had given him a mauling.'

She broke in, 'Tell me, Jakob, where did they grill him, it wasn't at the apartment was it?'

Again he paused before replying, no use denying it, 'Yes, the apartment, which can't have helped. By a miracle Ruth was waiting with Michael to collect him after the interview, she saw him open the window and talked him out of it.'

She wiped a tear from her eye with the back of her hand and blew her nose before replying, 'Really it's been as bad as it could be for poor Peter. Can you imagine any worse way for him to find out that I'm not who he thought I was and that I'm a killer. Then to be grilled by those thugs in the apartment where we'd shared so much happiness and joy. Thank God Ruth was there! A miracle isn't overstating things, Jakob, not in the least.'

'He's on medication and receiving psychiatric treatment. But then he was here a week ago and you would have seen how he was, flattened by it all but mercifully showing *some* signs of improvement. He would have told you that both Ruth and Michael have been his towers of strength. Yes, Michael as well, psychologically *he* is very much on the mend.'

'Yes', she told herself, 'he feels safe with me holed up in jail.' And in no way did she blame him. Her affair with Peter had begun when Peter had thought his marriage to Ruth was well and truly over and that he'd better get on with the long delayed divorce. Then, after a severe illness – which she suspected her colleague Eugene had had something to do with – Michael had begun to come apart at the seams, with recurring violent nightmares brought on by fears of losing his father.

'And how are you Elizabeth? Your experience has been equally traumatic. I've no idea how I would respond to being incarcerated here.'

'The sense of shock hasn't worn off, Jakob. It seems a lifetime ago that Peter and I arrived at your house on a wet Friday night in February after a long drive across the width of France. I know Peter was under stress then but I'd hoped things would improve, I've always been a hopeful sort of person. It was a funny few days, Peter's mood-swings. Up one moment and down the next. On the Saturday we went all over Basel – it was one of his better days with the problem of Michael out of mind for a while but surfacing at times. Then, when he'd gone back to your house at the end of the afternoon, and I was having dinner in the hotel I surprised myself by agreeing that a stranger could share my table.' Gold noticed that a wistful look crossed her face.

'That was the man they were looking for afterwards?'

'Yes, Sam Charles, an American journalist, someone I could open up to. No, Jakob, I wasn't looking for someone to replace Peter, I just needed to talk to someone. And he turned out to be a good listener, so much so that I invited him to spend the Sunday with me in the Alps. I know you're an old friend of Peter's but I must tell you that Sunday was the most delightful of days. It wasn't sexual, or not overtly so, it was friendship, companionship, we never even kissed, no that's not *quite* right, he kissed me on the cheek when we said goodbye that evening and he went off to Hamburg.'

'And that was the last of Sam Charles?'

'Yes, apart from a postcard with the view from the Rigi that came early in March with the message:

"Elizabeth you are not forgotten. Don't lose hope.

Sam." '

'But apart from that he's vanished, the Swiss appealed for him to come forward and there was no response?'

'True. But I'm convinced that there must have been a good reason. Like Peter he was someone I felt I could trust, Jakob.'

'You must not lose hope, Elizabeth. You've got a good lawyer. It was the right decision to change to Sylvia Brunner. She has quite a reputation as a defence *Advokat*. And you know that I'm underwriting the fees, we want you to have the best.'

'I'm grateful, Jakob, very grateful indeed. But, and this may seem strange to, you, I've no wish to get off Scot-free. What I did was wrong and I deserve punishment but on the other hand there's the baby. I don't wish it – boy or girl – to spend long behind bars or to be parted from me after three years or so, that would tear me apart.' Tears were forming in her eyes and she hunted for a tissue to wipe them away.

Jakob was at a loss, he had no wish to utter platitudes, to give her false hope. Wisdom dictated that he should remain silent, so he did.

'Again, this must sound strange, Jakob, but I try not to dwell on the very happy times that Peter and I shared. Sounds ungrateful, perhaps? But what's the use, it's past. I'd only hurt myself if I thought too long about it!'

'That's probably wise, Elizabeth.'

'But I have taken Sam Charles' message to heart. I re-live that day in the mountains, sunshine, snow, scenery and excellent company. And I think of him, Sam Charles. It isn't beyond the bounds of possibility that he might surface one day and say, "See I didn't forget you!" '

'Elizabeth, do take care, don't build up your hopes on a flimsy foundation.'

'I'll bear that in mind, Jakob, but, do you know, I have confidence in Sam Charles, though how he could help is beyond me!'

Jakob decided it would be wise to change the subject, 'How do you spend your time here, Elizabeth?'

'In some ways it's not as bad as you might imagine. It's not solitary confinement but I have my own cell and so I've my own space, though I'm locked up from 5.45 each evening until 7.15 the next morning. Plenty of time for reading and thinking, you see! But there's also my time with the other women. That's been an eye-opener! Low life, some might say, but many of them have never had a chance. We try to help each other, I'm improving my German – mainline German, I'll call it and also your Basel dialect.'

He smiled, '*Kasch Du Schwitzerdütsch reede, Elizabeth?*' [Do you speak Swiss German?]

'*Nur ein wenig,* Jakob.' They both laughed. [Only a little, but in "mainline" German.]

'*Ai Sprooch isch nie gnueg.*'

'You'll have to translate, Jakob.'

' "Just one language is never enough." Perhaps you would like some text books and phrase books, after all you have time to become quite proficient.'

'Now that's a good idea, it would help me to communicate with the other women and give them some assistance. They've all manner of difficulties, prostitution, drugs, theft and the like. There's one girl who's here on a murder charge like me and she's going to pieces with remorse, something I can empathise with, and it would help to get through to her if I could master the dialect. So, yes please, Jakob, *Dangge*, I think that's it for "Thank you".'

'*Gääm gscheh.* You're proficient already, young woman.

The prison officer indicated that their time was up and Jakob rose, '*Guet Nacht, Elizabeth.* And, yes, do not give up hope.'

Chapter 5

Wednesday 2nd April 1997

Ben Friedman produced his US passport to the Swiss official who returned it after a cursory glance which satisfied him that the face matched the photograph, 'Business or pleasure, Mr Friedman?'

'It's Switzerland and I thought that business and pleasure here were the same thing! But the answer to your question is pleasure, I'm going to photograph your mountain scenery.'

'We are not as serious as you seem to think, Mr Friedman. There are occasions when we let our hair down. This evening I'm off to watch FC Basel play, though on their present form it might be fair to say that while it isn't business it isn't pleasure either, we're having a bad season. It's a different kind of football from the sort you're used to.'

'Sure thing. Very different but I like both so I'll be paying a visit to your team before long. Have a good game this evening!' He picked up his case and camera bag and made his way through the door into the arrivals area. Ben Friedman was what the passport said and the photograph matched, but he was in fact Noam Cantor, and his proper passport was an Israeli one in that name. The US passport was also made in Israel, prepared for him by Mossad. In the past he had done the odd job for them and they had been willing on this occasion to provide him with a set of false papers so that he could assist Sam Kagan. This was, of course, on the basis that their involvement was in no way to be admitted.

He had travelled from Tel Aviv by way of London where he had seen a few West End shows, mainly musicals. As a night club singer he tried to keep in touch with what was new on Broadway and in London, it helped to have new songs and routines – otherwise work became an unremitting grind. He missed his years of flying helicopters in the Israeli Air Force but an accident, for which he hadn't been responsible, had led to his grounding and early discharge. True he flew helicopters now and then for businessmen but there was none of the excitement he had experienced in active service over the Lebanon and flying over *Eretz Israel,* the Land of Israel.

His taxi took him along the road corridor from Basel/Mulhouse/Freiburg Airport into Switzerland proper. He would spend a couple of nights at a small hotel in central Basel, making contact with Sam the next day and then joining him in his rented house by the Rhein. It was unlikely that anyone was keeping tabs on him but, just in case they were, he was making sure that it would be hard for them to link Ben Friedman with Sam Kagan.

***

The next day he went to the *Marktplatz* and found the *Café Schiesser* opposite the *Rathaus*. He had made very sure that he wasn't being followed - not that he expected it - but it was important to be sure. Sam had said to be there at 10.00 a.m. and so just a little before that hour Ben made his way through the shop and up the stairs. The cafe was quiet and, with a good choice of tables, he took one by the window. His order for a pot of coffee was taken right away and he was directed to the counter to choose a pastry from the large range on display. He made his choice and turned to see Sam waiting for him at the table. Their greetings were low key - a quick shake of the hand - not the loud and energetic displays of manly affection that were usual between them, they had no wish to stand out and etch themselves on the memories of the staff or the other customers. Sam's order for coffee was taken and when he had returned from the cake counter they got through the formalities of asking how their respective families were, except that they weren't formalities but the genuinely concerned enquiries of two men who had worked well together in exacting and dangerous circumstances and were honestly involved in one another's lives.

' ... and he wants to come back to join me in Jerusalem, he doesn't like life in New Jersey, Sam. I've told him that he can come during the holidays but he must stay where he is until he's ready for college, when he can make up his own mind. It's better for Sarah to be looking after him, with the hours I work in the club he would see little or nothing of me except at the weekends - it's not that he doesn't get on with his mother but his one ambition is to get into the IDF and, you've guessed it, fly choppers!'

'They never learn, do they! You've taken Amos up in one?'

'You bet, Sam, and he loved every minute of it.'

'I wonder how I'd relate to a son - or daughter - if I had one.' Sam looked quizzical.

'I've never thought of you as a parent, Sam. But why not? Though with your job it would be unfair for a child to have a father at risk as you are in your work.'

'Was, not is, you mean. I'm on my own now - it's different.'

'Different perhaps and perhaps more dangerous! You don't have the ... ' he paused and made sure that no one was within earshot, 'you don't have the Institute to look after you any more - that could be more dangerous than before don't you think?'

Sam lowered his voice, 'Yes there's the Swiss to cope with, we mustn't fall foul of them, they don't like foreigners messing round in their country.'

'And the Russians, have you forgotten them? The woman was one of their agents. Hasn't it occurred to you that they might want her back, that you might not be the only one dedicated to her removal from Basel Jail? And if that's the case it could well be that we might bump into them at some stage of the proceedings.'

'The thought hadn't escaped me, Noam, and by the way you're going to have to be *Ben* from now on. It is possible that they may be around. And it is also possible that they might want her dead or alive - she shot one of their folk and the operation was fouled up. She's charged with murder on the first count and they probably think she's to blame for the whole fiasco. There's also the worry, for them, of what she might say in court or to her interrogators. Killing her would ensure that she kept her mouth shut. I'm planning to be around the court when she makes her monthly appearance there, when the prosecutor applies for her to be kept locked up, not just to see her but to keep an eye open for anyone else who might be showing interest. The main thing that militates against their taking a shot at her is that the Russians are busy trying to repair relations with the Swiss – I won't tell you why – and they aren't likely to want to make things worse. After all they need a safe haven for their money!'

'And so far?'

'Nothing has happened ... which suggests I'm right that they don't want any more trouble with the Swiss. That's just as well in case she fancies standing for a few minutes under the trees outside the court, just enjoying being out of the jail. When we had her under observation in England we noticed that she enjoyed being out in the country. I wouldn't like to be in her position, deprived of liberty and cut off from contact with the world of fresh air, trees, hills, rivers and the rest of it. It would hurt, I'm sure of that. How I'd long for a glimpse of Hermon, the Golan or Tabor!'

'I'm here to photograph the Alps, or so I told the Customs man at the airport yesterday. Do I get a chance to get there?'

'No problem, Noam, no problem at all. We are going to have time on our hands and it will be good cover to fly the chopper in that direction. I've got some literature on hiring the things from the airport, but leave that for the moment, we've got company.'

A couple of Basel housewives moved towards them and took the next table. They placed their Globus bags and carriers of vegetables from the market against the wall, took off their fur coats, placing them carefully over the spare chairs and sat down. The men's conversation turned to other matters - there would be plenty of time to discuss plans over the coming days. Another coffee, more general chat and they went their way - Sam leaving first - to meet the next day when Noam would be collected from his hotel in Sam's car and move into Sam's place for the rest of his stay in Switzerland.

***

Sam was in no hurry to return home and set off for a brisk walk up the hill away from the river and towards the university. The arrival of Ben had brought home to him the immediacy of the problem. Just how would they be able to get Elizabeth out of the Basel jail? He was aware that he was beginning to sweat, though the day was not particularly hot. The problem was getting at him. He was used to keeping tension at bay and remaining calm in difficult situations. He reflected on the night that Elizabeth had put the bullet through Eugene's brain and how with just a momentary display of panic he had handled the situation. He wondered if the others had noticed. He supposed they had - after all, like him, they were trained to observe, so noting the small signs of stress in people that the untrained were not likely to see. Yes, they had probably noticed and then seen how his calm, controlled self had reasserted itself. Now the consequences of that night were his immediate concern. It had put her in jail and brought him back here to Basel. He could not face the prospect of failure. He was a man obsessed with the task of her rescue and wondered how he would face life if failure were the outcome of his endeavours.

He passed near where the remand prison had once been. If only they hadn't built a new remand prison in the *Innere Margarethenstrasse*, a building that also housed the Public Prosecutor, things might be easier. The old prison and the Prosecutor's office had been separate, with prisoners being taken out at intervals for questioning, giving more opportunity for a rescue attempt. But he had to deal with things as they were and not as he would have liked them to be! There were the monthly visits to the court and the visits to the ante-natal clinic at the *Frauenspital*, surely they would provide the opportunity he needed.

He bought the local daily paper, the *Basler Zeitung* and then looked for a small restaurant near the university. He longed for the stimulus of the academic world, his time as a rabbi at the Hebrew University in Jerusalem had been a good one and he had relished the conversations with students on a wide range of topics. He had particularly enjoyed his time with research students when they had given him an insight into the abstruse areas of their research. Some of them had expressed concern at the moral implications of their work and it had been good helping them to come to their own conclusions rather than trying to make up their own minds for them. He wasn't atrophying mentally - he had his books - but he longed to return to the interplay of minds sharpened by study and by a concern for the good of their own people and for humanity.

He found the restaurant he was looking for, he had been there at the beginning of the year when he had first visited Basel, and it was as he remembered it. Students from the university were beginning to make their way in for a snack after their morning sessions. He made for a table at the back and sat facing the door. There was a vegetarian lasagne on the menu and he ordered it together with a carafe of Chianti. Kosher cuisine was out of the question with his sort of work but he did what he could to avoid going too far from what was strictly permitted. He surveyed the tables with groups of students, some in animated discussion. They were at an age where things did matter, where principles were felt as well as believed. He experienced a longing for his student days. His calling had resulted in the subjection of his innately humane principles to the overriding one that, in whatever way it had to be done, the determination of Israel's enemies to annihilate her was to be stopped. And yet that wasn't true: he was here in Basel because he had revolted at the operation to which he had been a party and because he felt compelled to do all in his power to restore Elizabeth to liberty. But he had known a lot about the compromise of his principles, of seeking the higher good, of the end justifying the means. But it had made him uncomfortable. So now here he was back in Basel faced with this self imposed and almost impossible task and he was playing by his rules and no longer those of Mossad. He wondered how his former colleagues were getting on. It was clear that the Institute was going through a rough patch with tensions within and meagre success without. The appointment as its head of a soldier, Danny Yatom, rather than one of its own men had angered many. He was glad to be away from such politics, it was bad enough to have enemies outside the organisation without being involved in civil war within. His thoughts were interrupted by a young woman looking down at him. She had evidently spoken to him and he in his preoccupation had failed to hear.

'I'm sorry but it's busy here. Do you mind if I share your table, please?'

He looked up and took her in quickly, a woman in her mid twenties, dark short hair, green eyes, a red sweater, probably designer jeans and a good figure to go with them. He had only needed a split second to absorb all this. He smiled, it was his automatic reaction to an attractive woman, particularly one who gave every appearance of being lively and intelligent. 'Feel welcome - take a seat!' He indicated the place opposite him with a gesture of his hand. 'Your usual watering hole?'

She nodded, 'I'm here most days at this time. The food's good and a morning at the university gives me an appetite.' There was a touch of America about her accent though he guessed that she was probably either German or Swiss. She scanned the menu and smiled, 'I don't know why I bother to read it, I expect I could recite it to you after months of coming here.'

He took the menu from her, 'OK lets see whether you really can!'

She started slowly and quickly speeded up, working her way through a variety of antipasti and on to a variety of spaghettis. He stopped her at the end of the first side of the card. 'OK, you know it well enough - one asterisk and one footnote missing, otherwise faultless. You can save time in future and order without reading it.'

'Probably not, it seems part of the ritual of eating out and you never know they might change the food or the prices.'

The waiter brought his carafe of wine.

'But they don't change them, do they?'

'No, they're always the same - so it's just routine, something I'm conditioned to do.'

'You don't look the type that's easily conditioned, well not to me anyway. Pavlov would have had a problem with you I think.'

'I'd agree with that, it's self conditioning, I suppose. Something more subtle - you're less suspicious of yourself than other people ... like you, for instance, I see you as a hot blooded male and I'm wary, wary though interested of course!'

'So you wouldn't be surprised if I offered you a glass of wine!' He turned her glass upright and filled it from his carafe of Chianti. 'You do like red wine, I hope?'

'Especially when it's offered by an interesting stranger. I don't know your name and you don't know mine!'

'Joe Black, I'm from Brooklyn, New York.' And immediately he wished he had told the truth. But no, the old habits of covering his tracks were as important now as they had ever been for him. But it did go against the grain, being forced into continued subterfuge and rôle play. He would be glad when this was all over and he could be Sam Kagan to whomever he met.

"I'm Liz Curtis from Toronto, Canada though the family

originates from a village near here. We're both from the other side of the Pond, then.'

'Yes Liz, we're agreed on geography, it seems.'

She smiled and lifted her glass, 'To the New World and its peoples!'

'The New World it is then,' he replied and lifted his glass in response.

She caught his gaze and held it. She had interested him from the beginning and now she set a tingle running through his body. Her eye was not that of the interrogator, though she was clearly summing him up in her mind and wondering whether to take him at face value, it was the eye of a young woman in love with life. She had a sparkle and a vitality that showed and transformed what might have been an ordinary face into one that radiated energy and intelligence. She lifted her glass towards the light, viewed the colour of the wine and turning back to face him took a sip. 'Mm, that's good after a morning's work at the university.' Once again she held his eye, 'Joe doesn't suit you. What's your middle name?'

'Sam,' the name slipped out, 'but generally I don't use it.' He was both annoyed at giving it away and relieved that things would now be simpler if she telephoned him. And immediately he asked himself why she should telephone him or rather why he should think of her doing so and he knew that he had been too long without a female companion and that this young woman would be good company, good company that he wanted and needed.

'I think I'll use it and call you Sam, that's if you don't object *too* strongly!'

'I think it might *just* be allowable. After all what's in a name?'

'What indeed, but I think you're more of a Sam than a

Joe. This reminds me of kids stories where someone has to discover the name of a tyrant, a dragon or something nasty like that in order to escape. Somehow the name is the key that opens the door of escape or that sort of thing. To have the creature's name gives you power over it.'

'And so you feel you now have power over me, to escape that is! But you aren't advocating that we live in some sort of fantasy world of cruel kings, witches and dragons, adults need the firm grip of reality.'

'Not the adult, but the child in us needs a world of rich inner fantasy wedded to a clear grasp of reality - that's the way to the balanced personality. Didn't you feed your imagination as a child, you know kids' stories - the sort of things that you knew were stories and invention and yet at another level they were true. Haven't you read any of Lewis' Narnia stories or Tolkien's 'Hobbit' or his 'Lord of the Rings'?'

' 'Fraid not Liz. So I'm emotionally underdeveloped? You'll be wanting me for a project on the effects of starving a child's imagination, I suppose.'

'No, I'm not saying that ... but as a child you missed out on something valuable, I'm afraid. Still if you ever want to borrow Lewis or Tolkien you'll find out what you missed as a child.'

'But going back to my name, Liz, you think you have power over me, perhaps to escape?'

'Not while there's some wine left in the carafe! And I've had enough of research for one day.' She called a waiter and ordered a pizza and another carafe of Chianti. 'That will keep us going for a while. You're not in a hurry to go I hope. Now that I've got your name I've decided to use my power to keep you here talking and maybe even take you to parts of this city you haven't seen yet. Now tell me what you're doing here in Basel, so far from Brooklyn and it's high murder statistics.'

'So you know something about violence in Brooklyn, then? It's not as bad as it was thanks to Giuliani's zero tolerance policy.' For the moment at any rate he would keep any disclosure of personal details to a minimum.

'I'm doing a project on criminology, the background from which murderers come, the things that encourage them into violence and so on.'

A thought struck him and for the moment he filed it away in his mind, to be worked on later when he would see whether there was any mileage in it. 'And what stage are you at?'

'Pretty early, trying to agree with my supervisor just what the outline of the project is and what material I need to gather and how. I need to get it sorted out in the next week or so. I doubt whether it will be earth shattering but then it might just be useful. I suppose most of us kid ourselves that what we're doing will benefit others when all the time we're only doing it for ourselves. In my case to get a higher degree so I can teach somewhere like my father.'

'And he's at?'

'MIT on advanced computer systems. Not my scene at all, Sam. Is it yours?'

'I have to admit some expertise in that area, I'm afraid. So you'll probably write me off as a desiccated calculating machine, Liz.'

'Somehow I don't think that the description fits you, Sam.' She reached out and touched his hand for a moment, 'There's plenty of life and warmth in you, that I can see.' They both laughed, glad that they had decided to eat in that restaurant and at the same time.

Both their meals arrived together and they set to,

satisfying their appetites. The litre of wine that they had ordered between them set their already free tongues off into lively conversation on the city and their plans for the rest of the day which, not surprisingly were in each case easily modified to accommodate those of the other. Double espresso coffees were a sort of antidote to the wine but both of them were able to hold it without ill effects. Liz made for the Ladies' room and returned after running a comb through her hair and a light application of perfume. It was just after 2.00 p.m. and the afternoon was theirs. She took his arm as they left and he was glad. He was at the same time concerned at the possible outcome of his latest action, his meeting with Elizabeth in another Basel restaurant back in February had brought totally unforeseen consequences. But besides Liz herself there was her research project and he wondered whether it could be used to serve his purposes. But would that be fair on her? He would have to give it serious thought. He salved his conscience with the thought that she might be a vital link in his plans to get Elizabeth out. But at the moment he could see no way of using her without her knowledge and co-operation. And the words 'using her' were objectionable to him. On the other hand how could he tell her what it was that had brought him back to Basel and what he was proposing to do? And he had to be sure that she was the genuine article and not a plant by the Swiss or anyone else with an interest in Sam.

Liz as a way to Elizabeth? It was possible ... but was it fair and right? An opportunity and at the same time another problem! That Liz was an attractive woman and intellectually stimulating were factors that might cloud his judgement.

Chapter 6

Friday 4th April 1997

The warm sunshine of a Spring morning was making the car uncomfortably hot and Ben wound down his window as they made their way past the apartments in the Basel suburbs and towards the airport.

'It's a pity you couldn't have run to a half decent car, Sam. A soft top or something with air conditioning. A blue Ford Escort definitely lacks style. It's not the sort of car I'd associate with someone who was once one of Mossad's top men!'

'That's just the reason I chose it. Ordinary and unmemorable. I don't want to stand out and I don't want my car to stand out. We just fade into the background and that's fine for what we're involved in.'

'Not James Bond, then?'

'Certainly not James Bond.'

'But there are the women, Sam! The one from Brooklyn, the one in jail that is causing us all this effort and the one you were out with last night. By my calculation that makes at least three and there may be others I don't know about!'

'The one I was out with last *evening* not last night. I was back just after twelve wasn't I?'

'And you can't get up to mischief before twelve? I expect she had a thesis to write by this morning and had regretfully to throw you out and get down to more academic pursuits! Hold on Sam, there's a shop! I need some cigarettes, just pull in if you can. And if you can't ... pull in just the same, I can't go without a smoke any longer.'

Sam pulled in and waited for Ben to make his

purchase. He kept a constant lookout, using the car's mirrors to scan the pavement behind while keeping an eye on the area in front. He was aware that he had not given up watchfulness with retirement, even without Ben's recent reminder that his old enemies in the SVR could be on the scene taking an active interest in Elizabeth he would still have been watchful: it was a habit he didn't feel the need to break for the moment. Throughout the journey he had been checking on the cars behind him, noting any which followed for an overlong period and feeling relief when they left his route, especially when he was then left alone with nothing to the rear. One day he would drive without this extreme wariness but it wasn't now, here in Basel he and Ben were on their own - there was no one to watch their backs or dig them out if trouble came. Though that itself was an advantage as well as a drawback, the more there were of you the larger the target you presented to your foes.

Ben returned to the car smoking a cigarette, 'I need this if I'm going to fly a chopper this morning, Sam.'

'Well keep that window open if you have to pollute the atmosphere, Ben. If the prospect of flying does that to you with all your experience of choppers just think what it's doing to me!'

'No need to worry, you'll be in a safe pair of hands. It's just that I always feel like this when I haven't flown for a while - as soon as I'm strapped in and ready to go the anxiety is gone and it's all fun.'

Sam waited until a gap appeared in the steady stream of traffic and pulled out. 'Safer here than in England, Ben, trust the Brits to drive on the wrong side of the road! It's as well that they didn't leave that behind with their letter boxes from the Mandate!'

'British letter boxes? Do you mean that they're still

intercepting our post and tapping our 'phones? Where are they?'

'In the Jewish Quarter of the Old City for one place, that's if you look carefully. It's all right, our Post Office looks after the things and there are so many layers of paint that you have to look real close to see that the Brits made it.'

They headed down the corridor of road through France to the airport, passing near the terminal and on towards their destination, Airport Helicopter Basel. The office was easily found and they parked beside it. Nearby were some light aircraft and a couple of helicopters.

'One of them's a Bell Jet Ranger III, Sam. I've flown them often enough, they'll take a pilot plus four passengers. I'd be happy flying one of them.'

'Have whatever you need, Ben, whatever you're happy flying, the ride's on me - I'm picking up the bill.'

Sam parked the car to the side of the helicopter company's office and stopped his companion from getting out. 'Hold it a moment Ben, let's be sure that you've got a convincing story and that your background's OK.'

'Damn it Sam, you've rehearsed me often enough. I'm used to an audience, to creating an illusion and I never forget my lines - or hardly ever and that's when I'm tired, bone weary, not relaxed like now with a cigarette in my hand.'

'Let's just be sure, Ben.'

'OK then, Sam, just for you, I wouldn't oblige anyone else.'

'I appreciate your co-operation Ben, I really do.'

Ben drew his wallet from the inside pocket of his jacket and took out an American passport and a Swiss helicopter pilot's licence. 'The Institute's works of art, Sam, which make me Dennis Mayer from Long Island,

New York. I first held a Swiss licence five years ago when I was flying for an American publisher who was doing a book on the Alps and wanted to do some of the photography himself, a sort of ego trip for the old boy that his fellow directors went along with and weren't too sad when he had a heart attack that killed him before the project was complete - hence no book. That OK, Alan.'

'It'll do OK, I'm glad you remember who I am! At any rate for the time being.'

'And who were you for the young woman last night?'

'The young woman last *evening* you mean, Dennis.'

'Last evening, Alan, I'm sorry ... but under what name does she know you?'

'As Sam, I'll explain later. But let's go, there's no point hanging on, so let's have an enjoyable trip. Better stub out that noxious weed you're smoking and make the acquaintance of the chopper people.'

The office was an unpretentious, one storied box of a building but once inside it they found that they had stepped from what had the makings of a hot day into the slight chill of air-conditioning. They looked around and took in the office and it's furnishing, considerably better than they had expected. A young man came from the Flight Office to their right.

'Guten Tag. Kann ich Ihnen helfen, bitte?'

'Hi there, I'm sure you can. It's Nick Schwander, isn't it? We spoke on the telephone yesterday.'

'Ah, yes, of course - you must be Herr Hendriksen.' They shook hands. 'And you are Herr Mayer, the pilot?'

The other nodded, 'Yes sir, Dennis Mayer from Long Island, New York. Good to meet you.'

'And you wish to hire one of our helicopters, Herr Mayer? You have a Swiss licence to fly helicopters, I believe.'

'Sure thing Herr Schwander, I needed it when I was flying an American publisher around to photograph the Alps for a book, only the book never got published - he snuffed it first. His colleagues thought it would lose money, invited the widow to subsidise it out of the estate. She declined, didn't want to waste money that she could spend herself and married her lover of several years standing within three months of the funeral. Still it gave me a taste for the Alps. My friend Alan is a keen photographer and he's agreed to do some photography for another friend who's a Geology Professor at Berkeley ... California.' He added the State in case Herr Schwander hadn't heard of the place.

'I know it well Herr Mayer, my sister recently graduated in law from Berkeley. That was last year. I've been there several times, it's a fine place.'

Sam winced to himself, why was Ben embroidering his story in this way? Too much detail and you stood a good chance of tying yourself up in knots, particularly if you were a novice in these matters as Ben most certainly was!

'Our friend has only recently taken up his post there, so they're unlikely to have met and in any case with a university that size ... '

'People could be there for a lifetime and never meet. Much too big really. Our University of Basel is much smaller, on a much more human scale. People meet other people from different faculties and that is good, good for them and good for learning.'

Sam had begun to relax again and decided that it was time to steer the conversation towards helicopters and away from issues that might lead to difficulties. 'My friend, Dennis, was admiring your Jet Ranger out there, Herr Schwander, we'd like to hire one, probably on several occasions over the next few months. We're having an extended holiday in Europe and we'll send the first batch of photographs to Berkeley and await instructions on whether he wants different angles, different lighting and that sort of thing.'

Herr Schwander nodded, 'Good, but first Herr Hendriksen it will be necessary for Herr Mayer to demonstrate to me his competence as a pilot. We owe it to ourselves and to the Baslers on the ground to ensure that only those who are fully competent are allowed to fly our helicopters.' He paused and added, 'But, of course Herr Mayer is an experienced pilot so that there will be no problem - simply a formality but a formality that has to be gone through. You have flown the Bell 206 Jet Ranger III, Herr Mayer?'

'Sure, I've flown them for oil and gas corporations. All over the place - the USA, Texas and other States, the Near East, Saudi, Jordan and even in Israel - though I wouldn't tell the Saudis that!'

The two men turned to technical talk and Sam was relieved. Ben knew all about choppers and was unlikely to compromise them if he kept to something factual and left the fiction alone. The talk was about the performance of the machine: range, speed and the like, and about air traffic control. There was also talk about exclusion zones, generally due to military activity, which varied daily.

Herr Schwander concluded, 'And if you're wanting to fly at the end of August you will have to avoid Basel's airspace. It's the first time that there has been such a restriction but it's due to the Zionist Conference, some centenary event, and we Swiss don't want the PLO or their friends spoiling the event. We and our bankers are not, at the moment very popular with Jews. You're not from the PLO?' He laughed and the others joined him.

Sam broke in, 'I once had Arab neighbours, in fact Hussein was a friend of mine and we went to school together. He seemed a normal human being, indeed all his family did. No we're not PLO members who've left their head-dress at home! You can see that neither of us is Arafat – Dennis shaved today and my beard is well beyond the stubble stage! If there are no restrictions today we can fly over Basel and see the city from the air, I'd like some photographs for my own collection. I've been viewing the place from ground level so it'll be a change to see it from above. Now, Herr Schwander, remind us of the hire charges, please.'

'They are very reasonable, I think I gave you details when we spoke on the telephone yesterday - per minute, and for the Jet Ranger, it is 15 Swiss Francs plus, of course 6.5 % tax, and there's also a 25 Swiss Francs landing tax to pay.'

'Ah yes, that's what I expected and you will take a card.' He produced an American Express Gold Card and handed it to Herr Schwander.

'If you don't object I'll leave it with our secretary, then if we don't come back she can charge your account for flying time as well as the cost of a replacement helicopter.'

Ben reacted as though he had been insulted and when Herr Schwander showed embarrassment he roared with laughter. After a can of Coke apiece Herr Schwander handed Ben a warm jacket and they made their way onto the tarmac where the blue and yellow chopper was waiting. Sam was sent back to the office to wait with the comment, 'If your friend wrecks the thing it would be better that you weren't on board!'

Ben's response was a snort of contempt, 'After the hours I've spent flying these things you would be safe with me in a fog with my hands tied behind my back - sorry I exaggerate - with one of my hands tied behind my back!'

As Herr Schwander saw to things on the other side of the machine Sam warned Ben, 'Just make sure you don't start inventing stories and get yourself into a fix!'

'No chance boss, it'll be all chopper-speak from now on.'

'I hope so!' muttered Sam and returned to the cool of the office to await their return.

A quarter of an hour later they returned to the office.

'Your friend certainly knows how to handle these things but with his experience of Vietnam it's not surprising.'

'It certainly isn't! I take it that he's now free to take it up again and impress me as well?'

'No problem, just put on a jacket and you can be on your way. How long do you want it for?'

'Another 15 minutes perhaps, I'd like to do some photography over the city as the light's good at the moment.'

***

They came in over Basel from the north west and Sam looked down on the scene below watching the river come towards them. Before starting out they had agreed that, as their conversations would be held on the cockpit recorder or somehow picked up, they would not refer to the real targets of their reconnaissance but to other adjacent locations. Also they would adhere to their assumed names.

'OK Dennis, take the *Morgartenring* and the roads that

follow it and fly over the *Zoologischer Garten* ... that's right the park that has roads on viaducts at each end. Fine ... now take her over the garden towards the river. Good, now swing round and bring her over the main railway station - as slowly as you can ... fine now hold her over the station for a moment. OK on we go.' He had filmed Zoo and station but more importantly he had also shot a dozen frames of the building that filled the triangle formed by *Viaduktstrasse*, *Binnigerstrasse* and the *Innere Margaretenstrasse*. Its postal address was *Innere Margaretenstrasse 18* and it housed both the Public Prosecutor's Office and the *Untersuchungsgefängnis*, the Remand Prison. Down there was Elizabeth, held for murder and here he was in the air with Ben, making preparations for her escape *if* they could find a way.

'Where now?'

'Follow the railroad tracks ... now take the one on the left as it swings north and follow it to the Rhein.'

They reached the river and ahead of them on the other side was the German railway station, the *Badischer Bahnhof*. A heavy barge struggled against the stream as it made its way slowly up river. A car sat on deck and a clothes line towards the stern suggested that the captain's wife had been attending to their laundry.

'That railroad station was German territory in World War II Dennis, they came here to buy armaments and do their banking.'

The news was greeted with a barely concealed expletive from Ben who then followed their flight plan and began to follow the river downstream, bringing the chopper back to the south west bank in order to let Sam photograph the red sandstone cathedral with its patterned roof tiles, the *Münster*, on its cliff above the Rhein. Sam also took the *Rathaus*, with it's painted front and more patterned roof tiles, facing the *Marktplatz* set out with fruit and vegetable stalls. Basel life went on below them and Sam felt an intruder, aware that if the authorities found out just what he was up to they would be swift to bring it to a halt. They were now nicely positioned for the *Kantonsspital* and the *Frauenspital*, it would be useful to see whether there was anything about their location that would help if they decided to snatch Elizabeth at a hospital appointment.

'You're doing well Dennis. How about the *Spalentor?* ... Ah yes, there it is ahead of us.'

They headed for the old gate that had once been an entrance on the west of the walled city but it was the building on the next corner that was their real interest, *Schützenmattstrasse 20*, the *Strafgericht Basel-Stadt* - the criminal court. Here she came each month so perhaps ... .

'Is that the lot Alan?'

'Sure, we've got it all. You can take this thing back.'

Ben called up air traffic control and headed back to Basel-Mulhouse-Freiburg Airport as it had now been designated.

Sam sat back and watched the cars moving like snails below, this was certainly a good way to travel, though it was far from cheap!

Back at Airport Helicopter Basel Ben declined the offer of a job, Sam paid for the two flights and after they had shaken hands with Herr Schwander they returned to Sam's Ford Escort.

'I'm sorry, Ben, this thing's going to seem even more pedestrian after the chopper.'

'That's OK, I've enjoyed myself, you've paid and now I can smoke.'

'It's a relief to get that over, Ben. You'll have to tell me about your war service in Vietnam some time.' And they both laughed heartily.

***

They drove without further conversation and Sam contemplated a session in the darkroom, developing the films and making big enlargements, real big ones, to see what detail would show itself of features not visible from the ground. A pity to have to spend an afternoon in the dark on a fine warm spring day but this evening he was meeting a young woman near the university, he knew why he had arranged to see her again and yet he wondered whether there was really more than one reason for the meeting. How mixed were his motives? He had always enjoyed female company, but did his interest in her go further than that? He would have to make sure that it didn't - things were complicated enough already without adding a further romantic element. It was Elizabeth he wanted, but when would that be, if ever? So perhaps it was wise and prudent to keep Liz, another Gentile as it happened, in reserve.

The prints. that emerged from the darkroom were good, clear and crisp. In fact he was amazed at the detail. First of all he studied those of the *Untersuchungsgefängnis*, the Remand Prison. He had cropped the picture and blown up the roof to A4 size. Through a magnifying glass he studied it with a practised eye. He was disappointed but not surprised: a network of wires, which were probably electrified, would ensure that any attempt to lift a prisoner from the roof was a non-starter. It was both a disappointment and a relief: he had been cautioned against anything that would endanger Elizabeth or her unborn child and a helicopter rescue would have been a risky enterprise. The morning's flight had definitely ruled out that option. So he turned his attention to the photographs of the hospital and the court. He had plenty of time to ponder them before dinner with a certain young research student from the university.

Chapter 7

Wednesday 16th April 1997

It was mid-afternoon when Elizabeth got back to the wing from the Women's Hospital. They had done a scan and she'd seen the baby move. The excitement had stayed with her and she wanted to tell someone about it. Andrea was the only one of the girls around and she wondered about her state, 'How are you, Andrea? Are things any better at all?'

Andrea looked as withdrawn as usual, 'No better and not likely to get any better, Elizabeth. I don't know why you trouble to ask. I'm not being rude but it's true. Once I'd killed him I wish I'd done myself in and that would have been the end of it all.'

'I suppose I'm the only one here who has any real idea of what you're going through Andrea. After all I'm here on a murder charge too.'

'Yes, but I killed the man I loved, I'll never forgive myself.'

'Have you ever spoken, really spoken I mean, not just answered police questions ... have you spoken about it, Andrea?'

'I suppose not, but I don't want to, it hurts too much.'

'But you could tell me something about it, after all I'm in the same boat as you are.'

'Yes but you've not taken it as badly as I have ... I'll never forgive myself for what I did ... I just can't live with myself!'

'Perhaps it would help if I told you how I feel about what I did ... perhaps it would help me as well. Shall I try?'

'OK have a go but I won't be able to open up, I know

that.'

'I'd known Vladimir for a number of years, he was a colleague – you know what my line of business was?'

'You were a Russian spy?'

'Just so. We worked in the USA, and Canada and then in England. Our job was to get hold of business secrets not military ones, secrets that were worth a lot of money. Vladimir and I had been lovers, we'd had good times together but it was going nowhere, you see he'd got a wife and children in Moscow. But Vladimir wouldn't end the relationship, he seemed to think that he owned me and could do just as he wanted. Back in London he tried to rape me but spies are trained to defend themselves and he regretted the encounter.'

'But you didn't use a knife on him, did you?'

'No, unarmed combat, which pained him where it really hurts and sent him home to recover.'

'But that's not what got you into this place, is it?'

'No, and it's very confused. It's a kind of blur, you see. He may have been trying to rape me again, but I don't know for sure. But what is clear is that I shot him in the back of the head. They found Vladimir dead on the floor of my hotel room and me passed out and the gun with my finger prints and no one else's on it.'

'Do you think you did it?'

'I can't see that I didn't and I regret it, I really do, Andrea. We'd had great times in the past and all in all he wasn't a bad guy. I certainly didn't want him dead. I think I deserve whatever they are going to punish me with ... I feel guilty and it's not going to go away easily. Having a baby on the way makes it worse ... you know, who's going to bring it up and that sort of thing?'

'It's Vladimir's baby?'

'No, an Englishman that I was hoping to marry – but

that's a story for another time!'

'Elizabeth I feel guilty and it's *never* going to go away.'

'But there were reasons why you did what you did, Andrea?'

'Of course but ... OK I'll tell you about it.'

'I'm sure it will help ... but only as much as you can face for the moment.'

'I've always needed to have a strong man around, it started with my father: he was the dominant sort laying down the law to my mum and if she didn't do what he wanted giving her a clout round the ear. She just accepted it and I suppose I assumed it was the normal way men and women got on. So when I met Bruno I wasn't surprised that he wasn't very gentle. We got on OK but his temper often got out of hand, he wasn't just rough ... he was violent and I had plenty of bruises to show for it. One evening he came home the worse for drink, and the meal wasn't quite ready. Well, he threw the frying pan at me, food and all and it scalded me on my hands. I'd had enough, I couldn't take any more. The French cook's knife was on the table, I picked it up to defend myself, he ran at me ... and the next thing he was on the floor in a pool of blood ... and he wasn't ... he wasn't breathing ...' She stopped, closed her eyes and began to cry.

Elizabeth put her arm around her, 'And then?'

She managed to speak between sobs, 'He was a gonner, I could see that ... I panicked, put some cream on my hands to stop the pain, walked the streets till midnight and then gave myself in ... to the police. Then I wondered if I could have saved him by calling an ambulance ... but they said that it wouldn't have done any good, the knife was right through his heart ... ' She could manage no more and her sobbing became uncontrollable. A prison officer came over and Elizabeth indicated that matters weren't out of hand and that she could cope.

'Andrea, you know I'm here for shooting a former lover so I understand ... '

'You shot him, that was clean. I had his blood all over me ... I dream at night that I'm still covered in his blood AND THAT IT WILL NEVER WASH OFF.' She had become hysterical and Elizabeth could see that she needed help. The prison officer returned, said she'd called for the prison doctor to come and suggested to Elizabeth that she'd better return to her cell. Andrea managed to control herself sufficiently to insist that Elizabeth stay, 'She's the only one who's any idea how I feel.'

The doctor arrived, they got Andrea back to her cell and onto her bed and gave her a tranquiliser. Elizabeth remained with her in case she wanted to speak further.

'Andrea, I can understand how you feel ... I feel guilty for killing Vladimir. But for you it's all too vivid, for me it's a muddle, I can't replay it like you. The drink problem is one I can sympathise with. You see I had a step-father who was on the bottle, he was violent towards my mother and myself and he tried to attack me sexually while I was still at secondary school. I went to self defence classes and then he stayed away from my mother and myself ... well most of the time. Then one day he was found floating in a canal and we were rid of him at last. So, Andrea, I can sympathise with you and what you've suffered. I know that you're seeing a psychiatrist, you've told me you are, but you can always talk to me, any time. My experience isn't the same as yours but there are similarities and I can feel for you. I'll see whether they'll let me eat in here with you tonight before they lock us up.'

***

Back in her own cell Elizabeth stretched out on her bed. The haze surrounding the shooting of Vladimir still puzzled her but it seemed preferable to Andrea's ultra-vivid memories. She knew that the suicide watch on Andrea would be stepped up ... she must redouble her efforts to help her. Perhaps music would help to sooth and calm her down, she would suggest it to her. And she realised she hadn't told Andrea about the scan and the baby's movement, but it certainly wouldn't have been the right time to do so.

Life here in the *Untersuchungsgefängnis* was very different from anything she'd ever known before. Elizabeth had a lot more in common with these girls than most people would have guessed and this stiffened her resolve to help them in whatever way she could.

Chapter 8

Saturday 19th April 1997

The service was coming to an end. Sam sat near the back of the Basel synagogue involved in the Sabbath service and yet keeping an eye on the man three rows in front of him. He had arrived there about three hours before and taken a seat in the row next to the back, waiting to see whether Jakob Gold would come to worship. If he hadn't shown up Sam would have had to call on him at home but he had preferred to make contact this way and attract as little attention as possible. The Additional Service ended and the congregation, which had begun to thin out some time before, began to disperse. Sam removed his prayer shawl went to the back and chatted to the Warden, discovering that he had come from England many years before. They discussed the *Chazan*, the cantor who had led the service, an immigrant to Switzerland from Israel - a singer of the songs of Zion in a strange land and a strange culture, very different from his *Chassidic* origins in the *Mea Shearim* quarter of Jerusalem. Sam wondered how the cantor, his wife and family were adapting to life away from the restraints that kept you on the rails, so that the strictest observance of the Jewish law with all its intricacies was a communal thing. They were away from that all pervading community where it required a positive effort by the individual to do anything other than be totally observant.

His quarry came towards them, nodded to Sam and the Warden and headed for the door. Sam bade the Warden farewell and followed. He would make contact in the yard, it would be more natural and not frighten him - with high security around the synagogue Sam did not wish to create fears of kidnap and a resulting disturbance. He closed in and, coming alongside the other man, touched his arm addressing him in Hebrew and German, '*Shabbat shalom!* Dr Gold? I wonder if I might have a word with you?'

Jakob Gold stopped, turned and looked at Sam. He took his time and then replied, '*Shabbat shalom!* Certainly, so long as it isn't business. If it is I'm afraid it will have to wait until tomorrow I value this Queen of Days and do not allow business to spoil it. You are American, I think? Yes, I am right - then perhaps you would rather talk in English, I suspect you would find it easier.'

'It would help if you were happy to do that, my German is useful up to a point but not beyond.'

'Good. And where would you prefer to talk, here in the yard or as I walk home? You see I haven't driven here, unlike some - no, I'm not being critical, better to have them drive here, or at any rate to a spot out of sight of the synagogue, than not come at all. But for me I'm happy with the old ways and I walk.'

'I'm more than happy to walk with you and keep you company, Dr Gold.'

'Call me Jakob, please.' He was surprised to hear himself say the words, he was usually a little formal with strangers, and he wondered whether it was a subconscious response to the stranger as an American. He dismissed the idea and decided that it had more to do with the man's character. There was something about him that aroused interest and inspired confidence.

'But you haven't told me your name, though you evidently know mine well enough - you are in pharmaceuticals I suppose?'

Sam paused before replying, he wondered how open he could be with this man. Would he respect a confidence and keep it? He would have to take a chance, though there was that about Jakob Gold to suggest that it was a risk worth taking. 'Sam Kagan from Brooklyn, New York, Sir.' He paused looked Jakob Gold in the eye, took a breath and added, 'Until lately an employee of Mossad but now thinking of going back to my old calling as a rabbi.'

He had expected Gold to show surprise but he showed none and it was Sam who was surprised by his reply, 'I've been expecting you or someone from the Institute to make contact. Come on let us be on our way and continue our conversation as we make our way home. We'll both have an appetite by the time we get to Allschwil and Paula cooked enough yesterday to satisfy several hungry Mossad agents, you are alone I suppose?'

'Alone and an ex-agent, Dr Gold, sorry Jakob. But how is it that you were expecting me?'

'My colleague Bernhardt Schmidt received a message from a friend in Tel Aviv that you were in Switzerland and might wish to speak with me. So I am to receive the blessing of a Cohen, even if it isn't one of the High Holy days. Out here in the *Diaspora* we have to wait for our blessings, they don't come Sabbath by Sabbath as in Israel.'

'You have but to make *aliyah*, Jakob, then you could have weekly blessings!'

'Is that the message from the Institute? Surely you're not on a recruiting drive for the Israeli drug industry or is Lekem back in business?' They both laughed, at ease with one another.

'No it's not a recruitment drive and Lekem wasn't one of our great successes. Jonathan Pollard's imprisonment in the USA is a constant reminder of that.'

'So Pollard was being run by your people, then?'

'No comment, and I would prefer you to forget that we spoke about him.'

'I have forgotten already, Sam. Strange how the memory plays tricks.'

'No, it's not an offer of a job here or in Israel. It's about a young Russian woman who is being looked after by the Swiss prison authorities.'

'The unfortunate Elisabeth Fielder, I presume.'

'Just that. I need to hear how she is and to try to get a message to her.' He paused again, 'This isn't for Mossad, at least not directly, it's personal, I want her out!' He was aware of his increased heartbeat and a feeling of agitation. He knew that it had showed in his voice and that Jakob Gold had detected it.

'She is an emotional concern? If so take care. I would warn you off - look at the state that Peter Lewis is in! Do you know him?'

'Yes, I know him and something of his problems, though he doesn't know me.'

'It seems that you are an observer of human beings but not one who is directly involved in them and their lives - I assume that your work makes it that way?'

'Affirmative - Yes, that's how life and work are so often ... '

'But this is different. You, at the moment anyway, are not the dispassionate though committed seeker of information, working night and day for Danny Yatom, if he is still the head of your organisation.'

'He's still there, I believe, but don't forget I've retired from it. I'm my own man now and on my own business.'

'But not without friends inside the Institute who will put in a word for you and perhaps give you assistance when you need it? They prepared me for making your acquaintance at any rate.'

'I don't want to involve you in anything that would do you damage or create problems, Jakob.'

'So you do not want to sign me up as one of your agents? I think that I would be too old for that.'

'I need to know how Elizabeth is bearing up and I need to get a message to her.'

'You said that you wanted her out of prison. I am not sure that I ought to be told anything about that - the less I know the less I will have to deny if your plans go wrong, or indeed if they go right! Supposing you were to get the young woman out of prison, you can be sure that the Basel police would be anxious to have a word with everyone who had even the slightest acquaintance of her - and that includes my wife and myself.'

'I wouldn't wish to involve either of you in that way - you mentioned your wife preparing today's food. It would be better if I didn't meet her, so I'll leave you before we reach your home.'

'No need. She went to visit her sister in Luzern yesterday afternoon. I am alone and we will be able to speak in confidence and without interruption. So let us leave the details until we have eaten - I am assuming that you have time on your hands and that you are not wishing to rush down to the *Waaghof* and blow a hole in the wall this afternoon.'

'Your assumptions are correct and I would enjoy a quiet afternoon at your house. I've walked miles around Basel recently and it will be pleasant just to take things easy.'

'And you can take the No. 6 tram back once dark has fallen, rabbis should set an example to others especially if they are Cohens! Now tell me about how things are going in Brooklyn with the *Lubavitchers* - do they still think that their late *Rebbe* is the Messiah. You come from that part of New York and you are a rabbi so your opinion will be worth hearing ... '

And so, deep in conversation, they continued their hour's walk towards Allschwil, lunch and an afternoon of discussing Elizabeth Fielder and her current situation.

***

Pickled herrings were followed by cold roast beef with a variety of salads and there was an ample choice of desserts - Gold clearly had a very sweet tooth and the walk to and from the synagogue had given him a substantial appetite. He was an hospitable man who was glad to share a meal with a visitor whose conversation interested and stimulated him. The activities of *Chabad* in Brooklyn had occupied their conversation well into the meal and Sam noticed that Gold was no mean Talmudic scholar. When he had remarked on this the reply had been, 'It interests me and it keeps the brain in excellent working order, I am a better chemist and, more importantly, a better human being for the exercise. And are you or, rather, were you a better agent because of your rabbinical training?'

It was a subject that had occurred to Sam from time to time and he was not surprised by the question, 'In some ways a poorer agent but, I think, always a better human being. Analysing problems and balancing opinions, that all helps but there are times when because you are a better human you are a worse agent. When moral considerations cause you to question what you are asked to do or when you find that you've been used by your masters in a particularly unpleasant way, where your actions, unbeknown to you at the time, have consequences that you consider reprehensible - well in situations like that you are a worse agent.'

'And that is why you have now left the Institute?'

'I might have said, "No comment", but, yes, that's why. I believe that will go no further, Jakob.'

'I've forgotten what you said already, Sam! I'm not probing but just one more question. Did that have anything to do with the odd things that were going on at the time that Elizabeth shot her Russian friend and a certain kidnapping and rescue took place?'

'In a word, yes. But I can't say more than that, Jakob.'

'I'm not asking for any more. But now we are back to the reason for your visit - and let me say I'm glad you came, I have enjoyed our conversation and it has allowed me to weigh you up - to ascertain your mass on the moral scales. I am impressed, you are certainly not weighed in the balance and found wanting! That being so I am prepared to trust you in a way that I would not trust the average operative from the Institute or from any of its allies or competitors. I have told you that I do not want to know what you plan in relation to Miss Fielder but I am willing to assist you in getting a message to her, though I must tell you that will not be at all easy.'

'But she is allowed visitors?'

'She is allowed visitors, yes. But there is no physical contact. The visitors sit in a small cubicle and are separated from the prisoner by a glass screen. They converse by means of microphones and loudspeakers. I repeat there is no physical contact. The whole thing is very claustrophobic, to me as a visitor it was frightening and I was just that, a visitor. To the prisoner it must be far worse, emphasising their captivity and that they are deprived of normal human relationships. There is no way in which a visitor could pass a message. There is no way in which a meaningful message and reply could be passed either in writing or by word of mouth - there is a police officer in the next cubicle and also they probably record all that is said. You see, it is forbidden for a prisoner to discuss the offence for which they are being held. The authorities think that it might somehow prejudice the case, result in the perversion or intimidation of witnesses. Gifts are left at the door, labelled by the visitor with the prisoner's name and examined by the authorities before reaching the prisoner. Post is censored - I doubt whether they read everything but there is always the risk that they might and that would be of no assistance to you.'

There was a pause before Sam spoke, 'And the lawyers, they are able to speak with the prisoners without a police audience or a recorder running?'

'Of course, but an honest lawyer is not going to be willing to be the go between for their client and someone who is planning a jail break or something totally illegal.'

'I am sure that an honest lawyer wouldn't be willing. But one who was rather less than honest and was in need of a good payment ... '

'Would be hard to find.'

'But not impossible?'

'Probably not if one knew where to look. But in any case Miss Fielder has Sylvia Brunner her own highly competent and honest advocate. I'll give you her business card before you leave.'

'But Elizabeth might need a second opinion and a less sensitive and proper advocate might be found?'

'Indeed but you have to first think of a reason why she might wish to obtain the services of another of the legal class. For instance who might try to persuade her?'

There was a silence and Gold refilled their glasses, emptying the bottle of *Dôle* which had accompanied the beef and the dessert. 'Well Jakob, how about a visit from a chaplain, a Russian Orthodox priest might be in order, someone with a beard to match mine.'

'They know she's got SVR connections, the papers made that clear, so they're not likely to view a visit from a compatriot without a great deal of suspicion. Once again she would have to be persuaded to ask for a visit and there's no reason why she should unless it was to baptise the child when it's born.'

'Their child ... and when is it due to arrive? A prison is hardly the ideal place for a pregnant woman. I assume that Lewis really is the father.'

'Yes, Lewis is the father, not that he's in much of a state for fatherhood at the moment, poor fellow. Though he did seem just a little brighter when he was here a week ago, perhaps he's beginning to recover. The shock of February's events on top of the problems they are experiencing with his son, those things coupled with a rather sensitive conscience have badly unsettled him. The hurt of being deceived by the woman he loved came as a severe blow, of course ... knocked his feet from under him. Then the divorce from Ruth that in prospect seemed so straightforward and amicable to him dropped out of sight when he realised the harm it was doing to Michael, that's their son. Michael was the first one to need psychiatric treatment and now it's Peter as well. I feel for the whole family.'

'And *Elizabeth*, how is *she* reacting to her situation, she must be in a distressed state as well as Peter Lewis.'

'You won't be surprised that she has good days and bad days, Sam. Though she seems to be bearing up pretty well. Of course, her pregnancy does not help.'

'So Elizabeth leaves the prison ... for hospital visits?'

'Yes, of course, and there are also court visits. They

have to take her before a judge each month to keep her locked up.'

'So I gathered and I might see her there ... from the distance?'

'Yes, I suppose so. There are railings round the place so I suppose you might be able to see her arrive. It's an afternoon visit around 2 o'clock and I do know when they take place, it's in my diary.'

'If I could see her so could the Russians ... that's a cause for concern.'

'You think they might have similar plans to yours?'

'That or snuffing her out as a source of embarrassment, I'm sure that they'd prefer not to have their activities made public in open court and they're sure to blame her for the outcome of their schemes.'

Gold looked at his diary, 'As it happens Elizabeth is due to make a court appearance on Monday afternoon. That will give you time to scout out the area around the *Strafgericht*, the court, before she makes an appearance, though I am unable to guarantee that you will see much of her.'

'That's a real help, I'd like to see her, I haven't done so since the day she shot her colleague. Mind you the more visible she is the more she is at risk from her old employers. And when's the child due?'

'They tell me it is some time in August. You have met her? You have just said so. So you were you the man the police were looking for, who had been with her on the Rigi just before she shot her Russian friend?'

'That was me but I had nothing to do with the shooting or any idea that any such a thing would happen within a couple of hours of leaving her. I ask you to believe me, Jakob!'

'I have already said that I trust you. In my eyes you are

a man of integrity. I just ask that you do not complicate things and make it any worse for her with a failed attempt at rescuing her. And if there's anything you know that might help her case in court you must make sure that *Advokat* Brunner her lawyer can use it.'

'And how am I to get a message to Elizabeth?'

'I have been thinking since the subject of her pregnancy came up that it might just provide the opportunity you need. I have already said that her outings to the court are not the only ones she makes - she also attends an ante-natal clinic at the *Frauenspital*, the Women's Hospital, here in Basel. You may have seen it, next to the *Kantonsspital* near *Die Drei Könige* ... which of course you know well!'

'Elizabeth and I ate there on our return from the mountains.'

'I thought so. Well, I know a nurse who works at the *Frauenspital's* ante-natal unit. She might be prepared to be your go-between.' He paused and fixed his gaze on Sam, 'She's thinking of making *aliyah* and it could well be that you or your friends at the Institute could make her settling in and finding work and accommodation a little easier than might otherwise be the case. *If* she is willing to assist you, then I will set up a meeting between the two of you but, and I must emphasise this, that will be the end of my involvement. The Swiss gave me shelter from the Nazis during World War II, I was one of the lucky ones who did get into this country, and I have no wish to become involved in a conspiracy against the country that has become my home. Also I have experienced the arrangements for visiting the inmates of the *Waaghof* and I do not wish to see Paula, that is my wife, sitting on the other side of a glass screen in a small cubicle making polite conversation with me once a week. I would make a bad prisoner and ... '

Sam broke in, 'And you would miss decent food and wine!'

'That and freedom. Freedom is something that I value highly and, as a Swiss Jew, I do so constantly and not just on Swiss National Day or at *Pesah*. Now how will I contact you to let you know whether the nurse is willing to help?'

'It would be better if you didn't know where I'm living. Perhaps if I telephoned you from a call box later in the week after you've spoken to her. Then you could give me her telephone number and she and I could arrange to meet, perhaps in the coffee bar across the road from the *SBB Bahnhof* - she could sum me up over a cup of coffee and decide whether she wished to hear any more on the matter.'

'I would not try to advise you on the techniques of persuading people to help you in your nefarious activities, I'm sure you do not need any help there, but it does seem a sensible approach. Well then, telephone me on Wednesday after 20.00 hours, Paula will be out at that time - I have no wish to involve her in this - and I will let you know whether I have succeeded in finding you a potential conduit to Miss Fielder.'

'Thanks, I'm grateful, Jakob.'

'That's dealt with. Now Sam tell me why you think Paula and I should make *aliyah* at our age rather than remain in the *Diaspora.'*

***

Sam ignored the tram and returned from Allschwil to Basel on foot. It was dark, Sabbath was over, but he needed to walk off the substantial meal and the wine that

Jakob Gold had brought to the table. He had enjoyed his company and their discussion but now had to give some serious thought to what he should tell Elizabeth. Her pregnancy was a complicating factor for him, both personally and also so far as the various options for ways of escape were concerned. Nevertheless it might provide a means of access to Elizabeth. Without the help of the nurse he could only think of trying to approach Elizabeth through her lawyer who would probably refuse the rôle of go between for an illegal act. Not only would the ante-natal visits provide an opportunity for getting a message through, assuming the nurse was willing to help, they might also provide the opportunity for the rescue bid.

He crossed the Rhein on the *Mittlere Rheinbrücke* and stopped to look at the water moving swiftly under the bridge and the lights of a large barge passing under the *Wettsteinbrücke*, coming towards him and perhaps heading for the sea at Rotterdam. He looked up and saw the spires of the *Münster* - somewhere there lay the remains of Erasmus, the Renaissance scholar from Rotterdam who had been an advocate of study in the ancient tongues, in Hebrew and Greek rather than in Latin translations. The reflection gave him pleasure, he was a scholar as well as a man of action and he appreciated true scholarship. One day he would have a look around the *Münster*, the city's cathedral, to see what he could find to mark the scholar's resting place. Yes, he would go and have a look, Cohen though he was.

The barge sped under him and was gone. He turned and watched it head for the next bridge. On the left the lighted windows of *Die Drei Könige* caught his eye. In a little over twenty four hours in February he had become even more the emotional captive of Elizabeth: he recalled the sudden decision to join her at her dinner table at the

Hotel International, the Sunday out together in the snows of the Rigi and then dinner at *Die Drei Könige*. But for that lapse of discipline and his efforts to tantalise Vladimir her colleague he would not be here in Basel standing on a bridge over the Rhein and wondering how to extricate her from the grip of the Swiss authorities.

His world had been turned upside down, he was now an ex-employee of Mossad - but then that would have been the case, Elizabeth or no Elizabeth, his masters had used him to do things that he could never approve and he had had no doubts about resigning, nor ever would - and he was almost on his own on this personal mission without much back-up or assistance. Still he was not totally without assistance, the Institute had prepared Jakob for their encounter and Jakob had set in motion what seemed a hopeful line of communication which might even prove to be the means of getting Elizabeth out. And he had Noam, alias Ben, as a helper in the project.

He realised that he was standing in the middle of the bridge watching the barge's navigation lights disappear in the distance while people were strolling past, mostly ignoring him - there were always plenty of sightseers who found the river interesting so he did not excite any curiosity. He hoped that this would be so when the time came for action and his rescue plan was put into action.

He resumed his journey and at the end of the bridge he reached *Klein Basel*, turned right and went down the steps and made his way along the river bank, the *Oberer Rheinweg*. He liked its trees, small fountains and old lamp standards. The houses were set well back from the river and were mainly terraced. He reached No 21a, a small three storied house with off-white walls, light gray windows and shutters and an oak door. He looked around carefully before he dug in his pocket for the keys. He was always cautious, it was second nature and he supposed he would never shake it off. There was no one around apart from an elderly couple standing looking at the river so he undid the two locks in the substantial door, quickly let himself in and relocked the door. It might be only *Klein Basel* and not very far from the red light district of the city but it was prime property and he was glad that the Institute had been willing to pay its rent. Yes, they must be expecting to get something in return for their investment. He was sure that their assistance did not stem from remorse over their actions in Operation Guineapig as it had been renamed at the debriefing at HQ in March.

Standing in the livingroom he murmured a prayer from the service for the end of the Sabbath:

> 'Blessed are you, O Lord our God, King of the universe, who has made a distinction between the holy and the profane, between light and darkness, between Israel and the nations, between the seventh day and the six working days. Blessed are you, O Lord, who has made a distinction between the holy and the profane. Amen.'

He knew that for himself the distinction between the holy and profane, between Israel and the nations, had become blurred as a consequence of his feelings for this young Russian woman, a gentile who was carrying the child of another man, conceived out of wedlock. And he knew, with total certainty, that it was not simply a matter of feelings but the result of a decision made with all the resolution of a subtle mind and a powerful will: he knew that he had now one object in life and one alone. He *would* get her out of jail. He prized her freedom for its own sake, or rather for Elizabeth's sake. Whether she would have him didn't seem to matter or at any rate not enough to affect the decision. If she did it would be wonderful - though there were many problems in the way of such a thing especially for a rabbi who was a Cohen. His origins seemed to be getting in the way of his relations with both the dead and the living! Never had he been so conscious of his priestly identity. Before he had borne it lightly and enjoyed its privileges. Now it had become burdensome for him.

Freedom, Jakob had spoken of how he valued it, Sam was totally with him in that, and what he wanted and guarded for himself and his People, he was determined to secure for Elizabeth. The concurrence of the desires of heart and mind and the knowledge that he sought it in an unselfish way, for her sake primarily, though nor solely, gave him strength and peace of mind. He had no doubts about the rightness of what he was planning to do. There was only one qualification - nothing he did must endanger anyone's life or do them permanent harm. However that might complicate the operation it was a principle he felt bound to follow.

The kettle boiled as he looked through the window and across the Rhine towards the *Münster* whose towers stood out against the glow of the city. He liked it here, it was a city that appealed to him with its university and old streets. He made a large pot of strong coffee and placed it on the table with a large white porcelain cup and a sugar bowl. He found a bag of St Gallen buns and put a couple on a plate. He settled down at the table. Tonight he would read, or rather study. He took up his copy of *A Guide for the Perplexed*, the work of Moses Maimonides - it amused him that Maimonides' philosophical work had been influential in the Christian world of the Middle Ages because they hadn't realised that its author was a Jew. Sometimes it was useful for your real identity to be hidden, especially if you were a Jew: for much of his working life it had been thus

He read well into the night, his own perplexities were not theological and philosophical ones but were over Elizabeth and escape plans. But he kept them completely out of his mind as he grappled with the writing of the old sage - philosopher, rabbi and physician - who lay buried in Tiberias, beside Kinneret, the Sea of Galilee. He could picture in his mind the entrance to the garden in which Maimonides' body lay buried and its sign 'Entry of Cohanim Prohibited' which had kept him out. In the days before they had mistakenly tried to beautify the place with a roof he had looked down into the garden and been satisfied to pay, from a distance, his respects to a man whose intellect and compassion he greatly admired.

Chapter 9

Wednesday 23rd April 1997

They sat in arm chairs angled towards the window of her apartment, with its view over the Rhein, and on opposite sides of a coffee table on which were the remains of a pizza and an almost empty bottle of *Fendant Blanc* from the *V*alais. The bookshelves in the room were inadequate to accommodate her library and in the corner were piles of books with paper slips marking significant passages: clearly it was a working library. Liz reached forward and poured the last of the wine into their glasses. She lifted hers in a toast, 'Here's to hoping that this won't dull our minds too much!'

Sam lifted his glass, 'Well it's certainly lubricated our tongues, though whether it's clouded our minds I don't know ... probably not.'

'Don't lets get on to probability theory, Sam! It's been enough discussing views on freewill! It's been like a brilliant seminar, but then you've had experience of just that.'

He looked startled for a moment, 'You're guessing at my background, Liz?'

There was a pause before she replied, 'Not guessing Sam, I know. Let me explain. But first of all let me say that you're not in any danger, I'm not from the other side but from your own. I know that you're Sam Kagan and that you've recently retired from the Institute.'

She sipped her wine but Sam didn't touch his, now concerned to keep as clear a mind as possible to deal with this bolt out of the blue.

'I appreciate the shock I've given you, Sam. So first of all I'll give you a couple of reasons why I've come clean and then tell you how I know. Firstly I've grown very fond of you, in fact I've found myself falling in love with you and I don't think that would be helpful for either of us.' She lent forward and touched his hand, 'Sam, I really am fond of you, and if you whisked me off to bed I wouldn't be able to say 'No'. But please don't do that! I know all about your feelings for Elizabeth and have no wish to complicate your life any further. The other reason is that I feel guilty spying on you – OK I'll tell you who asked me to do it in a minute – you don't deserve that kind of treatment.' She removed her hand and Sam wasn't sure whether he welcomed or regretted the move.

'Well, Liz, I must confess that I've enjoyed our meetings not just for the intellectual stimulus but for being with a lively and attractive young woman. I'll miss our meetings, Liz – if that really is your name! You've probably been briefed on my aliases and on Elizabeth's.'

'I too would miss our meetings, but it may be that they needn't cease if we exercise a little restraint.'

'Nice as that would be I can't give any promises - though it would be good if we could. But it's confession time, Liz. Who put you up to this and why?' He allowed himself a sip of wine, suddenly aware of how dry his mouth had become.

'It all began at a meeting of the Swiss/Israel Society – oh, by the way I *really am* Liz Curtis, I *do* come from Toronto and I *am* working for a further degree in psychology here in Basel – so I'm real!'

'Well, that's a relief!' he ventured.

'To go back to that meeting, Sam, I chatted with the Cultural Attache from your Bern Embassy, over a glass of Israeli wine as it happened, from somewhere in the Golan ... '

'*Katzrin's* the name of the place and they make some

very decent wines.'

'I thought nothing of our conversation and then a couple of days later another official from the Embassy 'phoned me and arranged a meeting, wanting to chat about my area of research ... which is precisely as I have told you, the motivation of murderers. After beating around the bush for a while he asked me to keep an eye on you and to report back to him. They engineered our meeting in the restaurant, following you and then calling me in. They hoped you would take the bait and see my research project as a possible way of getting through to Elizabeth. They thought you might want to use me in that way and I suspect that they hoped you would weary of the quest and fall for me. He didn't use any nasty expression like "spying" but that was what it amounted to. And in return I was offered some help with my rent. I didn't know anything about you but he filled in the picture. Said you were in danger of becoming a loose cannon and could endanger Israeli security and that I'd be doing them a real service if I could make your acquaintance and report back. I didn't know you then and, to be honest, I was flattered to be given the task. I know you now Sam and I'm not prepared to play their dirty game any more. I'll give you the details of the Embassy officials and you can check it out just to be sure I'm not a Russian plant. I'm sorry, Sam, though if they hadn't involved me I would never have met you, or probably not - back to probability theory, you see!'

'And of your freewill you're resigning from your assignment. It does seem a pity if you're going to lose your rent supplement, Liz. Perhaps the answer is to stay in post and feed them inconsequential information, nothing false but nothing vital. In the parlance of my old profession I would have *turned* you. Would that be acceptable, it would be poetic justice.'

'Let me think it over, Sam. I'm disposed to say it's a good idea. Let me sleep, on it.'

'And Liz, the other aspect – *our* emotional entanglement – because I admit I've strong feelings for you - we'll have to take care.'

'Yes, and I would like to keep our meetings going, Sam.' She came round to his armchair, 'Sam, you kiss me on the cheek when we meet … can we kiss properly just this once, it might help me to sleep - on the decision – not with you, I fear. But only if it's of your own freewill – whatever that may mean in the philosopher's mind! By the way you more or less gave yourself away earlier with a quote from Maimonides which I recognised, " … *all is foreseen, yet permission is given.*". My first degree, you see, was in psychology *and* philosophy.'

He laughed and pulled her onto his lap, it would help to resolve the tensions that her disclosure had created for both of them, adding for Sam to those already there, for he had hit an emotional low in his hopes of securing Elizabeth's liberty. He slipped his hand under Liz's sweater, 'Well, well no bra!'

'Can I assume that you're not objecting, Sam Kagan?'

'You've assumed correctly, Liz. But now that you've become a double agent perhaps I can reward you with some new lingerie!'

'Which I shall keep undercover, of course!'

Sam mused to himself: *undercover* was OK but not *under the covers*, they had agreed on that. He owed it to Liz not to go too far, something they could all too easily do. And, despite the absence of real hope, he had an obligation to Elizabeth to be faithful to her. But was it faithfulness to *her* or to *an image of her* that he had constructed in his mind? She had known him for but an evening and a day while he had known her for much longer but from afar. It was another area for a philosophical deliberation with psychological overtones! But he somehow felt that he would not be debating the issue with Liz.

She left his knee and stood up. She slipped her sweater over her head, faced him and smiled, 'It's OK Sam, it was getting in the way but this is the limit of the strip-tease – I promise you.' She wanted him to know that if his quest for Elizabeth failed, then she, Liz, was more than willing to be his partner.

***

An hour later he let himself into his place by the river and, as he waited for the kettle to boil, turned over in his mind Liz's revelation of the Institute's activities. There seemed to be several possibilities. He found a piece of paper and wrote them down:

1. The Institute had gone back on their offer of help, though earlier they had supplied the false documentation he had asked for and they were paying the rent for this house.
2. There were two separate camps within the Institute, pro and anti Sam factions.
3. Someone in the Bern Embassy was working for the other side, for the Russians, who were anxious to know what was happening regarding Elizabeth.

Tomorrow he would give it hard thought and decide which of those colleagues that he still trusted in Tel Aviv should be contacted. It was bad enough if the Institute were using Liz, far worse if she were the unwary pawn of the

SVR, and far, far worse if she were knowingly working for them. He was pretty sure that it wasn't the latter scenario but in security nothing should be discounted too quickly.

His thoughts returned to their evening together and especially the last half hour and how hard it had been to pull himself from her embrace and leave. But he knew that had been the right course, wiser than intercourse with her. He owed it to Elizabeth to stay chaste, or at least reasonably so ... and there he was back with his philosophical conundrum! And then it struck him that his former fiancée Mia had been absent from his considerations.

***

A few minutes later Noam returned home to be invited to join Sam on a stroll by the river.

'I needed to get out of the house Noam in case it has been bugged either by our people or by some other outfit, possibly Russian.'

'But our lot are paying the rent, Sam, they're giving a helping hand. Why would they want to bug us?'

'I'm just back from a very interesting evening with Liz. You remember the young woman I met up near the university, the research student.'

'With your interest in her I'm unlikely to forget!'

'Well, Liz was a *plant* by someone with an interest in what I'm up to in Basel! She's just told me that she's in the pay of our Bern Embassy. It wasn't just by chance that we met up the other lunch-time: I was tailed and she was then called in to make my acquaintance. She's come clean, didn't like spying on me, thought I didn't deserve such treatment.'

'You mean she's grown fond of you, Sam!'

'I won't deny that there's an element of that Noam but I think that she genuinely feels she's been used, and she doesn't like it. As I see it there are three possibilities ... ' And he read out his note that he had written. 'Tomorrow I need you to set up a meeting with Shimon at the embassy, get him to name a place and time where we can meet. I need to know who's behind this.'

'Will do, boss. It's not comfortable having to deal with this as well. Can you trust the girl?'

'I hope so, I can't see that she would have told me this if she hadn't been genuine. By the way I 'phoned Jakob Gold this evening and the ante-natal nurse is a non-runner – she left for Israel last week. It seems that the only way to get a message to Elizabeth is via her lawyer who isn't going to countenance anything illegal. We're no further forward, unless crossing off non-starters like the chopper-lift from the roof of the jail is progress.'

'Perhaps it is, Sam. I know you won't give up.'

'The other thing that gets me down, Noam, is that my streetcraft is getting rusty – after I left you at the Café Schiesser the other morning I thought I'd kept a wary eye open for anyone tailing me ... seemingly I wasn't good enough and that annoys me. We'll need to take more care in future,'

Chapter 10

Wednesday 21st May 1997

'Well you've had your afternoon in the sun Elizabeth ... was it worth all the trouble?' Trudi greeted Elizabeth on her return to the women's wing.

'I know you think that the trip to the court for the remand hearing is a waste of time but I enjoy it. I know we can exercise on the roof here but there are trees at the court and people going by – normal life, I suppose.'

'Doesn't that just rub it in that you're locked up here, Elizabeth? Going out just means that you've got to come back inside again.'

'That's true but I still like to get out for an hour or so once a month, Trudi.'

'And you've also got your trips to the Women's Hospital, you had one last week didn't you?'

'Yes, that's another break from here and away from the law. They treat me just like any other patient though I don't sit in the queue so I suppose I'm like a private patient.'

'And how is the baby coming along? I wouldn't know what it's like being *that* pregnant, I had my terminations quite early on. You know, I'd like to have a child, be a mum make a family, even find a husband. You see you've given me ideas, Elizabeth.'

'You're thinking about what I said Trudi? Do you want to give the secretarial and IT thing a go?'

'First I've got to get completely off drugs, Elizabeth. That's a plus of being here they do help you to give up ... and I want to, I really do, and I want to give up selling sex but I'm afraid of being dragged back into it.'

'My lawyer might be able to help, there must be some

organisations that could help you change direction, may I ask her?'

'That's typical of you Elizabeth, "May I ask her?" you may be posh but you're not stuck up and superior ... you're a helper, you don't patronise!'

'Well, well Trudi your English is coming on, our sessions are paying off. You're becoming quite fluent, I liked that bit, "You don't patronise." - you've been reading the books I gave you? ... I thought so. I've told you before, you're a clever girl and you owe it to yourself to make the best of things. You asked about the baby just now, well there aren't any problems. The hospital is happy with progress and it's due around the end of July. Then the problems will begin, this isn't the best place for a baby or an older child. And it's a murder charge that I'm facing and you don't just get a year or two for that. But how it happened is still confused, it's all a bit of a muddle. The shrinks are trying to help but they haven't achieved much.'

'How about your man, Elizabeth? Will he stand by you and look after the baby?'

'He'll do all he can to help. He's a good man but he's not my man any longer ... that's not his fault. Even before the shooting our relationship was beginning to fall apart. Shall I tell you the story, Trudi? OK, you're sitting comfortably so I'll begin. Peter had been separated from his wife for some time and they were planning a divorce. I got a job with his company, how is another story, and in a short time we'd fallen for one another and were talking about marriage. But then their son started to have problems, scared that his dad would dump him, that sort of thing, screaming nightmares. Then Peter began to go to pieces and I knew that our bliss was going to end. And then ... and then came the shooting and Peter discovered that I wasn't English or Canadian but a Russian and a Russian spy at that. So he's had a breakdown, he almost threw himself out of a window and his wife only just managed to stop him. And the only solution has been for him to return to his wife and son ... I wouldn't want him to do anything else, Trudi.' She blinked back a tear.

'I've never met a spy before, Elizabeth. It must have been an exciting job, do you miss it. Of course you do, if you were still spying you'd be out of this place. Might they swap you for a Swiss spy?'

'Very unlikely, Trudi! I don't expect they've got any Swiss spies in Russian jails although I'm sure they could pick up one if they wanted to. More important I have no wish to go back to Russia.'

'Poor, Elizabeth!'

'It could be worse, I might be in a Russian jail and I couldn't be sure of getting out of it alive. They don't like failed spies who shoot their colleagues.' She wondered whether to be open with Trudi and decided to take the risk. 'Trudi let me tell you something in confidence. I can trust you? ... Good. A lot of my time was spent in the USA and Canada looking for business secrets – they call it industrial espionage – well the best way to the secrets was often via the boss's bed and that was part of my job. So, Trudi, you can see ... I can understand how you've had to earn your living, it isn't pleasant being in bed with people you dislike. If you're willing we're going to set about changing things for you, for the better. Does that seem a good idea?'

Trudi had begun to cry quietly but managed to get out her thanks, 'Elizabeth ... this is probably the first time anyone has been open with me and understanding ... '

Chapter 11

Friday 23rd May 1997

Having completed their shopping, Sam and Liz sat in the *Café Schiesser*, for coffee and *Kuchen*. They had just left a small specialist lingerie shop where Liz had spent the best part of three quarters of an hour working her way through a large part of their stock. Eventually she had reduced the choice to three sets of lingerie and was having difficulty in making up her mind when Sam interjected, 'You'll look fine in all of them, Liz. We'll take the lot.'

'No, Sam. I don't want you to think I'm trying to force you into extravagance.'

'Don't look a gift horse in the mouth Liz. Make the most of your rôle.' He lowered his voice, 'It's your double agent remuneration for the next month or so.'

She'd squeezed his hand and took her purchases to the assistant who'd greeted her with a smile and murmured, 'Lucky girl.'

Yes, they are rather nice.'

'I don't mean the lingerie. I mean him!'

'Oh, just a friend.'

'I'd like one like that. Make sure to look after him.'

Their conversation had been interrupted by the arrival of Sam at the counter, wallet in hand to pay the bill and shepherd her back into the *Marktplatz* and into *Schiessers*.

Their pot of coffee arrived and Sam poured it into their cups. 'Not the only cups you've been concerned with this afternoon, Liz.'

For a moment she didn't get it, then she flushed very slightly, 'Sam K, you're a wicked fellow but I'm fond of you. I liked the way you paid in cash leaving no trace of our visit.'

'I expect that they're often paid in cash – unfaithful husbands kitting out their mistresses and not wanting it to show up on the credit card statement!'

'So that's what you've just been doing! I'll have to beware of you.'

'That's not what the assistant said, Liz!'

'Oh you heard then?'

'I've very sharp hearing which helps at times. But you think that we left no trace of our visit to the lingerie shop?'

'You paid in cash didn't you?'

'True enough, but isn't it likely that the assistant would remember you and she evidently noticed me, so that's the first thing. Rule one: don't stand out, blend into the background. What else, Liz?'

'You're the expert, Sam.'

'What about CCTV. It's there to deter thieves and catch them but it records all that goes on in the shop. We're on the tape, Liz. If someone wants to look at today's customers we're there playing a starring role! Though don't ask me how long they keep the tapes before wiping them and reusing them.'

'So it's hard to leave no trace of our activities.'

'Hard but not impossible. After all unless someone does an underwear audit on you there would be no trace of today's gift – nothing in your bank account for instance. And talking of bank accounts, I guess that your "rent supplement" from the embassy doesn't appear in your bank statements but comes in plain white envelopes?' She nodded her agreement.

Sam lowered his voice, 'Incidentally I'd like your permission to give your apartment a sweep. By that I don't mean a clean up but I'd just like to be sure it isn't bugged.'

She was startled, 'But Sam, who might do that to me?'

'There are various possibilities, Liz. But first we had better be sure that it's bug free.'

'When can you, what's the word? ... *sweep* is it? OK, when can you sweep it?'

'In the next day or so ... I'd like to be sure. We may find nothing and that will be a relief. Better safe than sorry.'

'What have I got mixed up in Sam?'

'I hope nothing very much ... just wait and see and when we go back to your place be careful what you say.'

***

As she put the key into the lock Sam cautioned her, 'Just take care what you say, nothing about Mossad or Elizabeth, in fact just keep it lovey-dovey.'

They proceeded to the kitchen and Liz checked the fridge, 'Good there's a bottle of Alsatian Riesling. Open it Sam and pour a couple of glasses, There are some olives and nibbles in the fridge as well. I want to try on some of the purchases, I won't be long.' She disappeared into the bedroom while Sam saw to his kitchen duties, taking the opened bottle and a couple of glasses into the lounge before returning to get the olives and crisps.

After about five minutes she emerged from her bedroom wearing a black shift dress. Sam gave her an admiring look, the sleeveless dress came to just above the knee and he detected a fresh but subtle application of perfume. 'You look stunning, Liz. Underwear OK?'

'Would you like to see, Sam? Of course you would! Here give me a hand with the zip!'

She turned her back on him and he didn't need any

further invitation. He moved forward and unzipped the dress, lifting it from her shoulders and letting it drop to the floor. She stepped away and turned to face him. She picked up her glass of wine, took a sip and, returning it to the table, asked, 'Well Sam, what do you think?'

He took in the pale pink lingerie which set off her figure to its best advantage, 'Stunning, Liz, absolutely stunning! Like an advertisement come alive.'

'So Rabbi Sam Kagan makes a study of ladies' underwear adverts!' She came close, put her arms around his neck and kissed him, 'And how do you want to view the other sets? You've yet to see the black and the silver/gray. It's a bit of a bore zipping up a dress only to have it unzipped immediately.'

'Enough for the moment, keep it for the future, Liz. We need to get out to eat.' He had to take care.

She was well aware that Sam's interest in her was sexual as well as intellectual. Liz had no doubt of the degree of his fixation with the woman in the remand prison but, if eventually Elizabeth were unavailable or unwilling, she, Liz, wanted to make sure that she was in the running for the title of "Very Lucky Girl"! The prospect of being Sam's consolation prize did not worry her. She would be patient, ensuring that she didn't precipitate a crisis of conscience for him but doing enough to keep the coals of erotic attraction glowing without them leaping into flames. She would play it cool, or at any rate warm enough to keep him interested. As a psychology student she would be fascinated to observe his reactions to events ... as well as her own! And if it went nowhere? Well, nothing ventured, nothing gained – she would have had the pleasure of his company and learnt a thing or two along the way.

***

As they left the apartment she asked him, 'Was your response for me or for the bugs?'

He replied, 'Both ... but if I hadn't suspected bugging I would still have responded as I did. And when you next see your contact from the Embassy let him know about today's shopping spree. And, before you ask, I'd have bought those things for you anyway.'

He didn't tell her that the embassy contact was himself now under close surveillance, to establish whether *he* was a loose cannon with a grudge against Sam or in the pay of the Russians. As it turned out it was the former: he had thought there was advancement for himself in keeping an eye on Sam. That advancement took the form of a summons back to Tel Aviv and several years hard slog on the Records Section. Sam had decided to limit his meetings with Liz to cafes and restaurants as being safer venues for them both. Their philosophical seminars were kept going as a mutually valued intellectual stimulus. Both knew that Sam wasn't slamming the door on a future relationship if Elizabeth proved not to be available, though how long Sam would be prepared to wait, in the event of Elizabeth receiving a long sentence, he wasn't sure.

Chapter 12

Thursday 12th June 1997

They strolled uphill along *Spalenberg* making their way towards the University of Basel. A man and a woman engrossed in conversation and taking in little of what was going on around them. It was a fresh sunny June afternoon with small white clouds hurrying across the sky. Mia had arrived in Switzerland four days before, having flown into Zurich on a flight from New York. Tomorrow she would be heading for England to attend a medical conference. Once they had been engaged to marry but she had broken it off. The previous year Mia had begun to notice a change in Sam. It had come to a head that winter. Was it in November? No it had been late in December, just after her father's *Jahrzeit*. They had spent an afternoon at the Metropolitan Museum of Art in Manhattan and she had sensed then that there was something troubling Sam, something which was casting its shadow between them. She had been conscious of his slight uneasiness with her for some months but now it could no longer be ignored or pushed to one side. She had suspected that he had met someone in London or wherever it was that his work took him - that he was deep in a relationship with some other woman. She had discovered from him that a woman was involved but that she was a woman who knew nothing of Sam, who didn't even know of his existence!

And so their engagement had been terminated. Mia had taken the initiative in order to save face, not hers but his. She had not wanted him to incur opprobrium among family and friends for dumping her. But despite this, and the fact that there had now been five months when they had not seen one another, their ties had remained strong. In part this was due to their shared interests, he had introduced her to Western art. It was an area omitted from her education in a Brooklyn *Chassidic* community and he had taught her to enjoy it and not to feel guilt at doing so. Her community found danger in the depiction of people and animals in art. One day she and Sam had stood before a painting of the Israelites before the Golden Calf. She had said to him, 'And isn't that the danger for us, Sam? Mightn't all this distract us from our Creator?'

'But Mia we're not involved in the worship of these things, no more than you are involved in the worship of the last *Rebbe* when you carry that card, with a traveller's prayer on one side and his photograph on the other, in your handbag!'

She had flushed before replying, 'You're very observant Sam. It's true, *Chabad* has no problem with photographs and televising its gatherings world-wide. These are ways of forwarding God's work.'

'And the artist is involved in speaking to us from his experience, perhaps in a way that depicts creation or people in a realistic way or perhaps in an abstract way that tries to convey a more complex message - personally I treat abstract work as a sort of puzzle to be solved. But the worship of the Golden Calf is something else, and that's not the way we're going.'

This had come back to her that afternoon in Basel as they had stood in the Historical Museum in the *Barfüsserkirche*, looking at the Basel *Dance of Death*. She had been repelled by the macabre theme and had said so.

Sam had agreed but added: 'It comes from an age when death was a constant caller at people's homes. Plague and war were always there, just at your elbow, in

14th and 15th century Europe. They were impossible to avoid. So death was a subject that fired the imagination, the repulsive became irresistibly attractive, a bit like the feeling you get as you look over the edge of a precipice. And the idea of the dead as skeletons calling the living to join a dance ending in death appeared in art - paintings on church walls and the like. Not much consolation but a statement of how things were! For our people of course, as well as for the *Goyim*, death was a constant visitor - we had pogroms added to the other killers. You've read Isaac Bashevis Singer's *The Slave*? No? You should. It's set in 17th century Poland and he refers to a song, "What is life but a dance across graves?" The character in the story remembers it being sung by a Jewish wedding jester! They obviously took their pleasures seriously! Certainly no life for a *Cohen*, Mia!'

They had laughed and left the *Barfüsserkirche*. But the image of death had stayed with her for the rest of the afternoon. She had let him go emotionally but she couldn't dispel her concern for his safety. It had worried her ever since he had begun to work for Mossad, he'd never said who he was working for in so many words but she had known all along what he did for a living. She was concerned now and she took his arm, 'Sam stop here a moment. Promise me that you aren't in danger from what you plan. You want this woman - you want Elizabeth out - promise me that you won't risk her life, yours or anyone else's.'

'I can promise that, Mia. I'm determined to put no one at risk. If it can't be done without endangering people then it won't be done.'

'And you will remember that Elizabeth is pregnant, that you have to think of her child as well as her. Any violent rescue could cause a miscarriage and might even endanger Elizabeth herself. What sort of ideas are you working for her rescue?'

'At first I thought of using a helicopter to lift her off the roof of the prison but it's got wires stretched over the exercise yard - you couldn't land on the roof - a rope with a harness might just possibly work but the wires may be electrified.'

'If you care for her you *will* forget that idea, its no way to treat a pregnant woman, Sam.'

'I was on my way to that conclusion, Mia.'

'That's just as well, Sam. So what *sensible* ideas do you have for getting her out?'

'I've established that Elizabeth attends the ante-natal clinic at the *Frauenspital*. I'd hoped to get the assistance of a nurse there but she's just left the hospital and gone to Israel. Perhaps my contact can find me another nurse as a go between. You see the first problem is making contact with Elizabeth, any kind of contact. OK she has visitors in prison but the meetings take place in a cubicle divided by a glass sheet, so there's no chance of physical contact or of passing a note, and there's a police officer next door. And there's no way they would let a stranger in to see her in case it was an attempt to prejudice the trial and, in any case, you could hardly discuss an escape attempt with the police listening in - and the cubicle's almost certainly bugged by the authorities!'

'And Sam Kagan would never use such techniques!'

'*Touché!* I agree that I'm in no position to complain if they listen in.'

'So no one sees Elizabeth in complete privacy?'

'Only her *Advokat*, her attorney that is, Sylvia Brünner. And she's not going to facilitate an escape attempt by one of her clients. She has responsibilities to the Court and just imagine a botched escape attempt and someone implicating her - I wouldn't put anyone in that sort of position, Mia. She would end up in jail and it would be the end of her legal career.'

'Good, Rabbi Sam Kagan is alive and well and hasn't sold his conscience to Mos......... Sorry Sam, enough to say that you're still the upright man you always were.'

'We would both do well to forget my old employers, Mia. Certainly they shouldn't be spoken of publicly.'

'I'm glad that you've left them, Sam. I know that they're essential to the survival of Israel but it can't be easy to work for that sort of organisation and keep your hands clean.'

'Not easy, Mia, but not altogether impossible. Though you can find yourself unwittingly doing other people's dirty work. But forget all that. The situation is that only Elizabeth's attorney has genuinely confidential access to her and there's no way I'd use Sylvia Brünner to try to persuade Elizabeth to escape. Perhaps I might use her to get a message to Elizabeth, something to encourage her.'

'Tell me about her Sam. You once mentioned the impression she made on you on a railroad station.

'Yes, it was on Finchley Road Station on the London Subway. It was strange, she did it with a turn of her head, it was entirely spontaneous and unaffected. She was waiting on the platform for her train, smartly turned out but not showy. Somehow with that movement of her head, and her brunette hair swinging out and back into place, she exuded life and happiness. And unknown to her she captured my affections far more surely than if she had set out to seduce me!' He smiled to himself as Mia, without thinking, adjusted her head scarf at the mention of hair.

'And was she really happy, Sam?'

'Yes, Mia. I think it was that she felt she was settled for

a while and that her apartment was hers to turn into a home to her taste - that it wasn't simply a place to sleep. And her job involved her being there waiting rather than being actively involved in espionage.' He lowered his voice, 'You know, Mia, however experienced you are at that sort of work there are times when you suddenly feel at risk, you start looking around and suspecting all manner of people are following you. You begin to see white mice - that's how they put it, or so people involved in activities of that kind tell me.' He caught her eye and raised his eyebrows and smiled. 'So she was relaxed and, though her new job was nothing like as high powered as she was used to across the Atlantic, she felt relaxed in a way she hadn't been before. Well that's how I interpreted the situation.' He lowered his voice, 'And that's how I reported it. Mia, something I haven't told you is this: I was with her for most of the day before she shot her Russian colleague.' He had made sure that no one was near enough to overhear him and he had once again lowered his voice. Their faces were very close. 'We had a wonderful and entirely chaste day out together in the Alps and you can guess what a shattering blow it was to discover that, within an hour of my leaving her, she had shot a colleague dead and been taken into police custody! But enough of that, I'd rather not talk about it here.'

'It must be hard for you Sam loving her ... but not being able to communicate with her. Poor Sam!' She took his hand and looked into his eyes. She saw tiredness, sadness and frustration. Sam Kagan, not one to be short of a way out of a difficult situation was stuck for once. He couldn't see any way forward at all.

'Thanks for listening to me Mia. Spelling things out to a friend can clarify your thoughts but our talk has really confirmed the hopelessness of the situation. If there's a way of getting her out I haven't come within a mile of finding it. But ... I *am* convinced that there is some way I haven't thought of. The trouble is that the harder I work at it the further away the answer seems to be.'

'Perhaps you need to stand back and see things from a distance. Perhaps you should get away from here, from Basel, from Switzerland, for a while and have a break. Just rest your mind and your emotions, occupy yourself with something that engages your heart and mind. I know ... or I think I do ... you used to say that when you had the opportunity you would visit Poland and see what you could discover of your family's roots and fate there. Well if not now, when? Elizabeth's going to be in Basel jail until the Autumn, so you have time to put a plan into action, that's if you can come up with one which has a decent prospect of succeeding.'

'Perhaps you've got something there Mia. My mind has been turning to the past lately. I suppose it's being here in Europe. Being in Switzerland, on the doorstep of where it all happened. Here in Basel there are memories of Herzl and the Zionists' meeting in 1897 - it'll be one hundred years ago this August. And then there's the *Badischer Bahnhof* in *Kleinbasel*, the terminus of *Deutsche Bahn* - the German Railways - the Swiss allowed the Germans to treat the place as part of Germany during World War II. No doubt it made it easier for the Nazis to bring their money and looted gold here to make sure that reliable Swiss bankers would treat it with their customary care and discretion!' She noticed the bitterness in his voice. He continued, 'Yes, it's probably time that I confronted the *Shoah* head on and worked it out of my system. No, I doubt if it can or should be worked out but I have to face up to it.'

'Promise me that you'll take a break, Sam, make your pilgrimage to Poland and remember generations of Kagans and so many of our people.'

'I promise, Mia. Thanks for your help. I need something different for the moment, you've put your finger on it. And it has to be something serious, something worthwhile, weighty and not frivolous. The idea of going to Poland seems right, entirely right. Thanks again. How about a coffee, there's a good place not far from here?'

She took his arm and they continued uphill. A man and a woman who could be open with one another but who no longer could be classified as an item.

They sat facing one another across the small table in the café near the university. The room was filled with the buzz of animated conversation of students, young and not so young.

She looked around the room, 'They're fortunate Sam, the whole of life ahead of them.'

The waitress brought them two cups of Mocha coffee, a bottle of spa water and a couple of glasses.

'Yes but they face the constant pressure of exams and then the task of finding work at the end of it all. I'm happier to be a little further along the road of life, to have some small achievements behind me and some plans for the future - that's when the immediate problem is solved, of course. Again thanks for the idea of taking myself off to Poland, you've sold me the idea and I'll probably set off in around ten days' time. Elizabeth is due to make one of her remand visits to the Court in a week's time and I make a point in being there - outside the railing, of course - partly it's just to see her but there's also the practical point of making sure that the SVR don't take a pot-shot at her, I can't cover all angles and there's someone else who takes the other side of the courtyard, but I feel I ought to be there just in case. But enough of talking about Sam Kagan! Let's hear how you are, Mia. I still feel guilt over ending our relationship.'

'You shouldn't Sam. You know that I was the one who ended it.'

'That was to avoid me incurring the wrath of your family and friends, Mia!'

'In part - OK mainly - but there was always the tension that existed between your world and mine. I know you're Orthodox and observant - as far as your work allows - that's not an implied criticism, the *Rebbe* told me that if the security of our people necessitated your having to merge into the *Goyish* background then you had his blessing. It's simply that I've belonged to a *Chassidic* community all my life, it's part of the texture of things, it's the air I breath. They're my people, my family, and I know that if I had to leave the community I would find it very hard to adapt. I just would not be happy. I think you understand what I'm saying, what I'm trying to convey to you. *You* have never regarded us as alien "Blacks", you have always shown understanding even though our style, our life is not for you.'

'You mentioned "Blacks": it's strange but you probably suffer less antagonism in New York than you would in Israel where, sadly, things are very polarised, with the secular and the *Haredi* at one anothers' throats. It's a sad way for brothers to live! But it's the extremists from each side who cause the trouble.'

He paused before continuing, 'Yes, Mia, although the *Chassidic* life of *Chabad-Lubavitch* is not for me - I respect it and your people. For me your life would be a straight-jacket but for you and for many it's a joyous thing and I respect your piety and good works. I measure my own life by what I see in your community and often I'm dissatisfied by the comparison. But I need *my* space and I know that I wouldn't fit in or be a fulfilled person as a *Chassid*. There are times, I admit, when I sigh and tell myself that it would be so much easier to be part of a group like yours with very clear directives to follow but that's not too often these days. If you like, I'm a car and not a tram: I'd find the rails too limiting but that doesn't mean that I do just what I want, far from it! Like you I'm guided by the *Torah*, its precise stipulations and its principles. That's what gives my life meaning and direction. I admit that there will be real problems if I succeed in getting Elizabeth out of jail - marriage to a Gentile carrying a baby conceived out of wedlock isn't the best prospect for one who's observant, and a *Cohen* at that! But it's a problem to be faced in its own good time - I've to get her out of jail first of all and then find out whether she reciprocates my feelings.'

'I know your principles Sam and I respect you for them, you have to be true to yourself, just as I have. Out of the community I'd be lost. I'm sure of that now - and so the ending of our engagement is both sad and yet - dare I say it? - a relief.'

'But you ought to consider marriage seriously, Mia. That's a reason for guilt on my part, you've waited around for me for so long and now ... '

'And now I'm an established midwife who finds satisfaction in her work and is respected in the community at Crown Heights. I'm a fulfilled woman, Sam.'

'But you haven't closed to door to marriage. You would make a fine wife to a devoted *Lubavitcher*.' He observed her flush slightly and momentarily.

'Well Sam there is a doctor from the hospital who has suggested marriage to me but I wanted to be sure, I think

I am sure but I really want to be *surer* if you understand me, Sam.'

'I'm sorry if I have damaged your confidence, Mia.'

'No Sam, you haven't done that - in many ways you have given me confidence, widened my horizons and made me think for myself. The way you introduced me to literature and art and the New York galleries, that has really opened my eyes. It's enriched me and I'm eternally grateful to you. And another thing, Sam. If I marry I still want to maintain our friendship. It will be lovely for us all to meet - Elizabeth and yourself with Shalom and myself.' Sam saw her flush again and knew that she had been wanting to introduce the name of her doctor friend for a while.

'A man whose name is a blessing, Mia. That bodes well for your future. You do promise to let me know at once if you do decide on marriage?'

'Of course Sam and I would want you to take part in the service.'

'He's a *Lubavitcher*?'

'Not exactly but he's very sympathetic and would be happy to join the community to make his bride happy.'

'And you really haven't yet decided whether you will marry?'

'I told him that I would let him know when I returned from Europe. I wanted to see you first and be completely sure how I felt ... about you and the past, to be sure that it really was the past. And now I know, I'm sure, that both you and I have been able to finish what once seemed a relationship with marriage as its destination - not without some wounds and remaining pain - but, despite that, with a genuine sense of finality. Though we seem able to keep our friendship going and I value that, Sam. Very much indeed.' She lent across the table and kissed his cheek.

'Not the way for a good *Lubavitcher* girl to behave.' They both laughed. 'Tell me about Shalom, Mia.'

'Shalom Posner's a year older than I am. He hails from the Midwest, just outside Chicago, he specialises in eye surgery ... '

Several cups of coffee later most of the students had gone their various ways and the café was a good deal quieter. 'Thanks Sam for seeing me and for your blessing on my plans. I'll call Shalom this evening and let him know. It seems odd to have told you the decision before my intended husband but it also seems right, but you won't let on that you know already will you Sam?'

'Of course not Mia, my work has involved keeping secrets and I don't think I will stop doing so. By the way is it Mia or Miriam from now on?'

'You gave me the name Mia and you can still use it, I want you to.' He looked at her and smiled. Throughout the afternoon she had blossomed and grown in confidence. He could see that she was a woman in love and he was glad, extremely glad and relieved. For him it was a burden lifted and he could rejoice with her.

'And you Sam look after yourself and look after Elizabeth. None of the crazy schemes they have in films. Remember she's pregnant and take care of her and the child. By the way Sam, who's the child's father - obviously not you!'

'No not me, that's certain! An Englishman, he was Elizabeth's boss. They had a genuine loving relationship but in the end his son's psychiatric problems, which seemed to stem from the break-up of the marriage, meant that he had to go back to his wife. They're making a go of it, I'm told, and the boy's improving.'

'And Elizabeth is to be left holding the baby?'

'That's where I come in!'

'You'll have to find some way of letting her know of your intentions - but that's something for the future once you've explored the Kagan past.' She opened her handbag and took out a card. 'Don't laugh Sam, it's the card that you mentioned earlier. The *Rebbe* of blessed memory gave it to me. Somehow it got put away and I found it the night before I flew here so I brought it. I know you're unhappy about the cult of the leader - that's a very emotive word for our people, of course - but the *Rebbe* meant a lot to us, to my father and the family. I certainly miss him and it's strange not to have a successor - seven of them in a row and now none at all. It doesn't seem right, something's missing. The *Rebbe*'s death was like the loss of another father.'

'But if you're waiting for him to return as *Moshiach*, Mia.'

'I'm not certain that I am. Sure, some are, my brother Lieb is one of them. I keep an open mind but don't want to create rifts with our fellow Jews over it. It's enough to be able to say, " ... I await *Moshiach's* coming each and every day." '

'Amen, Mia. It would certainly ease the workload of my former colleagues!'

'Whoever they might be, Sam'

'Whoever they might be, Mia.' Both laughed, at peace with one another and relieved that it should be so.

'Sam picked up the card and turned it over in his hands, 'So on one side I have the photograph of Rabbi Menachem Mendel Schneerson to travel with me and on the other I'm told to pray for protection from "every enemy and lurking foe, from robbers and wild beasts on the journey". Fine, I can do with such protection in Poland, here and anywhere else, Mia.'

'And Warsaw was where the *Rebbe* married his wife in 1929 and later the *Lubavitch* headquarters was transferred to that city - you're going into the *Chassidic* homelands, Sam.'

'Married Warsaw 1929 and arrived in USA June 1941 from Marseilles. A fortunate couple to get out of Vichy France. You'll have to remind me some time of the remarkable rôle of the half Jewish Major Ernst Bloch of Admiral Canaris' Military Intelligence and fill in the detail of all that happened, Mia. I can't remember whether it was your *Rebbe* or his father-in-law who got out of Poland the year before.'

She took his hand, 'Take care Sam.' Once more he saw the concern in her eyes.

'I will, Mia. And for you and Shalom, "The Lord give you both peace." '

'A C*ohen's* blessing, Sam?'

'A C*ohen's* blessing and a heartfelt one, Mia.'

***

Elizabeth and the women in the wing rounded off their evening meal with the cake that Jakob Gold had provided for her 33rd birthday. They sang happy birthday in English and adjourned to their cells for the night.

She lay on her bed. Being here was certainly not something to make for a happy birthday! Only a year ago she had spent the evening with Peter at a concert of Chopin's piano music at the Wigmore Hall in London. It had been the very beginning of their relationship. She remembered that wonderful evening when she had renewed her acquaintance with Chopin and Peter had encountered him for the first time. She thought of the apartment and the Steinway piano Peter had given as her Russian Christmas present. She knew he had not forgotten as there was a birthday card from him by her bed. For once she felt really down and she wept.

Chapter 13

Friday 4th July 1997

Ruth Lewis had arrived back home at around 8.15 p.m. after taking Michael to stay with a friend for the weekend. 'We're on our own this evening Peter, so wc're going to enjoy a candle-lit dinner, perhaps re-kindle a little romance,' she had announced

It was clear that this was something she had planned, and not some idea that had just come to her out of the blue, as the fridge immediately yielded up all that was needed for a quick but satisfying meal.

'A good idea Ruth, the two of us together like we were years ago in happier times. Perhaps memory can be turned into reality once again.'

'Yes, that was some while ago in the past which they say is another country. Let's see how well we remember it! Now Peter off you go and watch TV while I get the meal together. Have a small glass of wine, here's a Gigondas from a new producer, new to me at any rate, open it and pour a small glass for yourself – I know you're still on medication – and a decent sized one for me, I had a busy afternoon in Kilburn but we'll talk about that later.'

He did as he was told and retreated to the lounge.

***

Later that evening he sat in his bedroom reading a crime novel but thinking about their evening together. There had been a feeling of nostalgia which he had enjoyed, it hadn't seemed too strange after all. He felt relaxed and not yet ready for sleep. There was a light tap on the door and Ruth entered. She was wearing a pale pink negligée that he hadn't seen before, but then that was to be expected as it was some time since he had been a long term resident of the house. She came and stood behind his chair placing a hand on his shoulder.

'Peter, would you like to do it together tonight? It might help ... help both of us to return to normality.'

He remembered that a couple of days before she had come into the bathroom, not expecting him to be there, and found him, as he had put it, “releasing the tension”. 'I know what you caught me doing the other day, Ruth ...'

'I didn't *catch* you doing anything, Peter! I saw what you were doing and wasn't at all surprised. I take it you were thinking of Elizabeth?'

'Sorry, yes I was.'

'No need to be ashamed or to apologise, Peter, I understand, I really do. To have bliss suddenly snatched away and face celibacy can't be easy. I want to help, and Peter, I'm beginning to feel *I* need *you*. What you were doing won't do you much harm but at some stage you're going to have to let go of the past, possibly never entirely but eventually to a large degree.'

'My therapist agrees with all that: he said that it wouldn't do me any harm and it would be good for my prostate!'

'Did he now? I'm not going to force you Peter - I'd rather not face a charge of raping my husband - but if you fancy seeing how we get on in bed then I'm ready to give it a try. And, by the way, don't feel guilty if you find yourself thinking of Elizabeth some of the time. What do you say, Peter?'

He thought for a moment, 'OK we'll give it a try Ruth ... it can't do any harm and it just might just help ... and if I call you Elizabeth by mistake, please forgive me!'

'Don't worry, you're forgiven already.

***

The clock in the hall struck two o'clock and Peter surfaced. It was nearly two hours since they had put out the light. With a pleasure that surprised him he felt the warmth of Ruth snuggled close to him. Ruth stirred.

'Sorry, I've woken you Ruth.'

'No, I haven't really been sleeping, just waiting for you to come to the surface.' She had pulled herself up, slipped off her nightgown and lay on top of him. 'Once again, Peter, if you're willing. By the way you got my name right throughout our last encounter. You were on top last time now it's my turn and I can feel that you're ready. And so with your consent ... '

'Willingly given ... Ruth.' He had feigned struggling for her name and she appreciated the touch of humour.

'Well done Peter, it certainly helps to know who your partner is,' and she immediately hoped that he didn't think that she was reminding him of the Elizabeth/Lizaveta dichotomy that had shattered life for him.

Chapter 14

Tuesday 8th July 1997, 8.55 a.m. Warsaw, Poland.
To Brok - in search of a lost time and a lost people.

The heat hit Sam as he left the Hotel Bristol, it was prematurely hot, the day really hadn't had time to warm up to such a degree. He searched in his pocket for the keys and made for the hire car. From the road map the route looked straightforward. He wondered how he would react to the day's visit, the emotion of his experience at Auschwitz was raw in his memory, but today and tomorrow he would be confronting places directly concerned with his own family and its life and death in Poland. He took his knitted *kippah* from his pocket and secured it in place with a hairclip, it would be a day of prayer as much as anything else.

At a little before 9 o'clock he moved off into Warsaw's morning traffic and, after a wrong turn, found the road that took him to the *Slasko Dabrowski Bridge* over the Vistula and onto Route 18 through the Praga district of the city, past its two large churches, one of them Orthodox and the other Catholic, or so the guidebook told him. He had been across the river the previous day to see the vast Eastern European market that had grown up around a disused stadium, a seedy *entrepôt* with beaten up vans and buses from Belarus, the Ukraine, Russia, the Baltic States and any number of other places. So much of the merchandise had seemed cheap rubbish, clothes in cheap fabrics and unattractive colours, poor quality hand tools made by some smith in the former USSR, and similar goods - large quantities of them. But there had been no shortage of buyers, many of them reinvesting the proceeds of the goods they had sold. They would take their purchases back home to sell there. And so the cycle would continue.

He waited at a junction for the lights to change, glanced at the map beside him on the passenger seat and wound down the window to get some air - it was a heavy day and the humidity was getting at him as the sun beat through the car windows and the car was without air conditioning. The lights changed and he moved off, inhaling a lungful of fumes from an orange Trabant in the next lane. The old polluters seemed to soldier on even though the Eastern regimes had changed, not everyone was in on the projects that enabled the successful to flash around in their Mercedes and BMWs!

He proceeded along the dual carriageway and left Warsaw behind. The traffic thinned out a little and progress improved, the barman had said that the journey would take him a couple of hours, perhaps a little more, certainly not less. Before Radzymin the dual carriageway ended and roadworks for a new by-pass brought progress to a snail's pace. He opened the window once again and took advantage of the halted traffic to take off his jacket and push it onto the back seat. Once through the town progress improved but without the benefit of dual carriageway. He marvelled at the volume of traffic carried by Route 18 and then remembered that it led to Bialystok and to Minsk in Belarus. The use of the hard shoulder to let others pass in either direction made his hair stand on end and he found little time to attend to what seemed to be pleasant countryside beyond the road - the road itself and his survival required total attention.

With relief he took a right onto the 694 beyond Wyszkow and left the heavy traffic behind. He had driven on the roads of many countries but that one was among the most lethal and he hadn't enjoyed the experience. He was now by himself on a straight road through the forest with only the occasional car travelling in the opposite direction. He was able to give attention to both the road and the scenery. On either side were a variety of trees - tall pines, shorter silver birch, stunted oaks and small bushes. There were some trees with white flower, lilac he guessed. The sunlight filtered throught he trees and gave the scene a light and airy appearance but he realised that on a dull wet day the place would have a very different feel about it. The road and the woodland exerted a calming influence, he relaxed, slowed down and took it gently. The road made a change of direction now and then but it continued basically in a straight line to his destination. He saw the town come into sight and glanced at the clock, it was just after 11 o'clock, he was more or less on time.

As he drove into Brok alongside the river Bug Sam's mind went back over the events of the previous few days. The visit to Poland had proved well worth while, he was glad he'd come: he had wanted to get to grips with his roots, to form at first hand an idea of the country where generations of his forebears had been born, grown up, married, had children, lived their lives and died. And in particular where the more recent generations had *died.* He had seen what remained of Auschwitz and been appalled by the scale and horror of the place. Now he was in Brok, the town where generations of his Kagan predecessors had lived - Kagan the Polish form of Cohen, they were from the priestly tribe, something that brought both privileges and restrictions.

He had studied the Holocaust literature, both Jewish and Gentile, extensively and had discovered that, as the crow flies, Brok, was only eleven miles from Treblinka, perhaps fifteen miles by road. How, he wondered, had the

Jews of Brok been taken to the extermination camp? Had they gone there direct on foot or had they been herded into the Warsaw Ghetto and then marched to the *Umschlagplatz* to be taken to Treblinka in trains of cattle wagons? The effort to imagine those events tired and numbed the mind but he knew that he owed it to the victims to make the effort. It had been his duty to go there, to imagine their sufferings as best he could - however inadequately that might be - and to pray. For there they had sanctified the Divine Name in their manner of dying.

It is one thing to survey a battlefield, where the lie of the land is usually the most significant factor and the action can readily be recreated by the inward eye of the military mind, it is another to try to recreate the image of a vanished community. Sam had studied the sites of vital tank battles in the Sinai and the Golan as well as some of the Normandy battles of 1944. He had taken particular interest in von Luck's success in repelling the most massive Allied tank concentration of the whole campaign which had attempted to break out of Caen in July 1944 and had studied the Normandy terrain with professional interest. But here in Brok there was nothing he saw that spoke of a *shtetl* - a little town - occupied for centuries by Jewish families, generations of small farmers, horse dealers, shopkeepers, printers, teachers and their rabbis and kantors. A Jewish community which had lived alongside their Polish neighbours, sometimes at odds with them but generally getting along, buying from and selling to one another. Two peoples thrust together by history. For long periods both had been without a state, Pole as well as Jew. Polish nationalist and Zionist Jew had both dreamt of their own land and of being no longer under the heel of the oppressor. Tsarist Russia had been no friend to either community. But then, as Polish nationalism had increased, so had Polish antipathy to the Jews, seen as an alien people unwilling to assimilate fully and throw in their lot with the Poles.

Brok had once been for its Jewish community a place of work and family life, a place where men had studied the Holy Books and the women the books of their husband's businesses, a Jewish community with its charitable organisations, synagogues and burial society. A new bridge spanned the river to carry traffic to Belarus and beyond. Brok was now a place of houses, log cabins and holiday homes along the river Bug and among the trees. A place for Poles to holiday. There was nothing here for the imagination to work on, no bricks and mortar to build with. The Germans had made Brok *Judenfrei* - free of Jews - and *Judenfrei* it had remained. Nothing spoke to Sam of the thriving Jewish community that had lived there for so long - nothing, that is, except this old burial ground. He had found it almost by chance, among the trees and surrounded by a chain link fence with an ungated gap for an entrance. There were a few irregularly shaped stones with barely legible Hebrew inscriptions. Stones that cried out to him.

His research at the Yad Vashem Archive in Jerusalem had given him some idea of the *shtetl* that had been here in 1939 awaiting the tragic events of the next few years. A total community of some 3,000 of whom about 1,000 had been Jews with roots going back around 300 years. They had, said the record, run small businesses, fruit farming, hotel keeping and the like - one family had run the bakery supplying the Jewish community with *matzos*. Their's had been a very ordinary, humdrum sort of life, given shape by the seasons and the Jewish fasts and festivals. Many of the Jewish children had attended the Polish State

School in the village during the inter-war period but their attempted assimilation had not saved them. 8th September 1939 had seen the beginning of the end when the German army had destroyed many of the houses in the village, the timber buildings being like matchwood before the fierce gun-fire. From then on and with rapidly accelerating progress the Polish Jews had been slaughtered by the German oppressor, at first by murder squads who rounded them up, made them dig their own graves and then shot them. 'Progress' had come with the introduction of gas vans and eventually the death camps. And this graveyard from before the Holocaust was all that remained of the *life* of that community of 1,000 souls. The Jews of Brok, observant or non-observant, assimilated or separated from the mainstream of Polish life, had been indelibly and irredeemably Jewish in Nazi eyes and marked by the German authorities for total destruction. The stones cried out to him of a different, richly textured, past. Anger welled up within and he felt his heart pounding.

As a Cohen he ought not to have been walking around the burial ground, for he was forbidden to defile himself with close proximity to the dead, even those who had been buried well over half a century before. But such was his longing to *feel* something of his roots in this vanished community that he wandered among the stones, the ground dappled by the sunlight which found its way through gaps in the overhanging foliage. He picked out a few of the engraved words and thought that perhaps one day he would return to attempt to clean and decipher the inscriptions, to look for evidence of Kagan graves amidst this, the only sign he could find of the existence of a Jewish community in that village. They would be along the side of the cemetery, placed so that living Kagans would not defile themselves by walking over ground where bodies lay. He stood there and swayed gently to and fro as he prayed. He was not able use the *Kaddish,* the ancient Aramaic prayer led in the Synagogue by a mourner, for its use was restricted to congregational worship - perhaps on his next visit he would be able to bring a *minyan,* the necessary quorum of ten Jewish adult males. He felt the quietness, indeed there was an atmosphere of profound peace that pervaded the burial ground, some distance away from the present day residents of Brok and its visitors enjoying themselves by the river and nearly sixty years away in time from the conflagration of World War II. Here his people had prayed as they buried men and women over the years, men and women who would mostly have lived a normal span of years, experiencing the varied joys and sorrows of life before returning to their Maker, blessed be He.

Sam set his imagination to work in an effort to recreate an idea of the Jewish community that had once thriven in Brok, rubbing shoulders with their Gentile neighbours. No doubt like any community it had been a mixed bunch of people with their individual likes and dislikes, friendships, and enmities, loves and hates. But he saw it as just that - a community. Easy, no doubt, to idealise that sense of togetherness. Some would have found its conformity constricting and taken whatever opportunity arose to leave Brok, to head for the big cities with their greater opportunities and relative anonymity. The more venturesome would have set off for Palestine (if they were Zionists) or Western Europe or they would have sailed from the Baltic for the New World. The older folk would have stayed, perhaps talking of following their children, but most would have been bound to Brok and the Polish soil by centuries of history, inertia and the fear of the unknown that lay beyond their familiar and regulated world. They would have waited with apprehension for the first letters back from the New World, for news of how their offspring were doing in New York or some other American city. Letters which would have assured the old folk that all was well, that the writers were making their way in life in the land of opportunity, the Land of the Free. They would not have been told of the reality of life in tailoring sweat shops and other manufactories in the Lower East Side of New York and such places in other cities or of the crowded accommodation and the incidence of illness.

He recalled communities he had known. The *Chassidic* community of the *Lubavitchers* at Crown Heights, Brooklyn. It was to this community that his former fiancée Mia belonged: Mia who had sent him on this pilgrimage, back to his roots. Very Orthodox and yet, at the same time, very American, welcoming and outward looking. He had liked and admired them yet known that their way was not for him. He questioned the dominance of the Rebbe, the leader, in such groups. He had always valued a certain independence of thought and action. The idea of consulting your leader on decisions that you should be able to make with your own God-given intelligence did not appeal to him in the least. He certainly didn't like the tendency in those communities to see things in stark black and white and, at the level of the adherents, though not of the leadership, to demonise rival groups. Though some of Israel's *Chassidim* were prepared to serve in the IDF most were not and sought and got exemption from military service. That annoyed him, it raised his hackles. It brought religion into contempt with secular Jews and created divisions in Israeli society. The idea that you couldn't bear arms and study Torah wasn't one that he accepted for a moment. He had had no trouble in combining the two and securing the respect and affection of his men in the Golani Brigade, you had to work at it but it could be done.

And then there was his kibbutz in the Northern Galilee. It wasn't a religious community but it had been tolerant of all sorts of opinions and all kinds of Jews. It was from that experience that he put together his idea of what it had once been like here in Brok. More religious than the kibbutz, no doubt, but mixed nevertheless. He could picture the Brok *Chassidim* going about in their black kaftans, some of them worn and threadbare. Men in a small minority with an other-worldliness about them, oblivious of things that took the time and attention of their fellow Jews. Sometimes attracting attention by the sounds of song and dance as their religious fervour overflowed. Looked down on, yet causing others to show a grudging admiration for their ways. Studying in their prayer halls, their beards deep in books, or engaging in learned debate with one another. Some owing allegiance to different Rebbes and going off to other towns and villages to bask in the glow of their teaching on the High Holy Days and other occasions. But most of the Jews of Brok would have been like his fellow kibbutzniks, almost fully occupied with the ordinary tasks of life - taken up with work and family life. Bakers, fruit farmers, shop keepers and the like by all accounts. Easy to idealise. But now all gone, disappeared without trace apart from the graveyard where he stood. Gone for over 50 years. Gone for ever. Wiped out with malice and calculated brutality.

And what of the Poles of Brok, those who had been there in 1939? After all they had been two thirds of the population of the town. He knew better than to label them all as anti-Semites - that was simply to trade in stereotypes, an evasion of genuine thought and understanding. Certainly some would have been that, with unfounded prejudices or past negative experiences of Jews, experiences set like a fly in amber and with the Jewishness of the offender viewed as the source of the offence itself. Difficult when two very distinct communities live cheek by jowl and do business together - especially when religion is a strong distinguishing mark of each, permeating the whole of life and culture. Jew and Pole, Jew and Arab. Solomon had been right when he said that there was nothing new under the sun!

But the history of Poland was a sad tale. At one time a country with a written constitution far in advance of the rest of Europe but at the mercy of its neighbours. Carved up in the late 18th century between Russia, Austria and Prussia, reunited early in the 20th century only to be carved up again in 1939 by Hitler and Stalin, before Hitler moved on to sieze the lot. And then the post-war years as a part of the Soviet Empire! The German *blitzkrieg* of September 1939 had been the same for all who had stood in its way, whether Pole or Jew. Destruction without mercy had come upon them. And so the seemingly unchanging life of Brok had given way to fear and tension as families waited by their radios hoping that the threat of war would go away and while they waited they had been overtaken by something far worse than they could have ever imagined. The Nazis had, of course, gone for the Jews as the first candidates for extermination but they had had their plans for the Slavic peoples as well. Sam remembered the Medical Block at Auschwitz, next to the Gestapo 'Death Block' and forming one side of the yard in which Gestapo executions had taken place. Here sterilisation experiments had taken place on Jewish women to develop techniques for treating the Slavs. And would the Nazis, had they won the war, have been content to rely on such gradual methods of eliminating the *Untermenschen*? Sam doubted it.

Some of the Poles had shown great bravery in protecting the lives of Jews. Their own lives and the lives of their families had been at risk as a consequence and that required a high degree of courage. Sam wondered whether he would have stood the test. It was one thing risking your own life, he was no stranger to that both in the Lebanon and in his years with Mossad - how long ago that seemed, though it was only a matter of months - but to put your family at risk was something else. And then there had been those Poles who had been indifferent or hostile to the Jews. Some had been intent on ingratiating themselves with the German occupation and he had no sympathy with them. Others had simply been concerned to keep out of harm's way and protect their loved ones, that he could understand. And how did Pole and Jew relate now? Precious little personal interaction with so few Jews left in the country, though the irritant of unsettled claims for compensation for Jewish property appropriated by the post-war Communist regime remained. And in Brok today? People in retirement or on vacation oblivious of the past. 'After all it was a long time ago!' as a Pole had told him in Warsaw when he had remarked on his difficulty in finding the last remnant of the Warsaw Ghetto wall to the rear of Zlota Street. A long time ago. And much water had flowed down the river Bug in that time. But for many the memories lay heavy upon them and not just the first-hand memories of the survivors but those memories passed on in the spoken word and in print by eyewitnesses to later generations.

He left the burial ground glad to have found something tangible there in Brok, stones which assured him that his people's sojourn in that *shtetl* was historical fact and not rumour. When he got back to Basel he would visit the synagogue's *mikveh* - the ritual bath - the defilement of the burial ground required purification. Those were the rules for the observant Cohen and, wherever he could, he stuck to them. There were many occasions when this was not possible but his work for Mossad, safeguarding the survival of his people in a hostile world, had justified his inability to comply fully with orthodox practice - there were plenty of places where donning the knitted kippah that he was wearing and which he had worn throughout his time in the IDF would have been fatal for him.

Chapter 15

Tuesday 8th July 1997, 12.35 p.m.
Brok to Treblinka, Poland,
The Production Line of Death.

" .... I hereby charge you with making all necessary organisational, functional and material preparations for a complete solution to the Jewish question in the German sphere of influence in Europe."

Hermann Göring's letter of 31 July 1941 to Reinhard Heydrich.

It was only 12.35 p.m. and though his visit to Treblinka had originally been planned for the next day he knew now that he must go on and see it that afternoon. Besides he did not relish having to take to Route 18 again the following day. He continued eastwards on Route 694, through the flat landscape with its fields and woods, and parallel to the river Bug. His mood was of increasing apprehension, he knew that the experience awaiting him would be painful. The pain of the visit to Auschwitz was fresh in his mind.

He had vivid memories of being taken by his father as a fifteen year old to Yad Vashem, the Holocaust Memorial and Museum in Jerusalem. It had been shortly after the family's move from Brooklyn to Israel. His father had said that there were dark things from their people's past - sufferings beyond the descriptive power of human words - that had to be known and understood if Sam were to begin to grasp the need for the State of Israel and their presence there as new citizens. Things that he had long known intellectually as facts he had *felt* that day as he had never felt them before. Indelible in his memory was the sight of his father standing in a gallery of the historical museum, before them had been a pillar recording the murder of a million and a half children. In a glass case attached to the pillar was a child's shoe, picked up in one of the extermination camps. He had grasped his father to himself as the old man had been convulsed with sobs and the tears had run down his face. His father had not been an over emotional man and his reaction had made a lasting impression on Sam. Two words that his father had uttered had remained with him - 'Never again!' He had looked at Sam, the tears running down his face, and repeated them, 'Never again!'. Those words had shaped Sam's life and career from that time on. Those words and his father's warning that such evil should be resisted with uprightness, that even in a life and death struggle for survival their people, while doing all in their power to resist, must never fall into the ways of the *sitra achra* - the 'other side' of darkness and evil. When Sam had asked him to explain the expression he had said that it was in the Cabalistic writings of the *Zohar* and that, though mysticism wasn't his thing, he believed it was an accurate description of powers that were really at work spoiling the world.

At Malkinia Gorna he took a right turn onto Route 63 (South) and found a sign to the Treblinka Memorial. He knew he was at the rail junction to which the trains bringing thousands of Jews, including the entire Jewish population of Warsaw, had come. He bumped over a couple of level crossings and headed south towards Siedlce. Traffic lights halted his progress at a narrow wooden decked bridge shared by road and railway. Some cars and a lorry heading north cleared the bridge, the lights changed and he set off along the bridge. Suddenly it came to him that this was the precise route taken by those destined for slaughter at Treblinka. Was it the same bridge or a replacement? It didn't matter, the route was the same and it hit home emotionally. The sun continued to shine with penetrating heat on the quiet countryside which seemed to protest its innocence of the horrors perpetrated there half a century before.

Through the village of Treblinka and then through another small cluster of houses which had been fortunate not to share their name with the death camp just along the road. At last a sign to the right pointing over a railway line. The road disappeared into the trees and ran for a kilometre to the parking lot. Treblinka was well hidden from public view, and that was what the SS had wanted. Sam parked the car and sat there for a few minutes, overcome by feelings of lethargy, not wanting to subject himself to what lay ahead but knowing that it was for this that he had come to the place. His mind turned to an historian's account of his first visit to Treblinka nearly forty years before, when it had simply been a large clearing approached by way of an abandoned railway line and when the sandy soil had been darkened by fragments of human bone. Sam shivered, despite the heavy weather the atmosphere of the place was getting to him already. Once again it wasn't the place for a *Cohen* but he knew that he had to be there and experience it. Had the camp an enduring atmosphere with an existence independent of the observer's mind and feelings?

Sam got out of the car and surveyed the scene. He found the lavatory and then made for the refreshment kiosk in the corner. He knew he was delaying his encounter with his family's past but he felt in desperate need of a coffee. It was a small wooden building that styled itself a '*bistro*'! The proprietor was sitting outside on a log that served as a stool smoking a cigarette and he followed Sam into the small building. He had no useful English and Sam had no Polish but a black coffee and a bag of biscuits was ordered and delivered. He was aware of a mild headache and his need for a stimulant. The coffee was hot and he sat gazing out through the doorway as it cooled: the feeling of inertia lingered. There was only one other car parked on the sun baked tarmac. He would have Treblinka to himself. At one and the same time he was pleased and angry, there wouldn't be hordes of tourists getting in the way and behaving inappropriately but at the same time he resented the seeming lack of interest in this place. He nodded to the proprietor and left. Sam adjusted the hairclip securing his *kippah*, once again it would be a time for prayer as well as for seeing and imagining.

He noticed the museum nearby, really a long shelter with a display of photographs. From the kiosk at the end he bought a ticket and a book on the 1943 break out. He sat there while the girl in the kiosk played the taped commentary in English. There was little that he did not know already but he listened intently. He made his way along the cobbled path through the trees and came to a stone panel made green by the weather, it recorded the murder of 800,000 Jews in a 16 month period in 1942/43 in the Extermination Camp, the revolt of 2nd August 1943 and the death of 10,000 Poles in the Forced Labour Camp a little to the south. The figures were enormous, he simply couldn't take them in. He wondered whether anyone could do so. Contemplation of what that meant by way of the piles of corpses was indecent.

He continued along the cobbles running parallel to where there had once been the railway line bringing trains into the camp, its route was now marked by concrete blocks. Birds sang, a butterfly flitted past, the scent of pine was strong and there were wild flowers in the grass. If he hadn't already known what this place was he would never have guessed. A moment of fierce anger surged through him: why should nature seem to be so amnesiac about such crimes? If the blood of righteous Abel had cried to God from the earth surely a vast chorus of anguish ought to rise forever from this place! But future judgment was certain. The Prophet Isaiah had said:

> "For, behold, the Lord cometh out of his place to punish the inhabitants of the earth for their iniquity: the earth also shall disclose her blood, and shall no more cover her slain."

The weather was breaking and he heard rumbles of thunder in the distance. For a while he wandered around the clearing, inspecting the small memorial stones, each bearing the name of a town or village whose Jews had been murdered in that place. He tried hard but could not find that for the Jews of Brok though he knew it must be there. The first drops of rain began to fall but he hardly noticed them. He saw where the railway siding had been and the platform where trains had delivered his people like sheep to the slaughter. He saw the site of the gas chambers, now marked by a great stone memorial, shaped rather like a mushroom, depicting a tangle of heads and arms on three sides and a *menorah*, the seven branched candlestick, on the fourth. Here the killing had taken place using the exhaust fumes from the engine of a captured Russian tank. He wondered how long it had taken for the victims to die and was sickened by the thought. There was now a heavy downpour, a wind was beginning to gust across the clearing and he was already wet through, but he ignored the weather. He noticed that he was shaking and knew that it was more from emotion than the wet - the intensity of his emotion and the physical symptoms surprised him, he wasn't usually an emotional man. More accurately, he rarely showed his emotions, in that he was his father's son. He knew that here they had buried the dead in vast pits. And here, later on, they had dug up the rotting bodies and burned them in a bid to remove the evidence. The re-creation of a long cremation pit, filled with burned wood, was a vivid reminder. The final twist of horror was that it was his people, the Jews who had been forced to do the digging and the burning - disposing of the remains of fellow Jews, in some cases their close relations. An anguishing job, though they had not had to live long with the anguish before they they too had gone the way of all Jewish flesh that encountered the murderous Nazi hatred of their race, meeting death and destruction in their own turn.

Next to the great memorial was a smooth stone block, rough at the lower edges, with those words *'Never Again'* in Hebrew, Polish, Russian, English, French and German - six languages in all. Those words his father had once used, words that hit home and once again reminded him of his father and his senseless death from a *Katyusha* rocked fired from over the Lebanese border. For some, Jews were still marked for destruction.

His mind went back to the break out from Treblinka in August 1943 when his father had been among the escapees. He reminded himself of what had happened. Prisoners had got into the camp armoury and stolen hand grenades, rifles and hand guns which they had distributed through the camp. Buildings which should have been sprayed with disinfectant had been sprayed with petrol and then ignited. The Jewish prisoners had killed the chief guard and fifteen other German and Ukrainian guards and over one hundred and fifty or three hundred prisoners - accounts differed, no one had stood by with a muster board to count them out - had escaped from the camp. Although some of the escapees had been shot outside the camp as they fled, there were many who had succeeded in their escape. And his father had been one of them! A Pole, Stanislaw Siwek, had helped some who had reached the river but his father had had the advantage of knowing the area - Brok was after all only a few miles away, that had been his father's good fortune - and he had been sheltered by the family of one of of his fellow pupils at the Polish National School. Sam tried to picture the break out. Long years had passed, there was little to show what the place had once been but he could somehow see the events in his mind's eye with a clarity which startled him. Was it that he was used to action and war, first as a soldier and then as a Mossad agent? Was it that the memories still haunted the place and were like recordings waiting to be played in the sympathetic mind of one who came to feel and pray. He felt his spirits really lift for the first time that day. He felt pride at those who had sought freedom and dignity, even if it had meant death in the attempt. He was glad that justice had been meted out to some of the Nazi barbarians. He was glad too at the involvement of Stanislaw Siwek and the family who had sheltered his father, at the reminder that at great risk to themselves there had been Righteous Gentiles who had risked their lives for Jews. He was glad that the avenue of trees that led to Yad Vashem was a reminder to all - Jew and Gentile alike - that the whole world was not against the Jew, that some had been prepared to risk their own lives to save his people. It was a healthy reminder and a corrective to the paranoid attitude of some of his people who regarded the whole non-Jewish world as hostile. He remembered too the murder of around 10,000 Poles in the Forced Labour Camp. Despite the dark history of Treblinka the events of August 1943 were for Sam life-affirming, he couldn't live without justice and compassion. For him the two had to go together.

'Hear, O Israel ... ' the prayer would have been on the dying lips of many of the three quarter million or so victims of the place. And there had been Gypsies as well as Jews and Poles, united in suffering and death at the hands of those who regarded themselves as racially superior. Sam stood and swayed slightly as he prayed, oblivious to the rain which was now blowing in sheets across the clearing:

'O Lord. thou God of vengeance,
thou God of vengeance, shine forth!
Rise up O judge of the earth;
render to the proud their deserts!
O Lord, how long shall the wicked,
how long shall the wicked exult?...

'Can wicked rulers be allied with thee,
who frame mischief by statute?
they band together against the life of the righteous,
and condemn the innocent to death.
But the Lord has become my stronghold,
and my God the rock of my refuge.
He will bring back on them their iniquity
and wipe them out for their wickedness;
the Lord our God will wipe them out.'

He hadn't been able to find a memorial to the Jews of Brok so he placed a pebble on the stone inscribed *Polska*

Poland - and made his way back to the station platform from which the cobbled path led out of the clearing. There, on the platform, he turned to take a final look, to ensure that the detail of the scene was etched on his memory. But he couldn't leave without further prayer:

> 'Thou, O Lord, art mighty for ever, Thou quickenest the dead, Thou art mighty to save.
> Thou sustainest the living with loving-kindness, quickenest the dead with great mercy, supportest the falling, healest the sick, loosest the bound, and keepest Thy faith with them that sleep in the dust. Who is like unto Thee, Lord of mighty acts, and who resemblest Thee, O King, who killest and quickenest, and causeth salvation to spring forth? Yea, faithful art Thou to quicken the dead. Blessed art Thou, O Lord, who quickenest the dead. Amen.'

His blessing of the name of God raised his spirits once more and brought to him a quiet joy at odds with the place and its memories. He still didn't know the answer to the question 'Why?' but he was content to believe that there was an answer. Eventually he knew that he would return to ponder the question but he was satisfied for the time being even if it were only on an emotional level. And he was well aware of the contrast between then and now. So easy to bless the Almighty when you were alone and unthreatened in this clearing in the trees with the Nazi killing machine merely one fact of history among many. How different it had been for those who had faced death bravely in this place. There were those who had revolted and meted out a just vengeance on some of their captors, would that there had been more of them! And there had been *Chassidim* who had faced death with dancing and song. The horror of their immediate situation had made not a whit of difference to their confidence in the Almighty. The remembrance of both sorts of bravery humbled him and once again he was moved to tears.

He dragged himself away from the platform. He had visited Brok and now Treblinka, places where many of his forebears had lived and died. There was no more that he could think and feel. He was totally drained in heart and mind, as well as soaked to the skin. And so he made his way back to the car. How many of his relatives had perished here? He muttered to himself, 'Never again. Never again' - it was as clearly incised on his own mind as on the stone in the clearing. This conviction had caused him to accept the invitation to join the Mossad after his father's death and yet he had now quit. He had his standards, the standards of what was just and right - victory at any price was not worth having, that his father had taught him - for he knew that he would one day stand before the Judge of all the earth who did right and required the same of His people.

The water ran from his jacket as he dumped it on the floor of the car and he felt cold. With the downpour the temperature had dropped. There was nothing he could do about his shirt and trousers. Make for the local town and buy some replacements perhaps? A hot drink would have been sensible but he did not want company for the moment. He drove northwards on Route 63 and by the time he crossed the wooden decked bridge the sun was attempting to break through. He passed through Malkinia Gorna and onwards through open country and patches of forest. He passed a wooden farm cart shaped like a boat and drawn by a horse. How little had changed here in 50 years, his father must have seen many carts of that sort when he had lived and hidden there. He reached Ostrow

Mazowieka, set astride Route 18, and bought a cheap pair of trousers, a shirt and some underwear in a shop where he changed and placed the wet clothes in a plastic bag. He found a restaurant which at 4.05 p.m. was still serving food. Again it was a triumph of sign language as he indicated, by pointing to his *kippah*, drawing a pig and shaking his head, that he didn't wish to be served the ubiquitous pork. Beef arrived and he was pleased with himself at his achievement. No alcohol! He had the frightening Route 18 to survive as the road back to Warsaw and he would not risk it. The waitress stood by the bar and watched him eat. It struck him that she was the best thing about the place and he wondered whether all Polish waitresses wore mini-skirts. Attractive as she was she lacked the mature beauty and personality of Elizabeth. It came back to him that this visit to Poland was an interlude in his attempt to get her out of Basel prison. He experienced in the pit of his stomach a momentary feeling of despair before his customarily optimistic nature reasserted itself. He felt, he knew, that he would succeed though he still didn't know how. He was aware that he might be deluding himself but somehow he didn't think so.

Chapter 16

Tuesday 8th July 1997, 6.45 p.m. Warsaw, Poland.
The cry of the Ghetto and the march of the doomed.

"No peace or solace,
Just hardship and pain.
What will become of us?
What will be our fate?"

From 'Moments of Despair' by Mordechai Gebirtig, born 1877 and died 1942 in the Krakow Ghetto, a victim of the Nazi barbarism.

Back at the Hotel Bristol in central Warsaw Sam surprised the receptionist by his bedraggled appearance and his non-designer label clothes and asked for a double vodka to be sent up to his room. While his bath ran he added the spirit to a coffee and enjoyed the warmth that the drink generated. Then he stretched out in the hot bath and reflected on the day's visit and the immediate task facing him in Switzerland. One more visit in Warsaw and then he would be ready to make his way back to Basel. The problem returned as it always did and he wondered why he was persisting with the project - there was no way he could see of getting Elizabeth out. He was frustrated and angry, never had he felt so ineffectual and at the same time been so emotionally committed. The optimism of the afternoon had gone and he was surprised at the volatility of his feelings, perhaps he was emotionally washed out after the day's experiences. Failure was not something he had encountered as a skilled operative and it galled him, even though he was working on his own and no longer for Mossad. Why not drop it, go back to Israel and take stock of life there? There were a variety of things he could do with the rest of his life. There were plenty of options after all. He wished that he had a choice in the matter but he knew that he had none. She had permeated every area of his life and thought, even to the exclusion of Liz. He saw no future for himself without Elizabeth. None at all. Rather than shut himself up to despair he would keep going, hoping against hope that he would find a way of releasing her from the hands of the Swiss authorities - action, like nothing else, relieved the mental and emotional pain.

As he dressed and got ready for dinner he noticed a slip of paper on the coffee table. He picked it up and wondered how he had missed seeing it until then. It was a telephone message from a Simon Bloch - they had met the previous week when Sam had made a conducted tour of what remained of the Jewish sights of Warsaw - an invitation to supper and a song recital at an address on the edge of Warsaw. He looked at his watch, 7.35 p.m. - the evening would just be getting under way, better to have dinner in the hotel and make an early night of it. He took another look at the note, it was a recital of Yiddish songs. He was surprised that he hadn't picked this up at the first reading, but then he had almost missed the note itself. He was normaly so sharp, so quick and accurate in his observations, was it the solitude getting at him or was it his fixation with Elizabeth? He knew that he had to accept the invitation, get out and socialise - after all it was to explore his Jewish roots that he had come here and a recital of Yiddish songs might bring him into closer contact with the culture of his forebears than he had experienced so far. Besides he had spent a moving afternoon at Treblinka without anyone to speak to and share the emotion. A telephone call to Simon Bloch supplied the directions for the taxi driver and the assurance that they were about to eat so that Sam would not be too late for food or miss any of the songs.

Twenty minutes later Sam paid the taxi driver and entered the lobby of a slightly down at heel apartment block in the Western suburbs of Warsaw. He took the graffiti scarred elevator to the fifth floor and found the door of No. 504. There was no doubt this was the place, the door was ajar and there was clamour of voices from within. He knocked and then pushed the door open to find Simon Bloch waiting for him.

'Glad you were able to make it, Sam!'

'Thanks for the invitation. I appreciate the chance of some company and food, not to mention the music. Here have this!' He thrust a bottle of vodka into the hands of his host.

'You needn't have brought that, it's you we're glad to see. Come and meet the folk, a lot of the neighbours are here - it's a chance to get to know them better, introduce them to our vanished culture and have them inside enjoying it rather than outside complaining about the noise!'

Sam was given a glass of red wine by a young woman but he parked it on a window ledge so that he could shake hands with the others. Introductions over, he took a plate, helped himself to casseroled chicken and rice and found a corner of the room to make his own, sitting on the floor as the chairs were considerably outnumbered by the guests. His companion was an earnest young economics post-graduate student from The University of Wisconsin at Madison doing research on the transition of Poland from a command economy to a free market one. Sam was all in favour of a free market but, such was the young man's fervour against the evil Reds of the past, that Sam found himself arguing their cause with a conviction that surprised him as well as the Wisconsan.

Plates were collected up and they were told to refill their glasses and get as comfortable as the cramped conditions allowed for the music. Simon Bloch introduced the young Dutch woman who was to sing and then spoke about the songs:

'... they are by a Jewish composer and song writer, Mordechai Gebirtig who died in the Krakow Ghetto in 1942, murdered along with his wife and daughters by the Nazis.'

A stillness took hold of the room and Simon continued. 'Before each song I will explain the meaning, in Polish and in English, I think that will be enough languages to enable all of you to understand.' They nodded assent.

So for Sam began an unforgettable evening for which he was totally unprepared and which stirred him to the depth of his being. The young woman singer stood next to an upright piano on the far side of the room. The piano was old and even Sam could tell that its tuning could have been improved. Yet somehow that very fact gave a feeling of authenticity to the performance. How often such songs must have been accompanied by just such an old piano. The combination of words and music, beautiful and disturbing by turns, with his experiences over the last few days in Auschwitz, Brok, Treblinka and Warsaw itself overwhelmed him. That the recital was being given in a land where there had once been such a substantial and thriving Jewish community, a community with its own rich culture and which had been wiped out in the most barbaric and wicked way imaginable, added its measure of poignancy. The songs told of the variety and vitality of life. There were lullabies, sad regrets for lost childhood, songs of the ordinary things of family life and celebration. There were also bitter cries of hurt from the Ghetto-Prison of Krakow. He found he was particularly moved by a song of protest from the workless 1930's:

"Ejns, tswej, draj, fir
ot azoj marsjirn mir
arbetloze, trit noch trit.
Oen mir zingen zich a lid
foen a land, a welt a naje,
woe es lebn mentsjn fraje,
arbetloz iz kejn sjoem hant,
in dem najem land."

"One, two, three, four,
so we march unemployed,
step by step.
And we sing a song
of a country, a new world,
where free people live,
nobody is unemployed
in this new free land."

Gebirtig hadn't lived to see that country or be a free person. Sam was very conscious that he had enjoyed the benefits of life in the New World and in the new State of Israel - new so far as his forebears were concerned. Gebirtig and his people had longed for proper work and freedom. They had been denied both of these, being given instead captivity, slavery and death. He remembered Primo Levi's comment that the wages for his slave labour at Auschwitz Monovice had been paid not to him but to the SS as, after all, you don't pay a horse or mule for their work. He felt tears in his eyes and tried to hold them back. No, he had to grieve - the songs were the songs of his people, songs of their joys, sorrows and shattered hopes - it was those shattered hopes, hopes of a better world with dignity and fulfilment, that so moved him. He knew that it was for this he had come to Poland and that to hold back his tears would be a betrayal of both his people and of himself. His grief was expressed, but quietly, and he felt sure that none of those present had observed his emotion, after all he was safely in the corner with no one looking in his direction.

He realised suddenly that the recital was over and that the guests were beginning to move around and talk. And he knew that he must be alone, even though he had come out to socialise. He had to stay with the things that he had heard and felt in order to cherish and brood on them and then draw rational conclusions from the experience. He did not want to have them swamped by inconsequential chatter. He knew that his host would understand. So he made his way through the crush to where he stood near the door.

'Do you mind if I push off now, Simon? Normally there's nothing I would enjoy more than staying and talking but after Brok and Treblinka and now those songs I must be on my own with my thoughts and feelings.'

Simon nodded, 'Of course I understand. It can be almost unbearable. If you want a word later on you have the telephone number - call whenever you like, it doesn't matter how late it is, Sam.'

'Thanks and thanks again for the hospitality.'

Sam caught sight of the singer in the middle of a group of five or six young people. She had seen that he was about to leave and came over.

He took her outstretched hand, 'That was splendid, an

experience I hadn't expected. So much beauty, so much joy and so much sadness!'

'You almost stopped me in my tracks, I only just managed to finish one of those songs, you know.'

'How come?'

'Your tears! What else? I could see that you were profoundly moved and it got through to me as well. Of course it's always moving to sing these songs, particularly here in Poland, but there are times when I know that I've got through to my audience or at any rate to some of them and tonight was such an occasion.'

'I'd like to chat but at the moment I must be on my own with my thoughts and feelings. You're staying here? Yes? Then I'll telephone you tomorrow, if I may, to chat about Gebirtig and his songs and how you learnt Yiddish. By the way my name's Sam Kagan'

'Do that, I'd like it, Sam.'

'Tomorrow then, Lija.'

'Tomorrow. And for tonight Sam, *Shalom!*'

'*Shalom*, Lija!'

***

Sam Kagan made his exit and went down the stairs, not caring for the elevator, and out into the dark street. There were no taxis in sight and he walked for about half an hour before finding one. As it pulled up he wondered where he wanted to go - the luxury of the Hotel Bristol seemed inappropriate to his present mood.

'*Zamenhofa*, please.' The driver nodded and they set off. Sam sat silent in the back of the taxi with his thoughts. 'Why had he asked for that destination?' he wondered. He had planned to go there the next morning, before he flew back to Basel, not tonight in the dark.

They arrived and he climbed out and paid the driver. In front of him was the *Memorial to the Ghetto Heroes*, he had been there earlier in the week and had been disappointed at it's slightly shabby appearance with grass growing on the steps. He walked slowly around it, stopping on the park side of the monument. In the dark he could just make out the deep bronze relief panel with Nathan Rapoport's muscular heroic figures, male and female, armed with knife, hand grenade and rifle. Not so different he thought from the relief panels with heroic Polish workers and mothers that decorated some of the post-war Soviet inspired buildings in the city. It was a city of heroic resistance, Jewish and Gentile, and of vast destruction in 1943 and 1944. He knew that he had come here to celebrate the heroism of those who had risen in April and May 1943 against the Nazi might. Here too, as at Treblinka his spirits were lifted by the memory of those who had risen in revolt, turning in defiance on the Nazi beast, striking fear into tyrant hearts. Almost all had perished in the attempt - the command bunker where their leader Mordechai Anielewicz and the last of his comrades had perished was only a little way along the road - but he rejoiced that they had struck out against the oppressor and exacted retribution for their sufferings.

He walked round to the back of the monument which faced an apartment block across the road. It had a smaller relief panel, again by Rapoport, and like that on the other side it appeared at Yad Vashem in Jerusalem but there it was a bronze relief rather than the stone carving that now held his attention. He made it out dimly by the street lighting. The theme of this relief was different, very different. He remembered the title from Jerusalem, *'The Last March'.* A group of men, women and children being marched to the death camp, with the Nazi presence understated, but nevertheless chillingly there, depicted by nothing more than three military helmets and bayonets just showing in the background. Prominent among the victims was a heavily pregnant woman and a rabbi, face raised to heaven - as if interrogating the Almighty - and carrying the Torah Scrolls. His hand was held over the head of the pregnant woman as though in blessing. Sam's father's words, spoken when he had told the old man that he intended to receive ordination, came back to him, 'A rabbi must always be with his people, not a remote teacher above the struggles of life.' And that was how Sam had operated in his time as a rabbi, teaching at the University and exercising pastoral care over his students. His recollection of this period before he had joined Mossad gave him pleasure, perhaps that was what he would return to once he had sorted things out. And suddenly there came to him the answer to his perplexities over Elizabeth, imprisoned and awaiting trial in Basel. He now knew what he must do. The panel on the monument was but dimly visible in the dark but he knew with the clarity of full day what was required of him. His flock had narrowed down to one heavily pregnant woman - the woman who meant more to him than anyone alive. He experienced an immense feeling of relief. He now knew precisely what he had to do. It would not be easy, it would not in all probability be quick, but he believed it would be effective. He had come to Poland to discover his roots: at Auschwitz, Brok and Treblinka and at that evening's recital of Gebirtig's songs he had done so to an extent that surprised him. And now his perplexity over Elizabeth was at an end. An immense sense of relief continued to sweep over him, he felt liberated, he could have danced and this made him wonder if he had *Chassidic* roots. Relief, liberation, a way forward and joy needed more than simply a cerebral response. He would have liked to dance around the monument but he thought that there in darkened Warsaw it would attract attention, he didn't wish to spend the rest of the night explaining himself to the local police! He set off on foot back to the Hotel Bristol, he needed to be tired in order to sleep. He went singing a Psalm with quiet fervour:

"O sing to the Lord a new song;
sing to the Lord, all the earth!
Sing to the Lord, bless his name;
tell of his salvation from day to day.
Declare his glory among the nations,
his marvellous works among all peoples!
For great is the Lord, and greatly to be praised;
he is to be feared above all gods..........

"......for he comes to judge the earth.
He will judge the world with righteousness,
and the peoples with his truth."

Sam's hope was that the Swiss court would judge Elizabeth's case in righteousness and truth. Whatever the price that had to be paid he would see to it that *all* the truth was available to the court. There would be no putting off what he had to do. 'If not now, when?' It was the title of one of Primo Levi's books but he knew that it was taken from Rabbi Hillel and his mind went back to the passage where the words appear. He remembered that they were part of an obscure and variously interpreted sentence. Easier were Hillel's words a few lines earlier:

'Be of the disciples of Aaron, loving peace and pursuing peace, loving mankind and bringing them nigh to the Law.'

The words of his father and of Hillel, speaking from two thousand years earlier, had set Sam's immediate agenda. He would see Simon and Lija the next day and fly back to Switzerland the day after. There were benefits in being on your own - his former Mossad chiefs would certainly not countenance what he intended to do!

Chapter 17

Monday 14th July 1997

"There is no greater mitzvah than the redemption of captives."

The Shulchan Aruch, Yosef Karo, published 1565.

The waitress had served them with coffee and they resumed their conversation.

'Well Sam, what was it that you brought back with you from Poland as emotional baggage?'

'Auschwitz, as you would expect. Treblinka was moving for family reasons but it was the magnitude of Auschwitz that got to me, the huge number of victims, the size of the place itself - Birkenau was 425 acres in area - and the magnitude of the evil of it all. There were triggers that let loose the emotion. On the ramp at Birkenau - the railway platform where the SS doctors, doctors of all people, had conducted their selection between quick death in the gas chamber and a slow one as a brutalised slave labourer - someone had placed a single red rose there on the gravel. That moved me profoundly, far more than a bunch or mound of flowers. It was a holy act in a hellish place, Noam.'

His companion nodded and was quiet, he did not interject, Sam needed to get it out of his system.

'And the day after I had been to Auschwitz I was sitting on the railroad station at Krakow waiting for a train that was running late. There was a party of school kids, boys and girls round about ten years old, I suppose. A couple of teachers, a man and a woman, were keeping them in order and they were keeping me posted from time to time with news of the train as, despite my Polish origins, I couldn't understand the station announcer. One of the girls ran past, her pigtails flying, and I shuddered, horror overwhelmed me. Do you know why? ... No, of course you wouldn't. At Auschwitz, in one of the museum blocks there is a display of large quantities of human hair. What was it that the Red Army found when they liberated the place, was it five or eight tons? Five or eight tons!' He said it with a quiet intensity. 'And that was just the latest collection, waiting delivery to the manufacturers to assist the Nazi war effort! Well in a case there was a plait of a woman's hair they had removed entire before her death. It was etched on my memory and the sight of that girl in Krakow, full of life and energy, unlocked the emotion and moved me to tears.'

They were silent and once again Noam showed with a look that he understood and knew that Sam would continue in his own good time.

***

They climbed the hill from the tea shop in the *Marktplatz*, a quarter of a mile away, and looked down on the Rhein from behind the Münster. They watched in silence as a large barge headed downstream on its way to Rotterdam.

'And old Erasmus came from there to Basel and died here.'

'Who was he, where did he come from and what's it to do with us anyway?' Noam turned to Sam with curiosity on his face.

'To do with us? Nothing really but it's as well to know something about the history of where you are and to realise that it's as much by thought as by action that our world has been shaped. Erasmus came from Rotterdam -

the port that yonder barge is probably making for - and he lies buried somewhere in the cathedral behind us. But it was not just here that his influence was felt, Noam. He was a European scholar of stature, a Renaissance scholar, one of those who went back to the study of the ancient texts in the original languages, back beyond the Latin to the Hebrew and the Greek. So, although he was a Christian, I hold him in respect. No that gives the wrong impression. Start again. I hold him in respect as a Christian scholar who revered the original text, or at any rate, texts far nearer to the original than the Latin ones then in use.'

'The history of thought! And when was all this?'

'1536. Long, long ago, I know. He wasn't a Hebrew scholar but he did encourage the study of our language and for that I respect him. So it was appropriate that Herzl's first Zionist Congress should have been held here in Basel in 1897, our visit to the helicopters reminded us of that. I admire the confidence of the man, do you know what he wrote once he'd got back to Vienna?' Sam didn't pause for a reply but forged on:

"At Basel I founded the Jewish State. If I said this out loud today, I would be answered by universal laughter. Perhaps in five years, and certainly in fifty, everyone will know."

'Ben Gurion pretty well made it in time you see.' Sam laughed and Noam joined him.

'You carry around a lot of strange information in your head, Sam!'

'Well, it gives me a certain satisfaction relating one thing to another. Two more odd facts: one, the Zionist Congress met in the concert hall of the Basel Casino and two, Herzl insisted on the delegates wearing white tie and tails for the first session!'

'He would have had problems with modern Israelis - the Knesset and the Government included - on that score, Sam.'

'Indeed he would, we live in less decorous times but still momentous ones.'

For a while they watched the river until Noam broke the silence.

'OK Sam. You've come back with new ideas on getting Elizabeth out, just what are they? I ought to be told.'

'Sorry, Noam, I haven't forgotten you. I brought you here as a chopper pilot and you haven't had much of a chance to fly, just wander round Basel and cool your heels. Yes, there is a change in my plans - a radical change. You will have to say what you think. It came to me suddenly while I was in Warsaw. The emotion of the visit had got to me but the decision was not simply the product of emotion. How can I put it? The emotion opened my eyes to a possibility that I hadn't thought of. No, let's be honest, to one that I hadn't wanted to consider. The heart of the thing is to get the true facts of the killing before the court so that they can see that there were extenuating circumstances and treat her gently.'

'Sounds sensible, Sam. But why didn't you think of it before or, rather, why did you dismiss the idea?'

There was a pause before his reply, 'Because it won't be easy to put the evidence before the court in such a way that they can't avoid taking it into account. The evidence is in the tapes we made when we had her under surveillance here at the Hotel International as well as in England. And the tapes by themselves are unlikely to be sufficient ... I will have to be there in court to say what they are, how they were made and that they arc authentic.'

'And the Swiss aren't likely to be very enthusiastic about Israelis who bug rooms and telephones in their hotels!'

'*Gerade richtig*, as they would say - just right! They don't welcome such activity and I suspect that they could find several laws that I have broken, all carrying more than a few months in jail. But I don't have to label myself as an Israeli, after all I'm travelling on my US passport and perhaps that's how it will be when I deal with the Swiss. The USA can take the embarrassment more easily than little Israel and I have one or two things up my sleeve that might encourage the Swiss to take a lenient view about *my* activities. But I'll tell you about that some other time.'

'And my rôle, that's if I have one?'

'Firstly to watch my back, making sure that I'm not being followed. I don't want to find that when I make contact with the defence lawyer that she simply shops me to the authorities as a foreign agent and that they take me in. I'll go to court when I want and not when they decide.'

'And what else, Sam?'

'Generally giving a hand and keeping things in order - there will be enough to keep you from getting fed up. And besides I assume that the little French blonde is still around, the one who was getting your attentions before I went to Poland?'

'Still around and even if she weren't I would still want to stay in Basel to see you through.'

***

Sam and Liz sat in a quiet corner of a small restaurant on the edge of Basel enjoying a light dinner. It had been recommended to Liz by one of her colleagues. She had wondered how Sam had responded to Poland and the Death Camps and had been intrigued to find him in somber mood yet giving signs of having seen some way forward concerning Elizabeth. She asked herself how she would handle this. He had greeted her with a friendly kiss on the cheek and continued to show warmth towards her.

'It's impossible to come face to face with such horror and not to be affected by it, to be changed really. The enormity of it ... '

'I too must go to the camps, I didn't ask to go there with you as I knew that you would need to face it alone. There are certain things that can't be shared, where you have to stand by yourself, take it in as best you can and respond. What was your response Sam, that's if you want to talk about it.'

'Yes, I'll talk ... I need to get it out of my system, Liz. Probably not entirely out, I wouldn't want that, but attenuated somewhat so that I can live with it. My response? Grief, anger and the perennial question, Why? You stand there and face unanswerable questions ... ' His account was much as he had given to Noam earlier.

'And I've clarified my plans for my time here in Basel. I've thought about the case against Elizabeth Fielder. Standing back from the immediate situation, I've come to see her case as stronger than I had thought until now. And there may be some things I can do to help - it would be a worthwhile deed to help to free her.' He sounded confident but went no further in explaining: much as he liked Liz, the fewer the better when it came to knowing what he proposed to do.'

'While you've been away I've been doing some reading on the *Shoah*. The day you left for Poland I bought a book at the shop in *Aeschenvorstadt* opposite the *Bankverein* tram stop which has a lot of English language books.'

'Bider und Tanner?'

'That's the one. Have you heard of Gitta Sereny? No? Well she worked with abandoned children in occupied France in World War II and then in displaced persons' camps after the war. She turned to journalism in England and wrote about Mary Bell, a child who, aged 11, had murdered two little boys aged 3 and 4. Touches on my area of study you see. Well one of her other books was on Franz Stangl, the commandant of Treblinka. I can see that you recognise the name, Sam.'

'I do indeed, Liz. My father was in the break-out from Treblinka and survived. But it must have been grim reading for you.'

'Grim but necessary, Sam. I needed to know what happened to our people.'

'*Our people*, Liz. I hadn't realised you were ...'

'Jewish? Perhaps I hadn't told you. We're not an observant family, it's my mother that's Jewish not my father ... '

'Enough to have taken you to Treblinka if you'd been around in occupied Europe.'

'I'll lend you the book and then we can discuss it. The very interesting thing is that at the end of a long series of interviews Stangl came near to admitting his guilt and then he died of a heart attack the very next day. Quite amazing ... '

'Killed by his conscience, perhaps.'

'Perhaps, one would like to think so. The other interesting thing is that Stangl cut his teeth, so to speak, on the forced euthenasia project ... one vile thing leading to another. But tell me more about Poland and what you did there ... '

***

Liz stood looking out of her apartment window towards the Rhein pondering her evening with Sam. She wondered how he had taken the announcement of her Jewishness. Would he consider it a bid to increase his affection for her, making her a safer prospect than the Gentile Elizabeth, and would he then suspect her motives, motives that she herself knew to be mixed. She had previously determined on a low-key, unpressured approach and this she would maintain. Lucky girl? She wondered if she would be.

And how would his return to his family roots affect him? Clearly the grim reality of what he had encountered weighed heavy on him but, as regards Elizabeth and her predicament, there seemed to be a strengthened determination, a new sense of hope. Hope for him, potential disappointment for herself. Perhaps their relationship would never progress far beyond the intellectual, beyond friendship. Already she had staked out her claim for his affection with a measure of the erotic. She would continue to keep it low key and try not to scare him off.

***

Sam too was gazing over the river thinking about their evening together. He appreciated the mental stimulation that their meetings provided and also the pleasure of female company. In many ways she would be the ideal partner for him. And yet the news of her suitability had made no difference to the strength of his attachment to Elizabeth. It was to the good that his emotions had been clarified in this way: it was a problem that Liz, whom he liked and admired, might be badly hurt by the continuation of her relationship, such as it was, with him. He would have to take great care.

Chapter 18

Tuesday 15th July 1997

Sam sat in the restaurant waiting. The *Safran Zunft* was a pleasant piece of old Basel, the ceiling about 15 foot high with dark timber beams and the walls panelled with dark oak. Inside the restaurant it was quiet, the large windows had double glazed panes so that the passing trams in the narrow street outside were just audible and the diners were involved in discrete discussion which did not carry beyond their tables. A lamp at one end of his table cast a warm glow over the fine linen of the table cloth and he played with his napkin. The place soothed him and he was pleased with her choice of venue. With the previous day's telephone call he had committed himself. How it would work out for Elizabeth and himself he did not know. The call had been from a public call box. He wished to speak to Advocate Sylvia Brunner. What was his business? He had told the girl that it was confidential and important. She had tried to pass him off to someone else in the office but he had insisted, Advocate Brunner or no one, and the girl had grudgingly agreed to put him through. Fräulein Brunner had been quick to say that she could not in any circumstances discuss the case of her client, Fräulein Fielder. She had obviously suspected that he was a journalist. Not discussion, he had information. What sort of information? Information on precisely what had happened in the Hotel International on the fatal Sunday night. The night before Fasnacht, he had added. No, he was unwilling to come to her office. Somewhere neutral, let her suggest a place. A pause, while she had checked her diary, and then her suggestion of a restaurant in the centre of Basel, the *Safran Zunft,*

Gerbergasse 11, the next day. Would 12.30, for lunch be acceptable. He had known that she was interested, that her curiosity had overcome her wariness. Yes, the place and the time were fine. No one else to be there, he was firm, he wished to speak in total confidence. She had agreed to his conditions and concluded their conversation.

No companion, she had agreed but she would have one of her clerks, a retired Basel policeman, to keep an eye on things from a distance. She had no wish to be kidnapped, though if anyone had plans of that kind they had only to wait for her to leave the office for the homeward tram any dark evening. Still it would do no harm for her to look after herself. And besides she would be interested to hear what Otto made of her mysterious caller, Herr Barth indeed! This American seemed to know something of Swiss theologians. She had called the *Safran Zunft* and reserved two tables. She knew the manager, she had acted for him in legal proceedings the previous year, and he had agreed to the tables being close but not adjacent, with Otto's nearer the door. Perhaps Herr Barth would provide something to strengthen the case for Elizabeth's defence, it certainly needed a shot in the arm. The psychiatrists had been no help. True there was Elizabeth's present remorse which might help when it came to the sentence, but neither the prison psychiatrist nor the one appointed by the court had been able to discover anything to throw light on why she had shot the man. Her curiosity kept breaking through the surface of her thoughts that afternoon as she tried to concentrate on a commercial case. Why, at this stage, had Herr Barth suddenly come on the scene. Would it simply be a waste of her time, an encounter with some sort of American nut, or would it provide the vital element in a defence which needed every help it could get? She had less than twenty four hours to wait, that was a relief.

The waiter had shown Sam to Advocate Brunner's table and taken his order for a glass of Dôle, one glass would suffice, he wished to have all his wits about him for this meeting. He had just lifted it to the light and begun to admire the deep red of the wine when another waiter showed a woman to his table. He rose to his feet, taking her in quickly, early thirties, light brunette hair well cared for, and a smart navy suit with a lighter blue silk blouse with a high neck. Attractive and able, he decided. It was likely that they could do business and that they could do so in a pleasant enough way. They shook hands:

'Advocate Brunner?'

'And you are the mysterious Herr Barth, an appropriate enough name in Basel though you don't sound like a theologian from our university.'

'And you don't look like one from Zurich but then I'm not looking for a theologian but a lawyer.'

They took their seats opposite one another with Sam facing the door. The waiter brought a glass of white wine which she had evidently asked for on arrival, either that or she was a regular and she had the same thing every time. Their glasses touched:

'Your good health!'

'Yours and Elizabeth Fielder's!'

'I have to tell you that I have to safeguard my client's interests and what she has told me in confidence as her Advocate. I could not disclose anything to you without her permission and I would advise her on whether to do so. I can, and will, listen carefully to what you have to tell me but you will find that there is a one way flow of information - from you to me - and you may find that unsatisfactory but that stems from the nature of my professional relationship to my client. But, first of all Herr Barth, who are you?' She took a sip of wine while keeping her gaze firmly on his face.

'An American whose name for the present is Barth. I'm afraid that for the moment I cannot be more forthcoming, not that what I have to tell you will lack candour and it may well be that eventually I will be able drop the assumed name and be more informative as to my identity, there may well be an apocalypse.'

She looked puzzled, was he some sort of nut after all with nothing to add to her case and possibly a source of nuisance value?

Sam read her thoughts, 'Sorry, I was playing with words, the idea of a couple of Swiss theologians or at any rate their namesakes ....'

She broke in, 'Authentic in one case assumed in the other!'

He could see that she was irritated and wished that he had kept his language simple and direct, 'Sorry, but as I was saying, the idea of a couple of theologians lunching together suggested the word - it simply means 'an unveiling' but it certainly has lurid connotations so far as the popular imagination is concerned and is better avoided. I hope to be able to tell you who I am eventually and I most certainly hope to be able to help you defend Elizabeth.'

'About that I am pleased because there is little enough ... ' She paused knowing that she had said more than she ought.

'OK relax. I'm not a journalist. I'm a genuine friend. Let me guess what you were going to say. There's little enough evidence to get her off, is that it?'

'In substance, though it's not exactly the way I would have put it. I don't get people off, I secure a verdict in their favour.' She paused and added, 'Not that she seems to want to be acquitted. But, of course, you haven't heard it from me!'

'Of course not.' Sam smiled, somehow there was an emerging rapport between the two of them despite the bumpy start.

'May I suggest that we order now? Their steaks and lobsters are good - steak is safe it doesn't come from here or England, the current source seems to be South Africa of all places!'

'Not lobster, thanks! It's cruel to cook them alive.' That was his view and it wasn't necessary for him to say that they weren't kosher.

'So I'll order two entrecôtes. Do you need another glass of wine, a bottle perhaps?'

'No thanks, this one will suffice - I'd rather keep a clear mind.'

'Then we'll have some mineral water, still or fizzy, is that the word?'

'Fizzy will be fine if that suits you, whichever you prefer.'

She turned to catch the waiter's eye but before she completed the movement he was on his way to her table. She gets good attention here, thought Sam. She must be a good customer who knew how to tip and besides she had a presence about her which commanded attention.

'Advokat Brunner, it is good to see you.' She smiled in response. He looked in Sam's direction and nodded.

'This is Herr Barth, a visitor to Basel.' She saw the waiter's eyebrow lift slightly and added, 'No sadly he isn't a relation of Karl or Markus.'

The waiter took the order for 200 gram steaks, checking how they wanted them done. He returned almost immediately with a bottle of gaseous mineral water and two glasses. When he had poured the water he announced that the steaks would be about ten minutes and left them.

'It would be welcome if you told me who you really were. You could have done better than choose a well known professorial name, Basel is after all a small community. Your real identity is going to be relevant in assessing the value of what you have to tell me.'

'That I can understand Fräulein Brunner and it may be that I will have to disclose my real identity in due course, but for the moment it has to be Barth.'

'Perhaps you would not feel at risk using your first name. It would relax our discussion, I think, if we were on first name terms.'

'OK Sylvia. I'm Sam.'

She smiled, 'Sam from the USA, then. And which part of the States might you hail from?'

'From New York, Brooklyn to be precise. And now you know as much about my background as I'm going to disclose for now.'

The steaks arrived, well done for Sam and medium rare for his companion. For a while conversation lapsed.

'And what do you make of our Swiss-South African steaks, Sam? How do they compare with the Brooklyn variety?'

'On quality and cooking, excellent. On size a good deal smaller, but that's no bad thing, we tend to over eat and show it.'

'Yes, it's often the fat American rather than the ugly American.'

'And you should see the Texans!'

She laughed. 'I'm glad you're not one of them, I wouldn't feel so much at ease with someone with six guns at his side. The Wild West come to the Restaurant

Safran! The staff wouldn't relish having the place turned into a frontier saloon and demolished by cowboys!'

'For a lawyer you have quite an imagination, Sylvia!' He wondered whether she was being herself or simply trying to put him at ease, to lower his defences and open him to saying more than he intended.

'Sometimes it helps to have imagination in my profession. To try to get into other people's minds, to see what might lie behind events and people's actions - to identify possible reasons for strange actions, hidden motives. To come up with reasons that my clients themselves hadn't grasped.

'Creating a fiction that might get them off in court?'

'Arriving at the truth of the matter, I would put it!'

'Of course!' He raised an eyebrow. She laughed and he joined in. They were both relaxed but at the same time still wary of one another. The sound in the background remained a quiet murmur and they attracted no attention apart from a man sitting near the door who caught Sam's eye and quickly looked away. Sam had seen him studying their table earlier and had suspicions that he might be her minder, early 50's, wearing a dark gray sports coat and a dark tie - possibly ex-police. Still it didn't matter, he had his own minder and there was nothing about the meeting that contravened Swiss law, he wasn't going to extort money or blackmail anyone. He was here to help her with what was evidently proving a difficult case to defend. Sylvia gave him the impression of a woman who throve on success and one who would not be happy with a messy and inadequate defence of her client in court. It was time to come to the point.

'A pleasant lunch, Sylvia but neither of us is here to eat and indulge in small talk. I will come to the point but first I have to have your assurance of complete confidentiality, your assurance that you will not pass on what I have to tell you to anyone unless I give you clear and specific authority to do so. Can you give me that assurance?

She nodded, 'Yes, I have nothing to lose have I? If you tell me nothing I get on with defending my client as best I can. If I listen then it is possible that lines of defence will open up which will make a very great difference to the case.'

'If I speak to you as my lawyer you would be bound to keep what I said confidential and not disclose it?'

'That is so Sam, if it helps I will act as your lawyer but only so long as there's no conflict of interests between yourself and Elizabeth Fielder. Is that satisfactory?'

'Very satisfactory. Our waiter is waiting further instructions, I think.' She looked towards him and he hurried over to clear their plates and take their further orders.

'Can I bring you cheese or dessert?'

'Cheese for me, Jules. And for my friend ...... '

"Dessert, a sorbet if you have one.'

'Orange, mango or lemon, sir?'

'Mango, please.'

'And would you like coffee now or later?'

She looked at Sam, 'Later, Jules when we have finished the next course. I'll have mine with cream and ....' She looked at Sam.

'Black for me, decaffeinated if you have it, please.'

'One cheese, one mango sorbet, coffee with cream and one black decaffeinated coffee?' They nodded and he was gone.

'Back to business then. I told you on the telephone that I had information that would help you defend Elizabeth and I will come to the point. I can provide evidence that she was attempting to save herself from being raped by the man she killed and that he had attempted to drug her to make her comply, rather that he had actually drugged her with that intent. Also I have evidence that it wasn't the first time that he had attempted to rape her.'

She had kept her eyes firmly on his, observing him and trying to make up her mind whether he was genuine or not. There was a pause and Sam looked over her shoulder towards the table near the door and caught the man in the dark gray sports coat hurriedly looking away.

'Sylvia, I would prefer that, when I am in session with my lawyer, she doesn't make me uncomfortable with an ex-policeman staring at me! You are wasting his time, I don't know whether he works for you but I suspect you're paying for his services. I am not here to rape you, kidnap you or do you any harm. I am here to help and, as your client, it would be a pity if our extremely pleasant lunch were spoiled by my being made uncomfortable. I don't mind the recorder in your purse, it saves you from having to make notes and take your attention off the meal.'

She paused before replying, 'And so if the gentleman at the table behind me is in my employ what should I do to send him away?'

'Send him a note saying that all is well and that he is to go back to your office or wherever he's from. I suspect that he won't do so and wait outside to see that all really is OK, but he won't be gazing at me and spoiling my lunch.'

She found her purse and took from it a small pad, wrote a note which she tore out and folded. She caught the attention of a waiter who took it to the gentleman in the dark sports coat. Sam watched his puzzled look, 'Look back and nod Sylvia - send him on his way!' She did so and her minder got up from the table, shrugged his shoulders and set off for the door.

'So you're picking up the check for both tables? He hasn't paid.'

'You are observant, Sam!'

'Makes for a good witness doesn't it?'

'At a good price?' And immediately she wished that she hadn't said it. As a look of anger, no it wasn't that, more a look of annoyance and disappointment, passed across his face.

'For free! I'm not selling anything! Do I look that mercenary. Sylvia?'

'Sorry, Sam. That was impolite of me, I'm sorry.'

'Apology accepted. Anyway I need to get on with my tale or we will be here for dinner as well as lunch.'

Coffee arrived in silver pots with mints. She looked at the waiter, 'Cognac for two, Remy Martin? Good.'

She smiled, 'That's a token of my sincere apology. I'm beginning to think that it wouldn't be a bad idea to continue our conviviality into the evening.'

'But first we'll see how the business goes. My evidence is on tape, Elizabeth's room in the Hotel International and also her apartment and telephone in London were bugged. I have the tapes and if they are of any use to you they can be used in court as part of your defence.'

'It might help if you explained how you came by the tapes - I hope you won't be affronted if I ask whether you were responsible for the bugging.'

'As I am speaking in confidence to my lawyer I can answer that I was responsible both here in Basel and in London.'

'She was a spy, working for the Russians, but you didn't hear it from me, of course!'

'Working for the SVR, the successor to the KGB, in fact.'

'And you are from the CIA?' She was watching him closely.

'That will do as a working hypothesis but, of course, if I were, I wouldn't admit to the fact. But I must make it clear that I'm here in a personal capacity and not because anyone has sent me.'

'You would make a good lawyer, Sam!'

'You're offering me a partnership, then?'

'Not for the moment though an informal one to progress Elizabeth's case would be welcome. But, to get back to what you were telling me ... '

'For reasons which I have no wish to disclose I was involved in keeping Elizabeth Fielder under close surveillance and that is why I have the tapes. But my guess is that the tapes will only be of limited use without me. They won't carry much weight if I don't stand there in court and testify about their authenticity will they?'

She paused. 'At some point, and we've probably already gone beyond that point, I shall have to tell you that I can no longer act as your lawyer - the conflict of interests between yourself and Miss Fielder is a glaring one. I've no doubt that your masters ... who sent you here ... '

'Not my masters, Sylvia. My former masters.'

She paused to gather her thoughts, 'So you are a disaffected spy, agent or whatever you called yourself?'

'In one sense, yes but probably not in the way you think. I'm not trying to get my own back on anyone. Not on my former masters, the SVR, the Swiss, you or anyone else.'

'Two points there, Sam. First let me complete the warning I was about to give: you have probably been advised that in taking the actions that you did in relation to Miss Fielder you were guilty of breaking a number of Swiss laws, your activities on behalf of a foreign government on Swiss soil were illegal as were bugging hotel rooms and telephones. Conviction for such offences carries liability to heavy sentences.' Her voice was low, she didn't want her fellow diners or the staff hearing.

'I was well aware of that when I came here the first time and I am well aware of it now. I will need advice on how to minimise the risk to myself and my liberty and when I want to have advice other than yours I will tell you. For the moment I want to deal with you alone to make sure that you get the information you need for Elizabeth's defence direct and not filtered through intermediaries.'

'OK but I will have to warn you each time we meet, that's if you are willing to meet me again - and I assume that you will be.'

'I believe I can trust you as my lawyer and Elizabeth's so you can be confident that I won't disappear.'

'And secondly, why are you here? Why were you ready to run the risk of getting in touch with me? To be blunt, what's in it for you? I have already apologised for suggesting that you might be after money - and I apologise once again - your face as much as your words was as emphatic a denial as I could have wished. But why do you want to become involved.'

'Let me ask you a question. I hope that you will feel able to answer me. What has Elizabeth Fielder told you about the events of the day of the killing?'

She hesitated and he continued, 'Were the police looking for someone who might have been able to shed light on her activities that day?'

'That helps me off the horns of a dilemma, Sam. Yes, there was a man who had spent the day, the Sunday, with her. in the mountains ... '

'On the Rigi, in fact. A day of beautiful weather. A day when we enjoyed each other's company in a glorious setting. A day of being together for the first time and ... ' He paused momentarily. She detected the longing in his voice and he, watching her reaction, noticed a shadow flicker across her face and he guessed that she regretted his emotional involvement with Elizabeth. He continued, 'Yes, the reason has to do with the emotions. That day is one that I have relived every day since then.'

'That was the last day you saw my client, saw Elizabeth Fielder?'

'No, I have seen her since then on a couple of occasions when she has attended the court, from the distance, through the railings.'

'You couldn't resist a look.' She had spoken too quickly. She felt cheap and blushed.

Sam ignored what lay behind her words, 'Yes, I had to see her and besides I wanted to make sure that her former masters in the SVR were not minded to remove her from the scene. What they were planning here in Basel went badly wrong and there are reasons for them to want her out of the way, either from motives of revenge or to silence her so that word of their activities doesn't get out. She is safe in Basel Prison and in court, there's good security in each of those places, but I have fears for her safety between the prison van and the court, especially when she takes the opportunity of enjoying the fresh air and sun for a few moments.'

'I will warn her of the danger, Sam. Will you continue to keep an eye on things?'

'A companion and I will be there but it would be as well for Elizabeth to take care. However you mustn't tell her about my presence, at any rate not for now. I'm sure you can look after that.'

They were the only customers left. Sylvia called for the bills for the two tables, at which Sam smiled to himself, paid by credit card and asked Sam to wait while she went to the Ladies' Room. 'The bathroom isn't it where you come from?' she said with a smile adding, 'Perhaps we could continue our conversation beside the river?' As he waited he reflected that if he hadn't fallen for Elizabeth he would have been more than a little interested in this woman who combined sharpness of mind with potent femininity. Another to join Liz!

'If you can stand my company for a while longer, Sam, may I suggest that we take a stroll up to the Münster, walk down the steps and then take the ferry over the river. Is that agreeable to you?'

'Perfectly. It's an afternoon for walking and it's a healthy thing to do after a good meal, which, incidentally, I've enjoyed immensely. I'm unlikely to tire of your company, Sylvia - particularly as we both have an interest in the outcome of Elizabeth's trial.'

'Typical,' she thought to herself, 'he flatters and at the same time he frustrates!'

***

Outside the restaurant Sam looked for Noam and with a nod sent him on his way. It didn't escape Sylvia's notice. 'So I wasn't the only one who brought a minder to lunch!'

'But mine kept well out of the way and didn't watch you eating, did he!'

'Manners in minders? Is it?' She laughed and took his arm. 'Say you don't mind. I haven't had much male company lately. But if your relationship with my other client means that you would rather not ... '

'An intelligent and attractive woman on my arm is an asset that I value.' He noticed that she had applied her perfume while she had been at the Ladies Room - it was stronger than when she had arrived at his lunch table. 'My relationship with Elizabeth Fielder? I'm not sure how to define it. Months of watching her from a distance and listening to conversations in her apartment, in her hotel room or on the telephone and then one day out in the mountains ... '

'And after the outing you had dinner at *Die Drei Könige* and after that ... '

'A chaste goodnight in the bar of the Hotel International, a Brooklyn address left with her should she wish to get in touch again. Then I checked out of the hotel and went elsewhere in Basel ... '

'And not to Hamburg. That, I believe, is where you said you were heading that evening.'

'Not to Hamburg. That story was necessary for me to extricate myself from any problematic entanglement with her. I went across town and later heard what went on in her room.'

'And were disturbed by the turn of events?'

'Shattered is more like it, Sylvia. You can imagine what it was like for me - we had spent a glorious day in the mountains, the Rigi covered in snow, lunch in the open air, the two of us getting on as though we had known one another for a long time ... '

'Though it was only one of you who had known the other for any length of time - Elizabeth knew nothing of you until that day?'

'Well not until the previous evening when seemingly by chance I had the opportunity to sit at her table for dinner and took it.'

'And if that opportunity hadn't come your way?'

'I probably wouldn't be here with you, though I can't be sure of that. You see she had made a profound impression on me long before. That day with her in the mountains, it wasn't something that I ought to have done. It was ... unprofessional.'

'Not the thing that CIA agents ought to be doing, sleeping with the enemy?'

'Not sleeping with her but being with her, and I didn't regard her as "enemy", which created problems. And, by the way, I don't own up to being CIA or even ex-CIA!'

'I take your point and I'm inclined to think that you're from some other agency, I have my suspicions which one but I won't jump to a premature conclusion but I'll keep my eyes and ears open. I like a puzzle and as your advocate I've got to think how you can say as little as possible on the subject in court and still carry weight as a witness whose evidence is going to help my other client. So you can see that there really is a clash of interests. I want you there to testify and give authenticity to the tapes. But if you go there and say what you were doing you will end up in prison for a whole bundle of offences.' She paused and turned to face him, 'Unless your old masters can find some way to persuade the Swiss government to go easy. But I think you've already indicated that you're on your own in this, that you're a freelance now?' She took his hands, 'You must remember that I have advised you of this conflict. I don't want to let you down or Elizabeth and I don't want to be struck off as a lawyer, it's a job I like and ... though I say it myself, it's one I'm good at. It takes most of my waking hours.'

'And what takes most of your sleeping hours?'

'Sleep!' A shadow passed across her face and she turned away to face the river. The boat was about a hundred yards away and they were silent while it came alongside and they clambered aboard, taking their seats next to other passengers on a geranium decorated ferry. The ferryman cast off and let the stream take the boat back across the stream to the far bank, to Kleinbasel, the pulley ran along the steel cable slung across the river as the fast flowing stream did the work. They remained silent and watched the Münster recede. He gave her his hand as they clambered ashore then once again she took his arm and they headed along the bank towards the *Mittlere Rheinbrucke*. The trees between the bank and the houses facing the river – one of which was Sam's house - gave a pleasant shade and they stopped to look back across the river at the Münster perched on its cliff on the far side.

Sam broke the silence. 'And Erasmus lies quietly somewhere there.'

'Yes, he too sleeps alone.'

Sam was surprised at her vehemence and bitterness in her voice. 'Perhaps you would like to tell me about it.' His caring instincts had been aroused, he had seen this kind of distress when he had had pastoral care of his students at the Hebrew University of Jerusalem. 'Only if you want to talk and only as far as you want to go.'

'I came out of my office with plans to interview you, to find out as much about you as I could. I've found out a little and now you are offering to play the father confessor rôle!'

'I'm not a father confessor, Sylvia! All I suggested was that you might find it helpful to talk. I'm trained to keep my mouth shut and I once had pastoral responsibility for students and have acquired the ability to listen, to be non-judgmental and, I hope, supportive.'

'We will have coffee at the café at the end of the bridge after I have telephoned the office to say I won't be returning there this afternoon. Then, if the idea doesn't scare you, we'll take the tram to my apartment and over a light meal and a bottle of wine we'll begin the therapy.' She squeezed his arm and they set off for the café.

***

They had moved from the dinner table to the easy chairs and taken the remains of the Alsatian Riesling with them.

'And you have the tapes, Sam? I think I ought to hear them, don't you?'

'Here then, Sylvia.' He took two audio cassettes from his pocket and passed them to her.

'The originals?'

'No copies, the originals are too important to carry around. The originals are in safe keeping and I will have instant access to them when they are needed.'

She nodded her approval, 'Efficient and organised - like your former employers, I expect!'

He smiled, 'Quite so!'

'Which one first, Sam' He indicated the tape and she put it into the hi-fi, switched on and sat down. 'What are we going to hear?'

'A conversation last year between Elizabeth and Vladimir after he had tried to rape her in her apartment in London.'

They sat and listened to the telephone conversation between Elizabeth and Eugene.

'He sounded pretty wretched I must say, my client is a tough cookie, to use US-speak.'

'Which is why he had to drug her in Basel if he stood any chance of a successful rape there and even then, as we both know it was Vladimir who came off worse from the encounter! They had been lovers, of course, - that was in the USA and Canada - but the relationship had come to an end, at any rate so far as she was concerned, but Vladimir wasn't so ready to let go. He couldn't or wouldn't - I don't know whether there is such a distinction in these things - break free and he paid with his life.'

'And Elizabeth is likely to pay with her freedom! She feels guilty, so much so that she almost welcomes the prospect of prison as making some kind of atonement for killing the brute. I shall have to try to stop her asking for a substantial sentence, no it's not that bad, but she is too resigned to being in jail for some years to come and not over anxious that I should plead mitigation.'

He had another tape, made earlier the same evening in London, of the attempted rape itself but in it Elizabeth had warned Eugene:

"If you ever try to force me again the damage that I do to you will be permanent - that is a final warning and it's non-negotiable. Get that into your thick head and don't you dare to forget it!"

Sam had decided, however, to keep this to himself. In the hands of a smart prosecutor the threat of permanent damage might be read in an unhelpful way. He had no wish to present Sylvia with having to search her conscience over whether it should be disclosed to the court.

'Well let's hear the other one' She rewound the first tape. 'And this is the star exhibit? The recording of what happened in Room 219 at the Hotel International?' She removed the first tape, returned it to its case, put the other in the hi-fi, switched on and returned to her chair.

They waited for the sound to begin. She bit a nail and Sam noticed her slight agitation.

The tape began. There was background noise and then a knock on the door, a pause and then a woman's voice.

'Well, good evening Eugene.'

Then a few moments of people moving around followed but there was no return of her welcome.

'Pleasant enough but not up to the quality of your work.'

'Standard sort of thing for an international hotel. 'The workmanship is good but the choice of fabrics and paper lacks imagination, I feel.' A pause. 'I'm pleased that you agree - too much gold in evidence, I think ... Like a drink?'

'You haven't a Calvados, I suppose?'

'As a matter of fact I do.'

The sound of a drawer being opened.

'I brought some with me knowing that you liked it.'

'Well done Elizabeth, you do know how to look after a fellow ... in some ways ... You are always very thoughtful.'

The sound of more movement and a glass being placed on a table or other surface.

'Thanks, can I get *you* something?'

'An orange juice would do fine, please.'

The sound of a door, possibly of a refrigerated drinks cabinet being opened and something being poured. Silence once again now broken by the male voice.

'Where have you been all day?' There was a hint of anger in his voice.

'I might ask the same question of you about yesterday evening and this morning, but I won't.'

His angry reply.

'You might, but you bloody well won't. I'm in charge

and I *would* like to know where you have been all day.'

'That's easy! I met Sam Charles, a rather personable American at dinner last night and we spent today in the Alps. We came back to this hotel, changed in our own rooms, had dinner at the *Drei Könige* and said goodnight in the bar here, at which point we went to our respective rooms. It was all very chaste and, for that reason, very pleasant. He's gone to Hamburg on the night sleeper and that's that. And as for not letting you know that I was going out for the day, the fact is that I couldn't make contact with you before I went out after breakfast, no more than I was able to find you last night - when you were probably amusing yourself.'

Sylvia smiled. 'And Sam Charles is Sam Barth?' He nodded.

A short silence and then Eugene's angrier response.

'Don't be so dammed impertinent. This morning I was meeting another member of our team, a technical expert, and for the rest of the time I was following up a lead.'

'Not chasing a bitch in heat?'

'A bitch in heat is better than a frigid bitch! Sorry that was uncalled for ... but unlike you I've had a very difficult day, but I won't bore you with all the details.'

The sound of movement across the room and a door closing. Then silence for a while before someone returned from the bathroom. Then more silence.

'Just what do you think you were doing by going off for the day without a word, you might have been involved in an accident and anyway who was the fellow who picked you up?'

'Picked me up? I don't like the expression I'm not a tart looking for customers. Let me tell you again what happened! At dinner last night I met an American to whom I took an immediate liking, no nothing sexual, he was clearly good company and when he offered to go with me to the Alps, by train I would stress - not in his car - I was pleased to accept. I had no wish to spend the day here just waiting for the action to begin tomorrow whatever it might be that you've planned. As it turned out I was right in my assessment of him ... we had a splendid day out and the weather was simply glorious ... and he made no attempt to get me into bed with him. He was attractive and at the same time a complete gentleman, someone who respects women and doesn't take them for playthings!'

'He might have been from Swiss Security or the CIA!'

Sylvia shot a glance at Sam and raised a questioning eyebrow. His expression said nothing on the subject.

'And pigs might fly - he wasn't one of *your* sort, I've told you that he was a *gentleman*!'

Sylvia laughed at Sam's expense.

Silence once again.

'You are sure that you know what to do tomorrow?'

'*Really*, Eugene I'm not a novice and neither am I stupid. We've been through it all often enough. I'm to be available if needed but otherwise keep out of the way. I'll have the mobile 'phones in my handbag so I'll always be in touch if you need me. You have chosen to keep me out of your plans and I am very happy with that. Ask once more and I'll take the first 'plane to London and leave you to your own devices!'

The sound of a glass being put down.

'How old are your children, Eugene?'

'Evgeny is twelve and Sera ten. These are some recent shots of them.'

'They're fine kids ... you should be proud of them ... and you're not keen to go back home, I don't understand it.'

'The kids are fine, it's my wife who's the problem, you should know that, I've told you often enough! We just don't get on together any more and the kids, fine as they are, take her side. Besides, it isn't fair on them to make them take my side - they are on her side already and I'm not wanting to bring conflict into their lives.'

'They need a father!'

'I'm fully aware of that but I would bring more problems than benefits you know!'

A period of silence. Then they just caught him muttering.

'I'll just make a visit to your bathroom.'

Movement and a door closing. A sigh from the woman, then the sound of him returning followed by silence which he eventually broke.

'Besides I would rather be away from Moscow and life in the West is to my taste, especially when I can feel that I'm exploiting it for the benefit of our Motherland. It's the only job for which I've been trained. It's good to feel that you can enjoy life and at the same time be of service to your country.'

'You'll have to go back home for good one day!'

'I was given instructions today that we are both to return to Moscow immediately this operation is completed.'

His voice showed both triumph and anger. He was met with her silence before she spoke again.

'I don't know what they'll have for me to do next. What about you? Will they have another .... job in the West that's to your liking or will they have .... a desk job waiting in Moscow?'

There was something wrong with her voice and diction.

Then his voice, trying to sound calm and friendly.

'Please, Elizabeth, I want you in bed ... I want you now, remember the good times we had.'

His voice had risen, he was evidently having difficulty keeping control.

'Just a moment .... ' she was now fumbling for her words, ' .... I must get my lipstick.'

Movement.

'You're not having me! You've doped my drink! You want to rape me! You want to abduct me!' Sudden clarity and lucidity.

'No, Elizabeth don't!'

The sound of a commotion in the room, of frantic efforts to open the door and as he succeeded a noise little louder than that of a Champagne cork followed by someone falling to the floor.

'Oh, Vladimir why?'

Something hit the door and then there was silence both from the hi-fi – apart from light music on the hotel radio - and between Sam and Sylvia.

'That's it, Sylvia. I hope it's useful. But are you all right. He had noticed her reaction to the recording and that she had begun to sweat profusely once it became clear what Vladimir had intended. He got up and stood beside her chair and taking a white handkerchief mopped her brow. She looked up at him, anguish in her eyes. 'Sorry, I'll be back!'

She hurried out of the room and as Sam followed towards the hallway he heard her being sick in the bathroom.

Five minutes later she returned wearing a fresh blouse and smelling of soap and toothpaste. 'Sorry Sam. There was something that upset me badly about that.'

'I could see that, Sylvia. It's clear that you have had an

unpleasant experience of your own in the past. I'm sorry about that and that hearing the tape has distressed you. If I can help in any way ... '

'Not now Sam. Perhaps some other time. I'm sorry but would you mind leaving me now. I'm truly grateful for your bringing the tapes. They will make a huge difference to our case at the trial. Can I keep them, the copies that is, the ones you brought?'

'Yes, no problem there but I will want a word with my attorney on how I will stand if I appear in court to authenticate the tape evidence.'

'Thursday morning, Sam, about 10.00 o'clock. I can't attend to it until then. Tomorrow I've a simple assault case to deal with in court, a battered wife who fought back. I'll see you on Thursday if that suits you.'

'OK by me, Sylvia.'

She put her arms around his neck. 'Just hold me close for a moment, Sam. Nothing passionate, just to reassure me, I'm frightened.'

For two or three minutes he held her and then she moved away.

'Thursday, Sam'

'Thursday it is, or rather it will be.'

'I've already told you that you should have been a lawyer, Mr Charles.' He caught a flicker of a smile and then she closed the door behind him.

'When,' he asked himself, 'had someone tried to rape her?' The dis-ease that had first shown itself as they had waited for the ferry to Kleinbasel that afternoon clearly ran very deep. Life was never simple! He had supplied the evidence to strengthen Elizabeth's case but it looked as though he would have to lend support to her advocate as well.

Chapter 19

Tuesday 15th July 1997 (the conclusion of the evening)

Sylvia closed the door on Sam and retreated to the kitchen where she poured herself a stiff gin and tonic. She took a sip and then, with a snort of contempt, poured the rest down the drain. She had to keep off the stuff, it was no help in the long run. Drinking with friends and in moderation was one thing but this was another entirely. She ran a bath, poured in some bath essence and luxuriated in it for half an hour. The arrival of this surprise witness had brought a sense of purpose and excitement to life. In her bedroom she slipped on a long white night dress and a peach coloured dressing gown, she loved the feel of silk on her skin. She looked at herself in the mirror of the wardrobe and sighed. She was a good looking woman and she knew it. In earlier centuries men would have gone in search of the Holy Grail or fought duels for her. But this late twentieth century liberated woman hadn't been able to form a stable relationship with any male she had met. And her resort to therapy seemed to be making things more difficult.

She sat down at the small antique writing table by the window and took from the drawer a hard covered exercise book. On the cover she had written in copperplate *"Sylvia's Diary, Therapy Exercise."* How long had she been keeping this thing? She turned to the first entry, yes it was five months ago that she had started. How long before she had completed the process, understood herself and got rid of the demons from the past that returned so regularly to torment her? She turned to the last entry, drew a line under it and began:

"Tuesday 15 July. A day of very mixed emotions. A

productive morning in the office with good progress on G's divorce settlement.

Yesterday had a surprise call from a Mr Barth offering to provide evidence in the Fielder case. Had lunch with him today and discovered that he answers to the name of Sam. He has tapes of the events in the room at the International on the night of the killing. These he played to me. It's good evidence if he is prepared to testify in court but I'm afraid that he will get cold feet when it comes to it - he would be in danger of a substantial sentence himself for the way he got the evidence. So it was attempted rape, as I believed it must have been.

"And how shall I describe my personal reaction to his tapes? Sufficient to say that I was violently sick. The intensity of my reaction shakes me. But that is part of the therapy and once it's completed I'll be back to normal - whatever that is! I must make more time to work on it, to get back into my childhood and uncover those things that are the source of my problems. I must give time to it before I see Ursula next Monday or she will accuse me of wasting her time and my own.

"And Sam Barth? From the tape it's clear that he called himself Sam Charles when he took Elizabeth Fielder to the mountains on the day of the ~~murder~~ killing. So the Sam is consistent and possibly genuine. What his real name is I suppose we shall know if he appears as a witness. Occupation? A spy of some sort or is that too romantic (? wrong word - more like "the product of a fevered imagination", but then Elizabeth Fielder was certainly in the pay of some Russian organisation or so the Federal Prosecutor's interest shows, as well as what was said by the dead man on the tape). Mr Barth liked to let me think he was from the CIA but I'm not so sure and have my suspicions about where he's really from. Well

Sam Whoever, what am I to make of you? Elizabeth had it right when she told Vladimir that Sam was a gentleman, even though she seems to have got it wrong when she said that he wasn't in some security service or other, work which apparently doesn't usually attract gentlemen! He's attractive, attentive to a female companion and mercifully not a sex fiend on the prowl."

***

'That's enough', she mused. 'I expect he'll disappoint you like other men have'. Her thoughts went back to her father. Once, indeed until quite recently, she had thought of him with wistful love and affection. How she had missed him when he had died from a sudden massive heart attack four years ago. It would be four years next month. But in the last five months she had come to wonder. Ursula had taken her back to her childhood in their therapy sessions. 'Dig,' Ursula had said, 'dig deep, uncover the memories that you have buried, covered over in your mind because they were too painful to face, to live with! You have repressed them and we will work together to bring them to the surface so that they can be faced and dealt with.' It was horrifying, suspecting that what you had previously remembered as a happy childhood might have been nothing of the sort. That being bathed by your father, and having him sit with you in bed reading your favourite books together might not have been the simple innocent occasions you seemed to remember but events charged with evil when you were violated by him.

***

She turned back through the diary, reading at random

from the entries:

"Friday 21 February. First session with Ursula, I think I like her though she is a forceful character. I suppose I'm going to need that sort of encouragement and push to make the effort. She said that it would not necessarily be an enjoyable process - indeed that it could be a painful one as the spectres of the past, my childhood traumas, were brought to the surface, identified and addressed. She suggests one two hour session a week but cannot say how long the treatment will last. It's as well that Dad left me a useful legacy, bless him!"

***

"Friday 21 March. A hard session tonight. I shouted at Ursula and almost hit her. I suppose she's used to that sort of thing but I ended up feeling humiliated. When I told her so she said that it was probable that I had been severely humiliated in my childhood, subjected to emotional or physical abuse by my relations or friends of the family. When I laughed at her she said that I should read about women who had been willing to face up to such treatment in their childhood and sent me home with an American book to read. I'm to read it and discuss it with her next week."

***

"Saturday 22 March. I can't believe that parents could do such things to children, especially their own. It's a horrifying book and to think that for so many women it was all hidden away, locked up in cupboards in their memory and refused the light of day until therapy unlocked the door! No work from the office this weekend, I must read the book and then re-read it so that I can begin to make progress with Ursula next week."

***

"Friday 28 March. Came home from the therapy session totally exhausted and drained. Thank God for Ursula who said she will always be there to help me confront the memories. Perhaps we are beginning to get somewhere. We went back to when I was three and Dad and I went on holiday while Mum was nursing Aunt Trudi who was ill. Was it all innocent or was there something sinister about the way he dried me after we had been in the lake? I told Ursula that I was beginning to think that I might have been abused. She was pleased and said that, if that was what I thought, it was most likely that it had really happened. I'm not sure."

***

"Monday 5 May. I'm having nightmares and it's hard to sleep for more than a few hours a night. Thank God for Temazepam - without it I don't know how I'd get any rest. Did those things really happen to me? And I once thought that I'd had a happy childhood!"

***

"Friday 9 May. She's asking about Satanic rituals, says it probably didn't happen that way but we must be sure. She says that if Papa were still alive I would have to confront him with what he did to me in those early years, him and Uncle Stephan. But they're both dead, which is good as I'm spared the anger and stress. But Ursula says that it isn't good as I need to confront those who have robbed me of my innocence to show them my anger. I was angry with her and she was pleased, said that it must all be stirred up and come out. She said that it was right at this stage to hate Papa. She says hate is creative and therapeutic. Strange, it's his money that's paying for these sessions! But I can't bring myself to hate him, he loved and cared for me. Ursula says that I've got to face up to his abuse and not pretend it never happened. I wish this had never started (the therapy that is) I feel like I've been cut open by a surgeon and there's no sign of anyone ready to stitch me up again. Ursula makes me angry but I've got to stick with the therapy if I'm to get back to normal. Was I ever normal? I'm wondering now if I ever was normal! Or if my father ever was! Perhaps the same sort of things happened to him as a child? Ursula says that it doesn't matter and I mustn't forgive him easily. If I could only talk to him about it! Ursula suggests that I talk to my sister and if she denies that anything untoward took place in our family, get her to see Ursula - perhaps Paula will need therapy as well, maybe that's why her marriage failed last year."

***

"**Saturday 17 May.** Dinner with Paula at her apartment. Ended with a heated argument. She refuses to accept that Papa did anything wrong to us. She refuses to believe that he was a child abuser and hates me for bringing the matter up! She said that I'd become the abuser - abusing his memory - and told me to leave. Afterwards she 'phoned and apologised but told me never to mention it to her again and not to insult Papa's memory in front of others. If only she were right, but the things that Ursula's helping me to remember!"

***

She closed the exercise book with a sigh. She was in a state of emotional confusion and turmoil. Her memories of being abused were so vivid. How had her father been able to hide what he was doing from Paula? And yet ... and yet ... she still loved her father in a real daughterly, un-sexual way. She still mourned his passing, missed being able to discuss legal points with him and benefit from his wisdom and experience. Missed being able to share life's triumphs and failures with him. As she had often done over the past four years she put the Fauré Requiem on the hi-fi and let its soothing music surround her:

"Lux aeterna luceat eis, Domine: cum sanctis tuis in aeternam, quia pius es.

Requiem aeternam dona eis Domine: et lux perpetua luceat eis."

"Light perpetual shine upon them, O Lord: with all thy saints in endless glory, for thy tender mercy's sake.

Rest eternal grant them, O Lord: and light perpetual forever shine upon them."

As a devout Catholic she wasn't happy to be told that forgiveness was sin and that she must hate her father as a step to her own recovery. She couldn't being herself to hate him, whatever he had or hadn't done to her. Or at any rate she couldn't hate him for long, despite Ursula's prompting. She would still pray for his peace, if the memories were true she had even more need to do so. That thought and the music soothed her. She made a cup of hot chocolate, heard the requiem through to its end with its gentle *In Paradisum*:

"In paradisum deducant te angeli … "

"Into Paradise may the angels lead thee … "

She retired to bed and enjoyed the first night of unbroken sleep for months. The calming impact of the music and the sense of moving in a positive direction with the Elizabeth Fielder case had relaxed her: she would try to sleep without a pill tonight.

***

Sylvia woke considerably refreshed and glad that she hadn't taken a sleeping tablet. It was Wednesday and she would be seeing Sam Whoever tomorrow. She laughed aloud at the name she had given him. Elizabeth's case had been interesting from the first, it was going to be even more interesting from now on. Sam, she felt would be more than just a witness, more than just the vital witness - she felt that with his help she could call up the reserves of intellectual and emotional strength that she needed to bring the case to a successful conclusion. Only recently she had been beset by doubts about its outcome. How she had missed having her father to discuss it with! Perhaps Sam would be her sounding board and support in the weeks ahead.

Chapter 20

Friday 18th July 1997

Elizabeth sat in the windowless room and waited for her advocate. Another routine meeting, no doubt. What had happened on that February evening had been very simple, frighteningly so, even with her muddled recollection of events, but it was amazing how complex and seemingly unending were the legal consequences. She liked Sylvia Brünner: understanding, to the point without being brusque, but willing to give time to her and concerned that she was being looked after properly in jail, and clearly very able at her profession. They had already gone through the events of the day before the Fasnacht Carnival on several occasions. She was soon to meet the psychiatrist appointed by the Court and, no doubt, Sylvia would want to talk about that today.

The door opened and Sylvia was shown in. The prison officer closed the door and left them alone, unlike when you were visited by friends, interviews with lawyers were completely private with no one listening in. That was what they said but she wondered, knowing how little faith she would have placed in such an assurance back home in Russia. And she had often wondered how long she would have been kept in custody by the SVR before they would have found some way of disposing of her: just long enough, she supposed, to be sure that they had extracted all the information they could. Elizabeth and Sylvia shook hands, greeted one another, and took their seats on opposite sides of the table.

Sylvia took a legal pad and some typed notes from her brief case. She also placed a small battery tape recorder on the table. She glanced at the notes and began, 'You will probably find this a little tedious, Elizabeth, but I would like you to go through the last 24 hours or so before the killing - but with this difference, that you are not preparing a statement for your lawyer, the Public Prosecutor or the court but telling a friend - I hope that you can regard me as a genuine friend as well as your advocate.'

'No problem there, Sylvia. You've proved that you're that. You've made sure that they are caring for me - as much as this sort of institution can do so. Your efforts to get me music therapy have paid off at last, the first session was on Tuesday and it relaxed me wonderfully. I'll tell you about it when we've got the biographical bit out of the way. You said the 24 hours of so before? Right. So you want the previous evening - from dinner onwards, I suppose?'

'That will be fine. Away you go and don't forget that you're telling it to a friend. I want to hear of feelings as well as facts, not that genuine feelings aren't factual.'

'OK away we go. I had come down to dinner at the Hotel International rather later than I'd intended, Peter had been with me for the day.'

'Peter Lewis, your boss and lover?'

'It's as you say, he had both those rôles in my life but both were coming to an end. My Russian masters wanted me back home in Moscow, not that I would have gone, and the love side was really in tatters. I don't blame Peter for that. It was lack of nerve on his part, he's unable to be ruthless in his relationships or in business. The old ties to Ruth, his wife, simply were too strong and with the way it was affecting Michael, their son, he couldn't cut loose. I suspect that if Peter had gone through with the divorce he would have ended up with a breakdown worse than the one he's had. No, he hadn't been using me. He started the relationship in better faith than I did, he made no secret of his broken down marriage when we met. I was the one who was deceiving the other, it began because I thought that was what my masters wanted - though it very, very quickly turned into something genuine on my part. Peter's fundamentally a very decent individual and the mess that we've all got into has hurt him terribly. It's one of life's unkindnesses that those with tender consciences so often punish themselves while the rogues who couldn't care a damn sleep tranquilly, oblivious to the harm that they've done in the lives of others. Sorry, you asked for the emotional element not the moral and philosophical!'

'Never mind Elizabeth, it was worth saying. Just one thing. The baby you're carrying - it's Peter's child and he's aware that it is?'

'Yes. His child and he knows about it. But I've made clear to him that it was my fault that I conceived. I haven't told him this, but it was a foolish effort to try to get him to make up his mind whether to return to his family or stay with me. Things seemed to be moving in my direction at the time and I persuaded myself that it might swing things. And I'd said to myself that I could always go for a weekend in the country - that's our Russian euphemism for having an abortion, you know - but it wasn't long before I knew that for me it wasn't an option. Peter or no Peter, I became determined to have his child, our child. Though how it's going to work out if I'm locked up for years I don't know. They won't let me keep it with me for long will they? And in any case how could you bring a child up in jail, what sort of an upbringing is that? Peter will give all the help he can, he's not poor and he'll care for it. But he lives in London and the child's going to have to live here in Switzerland. I sometimes wonder if my mother could get out of Moscow and come to care for her grandchild. It's a dream I have. And it would get her out of the mess that my country has become, her pension's almost worthless, even if they have the money to pay it. But I doubt if she'd ever want to leave. Though perhaps the prospect of looking after a grandchild would make all the difference. But they wouldn't let her out anyway. For one thing they have a hold over me if she's there. Sorry to digress, Sylvia.'

'No, it's all relevant. Your ante-natal visits to the *Frauenspital*, how are they going?'

'Fine, they're very good there and the child's developing properly. There's no shortage of time here in Basel Jail for my ante-natal exercises.'

'Good. Let's concentrate on dinner that Saturday night. You got to the restaurant later than you should?'

'Yes, Peter had stayed as long as he could. After a day looking around Basel we'd ended up in bed. The sex was good but - I don't know whether it's with hindsight or whether it really was so - but anyway as I look back my memory is of a sense of farewell, a gentle, loving farewell but a farewell nonetheless. Peter went, we weren't due to meet until the Monday evening of the Carnival. He would be with his family and his hosts until then.

'I stayed in my room, half watching the television and half thinking about Peter and myself. Then I went down to the restaurant and found that it was very busy, but I was lucky and got a table to myself. I'd just started my soup when I was aware that a man who had just arrived was looking in my direction, he caught my eye and my eye held his gaze. The next moment the waiter asked whether I would mind sharing with another guest and indicated the newcomer. If he hadn't caught my eye I might have refused but I found myself saying that I would be pleased to have his company. He apologised for intruding and introduced himself. It was immediately obvious that he was an American, a New Yorker as it turned out, from Brooklyn to be precise. Sam Charles, a journalist covering the carnival for some US newspapers that targeted Swiss communities. How did I feel? Immediately at ease with him. We were sitting opposite one another. He was the best sort of American, lively, intelligent, good company and stimulating. We chatted away about all sorts of things, the USA, Switzerland and I don't know what else. I told him about my job and even about my relationship with Peter and all our difficulties - I know, it's hard to credit that I'd be so open with a complete stranger and a male at that! But that's how it was. He wanted to know about the piano Peter had given me for Christmas, where I kept it in the apartment and that sort of thing.

'Suddenly it was 10.30. I'd planned an early night, with a trip to the mountains the next day, on the Sunday. To my surprise I found myself asking Sam if he'd like to go with me to Luzern the next day. And, of course, he accepted.' She smiled and threw her head up with pleasure at the memory.

'You clearly liked him, then?'

'You're right about that Advocate Brünner your forensic insight is phenomenal!' They both laughed, a sound uncommon in the interview room. 'Liked him and knew that he'd be good company. And I also knew instinctively that he wasn't a wolf waiting to pounce.'

'Now about the day you spent together on the Rigi, your Sunday together ... '

'Fine, Elizabeth. I'm grateful for all you've told me. Now let me tell you something. I've found Sam Charles, or rather he contacted me.'

Elizabeth looked at her in amazement, 'You're sure it's him? Sam Charles from Brooklyn?'

'Totally certain, though I'm not certain that his surname really is Charles. We had lunch together on Tuesday.' She caught the look on Elizabeth's face, a fleeting expression of shock with just a touch of envy. 'You last saw him on February 16th? Well he's seen you several times since then, watching you arrive at the court each month. And, by the way, he's not really a journalist. He's in the same line of business that you are, though he's not too keen to say exactly who his employers are! But the important thing is that he has evidence which will help me with your case. Your room at the Hotel International and your telephone were bugged and so was your London apartment. You remember his enquiries about where your grand piano stood? Well he had been listening to you play and wondered just where the piano was in your sitting room. He'd done the bugging so he knew the plan of the apartment. You've given him a good musical education, Elizabeth. The important thing, music apart, is that he's got tapes of what happened in your hotel room on that Sunday evening: Eugene had definitely drugged you as a prelude to rape. And there's a tape recorded in London, some time before, of you being telephoned by Eugene after he had tried to rape you and you had dealt with him pretty effectively. They're vital to your case and I'm relieved that he's turned up.

'He's sent you a message, Elizabeth, I shouldn't have brought it into here but read it and I'll keep it for you afterwards, I promise to re-seal it - I won't read it. Oh, there's this as well, though you won't be able to take it back to your cell' From her case she took a bottle of perfume, 'I think the name is some kind of message to you, though I don't give him high marks for subtlety.'

Elizabeth took the bottle, 'Calvin Klein's *Escape*.' She smiled, and sprayed some onto her neck, 'Just as well that he didn't ask you to deliver *Poison*!'

'I'm sure he wouldn't do that Elizabeth. He's in love with you, deeply in love, even after enjoying your company for a little over 24 hours.' She paused, 'You're a fortunate woman, you may be here in the *Untersuchungsgefängnis* awaiting trial for murder but, Elizabeth, I envy you, I really do. Sam Charles is the genuine article even if he works for a firm that's a rival of yours and even if the name he gave you was an assumed one. But then I don't expect that you gave him *your* real name!'

There was silence while Elizabeth studied Sylvia's face. Sylvia read what was in her mind, 'Elizabeth, I don't need to be a psychiatrist to know what you're thinking. You're concerned that I will make off with Sam Charles and that he will vanish from your life once again. I hope his letter will reassure you - no, I don't know what's in it but I can tell a man who's in love with a woman. And this particular man is a very resolute character. I have the feeling that what he wants he gets and what he wants, and will do almost anything to get, is you. I say almost anything because he's a man of strong principle, something which must be difficult in the line of business you both pursue. You didn't know that he's a rabbi? No, something he said pointed to that - it came as a surprise to me as well. One more thing before you read the letter. He never really vanished from your life, you know. As soon as he found out that you had ended up here on the murder charge he set to and began to plan to get you out. Fortunately he's convinced that the best way is the legal way - which is a relief for me!' She passed Elizabeth the sealed envelope and immediately started to busy herself with making notes so that Elizabeth would not feel that she was under scrutiny. Still she couldn't resist the occasional glance at her from the corner of her eye. She saw an attentive reader, immersed in the letter. She saw a lively and beautiful young woman basking in the warmth of being loved and growing in assurance and confidence as she read.

***

The officer who took Elizabeth back to her wing reported to the office and Elizabeth was called in. 'Perfume is against the rules, you know that. Do you have the bottle with you?'

'No, it was my advocate's perfume. She took it out to spray herself and I - I helped myself. I really hope she won't make a complaint to the *Direktor*.'

'You're normally - no, that's not fair - you're *always* one of the well behaved ones, Elizabeth. Nothing will be said this time, but wash the stuff off as soon as you can.'

Elizabeth went back to her cell, passing the time of day with the other women as she went. She lay on her bed deep in thought. How different things seemed from when she had gone down to see Sylvia! So Sam was not a mere memory destined to become more and more feint with the passage of time. He was here in Basel. He had watched her from a distance when she had made her monthly visits to the court. And as she thought she suddenly remembered the bearded man who had been looking through the gate at her on her last visit. Not too far in appearance from her idea of a rabbi. So she had an angel to look after her, one that was a rabbi in the CIA or some other western security service. She smiled to herself - life really was stranger than fiction. Before she joined the other women for lunch she regretfully washed off the remains of *Escape*. A sacramental gift, she thought and wondered whether rabbis had sacraments or anything of that sort.

***

After lunch Elizabeth lay on her bed. She had excused herself from the toy making session that afternoon. She had to give time to thought. She had told the officer that she needed time to prepare for her next meeting with her advocate, which indeed was the case. Her prospects looked very different now from what they had been earlier that day! Sam Charles was no longer the memory of a man who had come into her life for 24 hours and disappeared for ever. He was here in Basel! He had seen her and she, unknowingly, had seen him and his beard. Somewhere, out there in the city he was living and working for her release. But who was he and who were his masters? He hadn't put that information in his letter. Of course not! But she needed to know what she was being drawn into. Assuming she got off the murder charge and spent a short time in jail or was released, what then. It wasn't likely that the Swiss authorities would say, 'Welcome Elizabeth, how about settling here?' They would want her out of their clean, tidy little country double quick! And her Canadian passport would be no use to her. The Canadians knew all about her and might well have scores to settle. Either that or they would simply want to forget her and there would clearly be no refuge there for her either way. Sam in his letter had spoken of 'arrangements' once she was out. He would have to be more specific. A Swiss jail was at the moment preferable to the reception the SVR or the Russian *Mafiya* might have waiting for her back in Moscow. So where would Sam be taking her when she emerged from the *Untersuchungsgefängnis*? He and his masters must have a plan for that.

And now there resurfaced something that had been lurking in the back of her mind for a long time. Its force surprised her and at the same time she recognised it as a thought, a sentiment, a conviction that had been there all along, a familiar companion in her captivity. Now, with the coming of a hope of liberty it had acquired greater strength. *She wanted to be punished!* She *felt* the guilt of what she had done. It wasn't something to be shrugged off and forgotten. She had killed Vladimir. For all his faults, his drinking and his lecherousness she had liked him. They had been friends, in the past they had been lovers. Never before had she killed anyone. She wouldn't have imagined herself capable of it. OK they had trained her to kill, but as to doing it, that was something utterly different.

Looking back to the events of that evening in the Hotel International she still couldn't remember things with the clarity she wanted. But she did remember a blind fury, somehow she thought of it in terms of colour - at times a blur of red and at other times of darkness. *She was a killer!* She had killed a friend. At times he had behaved badly, very badly, but she couldn't expunge from her mind the conviction that she had killed a friend. She couldn't easily forgive herself - in that she was like, Andrea, one of the other girls in the wing who had killed her lover and now suffered in quiet withdrawn agony. All this was at odds with the unalloyed joy and delight she should have been experiencing at the news Sylvia had given her and from what Sam had said in his letter. She felt deep within the need to atone in some way for the killing. She recognised the need to make amends. Killing was something monstrous, utterly monstrous, unnatural and inhuman. In killing Vladimir she had distanced herself from civilised conduct. How was she to become reconciled to herself and to humanity? Though now she knew with certainty that he had drugged her as a prelude to rape and she would have to let that colour her thinking.

She recognised the power of the conviction within her that she must make amends but knew that it must not be allowed to overwhelm her as it had Andrea. Sam had evidence that would help to get her out of here. His letter had left her in no doubt that he was deeply bound to her emotionally and that he was here in Basel on that account and not in response to the orders of his masters. He seemed to be suggesting that his masters were no longer directing his actions, so how could they help relocate her on release? And that thought raised the question of whether he had a viable plan for her future. Where, indeed, did he plan to take her and her child? The child she was carrying and to which she would soon give birth. That child had first call on her. As if in response to her thoughts she felt the child stir within, releasing within her feelings of tender love and concern. She felt a longing to hold the child in her arms. To tell it how much she loved it. Her pregnancy had created problems and they would remain but she lay there and rejoiced at the new life within. The medical staff at the Frauenspital had been encouraging and reassuring about the child's development. It couldn't be in the infant's interest to have a mother in jail. She would go along with whatever Sylvia wanted to provide a powerful defence. But once out she would have to deal with her feelings of guilt. She knew that they were likely to remain, whatever the verdict of the court might be. As judge and jury in her own case she pronounced the guilty verdict on herself. And she would have to live with it, to contrive somehow to live in amity and harmony with herself. A self that she now knew was capable of the extinction of the life of a friend, not the best of friends but one who had been by no means the worst. Poor Vladimir! And how were his family faring? Were his old masters the SVR providing for the widow and the children left behind? Somehow she doubted it but she also had doubts about whether Vladimir would have done much for their welfare had he lived. Perhaps she shouldn't have them on her conscience as well as Vladimir.

Chapter 21

Monday 21st July 1997

Peter Lewis waited for Elizabeth to arrive on her side of the glass screen. Jakob Gold had brought him to the *Untersuchungsgefängnis* and then gone off for a coffee at a café near the SBB Station. Peter was grateful for Gold's moral support, especially when he came away from these visits feeling empty and sad.

A prison officer showed Elizabeth to her side of the glass and she gave a restrained smile before taking her seat, 'Thanks for coming again Peter. It's a long way to come from London for an hour's meeting. I'm truly grateful to you.'

'Well, despite all that's happened, Elizabeth, the past doesn't just drop away and disappear, does it?'

'No, you're right. The problem is relating it to the present and to the future. The past is still there, it was real and it was genuine, well most of it anyway. I've told you how sorry I am for deceiving you and hiding my real identity. I'm especially sorry over Vera's death ... I swear to you that I had nothing to do with it, no knowledge of what was planned. How are her family, her son and husband?'

'I saw them last week, sorted out a plumbing problem with their apartment and took them out for a meal. How are they? Still grieving and it hasn't helped having the police tell them it was probably murder rather than an accident caused by a wild motorist.'

'Good kind Peter, I knew you wouldn't forget them. And how about yourself? How are you bearing up? Does the therapy help, or shouldn't I ask?'

'Yes, I'm glad you have, there's no point pretending

about things. Therapy and pills have helped to deaden the pain, though the pills have done it by creating a sort of numbness, physically and emotionally. But I can report progress, slow but sure.'

Tears were forming in her eyes. 'It's only a passing thing, Peter. I'm sure it is, the intensity anyway. Given time things will normalise.'

'And Ruth and Michael have been wonderful, real towers of strength. You remember that at first I couldn't face work? Well Ruth dropped the day to day running of her wine business and took over keeping the glassware going. And she did it in the nicest way, consulting me, really more often than she needed, to make sure that I didn't feel useless and so I had something to contribute. That's helped a lot ... I've done a day a week back in Kilburn and I'm going back half time next week. By the way the team there send their best wishes ... they really liked you, Elizabeth.'

'Send them my greetings then and say thanks.'

'And Michael's been amazing, utterly amazing. He took a lot of flack at school but he survived ... it toughened him up, not unpleasantly, but it made him stand on his own two feet, stand up for himself, which is no bad thing. He made sure that our football trips didn't stop and he drew up a programme of visits to museum's and other places and made sure I didn't say no. He's been a real brick.'

'And his nightmares?' She had wondered whether to ask.

'Nightmares ceased and psychiatrist discharged! Only one member of the family in the hands of the shrinks at a time is best!' He forced a wan smile.

She wasn't surprised, Elizabeth knew that, with herself behind bars in Basel and Peter back home, the causes of

Michael's distress had been eliminated. No point in hiding it, 'Having me out of the way has done wonders for him then?'

For a moment Peter looked sheepish. He collected his thoughts together, 'Yes that's so.'

'And you and Ruth, how are things? Be honest, Peter.'

He began diffidently, unsure how much he should say and struggling to find the right words, 'You ask how things are between Ruth and myself ... ' He paused.

Elizabeth waited and then broke in, 'Between you as man and wife, Peter, not as between the proprietor of a business and his valuable assistant!'

Again there was a pause until he summoned up the courage to continue in a lowered voice, 'Well, a couple of weeks ago she came into my bedroom, we'd had a pleasant meal together, I suppose that was the trigger, well she came in in her nightgown – Michael was away at a friend's place ... ' He paused again, striving to get the right words and not look foolish. 'And she asked if I'd like to do it with her, I think that was how she put it. And she added, “I know how you relieve tension” – well she'd caught me doing it in the bathroom the previous week, much to my embarrassment.' He paused again.

'You once told me that you did it thinking of me, Peter.'

'And I still do ... sometimes.'

'With the permission of your therapist?'

'Well, yes.'

'Though I haven't been consulted on the subject, Peter.'

'May I have retrospective permission, Elizabeth.'

'And continuing permission?' She smiled, 'OK I give you both retrospective and current permission.'

'And for the future?'

'To be reviewed in twelve months time, Peter. I'm not

giving it for life.'

'Well Ruth and I hadn't made love for about three years and I thought why not? - after all we're married. Then she said, 'Peter, if you want to think about Elizabeth while we're doing it you have my permission. You're going to take a while to sort yourself out emotionally and I won't mind.' And so we made love and I thought of you. And Ruth and I shared the same bed for the night.'

'And it was good sex, Peter? I'm not asking you to give star ratings or to compare it with our time together.'

'Good enough to want it again.'

'With Ruth?'

'Yes with Ruth.'

'And with some thoughts of Elizabeth?'

'Yes, for the time being at any rate.'

'Well I'm pleased that you and Ruth are in the same bed, Peter.'

'But the problem for me is how to deal with what we, you and me, Elizabeth, what we were to one another. Despite your hidden identity our love was real! No we must talk about it, Elizabeth! We've got to work out how to live with what was a real part of our past, yours and mine. And there's our child's future to consider. I don't intend to dodge my responsibilities and I've told my solicitor to look at ways I can support him or her. I'll set up a decent trust fund but in which country depends on where you're going after here.'

'If I'm going anywhere, Peter. It's a murder charge that I'm on! It could be some time before I'm out and the child will only be able to stay with me for around three years ... and that's a real worry. Can you imagine, having bonded with my child, our child, to have it torn away from you while you complete your sentence?'

She had become agitated and he wondered how to,

respond, 'Of course I'll take full responsibility for the child but I don't think that would take away your hurt if it happened that way. What does your lawyer say about your prospects? They're good at defence, I hope?'

'Your good friend Jakob Gold has seen to that. He found one of the best, Sylvia Brunner, who's got a record of success in the Basel court. She's impressed me with her grasp of things and I like her manner, I like her as a woman.' She didn't mention her recent concerns that Sylvia seemed to have become stressed and preoccupied.

She had been weighing up Peter's responses: yes, he did show signs of being on the mend and he was sleeping with Ruth. There were things he ought to know sooner rather than later, 'Peter there are new developments affecting me and the case but we've no privacy here. Jakob Gold knows about them and will tell you if you say I've told you to enquire of him. He'll tell you all I would have said if there hadn't been the risk of being overheard. Don't ask me about things now.'

'And how's the mother to be? What do the medical people have to say about your progress?'

'I've regular visits to the Women's Hospital. They're completely happy, scans and tests are fine. Blood pressure and so on are as they should be. So it's just a case of waiting until the beginning of August for her to be born.' She had let it slip.

'So I'm to be the father of a little girl, I'll leave you to find names for her but I'll want to be able to show her a father's love.'

Elizabeth was in tears and a prison officer hovered near. Elizabeth sensing her presence indicated that all was well. The officer told Elizabeth that they had five minutes of the visit left and moved away.

Peter's tears began to flow, perhaps he was on the mend but it would be a long while before his recovery was complete. The information that it was to be a girl and the mention of love had stirred him up. He produced a spotlessly white handkerchief from his pocket and mopped his eyes. Part of Ruth's caring for him had been to ensure that he remained smart, tidy and well dressed: she was sure that appearance and self respect belonged together. 'A bit of a mix up isn't it Elizabeth ... for all three of us! We'll just have to do our best.'

She would have loved to reach out and place her hand on his shoulder and comfort him but the glass window separated them and she wondered if she should after all have primed him to speak to Gold. But it had to be done and there was never likely to be a perfect time. 'See you next time Peter, do come soon. I need to see you, we both need to see one another. And you must be present at the hospital when our daughter is born. The beginning of August they think. I'm sure they'll allow you to be there. I will insist!'

'I'll be there Elizabeth, you can be sure of that. Bye.'

She nodded to him, forced a smile and turned to the prison officer who led her off back to her cell. He sat for a moment before getting up, leaving the building and setting off up the hill to join Jakob Gold for a coffee. How did he feel? Churned up, but mercifully not as much as he had expected. *He* could simply walk out of the prison: *Elizabeth* could not. And he felt sad for her as well as for himself and for their daughter to be.

***

Elizabeth lay on her bed back in her cell. She closed her eyes and let her thoughts linger on those happy days with

Peter in London. They were *her* memories, they were *good* ones, no one could take them away from her. But she knew that she must move beyond them, she had to move on emotionally, and she had asked Jakob Gold to inform Peter of the new situation. She wondered how old she would be when she left this place. She remembered the week when she and Peter had become lovers and the afternoon she had spent alone at Maiden Castle near Dorchester. That memory had come to her once before in this prison but she wasn't trying to conjure it back once again out of thin air. No, each time the emotion had come it has been unsought, a powerful gift, not something she had manufactured or worked up. On Maiden Castle she had looked towards Dorchester and seen the prison, with its connections with Hardy's *Tess of the d'Urbervilles*, over in the distance. She had never imagined being on the inside of such an institution. Another memory of a time in the open air was now a regular companion, her day in the Alps with the American Sam Charles: but that was the day she had shot Vladimir and she pushed away thoughts of the latter part of the day. It had been a day of very mixed memories and emotions.

She felt the kick of her daughter and placed her hand on her stomach, if only she could be sure of keeping her, of bringing her up at liberty. No good brooding, she had to be active. She sought out Trudi for one of her American English lessons. She hoped she was succeeded in weening Trudi off the idea of improving her spoken English in order to upgrade her clientele as a prostitute to wealthy businessmen and was instead moving her towards retraining in secretarial and IT work. To help one of these girls in a positive direction would be rewarding.

***

'Well Peter, how was it? How did Elizabeth seem?'
'Not quite as draining as I'd feared and she seemed quite buoyant, though there were a few tears. She said that you had something to tell me – she couldn't mention it there in the prison but she said that you would tell me on her behalf. I don't understand why she couldn't.'

'First of all a coffee? ... Good, what will it be? ... A double Espresso? ... Fine I'll get you one then we'll take a stroll – you need some fresh air - and I'll try to explain.'

They set off along *Aeschengraben* on their way towards the Münster, the cathedral poised above the bank of the Rhein. Gold kept the conversation going on a variety of technical topics until they stood behind the cathedral looking down on the river and the ferry making its way to the opposite bank. For a moment they watched its progress before Gold began, 'Elizabeth wanted to see how you were shaping up, Peter, she's still fond of you and cares for you. It seem she's judged that you're ready to hear this, otherwise she would not have told you to ask me for her message. Elizabeth was unable to tell you this in the prison because she could not be sure she would not be overheard or recorded, it's a very public place for conversation as you know. As you will see this must be kept confidential, for the moment at least. So I must ask you to keep it to yourself, you must not tell anyone else, not even Ruth. It could have a significant effect on the outcome of her trial.'

'I give you my solemn word, Jakob. What you say will remain with me.'

'Peter, one of the things that shook you up after Elizabeth's arrest was the fact that she had spent the day of the killing with an American journalist, Sam Charles. You will remember that they had met on the Saturday evening at dinner, spent the Sunday on the Rigi, eaten at *Die Drei Könige* and then parted. Elizabeth insists that it was a chaste encounter, that they never saw the inside of each others room. Can you accept that, Peter?'

'Yes, Jakob, I can – we were so close that Saturday during the time we spent before I came back to your place in Allschwil early in the evening. I don't believe she would have cheated on me, especially as she was pregnant by me. OK she cheated about her true identity and her rôle in all this but I believe that sexually she was completely faithful.'

'One more thing, Peter, are you convinced that your affair with Elizabeth is over, never to be resumed.'

'If you had asked me a couple of weeks ago I would have said I didn't know for sure but now I can say that I have accepted that it's finished, Ruth and I have begun a sort of second courtship and we're sleeping together again. Michael is well on the mend. Mind you I won't shirk from my responsibilities for our child.'

'Nor should you. I'm really glad that you're back with Ruth – you need each other and Michael needs you both. But let's move on ... you may remember that Sam Charles left Basel for Hamburg and was never seen again though the Basel police wanted to interview him. Well, he's reappeared.'

'Elizabeth has seen him? At the prison?'

'No, Peter, that's the point about all the confidentiality. The police would still like to interview him and for a good reason that is something he wants to, no, something he must avoid.'

'He had a hand in Eugene's death?'

'No, but he knows exactly what happened in that hotel room leading up to the shooting and the evidence, if he is able to give it, could mean all the difference to Elizabeth's conviction and sentence. And, Peter, the future of Elizabeth and her child ... your child.'

'*If* he is able to give it?'

'Well, yes, there is a problem ... the evidence was collected illegally ... Elizabeth's room was bugged because Sam was no journalist, he was working for another security service, not the one Elizabeth belonged to. He needs to be sure that the evidence stands a chance of being accepted by the court before he makes himself known to the Basel authorities.'

'Jakob, it was complicated enough before, now it's even more so. Now that's the legal side, there's more isn't there?'

'Yes. I've assured you that his previous meetings with Elizabeth were chaste but that's not to say that he didn't make an impression on her. She told me that she was convinced that, like you Peter, he was a man of integrity, an upright man. And the fact that in giving evidence on Elizabeth's behalf he will endanger his own liberty – we Swiss do not like rooms and telephones being bugged! - certainly supports her assessment of his character. She doesn't think she's in love with him, not yet, but she is attracted by him and it could be the right thing for her especially as she has to find a safe haven to settle in once she is released, she can't stay here in Switzerland and Russia's the last place she wants. Elizabeth would have much preferred to tell you all this herself but you can see why she has had to use me as her messenger.'

'Jakob, all this has come as a shock ... I'm sure you expected it would ... thanks for bringing me here rather than telling me in the café. I need a while alone, give me a quarter of an hour, please. I'm going to sit in the Münster for a little while, I'll be back shortly.' He set off round the corner of the building to the main door of the cathedral.

Jakob Gold remained standing looking at the traffic on the river, the ferry going to and fro while a heavy barge with a tiny car on the stern moved slowly up-river from Rotterdam. He ignored a bearded man sitting nearby immersed in a copy of the *Basler Zeitung*. The man pulled on a raincoat, produced a hat from a carrier bag and changed his reading matter.

'OK Jakob. I've thought about it and I'm reconciled. If he can get her sentence reduced, find her somewhere safe to live and make her happy, then he has my blessing.'

'You're sure of that, Peter, really sure?'

'Completely sure, they both have my blessing.'

The bearded man had got up and strolled slowly past taking in Peter's demeanour. He disappeared across the *Münster Platz*. Sam Charles had heard every word of their conversation: Jakob Gold had been wired for sound. He had agreed to it reluctantly but had been convinced by Sam, who had insisted that he had to be sure that Peter had really drawn a line under his affair with Elizabeth. It would have made no difference to his willingness to testify in court but it did clear the way for the possibility of romance, for the fulfilment of the infatuation that he had lived with for over a year.

Chapter 22

Friday 1st August 1997, Swiss National Day

Elizabeth and her daughter occupied a private room in a wing of the *Frauenspital*, the Women's Hospital in Basel. Her prison guard, having checked that the windows were secure, had made herself as inconspicuous as possible in a room next door – after all the prisoner was unlikely to try to flee with her new-born.

Elizabeth snuggled the baby in her arms and began to get to grips with breast-feeding her. The midwife, satisfied herself that Elizabeth had got it right, departed and left Elizabeth and Peter Lewis on their own. Lewis sat quietly watching, taking in the tranquility of mother and child – the child that was also his. Never would he have guessed when she had told him way back in January, on Russian Christmas Eve, of her pregnancy that she would be giving birth in custody.

'Well Elizabeth we can be grateful that you've brought a good healthy child into the world.'

'So far the medical people are completely happy with her, there may be more tests to be done but, thank God, they haven't found anything amiss.'

'And how about you, Elizabeth, how are you after it all?'

'Six hours of labour and no shortage of medical staff. It was hard work at the end but that's only to be expected ... when you're expecting!' She laughed, glad to have got it over successfully.

'I'm glad they let me remain with you throughout, Elizabeth, though I'm a bit confused about my status in all these events!'

'No need to be Peter, with or without a certificate

you're the father, Little Olga was conceived in love and born in love, the love of us both Peter.'

He leant forward and gently felt the warmth of the little head. He rested his hand on Elizabeth's arm. 'However difficult it's going to be she will have the love of both her parents ... that I promise.' The tremor in his voice betrayed his emotion.

'You're happy with the name Olga?'

'Of course, it says something about her roots, doesn't it?'

'Do you know, Peter, I fully expected it to be a boy and to have a British Birth Certificate. It shows just how wrong you can be!'

'Yes life's certainly taken some strange turns this year.'

'Peter, I've been thinking about a second name for Olga ... today's Swiss National Day and it struck me that I might have been tempted to call a boy William after William Tell ... well for little Olga how about Wilhelmina? It's just a thought, Peter.'

'A generous gesture to your Swiss captors, Elizabeth? Well lets turn the idea over before we decide. Tomorrow or the day after I've got to go to the register office and register little Olga and ourselves as her parents. Thank God she was born here and not the prison ... that wouldn't have looked too good on the paperwork!'

'Maybe not but that's where we're both going to be in a few days. Back in the *Untersuchungsgefängnis* but that's not something you've got to spell for the birth certificate! It's going to be odd being there with a child. I just wonder how the others will take it.'

'She'll be safe there?' Peter felt a sudden sense of fear for the child.

'They'll keep her in the hospital section of the place

which will mean a change to my routine but I'll still see the other girls, I wouldn't want to miss out on that ... I think I can give some of them a bit of help.'

'Any parents among them, Elizabeth?'

'A couple of them are mothers but they've lost contact with their children, the result of their disordered lives, I fear. Several have had abortions ... it's not a place to look for much evidence of family life, I fear. But I like most of the girls and I think I can do some good.'

'And you know that when you do settle somewhere I'll set up a trust fund there or wherever it suits you for Olga. You've no idea, I suppose ... '

'Where I'll end up?'

'Yes, wherever that might be. But please let it be where I can visit little Olga. I suppose you've no idea where Sa ...'

She put her finger to her lips to stop him, shaking her head, 'Quiet on that score, Jakob will let you know if there's anything to report. Here, you ought to hold your daughter, safe to take her? ... Good, ready?'

She handed over Olga to Peter, buttoning her night gown and pulling her dressing gown around her. Peter took the little pink bundle, holding her gently, feeling again the warmth of her head and taking in the smell of milk. They sat for a while, each with their own memories. A couple of months ago Peter could not have faced this but now he was on the mend, though he had still quite a long way to go.

Elizabeth broke the silence, 'It happens every day all over the world, thousands upon thousands of children are born yet every one is a miracle.' She blinked back a tear, 'Thank you for giving me her, Peter, I will always take care of Olga as someone very, very precious.'

'Precious to us both ... ' He choked and couldn't say

any more.

'One question, Peter, how is Michael going to take the arrival of a sister?'

'I don't know for sure but as we do plenty of male things together, I somehow don't think that a little thing in petticoats will disturb him unduly ... time will tell! By the way, Ruth has sent some baby-grows and some little dresses.' And he indicated a large carrier bag hanging from the coat peg on the opposite wall.

Chapter 23

Friday 8th August 1997

'So your legal conferences and courses are really group therapy sessions, Sylvia?'

'I'm afraid so, Sam. And I'm not sure if they're doing me any good. I'd like your advice sooner rather than later.'

'I'm no expert in that area. As I've told you I've had the pastoral care of university students in the past but not as a shrink, just as someone who had some experience of life and could give sensible advice.'

'That's just the sort of person I need. Someone who can stand back and see what to make of it all, someone who's sound and sensible.'

'Sound and sensible? If I were that I wouldn't be here!'

'And two women - Elizabeth Fielder and myself - would be the worse off!'

'Yes you badly want to get her off - sorry, to have her acquitted - don't you?'

'As an advocate I want right to be done. But, yes, as an individual and as a woman I want her a free woman. My professional pride will be affronted if she ends up with a heavy sentence. Thank God there's no death penalty. Just imagine what it's like spending months, years even, with a client. Toiling through the court proceedings, sweating while the judges are out and then having to listen as a death sentence is handed down. Then appeals and having to tell your client that they've come to the end of the road, no more courts, no more appeals for clemency, that nothing beckons but their execution. Then having to see them before it's all done and then emptiness, anguish and revulsion. I couldn't practise as a criminal attorney in your country, if it's the USA that you really come from. It's barbaric there. You've read Grisham's 'The Chamber?' Yes? Didn't you find it sickening?'

'What a speech, Sylvia. You obviously feel strongly about it. And, yes, I have read 'The Chamber' and, yes, I agree that it's sickening.'

'But it's not just as Elizabeth's wonder witness, the one that I've got to keep under wraps and pray that he isn't run over by a Basel tram or otherwise put out of commission, it's not just as a witness that I'm glad you're here in Basel. I've found your company helpful and fun! I hope that saying so doesn't embarrass you but it's good to have a man around. Especially one who behaves as impeccably as you do! My therapist doesn't rate men very highly and you're a good corrective.'

'Your corrective from Brooklyn!'

'Or so you say. You're unable to tell me directly but what you've allowed me to believe, or rather what you've tried to get me to believe, is that you're a Brooklyn boy working for or retired from the CIA.'

'Sorry I cannot say.' Sam smiled. They had sparred around the point before.

'Some music, Sam? I've been sorting through some of my late father's collection of discs.'

'Fine. I'm a beginner in music appreciation, as I've told you I've learned to like Chopin by listening to the bugged version from Elizabeth's apartment in London.'

'OK some Bruch first - I'm no expert in music but lately I've found some of it quite soothing - but first let me fill your glass. Some more Pomerol or would you like something else?'

'The Pomerol's fine - no, that's not adequate praise, it's splendid. As is your company, Sylvia.'

She decided to ignore the complement for the time, 'It's the better known of Bruch's two Violin Concertos. I hope you like it, Sam'

They relaxed, sitting in arm chairs on either side of the fireplace. She closed her eyes to concentrate the better on the music. This was proving a more helpful therapy than the one Ursula was providing. He watched her wondering what was going through her mind or whether she was in neutral gear, not thinking or at any rate not beyond the processes needed to appreciate the structure of the music and to enjoy it. In fact one part of her mind was deep in Bruch but with another she was wondering what his reaction would be to the next recording. As soon as she had seen it she had known she had to play it to him and see how he reacted.

The Bruch finished and she picked up the remote control, 'Now a less usual item. By Arnold Schoenberg, my father liked his music, though for me it does take some getting used to.'

To Sam *Schoenberg* was a name and no more.

She looked at the notes, 'It's called "A Survivor from Warsaw". There's a narrator, who uses something called "rhythmic declamation" – a sort of pitched speech - an orchestra and a chorus. Let's hear what it's like! She pressed the button on the remote control and the music began. As she sat back, ready to see Sam's reaction, the thought occurred to her that *she herself* was, in Ursula's words, *a "Survivor".* The thought jarred and she forced it into the back of her mind while she watched Sam's face.

Sam was gazing at a flower arrangement that occupied the fireplace and wondering whether the Warsaw events were those of 1943 or 1944. She saw him focus his attention on the music. The discord certainly contrasted with the Bruch that she'd just played. Like her he had listened to it in a relaxed state. She could see that the strange narration gripped him, the survivor's tale of reveille and being beaten by Nazi troops.

"You had been separated from your children, from your wife, from your parents. You don't know what happened to them. How could you sleep?" She noticed Sam's disquiet. There was discomfort on his face and his hands were clenched.

"They are all dead", the soldier's words, spoken in a bass-baritone by the narrator after Jews, already felled by blows, had been beaten on the head, brought a chill to her own heart. She saw Sam begin to sweat. His nails were digging into the palms of his hands.

"There I lay, half conscious, it had become very still, fear and p a i n!". The anguish of the Survivor.

Suddenly out of the orchestral din the narrator cried, *" ... they began singing, "Shema Israel." '* And the chorus took up the words of *"the old prayer they had neglected for so many years, the forgotten creed."* She saw Sam unable to contain his anguish any longer, he let out a cry of pain and was on his feet. She found the control and stopped the record. 'Sam, are you all right ... I had no idea ... '

He had fallen back into the armchair and sat staring at her. She brought him some water and knelt beside the chair. She took his hand, 'If I'd known ... '

He didn't take his hand away but drawing on his inner reserves he gave her a pale smile, 'Last month I was in Warsaw, Treblinka, Auschwitz and Birkenau. I found this quite shattering. There I had tried to imagine these events, your recording has brought it all home rather too powerfully.'

'I don't think so Sam. Not *too* powerfully. The response of humanity can never be strong enough to that horror!'

'And when the member of the human race is a Jew ... with relations who died at the hands of the Nazis, killed by bullets or poison gas or simply beaten to death ... The pain doesn't go easily. And it isn't just something in the remote past. My father died because he was a Jew, stopped by a Katyusha rocket that some ill wisher sent in his direction from the Lebanon. But I'm telling you much more than I ought.'

'I'm your lawyer and what you tell me doesn't go any further unless you instruct me to do so.'

'You'll represent a Jew?'

'Whyever not. I already do so.'

'You have other Jewish clients, then?'

'Of course. I don't ask my clients whether they've had a close encounter with the *mohel* when they were younger and then send away the ones who had!'

'But in the one case of which *I* have experience you were once *nearly* in a position to check on the matter!'

'That was not the object of the exercise - that's not the apt word for what nearly happened then - but you know what I mean. Thank God you're looking better, Sam. I swear that I had no idea what that record would do to you.'

'I believe you, Sylvia, honestly I do! I myself wouldn't have expected such a reaction but having just been there, to Poland that is, has done something to me.'

'I want to hear about it, Sam. About your family, about your father, about your visit to Auschwitz and the rest. But now?'

'If we could hear the recording from the beginning and right through to the end this time.' He paused, 'And if you wouldn't mind me wearing this.' He produced his knitted *kippah* from his pocket, 'I wore it in the ... Army.'

'In the Israeli Army, what's it called?'

'The IDF, the Israeli Defence Forces.'

'In confidence, to your lawyer! And your lawyer suspects that you aren't from the CIA but from Mossad, which is much more exciting. But you needn't confess to that yet, though what you tell the Court will be interesting.' She picked up the remote control, 'Are you ready for the next seven and a half minutes?'

He nodded and the discordant music and powerful narration began again.

When it was over they were silent for a while until Sylvia played the slow movement of the Bruch Violin Concerto once more but this time very quietly.

When it had finished she caught Sam's attention. 'I'm a "Survivor" too in a sense, or so my therapist tells me. I'd be really grateful if you could help me with it ....'.

'Once you've told me what you know about the work of the *mohel* and circumcision!'

'Completely professional, I can assure you, Sam! I acted for a parent who was suing a local *mohel* for work badly done on his son. A really fascinating case to present in court - I think I got the case because the Jewish lawyers didn't want to get involved in a dispute with the *mohel*, one of their own folk and one whose services they might require. We had a variety of witnesses, medical people dealing with the physical discomfort to the child and psychiatrists on the potential loss of sexual enjoyment aspect. And the best thing was the choice of President, the judge that is. He was a real prude but also very thorough and conscientious. He spent a very uncomfortable time while the evidence was being given on the functions of the penis, especially by the author of a very explicit German sex manual! We all learnt a thing or two and our Court President rather more than most!'

'So I know where to come if I ever need to sue a *mohel*! I won't make a note because I'm not likely to forget and it isn't likely that I'll need to do so - our people have years of experience at it! Still, just in case, I've filed it all away in my mind. Now what do you mean about being a "survivor"?'

'It began around a year ago. A long term relationship had come to an end a couple of months before and, after the sense of freedom, a feeling of desperation set in, something I'd never known before. Perhaps it was my age, I'm thirty four by the way, and a sense that I ought to be settling down. But there was no one in prospect, no one who really appealed to me that is. My father had died three years before and I now came to miss him very much, he had been a lawyer working for a local pharmaceutical company and we used to discuss difficult aspects of my cases. He was good at helping me to come to my own conclusions, you know he would chip in with the comment, "Have you thought of ... " and there would be some element I'd ignored or played down which, on closer consideration, made a lot of difference to the case we were discussing. Not just business though, he was a great talker, the sort of person who enthuses about a subject and you want to know more. He was well read in Catholic theology, he knew Balthasar. I don't know if you've heard of him, Hans Urs von Baltasar, a Catholic priest - he'd once been a Jesuit - who ran the Institute here in Basel. He was known as the 'most cultured man in Europe'! Something to live up to wasn't it! You can guess how widely their conversations ranged. I've read many books on Papa's recommendation and read them carefully and with real enjoyment knowing that we would discuss them afterwards. Well suddenly I was very short of company, Gustav gone - he was my lover - and Papa gone. Somehow I began to lose confidence in myself, why I don't know - after all my legal work was going well, with a string of successes in Court and certainly no shortage of clients. But my confidence was ebbing and I was having to push myself harder to achieve the success I'd always enjoyed.' She paused, 'A drink, Sam?'

'No thanks, just keep going for the time being. When you feel in need of one, *then* I'll join you.'

'I began to experience panic attacks. Fortunately never in Court, somehow the adrenaline kept flowing there and my attention was on my clients and their cases and not on myself. Six months ago a girl friend in whom I confided suggested that I should see Ursula, her therapist. So I did and things seem to have become even more complicated since then, though I'm sure that it's all for the good ... ' Her voice trailed away.

'OK Sylvia. Drinks all round. Nothing too strong how about lemonade with a dash of that Czech stuff you have in the fridge?'

'You mean the Karlovarska Becherovka? A Czech client insists in giving me bottles of the stuff whenever he calls at the office.'

'Yes, that must be it if you say so - but only a dash mind! Lubrication for your vocal chords, not befuddlement for the brain!"

She brought back two hi-ball tumblers from the kitchen, each with a slice of lemon on the top. Cheers, Sam. Thanks for being a good listener.'

'*Le Haim* - To Life! If I can help you by listening and perhaps making the odd suggestion or two I will be well satisfied, Sylvia. I'll not be trying to direct you in your choices and decisions. That's for you and, in any case I respect your judgement as a mature woman who's a successful lawyer.'

'Mature woman? Since I've been in therapy that's the last thing I feel! But let's go back to my early sessions with Ursula.'

'Sessions?'

'Generally once a week and there is also group therapy session once a week in Bern - I wouldn't want to be involved with Baslers, not when I practise law here!'

***

'It's late Sam. Your description of Auschwitz and the other places will have to wait. But I think you need to get some of it out of your system. You weren't on a sightseeing trip were you. More like a pilgrimage I should imagine. Am I right?'

'Yes, you're on the right lines. There wasn't a lot for me to do here and I suddenly felt compelled to take off for Poland to see what I could discover of my roots. Mia, my former fiancée from Brooklyn came up with the idea but I went on my own. My family came from there, from Poland, of course.'

'But moved to Brooklyn?'

'What was left of the family did. My father lost pretty well all his relations. It was his good luck to be part of the *Sonderkommando* - I'll tell you what that was, but not tonight - at Treblinka at the time of the revolt in August 1943 and it was also his good luck that his home town was Brok, fifteen kilometres away. He knew the area, he had friends - Righteous Gentiles - and he survived. It's quite a story and it's also for another occasion.'

'Auschwitz, Sam. What's it like? What moved you the most? What stays in the mind and the emotions?'

'At random, let's see. First of all the size of the place. Auschwitz was a huge complex of camps with three main ones. The death camp was Birkenau - you know the one with the railroad running through the gate? Yes? Well it's 425 acres in area, a huge death factory. But the thing that hit home emotionally was a single red rose that someone had placed on the ramp - the platform onto which the victims descended from the trains, three quarters of them to go straight to the gas chambers and the rest to be slave labourers until it was their turn to die.' He paused to control his emotions, 'I just don't know why but I found that single rose incredibly moving. Leaving flowers isn't a Jewish way of commemorating the dead - you pray and leave a pebble on the memorial - but I felt that whoever had placed it there had performed a holy act in a hellish place, a *mitzvah*. That's roughly a godly act that benefits the doer and the whole world.' He had said much the same to Noam and to Liz but that was how it had been there was no need to embroider his account or to subtract from it.

'A small thing but ... '

'But of genuine significance. The world needs more hearts and minds touched by such things and determined that there will be no repetition. But I'm preaching and my response that afternoon wasn't cerebral but simple and direct, from the heart. The sight of that flower lifted my spirits as nothing else in that place had done.'

'What else?'

'The gallows where Hoess, the SS Commandant, was hanged by the Poles in 1947. In the original Auschwitz camp, between the gas chamber/crematorium and his house. Here justice was done, that too spoke to me of cleansing. I know what we said earlier about the death penalty, but if ever there were candidates for the gallows they were people like Hoess and his masters. They say that you Christians stress forgiveness and we Jews justice but, I put it to you, Advokat Brunner, it is possible to speak too readily about forgiveness. The offence of the Nazis was so immense, so heinous that only the ultimate penalty was appropriate. And in any case *we* the survivors are not authorised to offer forgiveness on behalf of the victims of barbarism.'

They were silent and Sam resumed, 'One last memory and that will do for tonight. By the way thanks for letting me get some of this out of the system. It was the next day when I was sitting on the station platform in Krakow waiting for the train to Zakopane in the Carpathians - that's the eastern end of the Alps, I think. There was a school party. You know, lively kids, boys and girls - about the age of ten I suppose - with a couple of teachers, a man and a woman who were keeping order and letting me know how late the train was likely to be - the station announcements were in Polish, of course, and, although my origins are Polish, I had no idea what was being said. Well, one of the girls shot past with her pigtails flying and I shuddered. And why, well the previous morning at Auschwitz I had seen a vast quantity of human hair in one of the museum blocks - the Red Army found five and a half tons of it when they liberated the camp - but it's not just piles of hair that make such an impression. In a case there was a blonde plait of hair, intact, just as it had been cut off from a girl or young woman who had then gone to the gas chamber and the oven. She would probably have been an assimilated Jew rather than an observant one as it happens. My reaction there on Krakow station the next day to a lively girl with similar hair was proof of just what a deep impression Auschwitz had made on me.' He was quiet again and looking up noticed the moisture in her eyes, 'Thanks Sylvia, you're a good listener. And now I really must be on my way. But I promise you that we will give deep thought to your therapy and whether it is helping or not. That will be our agenda and nothing else when we next meet'

She smiled her gratitude and kissed him on the cheek, 'I'll be grateful for that, very grateful, Sam.'

***

As he went his way Sam realised that his report on Poland had been very little different from those he had given to others – to Noam and to Liz – but could it have been otherwise? His experiences were etched so deeply on his memory and consciousness, Poland had been a defining experience, a series of such experiences, which would never leave him. And he was deeply grateful to Mia for having suggested that he make the pilgrimage. And he prayed for her happiness.

Chapter 24

Sylvia's Journal: Monday 21st July to Sunday 31st August 1997

Monday 21 July. A long and stormy session with Ursula this evening. Told her that I was beginning to have doubts about my memories and she said that this sometimes happened: the wish to brush what had happened under the carpet was simply reasserting itself, I was into denial. When I began to say that there was no evidence of any abuse having taken place she said that the memories were evidence enough and the absence of other evidence was merely the measure of my father's cunning. Had I read any of the books lately? Then I ought to re-read them to see just how like others' experiences mine were. What I needed, she said, was to join the therapy group so that I would have others to support me and share their experiences. When I said that I wasn't enthusiastic at sharing intimate experiences with a crowd of women she became very angry and accused me of disparaging women, how could I be a properly integrated woman if I despised my sisters? And after all that men had done to me! And when I said that all that I could place under that head were some memories of my father which might or might not be genuine and that my experience of men was generally not much different from my experience of women she became remote and suggested that we were both wasting our time. Did I want to get better, to become an integrated personality instead of being an emotional cripple? I objected to her description and she asked me why I had come to her in the first place. We agreed that I would read the book again and see her next week.

Is she right? Am I just trying to push it back under wraps to avoid the pain of reality? Or is it pure imagination on my part? I want to believe she's right and at the same time I want to shout from the rooftops, "No it wasn't like that at all - Papa was a good father, the best of fathers. He loved me and cared for me and I loved him for it AND I STILL DO!" It's exhausting. I feel worse than when I started the sessions but then she says that it has to get bad to get better. OK back to the book tomorrow and also the new one of 'Survivor's Experiences' that she gave me tonight. Perhaps I should talk to someone about it and get their opinion. But who? It's not the sort of thing you want to share if you can help it. What's the phrase? 'Dirty linen'? Yes, that's it!

Sam Charles comes to mind, but discussing it with a man! Surely not!

Sunday 27 July. Can I afford to spend so much time trying to sort out my emotional problems? A whole weekend when I ought to have been thinking about M's appearance in court next Wednesday. Still I need a break from work. But this therapy business is harder than 'work'! Compared with it work is a rest, a break. It's a good thing that I <u>can</u> immerse myself in work, and put my emotions out of mind. If I ever find that I can't do so any longer I'll be in real trouble.

So what do I feel now, after the reading that Ursula set me? My memories seem more real and my doubts less. In a way, in every way, I'm sad at that! If only I could believe that there was nothing in the memories! So what next? I'm still reluctant to join the therapy group. Well I'll find out what Ursula says tomorrow.

Monday 28 July. A positive session with Ursula. She was

very supportive. She is very keen that I should join a therapy group and suggested one in Bern if I were afraid of meeting people I knew in Basel. That sounds a good idea. I could start next Saturday - that gives me the week to think about it.

Saturday 2 August. My first experience of group therapy was quite an eye opener. So much rage and anger in such a confined area! One woman, Jeanne, almost went wild as she denounced her father, brothers and mother. She even acted out castrating them, the men that is, and the other women cheered her on! She wouldn't have got through it if they hadn't helped her - egged her on, is perhaps more accurate. But that's the view of a sceptic, as Ursula told me afterwards. She was really pleased with Jeanne's performance and told her to keep up the intensity of hate as it was essential if she were to recover. I spoke to her afterwards and she admitted that she felt worse than she had a couple of months ago. When I remarked about it to Ursula in the car on the way home she accused me of being simplistic. Couldn't I see that Jeanne had suffered so badly at the hands of her family that she had every right to hate them and to show it? Unless she expressed what she really felt and let it all come out the pathway to recovery would for ever be blocked.

Saturday 9 August. Ursula encouraged me to tell the others about my childhood and to be honest with them and myself. She left the others to draw me out. I don't like this exposure but I think they all wanted to help. I started to tell them about what I remembered from a long summer evening in our garden when I was six. A tall man on top of me and then darkness .... I could go no further and began to shake. I tried to speak and couldn't. Then I was sick. When I came back they were supportive and Alicia said that it must have been a memory of oral sex. Then all of them said how horrific it must have been for me and how brave I was to face up to it. I just felt soiled and didn't take in much of what went on after that. Afterwards Maria asked me if I'd like to spend the night with her after next week's session. It's kind of her and I said that I'd let her know during the week.

Sam's willing to discuss my therapy. Can I really trust him? Well he appears to be selfless in his involvement as Elizabeth's star witness – that's if he does appear in court. Apart from losing face what have I to lose?

Saturday 16 August. Another group session. How they support one another, being a 'Survivor' seems to bind you together. There's a camaraderie, a sisterliness about belonging to the group. I didn't say much about myself although several of the others tried to encourage me. Ursula said that I possibly needed more time to really feel a part of the group and to be able to speak without any inhibitions.

Maria has a small but lovely apartment with a view of the River Aar. She's a good cook and we had a very pleasant dinner with a bottle of an excellent red Burgundy. Afterwards we talked and talked. She was abused by her father and grandfather - at times both together! She's been a member of the group for six months and doesn't know how she would survive without the support it gives. We walked up to the Parliament Building and looked out towards the Alps, the air was delicious. Maria came for therapy after a failed relationship. I sympathised with her, most women have trouble with men at some time or other. Told her she'd just have to find another. No, she said, since starting therapy she had been considering her sexuality and she had thought that she ought to consider whether she wasn't really a lesbian. She said that a number of the others in the group had discovered that this was their true orientation. So she was exploring the matter. As it turned out I was part of the exploration process! I wasn't expected to share her bed, nothing as blatant as that but this morning she brought me a cup of tea, sat on the edge of my bed, put her arm around me and asked if I would like to explore a relationship with her. I said no, of course. But is this really my orientation too? Has the abuse driven me in this direction? That I'm even giving it the slightest consideration shows just how my world has been turned upside down! In fact the idea revolts me and I told her so. She said that I ought to read what some women who have come-out as lesbians have written - *they* were revolted at first until they were able to work through it, accept their sexuality and celebrate it.

She let the matter drop and over breakfast we discussed how we had found our need for therapy and how it was going. She had already told me about her failed relationship, a French businessman who came to Bern during the week and went home at weekends. She had known that he was married but the arrangement was OK at first. Then she came to want him all the time and not to have to share him with his wife in Besançon. He promised her that he would get a divorce and spend all his time with her in Bern. The next month he didn't turn up on the Monday but she got his farewell letter - he was moving to the USA with his wife and kids. He had never told her about the kids before. She had been distraught and although she had tried to find another mate she found that she had lost all her old confidence and sparkle.

She had been in need of confidence boosting and individual therapy and then the group had seemed to provide the answer. We admitted to one another that we felt much worse now than when we had started the process. Neither of us could imagine how we would get by without the group and the support it gave. Both of us had become very dependent on Ursula. And she had assured us both that it was perfectly normal to feel worse before the therapy brought relief. Maria had been abused by her father and grandfather with the help of her mother. The very idea is sickening!

I thanked her for the meal and the chat but she didn't invite me back - she's probably working through the list of members of the group looking for a partner to share her newly discovered or, perhaps, suspected sexuality. I'm not one of them, at any rate I don't think so. No, I'm not going to give the thought house-room! Things have become messy enough without that. As I've recorded, the idea revolts me but then Maria said that it does so to many who then find that it's their authentic lifestyle! Felt glad to get back here by myself at 1.05 p.m. Pleased that Sam's coming for dinner - he's offered to cook it and I'll take him up on that. Things are getting messy. Yes I'll find out what Sam Whoever makes of it all. There's a mound of papers to read through before I go to the office on Monday.

Monday 18 August. A good meal with Sam last evening. He certainly knows how to cook, every woman should have a Sam around. A splendid antidote to stray thoughts of lesbianism! If we can get Elizabeth out of prison and she feels for him as he does for her they'll make a fine pair. She'll be a fortunate woman.

His reaction to the Schoenberg piece the other evening was quite dramatic. Going back to his Polish roots has certainly been a disturbing experience for him. He's promised to tell me more about his family and its history.

Told him about Ursula and the therapy and that I'm a Survivor. He was mildly sceptical about it all - which was disappointing. I wish he'd believe about my memories. Still it's men who take the lead in doing this sort of thing and it must be hard for a man like him to believe that - sure they can understand that men take advantage of older girls and young women but they must find it difficult to believe the things that I and the others are remembering with the help of Ursula and the group. Some had unspeakable things done to them in their cots! At one stage I got quite angry with Sam about it all. He stayed very calm and asked if I wanted him to go. Of course I didn't want that or for him to feel that he wasn't welcome here. He really was very calm about it all. Said that he was happy to listen, that he wouldn't try to advise me and direct me but that he would point out anything that seemed odd and about which I ought to think carefully. In a way very much like Papa's approach to the problems of life and work. If only I could feel one thing or another about Papa. If only I could hate him unreservedly or love him unreservedly - or at any rate hate or love his memory - but my feelings are so mixed and fluctuate so much!

Sam's promised to contact a friend with some experience of therapy so that he knows more of what it all involves. I'm glad he's turned up, even though his sights are on Elizabeth. He's lonely of course. He spent one day with her and since the night of the murder he's only seen her four or five times and then only for a few moments from the distance outside the Court! That's some devotion! And he doesn't know how Elizabeth will respond to him if we do get her out of prison. He just remembers their one day out in the Alps and relies on the vibes he picked up then! I thought it was women who were gifted with intuition! He's lonely and we get on well together. If he weren't smitten with Elizabeth I ~~think~~ know I would want to see where our friendship would lead. It went a long way beyond mere friendship the other evening but both of us pulled back at the last moment. Strange that we both did. It's not as though he's engaged to my client or anything like that. He just hopes that she'll respond to him and that she'll be free to do so before much longer. And why did I pull back? Looking after a client's interests? I don't know. A newly acquired distaste of men - the result of therapy? I don't think so. I just don't know. Perhaps it's the fact that I like him and respect him and don't want a good friendship to be spoiled by casual sex! Am I becoming a prude, then? Surely not. But I am glad that we stopped when we did. In some situations friends are more valuable than lovers and Sam has the makings of a good friend who'll be around for years to come.

Tuesday 19 August. As luck would have it the consequence of moving my appointment to this evening was that I met Anna B in Ursula's waiting room - she was waiting for her chauffeur to collect her. When we had both got over our embarrassment we fixed lunch together to compare notes. Why does a women like her need help from Ursula? Her husband's a highly successful accountant and the director of several big companies, they've two lovely kids and she's always the height of fashion, no expense spared. Well perhaps I'll find out over lunch on Thursday. Maybe she's wondering why I go there!

Ursula isn't convinced that I'm working hard enough to get my memories of the abuse clear. She keeps saying I've got to work harder at it - to try to see it in my mind's eye like a slide show or like watching the movies. To bring back the feel, the smells and tastes of childhood so that it's clear just what they did to me. I've got to work on the 'inner child' - she asked me what dolls or fluffy animals I had as a child and said I should buy some which resembled them, to recreate my childhood bedroom. I've got to make contact with the 'wounded child' within me, to care for it, for the real me and not to give a damn about what other people think. I've to find my real self and love that self, the innocent child within that was so damaged by all I went through. Should I turn the spare bedroom into a nursery? What would friends think if they found out? I could always keep it locked, a touch of mystery about the room with me as the keyholder and no one else able to enter. A place of safety for me. Is it all crazy or is it the way I'm going to get better? Am I going crazy? Nothing gets any easier! Perhaps Anna will be able to shed some light on it all - and then there's Sam, though I hardly feel able to tell him that I'm thinking of turning a room into a nursery for myself!

Wednesday 20 August. What began as an enjoyable evening with Sam turned decidedly unpleasant. Perhaps the problem was the fact that it was so pleasant and relaxed. It led me into being more open with him about the therapy and what it involved than I had intended. He is still very sceptical of it all. He doesn't believe me when I say that Papa abused me. At any rate he said that it was unlikely that I'd remember such things after all this time.

No, that's not quite his line. He said it was that it was highly unlikely that I would have ever been able to forget if anything like that had repeatedly happened to me as a child. I wouldn't put up with that! After all I'm no fool - I know what I'm remembering is real, the memories are so vivid and detailed - much more now than they were a month ago.

He was very dismissive of Ursula especially when I told him that I couldn't imagine how I'd get by without her help. 'Like you did before you met her when you were doing pretty well by all accounts', or something like that was his reply! There are a lot of women who depend utterly on her and I told him so. 'Brainwashed like you!', was his snide retort. So I hit him then, harder than I had intended, and drew blood from his mouth. I wish I hadn't but he deserved it. Where did I get such fierce anger? Must have been from the last group session when we were battering the life out of that dummy, that proxy for my bastard father who molested me for so long - didn't Maria congratulate me for the way I went about battering it with my fists and then a chair! I'd have castrated it if I'd had a knife! Thinking about that I'm afraid of what I might have tried to do to Sam if I'd had a sharp knife handy, though I certainly wouldn't want to hurt him in that way. And in any case I suspect he's been trained to deal with any serious assault. Men do seem to gang together though. Sam should have supported <u>me</u> and not attacked Ursula.

How am I going to calm down and sleep tonight? My sleep is getting worse - but Ursula's pleased that I'm having more dreams than I've ever had before. Last night's was more nightmare than dream though, I was frightened by the way my heart was racing when I woke up. I don't understand most of them but Ursula's studied a lot about their sexual symbolism so she helps me to understand. It's all coming to the surface and that way lies my healing.

A hot drink and then some relaxing music - they might do the trick. Schubert's 'Trout', that usually helps.

Wednesday 20 August (Continued). It's my weakness, I suppose, as a dependent woman. 'Phoned Sam and was lucky that he'd gone straight back home. Apologised and asked him to come back here. Which he did, asking when he arrived whether he ought to be wearing his American Football gear! He remains remarkably calm and has a really good nature so it's odd that he comes from the world of agents and spies. I apologised for calling him a Yiddish bastard and he just laughed and said that it was mild compared with some of the things he'd been called in his lifetime.

I asked him why he'd been prepared to return. His reply was that there were two reasons:

1. He liked me and my company and wanted to help, though that help wouldn't take the form of unquestioning acquiescence in the therapy I was receiving. He apologised for his 'gut reaction' to what I had told him and said that his friend had put some literature in the post and that he'd try not to be too dogmatic until he had read it.
2. He wanted to be sure that I was in decent form to defend Elizabeth in court.

Then he asked me why I had wanted him to come back to the apartment. So I gave him my two reasons:

1. I liked him and his company. It was good to have a man like him around, someone who respected a woman, gave real friendship and wasn't there just waiting to fall into bed with me! I added that I respected his willingness to question my therapy, though of course, I had no doubts

about my need for it. Certainly not after the amount of time and money that had gone into it.
2. I wanted to know why he was so critical of Ursula and what he knew about brainwashing.

So we had a very long talk. I told him all about my therapy, my sessions with Ursula, the group sessions in Bern, my reading about the subject and other women's experiences and their recovered memories. Baring my soul to him in this way seemed much harder than doing so to Ursula, was it because it meant having to tell about what the therapy involves? If it's all a waste of time what a fool I'll look!

He told me about brainwashing - he certainly knows plenty about it both academically and practically. He referred to some book by an English shrink that he'd read some time ago on brainwashing and how they'd dealt with post-traumatic stress sufferers from World War 2. He couldn't resist pointing out that the Swiss shrinks wouldn't have had too many patients of that sort! I rather think I'd like him to brainwash me and persuade me that Papa was really the kind, loving father that I once thought him to be! When I told him that he said he hoped to get there without brainwashing and that he wouldn't want to get me there any other way than by making me face reality and, as a lawyer, he stressed that, to take a good hard look at the real evidence. He's already been doing some reading on recovered memories and among the items in this morning's post was a large American book on the subject which is critical of much therapy in the area. He promises to read it over the next week and then let me read it so that we can discuss it together, 'have a seminar' as he put it.

He's keen to get me away from Basel and Ursula for a few days and suggested a week walking in the mountains. I told him about the apartment in Grindelwald I'd bought from what Papa left me. He seemed taken with the idea of walking in the Berner Oberland. If I can arrange to get away it's a good idea, most of the others are due to be in the office for the whole of August so it should be possible. They'll think I'm off there with a new lover! Well let them! I'm suddenly excited! Why? It could undermine all that I've achieved with Ursula - but then I'm beginning to feel unhappy about where it's got me. When I spoke of those achievements with Sam he just muttered, 'The king's new clothes!' The idea of getting out into the mountains and walking among all that scenery until my legs ache, of having intelligent conversation with a man who isn't afraid to say what he thinks and to work up a healthy appetite for good food (and a little good wine), that's just what I need at the moment. Thank God for Sam Whoever from Mossad or wherever!

It's 3.17 a.m. - but for once I don't feel tired. I feel hopeful. I only hope that my new hopes aren't dashed. I remember how I felt soon after starting with Ursula, how she seemed to have the way to solve all my emotional problems - and now ... Sam's different though. 'Look at the evidence', he says, 'including the evidence about your therapy itself.' We shall see!

Thursday 21 August. (Written the next morning after Sam had eaten breakfast and gone.) I'm glad I started this diary as well as the journal for Ursula. It's good to have a record for my eyes only, I wonder what she'd think if she read it! It's not for her and not for Sam either. He, of course, behaved very properly and spent the night on the sofa. Part of me wishes he'd behave a little less properly but, on balance, I'm glad he's the man he is. However I'm not sure I'd be too sad if Elizabeth gave him the cold shoulder and he became available!

Thursday 21 August. (Evening). A good day in the office today. There will be no problem in getting away next week to Grindelwald. They seemed relieved and several of them said that they'd wondered whether to suggest to me that I took a break. Elise my secretary seemed particularly pleased at the idea, genuinely so on my account. Not so much as for the prospect of having rather less work to do - she came up with a number of helpful tasks she could do in my absence - no, rather she felt that I was badly in need of getting away from it all. They'll phone the apartment if there's an emergency but only, they insisted, one that no one else can handle. Good for them! I'm feeling quite excited. I can hardly wait to get my walking boots on and out among the mountains. Feeling at least ten years younger. And Sam's my friend not my lover! What did he say last night? "Friendship, the 20th Century's most undervalued relationship."

'Phoned Ursula to say that I'd be missing a couple of the weekly sessions and the group session in Bern. She insisted that I must keep up working on my memories and not neglect the journal. If I became distressed I should find my 'safe place' and take myself there. She was always available at the end of the telephone line if I needed reassurance. Thanked her for this. I hope I'm not being disloyal or foolish and that I won't undo all that I've achieved with her help.

Sunday 24 August. (9 a.m.) Too tired last night to write things up. Told Sam that I needed to spend a while writing up my diary after breakfast and he's now sitting on the balcony reading his 'big book' on recovered memories. He claims it's a real eye opener. But I'm to read it and then we'll discuss it - not while we're here though, he insists, unless I'm ready for it.

And yesterday? He came for me at 8.30 a.m. and we loaded his car with food and drinks - he insisted on taking the Becherovka from the fridge, says he's hooked on it! I'll have to get Fritz Ellinger, my Czech client, in to keep supplies going! As quick a journey as the traffic allowed. Sam's a fast driver but his reactions are equally sharp and you don't feel in danger with him. In fact that's typical of him - you get a sense of security just from having him round. Sam's security service, I suppose! Every woman should have a Sam. (I think I've already written that recently - I've said it twice so it must be true - or was it three times per Humpty Dumpty?)

We arrived at 11.15, unpacked, opened the windows wide to air the place and had an early lunch. Then back to Wilderswil and up to Schynige Platte on the train. Once we'd done the Alpine Gardens we did the walk along the ridge to First. There we stopped for a *Kafi fertig* and a sandwich. The Gondelbahn ride down to Grindelwald was good though I miss the open chairs I knew as a child - then you sat in the open and all was silence, apart from the rattle of the cable over the pylon's pulleys and the chirping of the crickets below. Perfect weather and glorious blue skies.

We talked and talked. What about? About everything! About law, about war, about cooking, about books. And you know what? I forgot all about therapy, Ursula and the group! That's hard to believe. But I really did. They must have been back there in Bern working out their repressed hate and anguish - and we'd gone through Bern on our way here - and I had forgotten all about them! When I remarked over dinner about having been oblivious to it all, Sam said, "Well make what you like of that but I think it's significant." Then he insisted on changing the subject. Told me about his childhood in Crown Heights, Brooklyn, among the Lubavitchers, one of the ultra-Orthodox Jewish Sects (Sam called them *Chassidim*, said that they didn't like the 'ultra-orthodox' tag, ultra-religious if one had to put it in such terms). Lots of Yiddish spoken by men wearing big black hats and following their Rebbe. Made me want to see them and the place. He's very good at conveying the feeling of things, making places and people seem very real. Then he told me about life in Israel, insisting (with that smile of his) that he was speaking to me in total confidence as his attorney! Again he conjured up vivid pictures of the country and its people, Jew and Arab. I expected him to be anti-Arab but he isn't, though he's certainly critical of their leaders and against giving up some of the land that the Israelis took in 1973 (I think that was the date). He talks about growing grapes on the Golan Heights and says that it would be an inexcusable waste if the Syrians got the land back with its winery and vineyards!

Today I've got to tell him about my childhood. It won't be easy!

Sunday 24 August (Midnight). Tired but relaxed, wonderfully relaxed. We're fortunate with the weather which is ideal for walking. Today we got to Wengen and had a late lunch outside a hotel there before taking the cable car up to Männlichen. Then we walked down to Grindelwald. The views were magnificent, with the big peaks of the Eiger, Mönch and Jungfrau and over us an intensely blue sky - I don't think I've been so aware of the world around me for a long while. I think the reason why Sam's descriptions of things are so vivid is because the way he sees them is vivid. He's got an incredibly sharp eye for what's going on around him and takes in every last detail. He certainly noticed things that I'd looked at in the past without really seeing. Though the walk to Grindelwald was downhill it was tiring and my calf muscles are aching gently as a reminder as I sit here. There's a pleasant tiredness and an enjoyable ache and this is it.

This evening we had a cheese raclette sitting on the balcony and watching the sun set. Sam produced a bottle of 1982 Chateau Pétrus that he had brought, full of apologies for its having 'had violence done to it' in the hot trunk of the car on our way yesterday. I told him that if this was a damaged Pétrus I couldn't imagine what an undamaged one would be like!

He got me to tell him about my childhood. He insisted that it should be the pre-Ursula version. What I had always remembered. He wanted me to go into real detail, sights, noises, smells and how I had felt. He would make a good lawyer - he "led" me and yet he didn't. That is he was scrupulous not to put any ideas into my mind if he could help it, he somehow managed to coax out detail that surprised me. He must have had considerable experience of interrogating people, getting out of them more than they thought they knew. And at the end he said, "Right Sylvia, how do you rate your childhood? And I had to say, "I rate it pretty highly, I'd say that I'd been a lucky girl." He just smiled and suggested a night-cap before we retired to our rooms.

So I have two versions of my childhood. Which am I to believe? What is reality? Is there such a thing? To bed then and at the moment the good version seems the real one.

Monday 25 August. (8.05 a.m.). Sam's out buying a

paper and I must get it written down while it's fresh in my mind. No sooner had my head touched the pillow than I fell into a deep sleep - fresh air, exercise and 1982 Pétrus I expect. But I had a terrible dream during the night. There was something dark that seemed to hover over me and then press down on me. I was paralysed and couldn't move or fend the thing off. It hadn't got any face I could see, so I don't know who or what it was. I could hardly breathe, I was choking and I couldn't scream. Or not at first, because I eventually brought Sam into my room wondering what was wrong. He told me my screams were very loud and my distress was real - I didn't need him to tell me that! He calmed me down with the help of a wet face flannel and then sat on the foot of the bed and made me tell him every detail I could manage.

This morning I said to him over breakfast, "So you see it's real, I'm not imagining it, am I?" It was strange, I had a feeling of triumph. It had vindicated all that I'd done with Ursula, the time, the emotional distress not to mention what it has cost me! And his reply? "I agree the dream was genuine and so was the emotion but whether it had any basis in fact - I mean whether it was you remembering a real event from your childhood or something else - is another matter, something we will find out in due course." Of course I was angry with him. More so because I had hoped that the memories of the previous night were the real ones. In my disappointment I took it out on him. What were we doing here? Who did he think he was? Ursula had vast experience of these things and a lot of women were totally dependent on her for their well being. So on and so on. And he sat and took it all and then said, "I never said that it was going to be simple to get your memories sorted out but I know you will. I spent most of last night reading about Recovered

Memory Syndrome and it's fascinating, I couldn't put the book down, at any rate not until you called! But forget it, today we're going up the Schilthorn."

As he went out for the paper I shouted after him, "Going to do your James Bond act on the roof of the cable car then? Hope your employers have insured you properly for the trip!"

"Bond's as real as your fantasies, Sylvia. Both are illusory worlds, I suspect, and tonight you're going to tell me about any horror you have encountered in films and books or on TV." And he added, "That includes the books Ursula's given or recommended!"

He remains very stable emotionally nothing seems to faze him. How I envy him that stability.

Shall I telephone Ursula? After all she said I could call her if I needed at any time. No, lets see how the week develops. But if the memories are false what a fool I'll look! Still I'd be happy to look a fool and know that the things about Papa were all lies in my mind.

Monday 25 August. (10.00p.m.). Did our trip up to the Schilthorn and had lunch in the restaurant. What a view! Then down to Mürren. Told Sam that I first stayed there with my parents twenty years ago and that we had often returned. He insisted on stopping for a drink and quizzed me about my visits - the weather, others who were with us, walks, skiing in the area, what I had felt. As I told him at the end, they were good memories. Again he just smiled and let the matter drop. I thanked him for showing me the good things about my relationship with Papa and said that they would help to balance the negative memories. Perhaps, he said, it isn't a question of balance but that he lived only for your good. I would have argued but we were in a café with others so I left it till later.

From Mürren we walked along the ledge above the valley and then took the funicular down from Grutschalp to Lauterbrunnen. Then tea and torte before taking the train to Zweilütschinen and, after a few minutes there, another to Grindelwald. It's been a welcome change to have a few days away from the car and the city and be able to look around while we travel.

An early dinner - a light one of cold beef and salad and then we sat on the balcony and listened to some of the CD's I'd brought, a couple of the late Beethoven quartets. They were new to Sam but old friends of mine. The mood of the slow movements matched our own there with the immensity of the tranquil mountains before us. Sam thanked me for bringing him here and adding to his musical education. So I pointed out that this most glorious of music had been written amongst total domestic chaos and unemptied chamber pots. It seems that his musical education began via Elizabeth's bugged apartment in London. It's amazing what spin-offs there are to a career as a spy!

We retreated to the lounge for coffee and schnapps and he switched to Sam the interrogator. This time I was pumped dry on my therapy and what it had brought to the surface. He had a list of questions:

Why had I gone to Ursula in the first place?

What did the sessions with her involve?

And the group therapy, what was that like?

What literature had I read before and during the course of therapy?

What memories had I recovered?

When had the memories begun to return?

Had it been full and detailed flashbacks or had it been gradual?

Had I ever had any other traumatic experiences? I told

him about being dragged from a burning car when I was six. Had I ever forgotten that? No of course I hadn't! He smiled and moved on.

How did I feel - not now but, say, in the middle of last week?

How had I felt when I commenced therapy?

So I was going downhill? I refuted that - Ursula says that you have to get worse in order to get better. All right, I admitted it, but it's got to be like that to be effective.

Was I more effective as an advocate now than before seeing Ursula? I had to admit that I was a little less effective but only marginally so. He angered me by saying that this was how I saw things and that others might be more critical. He accepted that I had always been my harshest critic and that if I were ever unable to give a client the attention that their affairs deserved I would give up law for something else.

What else? Spying, I suggested, adding that it seemed a pretty relaxed occupation if he were typical of its practitioners. He offered me a job as a Colonel in the GRU, apparently Russian Military Intelligence. I countered with the suggestion that Mossad was more to my taste but he didn't bite.

He went back to how I felt. On top of the world at the moment, I told him. He let a look of satisfaction slip out - just for a moment.

And after recovering a new memory, how did I feel then? Devastated and then liberated, a sense of release, I said.

Wouldn't that have done? he asked Why not stop there? No, there was more to come. Ursula made me work hard, and as a result the memories had become more detailed, more specific, much sharper. And I'd been able to get further back - I'd been able to recover what

Papa had done to me when I was two, I wished I hadn't brought that up as Sam made me tell him about it, I felt dirty and ashamed. Again I lost my temper. How dare he, a man and, for all I knew, a molester of women and children make me tell about all this. Then I saw his face and he was suffering as well! I burst into tears and clung to him. He was like the brother I never had and always wanted. Plenty of men would have used it as an opportunity to get me to bed but he didn't - I won't say that nothing was further from his mind, I know I arouse him and I knew that I was doing so then but he was feeling <u>for</u> me. We took a break, had another coffee and strolled into Grindelwald in the dark. But we were both tired from the "interrogation" and soon headed back to the apartment. I'm just managing to keep my eyes open and hope that I'll get an uninterrupted night's sleep. Sam says that he's hitting the hay and that he'll finish his RMS book when he wakes in the morning.

Tuesday 26 August. (7.15 a.m.). Sam's reading, having brought me a cup of the very strong coffee he brews. An undisturbed night of wonderful sleep! Last night was a sort of catharsis. Is <u>his</u> therapy healing me or is he merely papering over the cracks? When I asked him he just said, "What therapy?" and left me to wonder about it. Today it's the steamer on the *Brienzersee*. Sam's fascinated by anything mechanical.

Tuesday 26 August. (10.15 p.m.). Another glorious day. How I'm enjoying this week! I can't remember anything like it. I wrote that he's fascinated by anything mechanical and today he had his fill. First of all it was the *Lötschberg*, the paddle steamer on the *Brienzersee*. We caught it at Interlaken. I just loved hanging over the rail watching the lakeside go by and hearing the splashing of the paddlewheels through the water. He was down below looking at the engines - triple expansion he called them. As if that meant anything to me!

Then Brienz, a lovely village of old wooden houses and shops with carved wooden things for sale. We spent the rest of the morning there and then he heard a railway whistle and that blew away plans for lunch near the lake. We just <u>had</u> to take the train to the top of the Rothorn! He asked me if I wanted to go but I couldn't have said no. He would have been too disappointed. There's a childlike quality that he's kept along with his sophistication and his this-worldliness. How can I describe it? Perhaps it's the ability to feel wonder, to show it to other people and not be at all embarrassed. He was just like a child with a new toy at Christmas - though whether that's an apt way of describing someone Jewish I'm not sure. (Why have I just written <u>'someone Jewish'</u> and not simply <u>'a Jew'</u>? Is it that so often when we say 'He's a Jew' we are being somehow derogatory, identifying someone different, foreign to ourselves and our experience, in a way that Fritz Ellinger my Czech client isn't. Is it centuries of Europe's anti-Semitism both hidden and overt. Does it make any difference to me that Sam's a Jew? Will it make any difference to Elizabeth, for that matter? I believe that, so far as I'm concerned, it makes no difference whatsoever and I am glad that it doesn't.)

He was full of questions for the driver and really disappointed that he couldn't ride on the steam locomotive. He said that he'd discovered that you can do so in some obscure place in Poland and that he's planning to go there again to do that. I'd love to see him enjoying the ride there. Anyway we took the train up the mountain and we <u>both</u> enjoyed the ride and the view down onto the *Brienzersee*. At the top we had a snack, looked down into the valley on the other side at Sörenberg and then took the train down. Not the first one - that was an oil burner and he insisted on one that ran on coal. Much more real, he said. Much dirtier, I replied. But coal it was. The driver told him that there was a similar locomotive in the back of the sheds at Wilderswil on our way back to Grindelwald and so, 'If you don't mind, Sylvia', (and of course Sylvia didn't mind) we had to break our journey and look for it. Sam found out from a man in the shed the date they would next be using it on the line up to Schynige Platte and I've agreed to come with him to do the trip - I wonder if I'll get invited to play trains with him in Poland!

We ate out, as we were late back to Grindelwald - fondue at a restaurant on our way from the station to the apartment.

Back at the apartment it was coffee and Cognac. Then he gave me a history lesson on the Jews and the Land of Israel. So much suffering and so many false hopes. To be concluded tomorrow or at any rate this week, he said. And then I burst into tears. Of course he thought it was the memories but it was the thought of all that hatred. I told him I was sorry, sorry that my country hadn't done more to help when it could during World War 2 and that it had resisted paying compensation for so long and sorry for the long years of hate and persecution. He said that he had been able to sense all along that his Jewishness was not a barrier between us, that I quite liked having a 'Jewish bastard' around the place. I told him I'd never said that, the expression had been "a Yiddish bastard". And then he stopped me when I tried to apologise for having called him that. We both ended up in hopeless laughter. I haven't felt so good for a long, long time. I've never had a friend like this before. The 'forgotten relationship of the Twentieth Century', he said. I believe he's right. And so to sleep, I'm hoping for an undisturbed night.

Wednesday 27 August. (10.35 p.m.). What a mix-up of a day! The glorious weather continues and in the mornings there's a wonderful clarity and the mountains are so clear that they seem no distance away. Not content with yesterday's steamer (paddle boat, that is) Sam wanted to take one on the *Thunersee* from Interlaken to Thun. His feeble excuse was that he'd seen Thun in a TV production of one of Le Carré's spy thrillers and that he wanted to visit the place. (So spies read spy novels!) But when we got to the quay at Interlaken West he began searching the timetable for something and it turned out to be another steamboat, this time the *Blümlisalp*. It was running in the afternoon and so we spent the morning climbing to Harder Kulm above Interlaken.

My muscles have toned up with the week's exercise and the 750 metre climb to the summit wasn't much trouble. The guidebook said that Wagner and Mendelssohn had both made the climb - anti-Semite and Jew, I wonder what they thought of one another and if they ever met, something to check out one day. Sam spotted the ibex and the marmots before I did, his eyes really are sharp!

Lunch at the summit, out in the open looking out towards the Jungfrau, we got through a bottle of Dôle and were sitting quietly viewing the scene when I heard my name being called. It was Maeve, the Irish girl from the Bern therapy group. At the best of times I would go a long way to avoid her but there was nothing I could do and so she joined us at our table. Usually she's very restless and edgy and today she was even worse. Clearly she wanted to speak to me on my own, so while Sam was paying the bill I went with her to the ladies. She was full of it - yesterday she had confronted her father with accusations of molesting her as a baby and for years afterwards. She was triumphant - she had done it at last - and he had just sat there not daring to say anything. He hadn't contradicted her, too ashamed to speak, she said. She had just looked him in the eye, told him how much she hated and loathed him and then got up and left his cottage in the Wicklow mountains for the Dublin - Zurich flight that afternoon. She should have been at work today but she was so excited at confronting him that she took the day off and headed for the mountains. She was so on top of the world and said that she'd never guessed just how great it would be to denounce him to his face. 'I'm getting free of it, free at last, let him carry the shame from now on, it was his doing and it's time he suffered'. She's going to leave him to stew for a while and then write saying that she's thinking telling his parish priest what he did to her as a child. 'Put the screw on him for screwing me', was how she put it. Of course I congratulated her but my emotions were very mixed. She said goodbye to me and ignored Sam, as a representative of maledom I suppose - she had kept back a little of her disdain to show to men in general. She gave me her business card and said I could always call her if I needed a chat.

Of course Sam wanted to know what it was all about and at first I refused to say. But she hadn't sworn me to silence so in the end I told him. He was horrified at what she had done. So I poked fun at him, telling him that men all stand together and treat women as gullible, emotional and empty headed. He just smiled and asked if he'd ever treated me that way. I had to admit that he'd never done so. Then he wanted to know about Maeve and her father, what I knew about the alleged molestation and about Maeve and her father. The answer wasn't much except that I remembered her celebrating her 40th birthday and saying something that suggested her father was getting on in years. So, said Sam, 'phone her this evening and find out all about it and then we'll discuss it.

We went down the mountain on the funicular and caught the paddleboat but it wasn't like yesterday. While Sam investigated the mechanics of the boat I stood there at the rail, looking out and somehow seeing nothing. Hearing Maeve's story had stirred it all up again. It <u>must</u> be real, Sam was wrong to pretend otherwise, I know he was trying to help me, I know, but he was wrong. Abuse <u>does</u> take place and it leaves its marks, physical and mental on women. I hadn't the option of confronting my father like Maeve, conveniently for him he was dead! Those were my thoughts.

Sam had been watching me, for a while it turned out. He told me he could see that I wasn't happy. We would get out at Spiez and get the next boat or train back to Interlaken. And this we did, getting a diesel boat back, or so Sam told me. We sat in the restaurant with coffees, saying little to one another and just gazing out through the windows. A spectator would have suspected a lovers' tiff and would have been wrong. We got back to the apartment just after 5 o'clock. Sam sent me off to have a good long soak in the bath with the door open so that I could hear Bruckner's Seventh on the hifi - he'd remembered me saying that it was the musical equivalent of a long walk in the mountains. Afterwards I felt better and he'd got together quite a meal which we had on the balcony. Smoked trout, salt beef salad and Carte D'Or cassis sorbet. Gewurztraminer followed by a St Emilion.

Coffee, mints and liqueurs. And I was feeling better. But then he told me to 'phone Maeve and get her full story. He went for a walk so that I would feel free to respond in my way to her story.

Well she was more than willing to tell the tale: molested from six months onwards by her father and a priest friend of his, right until she started primary school at five or six. She said that the two men were part of a Satanic ritual group and that they had had intercourse with her in front of the other members of the group. Her father's in his early 80's and has a heart condition. When I queried whether she was wise to confront a sick man, she was adamant and said she didn't care if he dropped dead that moment without the benefit of a confessor or the last rites. Though she couldn't see what he would gain from the ministrations of some dirty old priest who was probably messing around with kids just as her father's friend had messed around with her as a child! We talked generally and said we would meet at the session in Bern the Saturday after next. When I put the receiver down I was shaking.

Sam came back a quarter of an hour later to find me sitting on the balcony with a large Irish whiskey - I suppose speaking to Maeve had suggested that beverage. He poured himself a stiff Becherovka and we went back into the lounge and sat looking at one another.

And so, he asked, what would you have done in her place?

I would probably have confronted him, I said.

Just before flying home? Didn't give him much of a chance to question her or explain did it?

But he just sat there and took it. Doesn't that prove that he molested her?

How old is he?

80's, early 80's.

How well is he?

Not very well, he's got a heart condition.

And would you let the Basel police come along out of the blue and interrogate a man in that state, coming down hard on him and accusing him of unspeakable things done against his own daughter.

But it wasn't the police!

No, it was something far worse - the girl, the woman herself, his own child. Does it really strike you as odd that he said nothing. I'd have been struck dumb if it had been me who was being denounced. Just put yourself in his shoes or, more probably, slippers.

I'd have given him more time and been gentler.

Good. Now here are two things for you to think about. First children's brains develop over the years and memory is the function of the more mature brain - children don't remember very much about events before the age of four or five.

And so Maeve's memories of things happening when she was six months old ...

Are highly suspect, I'm even prepared to say impossible. OK she thinks she remembers things but how the so called memories got there is another matter.

And your second point?

Satanic ritual abuse.

But I've read about it in books and some of the girls at the therapy group have had it done to them - have been the victims of covens and that kind of thing.

What kind of thing?

Oh, you know, where they breed babies for sacrifice to the devil and make the initiates eat human flesh. Unspeakable things that I don't want to talk about.

But you've never had memories of that kind.

Thank God, I haven't.

And if I told you that the FBI have never been able to find any evidence of such things despite plenty of recovered memories of satanic ritual horrors, murders and the like?

I'd be amazed.

And then if I told you that a study by a British academic, funded by the British Government, had come to the same conclusion and said that such accusations tell you more about the theology of the accusers (and I suppose that the psychology that the therapists follow is a kind of theology, it's certainly their belief system) what would you say?

I'd be totally amazed and want to read the book.

You'd be rather careful before making any accusations in the circumstances?

Very careful indeed.

Good. You mustn't take my word for it. I finished my big book last night so it's yours whenever you want. Now or after the week here is over.

Now. At once. You've totally unsettled me. Are you saying that I've been taken for a ride.

That's for you to judge. I'll get the book.

And so once I put down my pen I'll start reading Sam's big book. I just wonder where it will all end up.

(It's probably my legal training but I'm sure that this note is almost verbatim and that if I'd written it down at the time it wouldn't have been much fuller or more accurate.)

Maeve rang at 11.20 p.m. - Her father had a stroke this afternoon and died at 10.30 p.m. They told her he hadn't spoken a word after she left him yesterday. She asked me if she had done the right thing. I told her that I hoped so. I'm so glad it wasn't me. She had lost all the nervous excitement that she had shown when we met at Harder Kulm and when we spoke on the 'phone earlier this evening. She sounded quite down. I really hope she'll be all right. I've agreed to call her tomorrow morning.

Thursday 28 August. (9.30 p.m.). I'm exhausted, totally all in. Read until 3 a.m. this morning and then slept until 10.00 a.m. Awoke to the sound of Honneger's *Pastoral D'Eté*. I must have told Sam I love the piece, though I can't remember when. Outside it was the most perfect day imaginable. I stood on the balcony and declaimed, *'J'ai embrassé l'aube d'été'* Sam remarked about the lady being poetic and I impressed him by saying that I was quoting Rimbaud. Then he pretended that I'd said Rambo and wanted to know what Stallone had to do with it - I <u>think</u> he was pretending but you never can be sure with him. 'Summer morning I embrace thee!' I told him and suggested that he read the notes with the CD!

No reply from Maeve on the 'phone so I left a message for her.

Breakfast on the balcony and I tried to discuss the book with him but he wouldn't. I must read it all and entire before talking about it. I needed several cups of coffee to get my mind working but it was good just sitting there in the sun and watching the small fluffy clouds moving slowly across the deep blue sky above the mountains. I was glad that I'd used Papa's money to buy the apartment and, of course, thinking about him started off all the things that are tearing me apart, all those things that gnaw at my innards, stir the bowels and disturb me.

Sam suggested that we should spend the rest of the

morning walking locally and have a light lunch before coming back to the apartment and getting on with the book. He was good at making me use my eyes to look for plants and flowers we'd seen at the Alpine Gardens earlier in the week. He's bought a book on them and so we had to attempt to identify as many as possible. I like his ability to enthuse about such different things. It took my mind off my problems and Maeve.

By 5.30 p.m. I'd finished the book. Told Sam that if it was true it was devastating. He agreed and suggested that I read it once more and then discuss it with him. He doesn't want me to jump to any wrong conclusions and encouraged me to be critical in my evaluation of it. He suggested that I spend the next two days reading it with a pen and legal pad handy so I could make notes. I said I'd do that on one condition - that he would come here with me again and walk the legs off me in the mountains. He readily agreed. I'm glad he's keen on friendship but I'm beginning to wish that he was looking for something more! Better make sure that he doesn't see this or he might feel threatened. So Friday and Saturday with his big book but I'm insisting that we have a day off on Sunday and get out once again - it will be the last day of our holiday and there's bound to be work to catch up on when I get into the office on Monday. And there's a court hearing in J's case on Thursday - that's exactly a week away - and I must be properly prepared, it's the second time he's been before the court on a drugs charge.

Maeve rang during the evening. She'd been to Basel to see Ursula who told her that I should have been more supportive and suggested that I wasn't taking the therapy seriously enough. I was lacking commitment to my recovery and to my fellow Survivors! I almost told her what I'd just read in Sam's book but restrained myself.

She's in a big enough emotional stew already without my adding to it!

No doubt she reported Sam's presence as my companion, 'Sylvia's got a lover on holiday with her' or some such comment - of course, a lesbian relationship would be acceptable to them! Her father's funeral is on Monday and, despite everything, she's flying out on Saturday. Her step-mother accuses her of being responsible for the old man's death so Maeve won't stay with her. Apparently she didn't hear what went on between her husband and Maeve before she left for the 'plane but she saw that there was a disturbed altercation going on between the two. I warned her that, if there are any enquiries by the police or the authorities, she must be very careful what she says and that she should have a good lawyer with her. Fortunately she doesn't want her accusations in the local and national Irish papers so I think she'll keep it under wraps, I hope so for her sake and the sake of her father's reputation not to mention the step-mother.

Friday 29 August. (10.10 p.m.). Two long sessions on the book today with a walk in the afternoon. Made a lot of notes and will have to check on the American court decisions where therapists have been successfully sued by their clients for giving them false 'memories'. I'll get Henry in Chicago to do that for me on Monday, he can E-mail it to me. Sam's getting me the book by the English academic that claims that the sort of Satanic ritual abuse that Survivors remember just doesn't happen. Or is it that it just doesn't leave any trace of its existence?

Saturday 30 August. (11.50 p.m.). Heavy rain in the morning but as I was working through the book it didn't matter. Lunch at the apartment. Melon, smoked chicken salad and then a choice of sorbets. Just right. Sam's a good caterer and he enjoys the rôle. He's been working through a pile of books on all manner of subjects including one on brainwashing - I told him that he was obviously keeping up to date for his Mossad work. He shook his head and put his finger on his lips and I promised not to mention that organisation in public again (we were on the balcony at the time).

Finished the second reading and my notes just before 5 p.m. and accepted Sam's suggestion that we take the cable car up to Männlichen and then down to Wengen for an early dinner. Great to get out into the open air, walk to Grund and then sail through the air to the top of the Holenstein before catching the next cable car down to Wengen. A good meal - perfectly cooked filet steak and a bottle of Israeli wine. Sam got quite excited when he found it on the wine list. A Cabernet Sauvignon from the Golan's Gamla winery. I remember that because he told me how the inhabitants, men women and children, of the town of that name had thrown themselves to their deaths from the citadel rather than die at the hands of the Romans. I said 'Wasn't that Masada?' and he said, 'The same thing happened in both places.' He added, 'They're powerful stories. But our watchword now is 'Never again!' He's going to elaborate when we've dealt with my problems - his Jewish history lesson has yet to be completed.

Back at the apartment we worked through my notes from 9.10 until 11.00 and dealt with most of my points and objections. He really has a good grasp of what he's read and knows how to present a case. But he didn't try to pressure me into a conclusion, 'You've got to be persuaded in your own mind, not browbeaten, Sylvia.'

Sunday 31st August. (10.30 p.m.) The last day of a holiday I wanted to never end! Sam insisted that we forget all about 'memories' and his 'big book' and simply enjoy the area. A leisurely breakfast with hot oat cereal laced with some Scots brew he'd brought, Drambuie seemingly. Then rolls, croissants and fruit. All washed down with his strong coffee.

We repeated the walk we'd done earlier in the week. The train to Schynige Platte then along the ridge to First. There again we stopped for a *Kafi fertig* and a sandwich, ending with the Gondelbahn ride down to Grindelwald. Once more with thoughts of childhood but now untainted by 'memories'!

After we had packed up for our return to Basel we stood on the balcony.

'Well, Sylvia. A week well spent?'

'Never better, Sam. You've worked magic.'

'No magic, I don't deal in that sort of thing, Sylvia. I'd say that all I've done is to help you to apply your considerable forensic powers to the situation. There's more to be done but it's beyond my competence. However I know a therapist who specialises in this sort of thing. I've been in touch and he's prepared to help. He's based in Paris but doesn't mind the occasional trip to Basel. If you're agreeable to seeing him, of course.' He paused, 'Incidentally he's my younger brother David.'

***

Sam hadn't added that they had been estranged for several years and that he had struggled hard with his principles to break the ice and commence a reconciliation in order to secure David's help.

Chapter 25

Saturday 6th September 1997

Sylvia Brunner looked at her watch once again, it was 6.50 p.m. She had got through a lot of work that Saturday afternoon but the last half hour had dragged by very slowly. She began to restore some order to the desk in the corner of her lounge, making neat piles of the papers she had worked through and of those still requiring her attention. It would be easier to use the spare bedroom as a study, she wouldn't have to tidy up for visitors, but then she preferred to work in the main room of her apartment, enjoying its spaciousness and light, feeling relaxed and at home, otherwise she might as well have gone to the office. And, in any case, apart from Sam she had been short of visitors for the last year or so. It wouldn't be long before he arrived together with his brother David. His younger brother, Sam had said, a psychiatrist working in Paris for a United Nations agency. She hoped he'd be able to complete the process Sam had begun. The process of restoring her and her emotions to normal, of mending the harm that Ursula's therapy had done. Her soul had been ploughed up, now she longed for the process of healing and restoration to be completed.

She suspected that, if only it had been possible for a relationship to develop between Sam and herself, the healing process would have soon been over. But he was in thrall to Elizabeth Fielder and her only hope in that direction was that when they met again - Elizabeth and Sam - his love would not be reciprocated. And she knew that in this situation were the seeds of further hurt and pain. She was already wounded enough within. But it made good sense to safeguard the relationship that had grown up between herself and Sam, that of friendship. She had found it very enriching, far more so than she would once have thought possible. Much better to safeguard their friendship than hazard it on the rocks of *amour*. Would she ever again know a really quiet mind, a tranquil heart? Oh to get on with life on a level keel of emotions! The fact that Sam was not available as a lover emphasised her own loneliness when she looked at her situation in the long term, she certainly wasn't getting any younger. Nonetheless it was reassuring that they both wanted their friendship to endure; it was a relationship within which both of them gave and received.

The bell rang and she went to the door of the apartment to check the caller's identity on the closed circuit TV. Sam was there on his own. It was 6.55 p.m. - he was a little early. But for the first time she experienced disappointment on seeing him. His brother wasn't there. Perhaps his flight had been delayed and Sam had come in advance. How tender her emotions were! David's absence hurt her. She was pinning so much hope on his ability to get her back to normal. She pressed the button to unlock the outer door and spoke to Sam over the intercom, 'OK Sam, come on up.' She opened the door onto the landing and waited. The lift made its slow way to the top floor. The doors opened, he looked around, saw her and crossed the landing.

'He's delayed?' she asked.

'No, he's parking the car and will be with us in a few minutes.' The voice was familiar and yet different, the pitch a little higher and the accent more European. Then she realised that he hadn't a beard. 'You must be Sylvia Brunner, if not I'm in the wrong block! I'm David Kagan, it's good to meet you.'

She stood there dumbstruck for a moment and then

laughed, 'I thought you were Sam. The pair of you are so alike, apart from your lack of a beard. I know you're brothers but you're like peas out of the same pod.' And now she knew Sam Whoever's real name, unless this brother also used an alias!

'In a sense we are Miss Brunner, we're twins - identical twins in fact. Hadn't he told you?'

'That he hadn't. But you're no less welcome for the revelation. It's just as well that one of you has a beard and the other uses a razor.'

'There are times when there hasn't even been that difference to distinguish us and, for me, that has been a source of concern - in case anyone with a grudge against my older brother wished to take it out on me.'

'Or perhaps the other way around. You're a shrink after all and your profession has some dissatisfied clients at large.'

'Like the clients of other professions, Miss Brunner. You're a lawyer and I'm sure that, although all *your* clients are appreciative of what *you* achieve on their behalf, there must be some clients of *other* lawyers who would like to murder them.'

'OK I'll admit that. I do have *some* clients in that category myself. But my work is not with the emotions and yours is. There's greater potential for trouble in your profession than mine. But I don't know what we're doing here on the landing, come on in and we'll wait for Sam in comfort.'

They went into the hallway and she took his raincoat and showed him into the lounge. 'A drink, perhaps, Mr Kagan?'

"David, please! And perhaps I can call you Sylvia? Good. Lemonade and orange juice, if you can manage it. Otherwise some mineral water. No, unlike my older brother the Rabbi I keep off alcohol but do eat bacon.'

'The Rabbi! - so he really is! But I thought he was from Mos ... '

'We don't mention that if we can help it, though I've already hinted that there are those around with grudges against him.'

'An evening of surprises, David. Surprises indeed.'

She went into the kitchen, mixed him a tall tumbler of orange juice and lemonade and poured a couple of Becherovkas for the rabbi and herself. So she'd almost been in bed with a rabbi. She couldn't help laughing aloud. It was as well that things hadn't gone very far and that they'd both pulled back. Interesting how you immediately put a minister of religion into a different category from other people.

Sylvia gave David his drink and sat down in an armchair facing him. 'Sam did tell me he was a Cohen, is that some sort or rabbi then?'

'Not really, Sylvia. You're born into it, it's a family thing. I'm a Cohen, it means a priest, a descendent of Aaron. Some of us take it more seriously than others. Sam takes it much more seriously than I do. I married a Gentile. He wouldn't do that or take a Jewish bride from one of the categories forbidden to a Cohen - a convert, a divorced woman or that sort of thing. It's one area where we've disagreed violently. To marry a woman who isn't Jewish is for him perpetuating what Hitler started, doing away with the Jewish people. You see under Jewish law whether you're Jewish or not depends on whether your *mother* is Jewish. In Orthodox thinking the status of the father doesn't come into it. To Sam, the watchword, 'Never again', applies as much to mixed marriages as it does to defending Israel from those who would push all her people into the Mediterranean. Though we haven't discussed the issue lately. But then the suicide of my wife, Thérèse, has made it somewhat academic.' He had said her name with difficulty and now was silent, his gaze fixed on a table lamp that had just switched itself on, and Sylvia, sensing that he was still hurting inside, respected his silence.

He took a sip from his glass, put it down, resumed his composure and continued, 'Although it was two years ago the pain's still there. And, do you know, sometimes I'm glad that it is. It speaks of the value and reality of our marriage. When I see how easily so many of my friends give up on their relationships, heading straight for their lawyer and the divorce court - no insult intended to your profession, I assure you,' he smiled at her, a rather sad smile but a smile nevertheless. 'Intent on going their own ways instead of working together at overcoming their problems - it makes me very sad.'

'You have children?'

'No, a source of sadness but also of relief when I think of how they might have been affected by Thérèse's death. But I do long for my own kids. Some day perhaps. There's Sam, I expect, unless it's a party that we've been invited to this evening.'

The bell had rung and Sylvia went to the door to receive Sam. He gave her a kiss on the cheek and apologised for the delay, parking was difficult that evening. She showed him into the lounge and the brothers nodded to one another.

'You'll sit next to David on the sofa and then I can compare the two of you and see whether there are any differences apart from the beard and your preference in drinks. Hold on, I've poured you a Becherovka, Sam, but I've left it in the fridge, I'll go and get it. Make yourself comfortable while I do.'

She took the glass from the fridge and closed the door. She stood for a moment and thought. So it would have been doubly difficult for there to be any relationship between herself and Sam. And then it came to her: exactly the same applied to Sam and Elizabeth. A tear came to her eye, she felt dreadfully sorry for him. Amidst all this he must be experiencing an inner conflict as emotion and passion were ranged against loyalty to his people, religion, family and principles. And he had let none of this show! He had been the model of a caring gentleman, totally taken up with the problems of herself and of Elizabeth. She had known he wanted Elizabeth but he had given no hint of the inner turmoil that was his. She took the glass into the lounge, handed it to Sam and resumed her seat.

'When you said, Sam, that David was your younger brother ... '

'I didn't tell you that my arrival in this world preceded his by twenty minutes. Sorry, to have surprised you like this. I must remember in future.'

'He won't Sylvia, he's done it before. It amuses him, I think!'

'Does it now? You haven't any other brothers born at or about the same time have you David - at the moment I trust you more than Sam.'

They laughed, suddenly at ease with one another.

'OK Sylvia, once I've finished my drink and made sure that my younger brother is comfortable I'll be on my way. After all he's here professionally and I'm sure you both want to talk. I'll be seeing you on Monday for one of our working dinners at the *Safran Zunft*.'

A little later Sam left and Sylvia and David began their first session. She did most of the talking, detailing the therapy that had brought so much distress to her and then going further back to the loneliness that had caused her to seek therapy in the first place. He guided her through her account with the minimum of comment but she was conscious that he was succeeding in drawing out of her much that she had gone through and how she felt.

***

David stood looking out of the window of Sam's apartment. The Rhein lay before him flowing powerfully and ceaselessly towards the sea at Rotterdam while high up on the opposite bank the spires of the Münster stood out against the night sky. Ceaseless movement and solid immobility. He sipped the tonic water and wondered whether he should take the lead and break the silence. He had reported positively to Sam on his conversation with Sylvia, confirming that he ought to be able to help her back to emotional health and stability, though he showed the professional's reticence to discuss a client. With a measure of satisfaction he had told Sam that he had been right on target in getting him to see Sylvia - his experience in deprogramming people who had escaped from the clutches of cults would be of use in helping this 'refugee from the Survivor Cult' as he had called her. She wasn't really his client, as he had refused to charge for his services, pointing out to her that he wasn't allowed to practise in Switzerland though that wouldn't stop him from giving her whatever help he could. Nevertheless she had insisted on paying his fare and he had accepted the payment, it would somehow ensure that she would cooperate and work hard on her cure.

Sam broke the silence, 'At last we're together David. How long has it been?'

'Five and a half years, Sam. You know as well as I do.

I won't deny that I was surprised when you first telephoned me. A voice from the past but a most welcome one. You clearly must have been very concerned about Sylvia for you to make contact again after all that time. You had written me off as dead and said *Kaddish* for me, hadn't you?'

'No David, I hadn't, I won't deny that it had been in my mind but I never could bring myself to do that. But I won't deny that I'm concerned that Sylvia recovers quickly from the mauling she's received from her therapist. Yes I'm concerned for her but I'm also concerned for her client Elizabeth. It's on account of *her* that I'm in Basel after all.'

'So the Institute has given you the job of trying to get one of its agents out of the clutches of the Swiss?'

'No you're wrong there, twice over, though both your assumptions are very reasonable ones.' He found that he was speaking more quickly than he wanted but he let the words rush on. 'First of all she's not one of ours, she was employed by the SVR, that's the new initials for the KGB - though I think there may have been a Russian *Mafiya* involvement in the operation that brought her here from England. It's a long story and I'll tell you in due course. Secondly I'm not here on behalf of my old masters. I've fallen out with them and taken early retirement. I'm doing this freelance because it's what *I've* decided to do, the choice was mine. I felt compelled to do it. And that's the other reason I wanted you here. I'm in love with her. No not Sylvia, that's friendship. I'm in love with Elizabeth her client. At the moment she's in jail here in Basel, about a mile or so away ... in the direction you were looking just now.' He paused and continued. 'She's a Gentile and I wanted to apologise to you for the way I responded to your marrying Thérèse ... and that I refused to come when you ... when you buried her and needed me.' His voice had thickened with emotion. There was silence once more and David looked out the window again before turning to face his brother.

'So the love of your life is in jail a mile away, her lawyer's in an emotional state and has to be got right to defend her. Is that correct? OK fine. Not only that but Sam Kagan, rabbi and Cohen, is in love with a Gentile. From every point of view it's a mess Sam, a real mess! You've taken early retirement to deal with the situation and you're struggling with your conscience. Am I right, Sam?'

'Right, David. Exactly right. Though, in fact, the struggle is over and I've made my mind up. To continue debating with oneself is a waste of energy, new facts and arguments just don't come along. You can't keep raking over the same material, covering the same ground. If my job with the Institute taught me anything it's that once you've made your mind up on a course of action you get on and do it - unless, of course, something vital happens to force you to reconsider.'

'If you were still trying to make up your mind I *might* have told you that you're the religious one and that it was up to you to sort it out according to your laws - OK I know you don't think of them as yours but of Divine origin through Moses - and I *might* have said, "It's your problem, Sam, get on with it" ... but I won't do so now. And I probably wouldn't have done so anyway. I feel for you. Your life's in danger of falling apart. You may have made up your mind but you are still finding it hard to live with yourself. At times you think of throwing it all overboard, all your beliefs, all your observance of *Halakha*. But then you know that you couldn't. So you've got to find a middle way for yourself, a less observant Judaism or something. Perhaps 'observant' in a different way. But then you probably wonder whether you could survive by embracing something to which you've always denied the name of Judaism. I feel for you because, although I'm not observant and never likely to be, I did face something of the same griefs over my love for Thérèse. Though I count myself as a secular Jew it still wasn't easy.' And at the mention of her name the tears that had been kept back when he had spoken of her to Sylvia welled up.

The room was heavy with their grief. The sorrow of two brothers, identical twins whose estrangement had been like a bereavement for each of them and nearly formally treated as just that by Sam. They faced one another and wondered why life should have become so complicated and seemingly so heavily weighted against them. For the first time in many, many years each of them had found that they understood something of the other's feelings. How far back into childhood did they have to go to retrieve the lively empathy they had once known? They understood one another and were determined to do whatever they could to help. Sam got up from his chair, crossed the room and put his arm around David's shoulders. Together they wept - each for himself and, even more, for one another. Their lost years of silent separation were at an end. They knew intuitively that from now on they could be completely open with one another, as they had been in their boyhood, growing up together in Brooklyn and in the Northern Galilee. That knowledge brought relief to them both.

Over coffee they began the task of telling one another of the previous five and a half years. Each knew that there was no longer any need to justify himself or be on the defensive, they had simply to tell it as it was and know that the barrier of judgementalism had dropped away to be replaced by a sympathetic ear.

'Would you believe it David, it's nearly three and we've still got a lot to say to one another! It'll have to be tomorrow, I'm feeling drained.'

'I'm with you there Sam. One word more, perhaps? Your problem has been whether to be a good Cohen or a good human being, anyway that's how I see it. You've chosen the rôle of the good human being and that pleases me. You mustn't think you've chosen second best. I think that you're a good Cohen as well!'

***

Sylvia lay in bed restless. She had written her personal diary hours ago. David, she knew would make all the difference to her recovery. But it was strange to find that your therapist was himself still in the throws of real grief, that he too was no stranger to heart ache. 'Physician heal thyself!' did not apply. Somehow the fact that he too was a wounded human being gave her confidence and hope. Here would be insight and understanding, not like the send up of a shrink in West Side Story!

She couldn't sleep so she got out of bed and made a milk drink. She found the old vinyl LP of the film soundtrack of the musical, much better than the 'authentic' Bernstein recording with opera stars whose voices had lost the sparkle and freshness of youth. She found the track with the drug store scene, dropped the stylus accurately at the beginning of the track and sat back enjoying the music and the lyrics. Then she returned to bed and started reading an American thriller set in Basel - perhaps it would shed some light on the sort of things that these people did, though she suspected that

Sam would have found such books something of a joke. At 4 o'clock she put the book down. The Mafia had just rescued the American banker from the custody of a prison officer as they walked from Basel's old remand prison to the Public Prosecutor's Office. That would have suited Sam! But with prison and Prosecutor now under one roof in their new building such methods were no longer available. So much the better - Sam's inability to devise a macho rescue attempt had made him turn to legal remedies and to her. And Sam had now brought David onto the scene. Non-observant Cohens were fine by her. She looked forward to sharing bacon and eggs with this one for breakfast! David Kagan as her therapist, to help heal the wounds inflicted on her by Ursula. And his wounds, the sadness which he still could only just keep below the surface? She longed to be able to help to heal them. And she sensed that there was a healing process beginning between the twin brothers and she was glad. 'All is well and all shall be well.' She said the words out loud. She laughed and murmured, 'Sylvia, you incorrigible optimist', switched off the light, pulled the duvet over her shoulders and was asleep almost immediately. But her optimism was something that had only recently returned to her after an absence of some months.

Chapter 26

Thursday 23rd October 1997

Elizabeth and Sylvia sat beside Olga's cot in the medical wing of the *Untersuchungsgefängnis*. They had been running through the court procedures for the trial which was a little over two weeks away.

'We'll cover it all in greater detail nearer the time, Elizabeth but I wanted to give you an idea of how it all works. You'll be relieved that it's very low key. It's not like you see in American films or TV.'

'That's something of a relief Sylvia, though it won't take the worry out of the proceedings.'

'And remember Elizabeth, express deep sorrow for what's happened but don't, please don't, plead for a heavy sentence. The prosecutor will look after that and I will do my best to counter his efforts. You owe it to little Olga to get out as soon as you can. My hope is to get a manslaughter verdict and a lenient sentence.'

At the mention of her name Olga began to cry.

'My little one's hungry again, Sylvia. Mother will have to respond!' She unbuttoned her blouse while Sylvia lifted the little one from the cot and held her while Elizabeth made ready to feed her.

'How old is she now? Eleven weeks is it?'

'No, all of twelve, and she's hungrier than ever!'

'She's a lovely little thing Elizabeth, you're lucky.'

'Some might not say so, Sylvia, but, yes, on balance I suppose I am. All right I'm not married to her father nor ever will be.' She paused, 'But I know he'll care for her and not stint on financial support. And there's Sam Charles, or Kagan as you now tell me. How that pans out we'll see. How long I'm inside is going to be a factor in it all.'

'I don't suppose you know this, Elizabeth but Sam has a brother, David. And not just a brother but a *twin* brother. I see him now and then, in fact I'm rather fond of him.' She wanted to speak about David and also to reassure Elizabeth that she wasn't in pursuit of Sam.

'He's like Sam?'

'They're like peas in a pod! The good thing is that Sam has a beard while David shaves.'

'Sam didn't have a beard when we met at Fasnacht, but I've seen a bearded man in the distance on my court visits. Sylvia, just now I referred to myself as mother and it seems strange to have that rôle. I've been thinking about my own mother there in Moscow. You know we've grown apart in recent years but now with my own child there's nothing I'd love more than for her to hold little Olga in her arms but I can never see that happening. They'd never let her out, not after what I've done!'

'Give me her address, Elizabeth. You never know.' She wondered whether to say it and decided to do so, 'You never know what Sam Kagan might be able to do ... he might just possibly have contacts. Don't get too excited but I'll mention it to him. Do you remember that I once advised you not to get too excited about Sam and was proved wrong? - so I hope that I'll be proved wrong this time as well!'

'Tell him not to run any risks, Sylvia. By the way I've got some good news: Andrea's far less suicidal now and Trudi's just passed her first IT exam. That's progress!'

Sylvia looked at her watch, 'I must go Elizabeth. It won't be long now before we know the outcome of all this. I'm hopeful but try to keep your mind on other things and don't spend all your time thinking about the court. Still with Olga to care for you have plenty to keep you occupied.' She kissed the little one on her fluffy head and left. Too late to make it to the lingerie shop this evening. It would have to wait until tomorrow morning before she flew to Paris.

Chapter 27

Saturday 25th October 1997

It was late October and they were in Giverny, Monet's garden to the west of Paris. The two months of sessions with David Kagan had transformed Sylvia's life. No longer did her emotions feel as though she had been under a surgeon's knife and her wounds left open. For the first month he had come to Basel each Saturday and spent the afternoon with her, leaving her to work over the ground they had covered during the following week. At the end of the month she had invited him to dinner on the Saturday evening and been pleased that he had accepted with alacrity. She had booked a table at *Die Drei Könige* and hoped that Sam wouldn't mind and feel that David was being special treatment. Then she remembered that Elizabeth had told her that on the fateful Sunday evening she and Sam had dined at *Die Drei Könige*. It would be as well not to take Sam there!

Over dinner David had explained that he wouldn't be able to visit Basel the following Saturday because he had to give a paper at a psychiatrists' conference in Paris. Hardly had she had time to feel her disappointment when he had added, 'But if you would like to fly to Paris for the weekend you could see what you think of the paper and join me and my colleagues for the closing dinner of the conference.' Seemingly as an afterthought he had added, 'And we could, I'm sure, find some time to work on your therapy while you're there.' She realised that her momentary disappointment had been at the prospect of not seeing David rather than at missing a session of therapy. There were two elements in Sylvia's healing process and the personal one had come to dominate.

She had flown out of Basel on the following Friday in the late afternoon and returned on the Sunday evening. And this had been her routine for the last month, though for the last two weeks she had not returned until the Monday morning. It had been wonderful to be taken round the city by someone who knew it well. Together they had seen so much, visited so many places, seen films and been to the Opera as well as the Opera Comique, done galleries and museums, not to mention the restaurants. And of course the therapy had continued, though it had been squeezed in between other events it had not been forgotten. Perhaps the lack of formality had helped its effectiveness rather than hindered it. When she had apologised to one of her colleagues for the late arrival one Monday she had been told, 'Don't apologise, Sylvia. You always do more than your share of the work and you're looking so good these days - we're all delighted. You're back to normal or perhaps its normal-plus?' So the 'normal-plus' *Advokat* had turned to her work with renewed enthusiasm, encouraged by the warmth of her colleagues pleasure at her progress. Her secretary had told her when pressed, 'Yes, we *were* worried about you. Not about your work, of course, but about you as a person. We're so pleased you're fine now.'

She and David stood among the late summer flowers in the garden at Giverny. The pink walls and green shutters of Monet's house formed the back-drop to the scene. They had come early on the Saturday morning to avoid the crowds and in this they had met with success. A fine rain had begun to fall and David opened the umbrella he had brought, *'Un des parapluies de Giverny, Sylvia.'* He smiled and she took his arm. They wandered slowly around the garden, a random perambulation. Their absorption in one another made their progress appear aimless. Despite the gentle rain there seemed to be something out of the ordinary about the quality of the light illuminating the garden. She wondered whether the magic was in the garden or in the light or whether it was in both. They had stopped by an old climbing rose, luxuriant with cream flowers, even though it was so late in the year, whose deep scent blended with the smell of the warm moist soil and the faint smell of cut grass in the distance. A profound tranquillity engulfed them, peace was all around them and also deep within. He turned to her and took her hand. 'I don't need to say a lot do I, Sylvia?'

'Nor me, David. I love you, that's it. A few words and yet everything.'

'And I love you, Sylvia. I'd been afraid that I'd never be able to love again, the scars seemed too deep, but you've made it possible, and I'm so glad, so very glad!'

He slipped his arm around her waist and they kissed. Light, colour, scent and joy were everywhere. If time wasn't standing still it certainly seemed to them to have slowed down to a snail's pace. She was aware of a feeling of light-headedness. Eventually they continued their progress around the garden, seeing and at the same time oblivious of much around them. How right he had been to bring her here before crowds engulfed the place.

'And we've got my brother the Rabbi to thank!'

'And Elizabeth as well. She's the first link in the chain. If she hadn't shot her friend Vladimir, Sam wouldn't have come back to Basel and neither would I have been her *Advokat* - and it's because of Sam that you came on the scene, David. His little brother, the therapist has been quite a find!'

'As ... therapist and ... lover ... '

'I'll take the lover part on trust, until now you've been

extremely chaste! It clearly runs in the family.' She realised what she had said and showed her embarrassment, 'What I meant to say is that Sam and I have never been other than friends - after all, as you have just reminded me, he *is* a rabbi, whatever else he might be.'

He was amused at her discomfiture but succeeded in keeping a straight face. 'Of course I now have a problem. It would clearly be highly unprofessional for me to be both your therapist and your lover. So you will have to choose which one it must be. What is to be my future rôle so far as Sylvia Brunner is concerned?'

Her anxiety had shown momentarily but as she looked into his eyes she saw the smile that he couldn't hold back. She pulled him close and looked up into his face, 'If Sylvia Brunner didn't say 'lover' she would be certifiable, wouldn't she?'

'In my personal, though biased opinion, yes. Undoubtedly so.'

They were standing on the Japanese bridge over the water lily pond. The sun was breaking through the cloud. They watched the reflection of trees and sky on the surface of the water. He broke the silence, 'It's interesting how we see it all through Monet's eyes, we look for the reflections, the distortions, the colours. Without Monet I don't think we'd do that or not quite in the same way. "My garden is my masterpiece," he said, but that's only part of the truth. He was a genius who painted his way from impressionism to early abstraction and all through the loss of his wife of many years. A miracle of vision, I call it.'

'David, in two months each of us has come to see life, ourselves and one another differently. I'd call that a miracle too.'

The tour buses were beginning to park in the road between the two gardens and sightseers were beginning to move around like a colony of ants.

'And I'd go along with you there. Well it's getting busy here. Let's go before the magic of Giverny wears thin. What about lunch in Vernon? It's a little way down river and on the other bank of the Seine. I know rather a good restaurant there.'

'Splendid you've given me quite an appetite - not only for food, David! I'd most definitely like to find out just how unprofessional you can be with a poor helpless patient like me. Dr Kagan do you think that you could book me in for a session on your couch some time later today, please?'

'Just so long as you don't run off to some clever female *Advokat* in Basel and sue me, Sylvia. Promise that and I'll be more than pleased to oblige.'

The rain had ceased. They took the subway under the road and strolled slowly, hand in hand, back through the flower garden and out into the car park. Both their minds were on their return to David's apartment at Saint-Cloud, but they were in France and the prospect of lunch in Vernon was also an alluring one. Nature's beauty, haute cuisine, wine and love - it was an intoxicating mix. David opened the door of the black MG for her before going round to climb in himself. He lent over and kissed her. 'Now Sylvia, we concentrate on the road. We owe it to ourselves and others to get home safely. Both Sam and Elizabeth are depending on your legal skills. Let's hope that they find the same happiness together that we have.'

'Well David, although I can't work miracles in court, I can tell you this for sure; Elizabeth's chances are far better now than they were two months ago. And we're only a couple of weeks away from the hearing. That's all your doing. You've got me back on my feet by sweeping me off them!' She placed her hand on his, 'But next it's lunch and then home.' She was glad that she had spent half an hour the day before shopping for lingerie in Basel. She had told herself that she was doing it to boost her morale and update her wardrobe, while knowing all the time that she was longing to please David.

Chapter 28

Monday 10th November 1997 - Morning

Murder is like most things in Switzerland, understated and almost anonymous - another statistic to be worried over or forgotten. Likewise murder trials are usually low key events. People would rather believe that such crimes do not happen and the court proceedings themselves are organised in such a way as to generate a minimum of excitement. For those wanting drama with adversarial lawyers, a red robed judge and the possibility of a death sentence at the end, a Swiss court is not the place to be. But if you are looking for a system which seeks to get at the truth in a calm and dispassionate way and leaves little room for the tactics and histrionics of the screen lawyer, then a court like the *Strafgericht* of Basel-Stadt has much to commend itself. But nevertheless a Swiss murder trial is not without considerable human interest.

***

The public area to the rear of the court was full and some newspaper reporters were arguing with the police that they should be allowed to stand at the back. The fifty or so seats had all been taken as soon as the doors of the court were opened to the public at 8.00 a.m. The beginning of proceedings at 8.15 a.m. had surprised the foreign journalists, as had the 6.00 p.m. conclusion to the day's proceedings. For courts to keep office hours, and long ones at that, was a novelty. Those involved in administering Swiss justice clearly had a longer concentration span than their opposite numbers elsewhere. One of the court officials conveyed news of the crowd of spectators to the Court President, Dr Bruno Schreiber, in his office in the former school that formed the court's administrative block as he drank a cup of the strongest coffee that his clerk could produce. When he wasn't in court he chain drank coffee through the day; it was something he missed when he was hearing a case. Another six months and it would be his turn to be the remand judge, a couple of years respite from actually hearing the cases. He felt in need of the break, though there would be plenty other things to keep him fully employed.

How the international media had heard of the trial was something of a mystery, the murder had been reported in only the sketchiest of outlines in the Swiss press, the Fasnacht Carnival itself taking precedence for press headlines, and there were no public committal proceedings, such as those before magistrates elsewhere, to give notice of an interesting trial. The President suspected that it had probably been *Advocat* Brunner but he had no way of being sure. In any case it did not worry him, there was no harm in public interest in the workings of the justice machine: indeed there was much benefit in the public hearing about what happened in the courts. It just meant that he would have to be more than ordinarily careful that nothing happened to lower the esteem of the court in the eyes of the world or of his fellow Swiss.

Advokat Sylvia Brunner was downstairs, below the court room, with her client. Her police guards were content to leave Elizabeth speaking with her lawyer across a table rather than lock her away in the cells. They had seen her every four weeks over the previous eight months and grown to like the young woman. They had often discussed her after she had left the monthly remand proceedings at the *Strafgericht*. She was unlike most of the prisoners who came there, they would have been happy to have her as a daughter or as something more exciting if they had been younger. A pleasant calm young woman who always asked them how they were and enquired about their families. They were hoping that she'd get a fair deal upstairs, but then you never knew with these cases - under the pleasant surface she might be a beast from hell deserving of the heaviest sentence the court could hand down, though they doubted it.

Neither the lawyer nor her client had slept particularly well the previous night but each was calm as they discussed the day's proceedings. 'As I've said before, Elizabeth, you won't find high excitement in court but I think you will find the judges are good listeners. But then an excess of excitement is something we can do without, it's the outcome that matters. Dr Schreiber, the President, is very thorough and very fair. Something happened to change him some years ago. Before that he was rather abrupt in his dealings with people but then he was taken ill and spent some months away from the court. When he came back he was a very different man, showing understanding and consideration to all. Appeals against the sentences of his court rarely succeed and indeed there are few appeals, we advocates know that generally to take cases that have been before him any further is a waste of time.' She didn't comment on Frau Berman, the Vice-President, who had been re-elected on a law and order ticket subtly presented by her supporters. She might be a real problem, particularly if the other three *Richter*, judges, on the panel followed her lead.

'I think they want us to go up to the court, Sylvia. Whatever the result I want you to know that I'm grateful for all you've done.'

'Don't sound as if you're about to face a firing squad or something out of Kafka, Elizabeth. I'll be sitting beside you throughout the hearing. In a sense we're both on trial - OK you're the one charged with murder but my forensic skills are also on trial. The other Basel lawyers and the world press will be keeping an interested eye on how I do. It'll help the adrenaline to flow and keep me on my toes. OK let's go!' They got up and walked to the door where two police officers were waiting to escort them up the stairs to the court, *Gerichtsaal 2*.

As they entered the court the conversation quietened and those at the back of the room strained to see the two women. Sylvia took Elizabeth's arm and guided her to a table and desk just in front of the public area. 'You sit on the left, I have the desk on the right. You know the geography of the place from what I've told you. Don't forget this isn't Britain, we don't stand when the judges come in and you're not placed in isolation like someone with the plague.' Elizabeth scanned the public area and located Peter Lewis towards the back. She caught his eye and smiled a sad smile of recognition. At the same time she was glad and sorry to see him there. Glad that he cared enough to follow this through but sorry that he was still hurting from the end of their relationship. Still he had every reason to be there to find out what was to be the fate of the mother of his child.

Behind them a British journalist noticed the smile of recognition but failed to identify Lewis. She turned back to read through her notes:

"More like a committee room than a court.

Tall room with pale gray walls. Unbroken wall on left. On right three doors, for public, prisoners and probably judges. Three large modern art prints on the walls, one on each side towards the front and one on the back wall, all are rather bland.

Behind the judges are high windows draped with net curtains through which a garden can be seen with plants growing up a wall.

Dark mahogany furniture. It looks as if the judges will sit in a line facing the accused.

Accused sits facing the judges with her lawyer beside her. NB No dock!"

She began to write once again:

"8.10 a.m. Elizabeth Fielder and *Advokat* Sylvia Brunner take their seats facing where the judges will be.

Neither displays any emotion and they are engaged in quiet conversation.

Elizabeth Fielder wearing a dark grey suit with a skirt to the knee and a dark blue sweater - no jewellery. Medium height to tall with a good figure. Mid length dark brunette hair. An attractive woman.

Advokat Brunner in a plum coloured trouser suit with a white silk blouse. Jacket with a diamond? brooch and small pearl earrings. Lighter brunette hair and an inch or so shorter than her client, also an attractive woman. She has a determined look about her.

Advokat Guillaume from the Public Prosecutor's Office, a tall man with graying hair and a navy blue suit sits at the end of an extension from left hand end the judges' desks. A young woman assistant looks after his files."

She was glad she had got there early enough to get a seat on the far left of the front row, she wouldn't see much of Elizabeth Fielder and her lawyer but if anyone was going to get a glimpse of their faces she was the one. She knew she would have her work cut out to keep this seat through the length of the trial. She hoped that her grasp of the German language was adequate to enable her to understand the Basel dialect of Swiss-German but no doubt there would be an interpreter, something to slow things down. Also there was the woman reporter from the *Basler Zeitung* beside her - they had struck up a friendly acquaintance right away when they had met a couple of days before. 'How about a trip to Switzerland', her editor had said, 'almost a holiday for you!' And here she was in this city without a mountain in sight and stuck in a court room from before eight to after six each day. By the time she'd written her piece and sent it each evening there would be nothing to do but go to bed! A two and a half hour lunch break would be her only recreation Monday to Friday. Some Swiss holiday!

Beside her the *Zeitung's* reporter sat with a blank notebook open before her, she had been in this court often enough and had no need to describe the place or its personalities. Nevertheless she somehow felt that this case had something different about it, the number of foreign journalists and other spectators testified to that. Whether it would make good copy and advance her career was another matter.

The furthest of the doors on the right opened and the judges filed in. Some of the foreign journalists stood up, realised that they were the only ones to do so and sat down looking sheepish. The judges made themselves comfortable, arranged the papers on the desks in front of them and waited for the President to begin the proceedings.

'I am told that we have here representatives of the world's press and we - my colleagues and I - are glad that you have been able to take time off from other things and come here to see our legal system at work, to see Swiss justice in action. I believe that you will find it undramatic but thorough and fair. Such proceedings do not always make good copy for journalists but I am sure that you will concentrate on essentials and not trivia and be as thorough and fair in your reporting as this court will strive to be in dispensing justice.'

He had been speaking in Swiss-German and an interpreter then translated his speech into English.

The President began again but now in English, a language with which he was clearly at home and which he spoke with only the very slightest of accents. He addressed the accused:

'And, Miss Feldman, what I have just said to the journalists I say to you with added emphasis: this court will seek to arrive at the right decision on the question of guilt and, if that is established, on the appropriate sentence. There is an interpreter here and I understand that you wish the translation to be into English, though (and this is something that we will touch on later) I understand that English is not your first language.'

'Thank you, Sir.'

'One further point before we start, Miss Feldman. I need to stress this - if at any time you are confused as to what has been said or about the form of the proceedings you must say so. It is absolutely essential that you feel that you have had a fair hearing before the *Strafgericht* of Basel-Stadt. We come to this trial with open minds seeking to do what is right. When you answer questions put to you in this court you must tell the truth and nothing but the truth. If *Herr Staatsanwalt*, the Public Prosecutor, or *Fräulein Verteidiger*, Fräulein Brunner your *Advokat*, require it you may be asked to give evidence under oath otherwise there will be no oath but that does not mean that we are not seeking from you, indeed requiring, the truth, the whole truth and nothing but the truth. You are aware of the contents of the indictment, the charge? Good, I will not therefore read it in full but summarise it before beginning to work our way through the evidence.'

Elizabeth nodded assent. She had warmed to him, there was a complete absence of judicial arrogance or stuffiness about him. He struck her as the sort of man who would make a good father-in-law. Neither she nor anyone else there knew that twelve years before he had sat and sweated at the back of a Thai court where his only daughter was held on suspicion of involvement in drug smuggling. Eventually her travelling companion had succeeded in convincing the court that he had acted alone and she had been acquitted. They had flown out of Bangkok within a couple hours of her release and arrived back in Zurich relieved but totally exhausted. Somehow the matter had escaped the attention of the world's press and they had been very relieved that it was so. He had needed six months to recover fully from the experience. What he had said to Elizabeth was spoken from the heart. He knew it was no light thing to be on trial in a strange land and in a strange tongue.

The British journalist opened her notebook to a fresh page and began her word picture of the President and the other judges:

"President Dr Bruno Schreiber, in his fifties with a full head of white hair. A tall man ?a little over six foot tall. Medium grey suit, white shirt and dark tie. No gown but has a larger chair than the other judges. Clearly concerned that fairness should be the keynote of the proceedings.

'Next to him on the right Frau Trudi Berman, the *Statthalter* (Vice-President). Also in her fifties. Dark suit, skirt to just below the knee, white blouse. Something austere about her and her dress style. Shaw's "vulpine under the veneer" fits very well - ?just my impression or is she really like that?

'Three others, lay judges - magistrates - a woman in her late thirties and two men (forties and fifties). They give away nothing in their faces. There's also the clerk to the Court, a young woman in her 20's.'

She turned back to her notes of the actual proceedings and prepared to take down what the President was saying. He was evidently summarising the charges against the accused. She could only grasp the general drift so instead of concentrating on what the words meant she attended to the President's manner and apparent attitude to Elizabeth Fielder. She decided that he was deliberately keeping things low key and avoiding any histrionics. He stopped and the interpreter took over:

'You are known as Elizabeth Fielder but you have stated that your name at birth was Lizaveta Feldman. You are a Russian citizen although you entered Switzerland on a Canadian passport which carried the name of Elizabeth Fielder. You have been charged in the name of Lizaveta Feldman and that is therefore the name that we must use in this court.'

Elizabeth nodded her head in agreement.

'Lizaveta Feldman, how do you plead in respect of the charges against you?'

Sylvia Brunner replied, 'My client pleads not guilty to

the charges under Article 111, Intentional Homicide and Article 112, Murder. However she does plead guilty to Manslaughter under Article 113.'

'Would the accused please confirm that.'

There was a slight pause before Elizabeth replied, 'That is correct, Sir.'

As the President began again in Swiss-German her thoughts turned to the question of her identity. Who was she really? Who did she feel herself to be? No, she didn't feel like Lizaveta any longer. Gone were the constrictions of life in the USSR, the shortages of basic necessities and the brutality of a drunken abusive step-father. Things certainly didn't seem to have improved in Russia under the post-Communist regime. Yet her memories were not without an affectionate regret for times gone by. She remembered her introduction to the arts and to music in particular. For some reason vivid memories came back to her of the first time she had seen Boris Godunov in Moscow, of sitting there at the Bolshoi sweating, not from the heat of the theatre but from the realism of the young bass' portrayal of Boris being driven out of his mind by remorse. Perhaps it was her sense of remorse for the killing of Vladimir that had prompted the recall of Boris. The move to the USA and Canada with the KGB had been like the metamorphosis from caterpillar to butterfly without the sleep of the chrysalis - Sylvia's earlier reference to Kafka had triggered off the thought in her mind. And as a butterfly she had relished the freedom of life in London and her time with Peter Lewis. And there he was some yards behind her. Neither of them could have imagined an event like this when they first met eighteen months before. Poor Peter! But she must keep her attention on the court proceedings, appearing to be bored or in another world would not do her any good in the eyes of the judges.

She looked at Sylvia Brunner, she was following the President as he worked his way through the statements and reports on the Public Prosecutor's files - copies of which had been supplied to her, as defence lawyer. She knew them well but nevertheless she attended carefully to the President as he read. She was alert to any inflection of his voice that might show what he was thinking, or where there might be doubts in his mind. She ticked off documents on the *Beweisliste* - the evidence list - as he progressed.

***

At ten o'clock the court rose for a twenty minute coffee break and Elizabeth and her *Advokat* were taken downstairs and again the police refrained from locking her in the cells. 'Nothing in particular to report, Elizabeth. It's going as it should. The President seems considerate, sympathetic even, just as I told you, so that's all to the good.' She wondered to herself how sympathetic the other judges and in particular Frau Berman, the *Statthalter*, would prove to be.

'Did you see Peter Lewis, Sylvia? He was at the back of the court. I knew that he would come but it was strange to see him all the same.'

'He is the father of your daughter after all and he's got an interest in the outcome of the trial apart from emotional ties to yourself. He's obviously concerned about where and how the girl's going to be brought up.'

***

'Well Peter it's under way at last and it will not be too

many days before we know what they decide to do with your young woman.'

'Yes Jakob, probably not very long - though with everything in two languages it's not going to be the swiftest of events. As for "my young woman" well she once was that but my nerve failed as you know, in the end I couldn't leave Ruth and the state Michael was getting into was the final argument for staying. And by then a child was on the way! I have a horror of Elizabeth and the girl spending years in a Swiss jail.'

***

'You look thoughtful Trudi, not of course that our task as judges requires less than profound thought.'

'As you have said Dr Schreiber, profound thought. There are complexities in this case, especially the foreign involvement, which seem to be avoiding the daylight. I would like to know much more about what she and her victim were really doing here in Basel. I think it unlikely that they had come for *Fasnacht* and the carnival revelries. You have seen all the Prosecutor's files, are we going to be told the whole of the background?'

'Only what is relevant to the prosecution. The Federal Prosecutor in Bern has advised throughout. There are things that he wants kept out of court and there are charges that have not been preferred against Fräulein Feldman - entering Switzerland on a false passport and transacting the business of a foreign government on Swiss soil are among them. If such matters are raised there is no difficulty in pointing out that the Public Prosecutor has simply concentrated on the most serious crime she is alleged to have committed here in Basel.'

'Perhaps, but I am not entirely happy about it, Herr

President. We ought to be presented with the complete picture.'

'Does anyone ever have the *complete* picture, Frau Berman? The complete picture of anything? I suspect not. We know in part and have to do as best we can on what we do know. Time to return to to court to arrive at as complete a picture as the circumstances dictate.'

'Circumstances or Swiss Security, Dr Schreiber?'

'Who knows, Frau Berman, who knows? But coffee sharpens the mind, perhaps we need more coffee and less verbiage in court.'

She laughed, 'One of these days Bruno they'll have to put you on a medical drip to keep you topped up with the stuff. They're supplying free drugs on public funds for addicts, perhaps you ought to register and have your coffee supplied that way.'

He laughed in response, 'I'm not mainlining yet, Trudi. It'll have to wait a while.' But the mention of drugs brought back memories of the court in Bangkok and the charges that had put his daughter's life at risk. It was twelve years ago but time seemed to shrink to nothing and the memory was potent enough even now to shake him to the core emotionally and cause his innards to churn. Yes he understood what the young Russian woman would be feeling, and she had only recently given birth to a child. For some people life became a mess, a real mess!

***

The return of the judges brought an expectant hush to the court room. The President returned to his slow and methodical journey through the Prosecution files. He read the report of the police officer who had been called to the hotel on that February morning, with its description of the position of the body at the door of the accused's room in the Hotel International. Just inside the hotel room the body of the accused had also been on the floor and he had thought that there were two victims. The man was clearly dead with a bullet hole in the back of his head - there had been substantial bleeding. But he had been relieved to find that the woman lying there was breathing and then he had seen next to her a small calibre pistol. Neither the Prosecutor nor *Advokat* Brunner had any questions for him.

The President moved on to the forensic report on the corpse. Time of death was given. The wound was in the back of the head and the pistol, the one found beside the accused and with her finger print on the trigger, had been fired at very close range, this was evident from burning on the hair of the deceased. The forensic scientist estimated this as between eight to fifteen centimetres from the back of the deceased's head. On the accused's hands clothes and face were found traces of the victim's blood, bone and brain material. This caused a *frisson* to run through the court and Elizabeth shut her eyes. The only question was from Frau Berman and was more a statement of her conclusions than a question. 'The victim was fleeing from the accused?'

'That's not for me to say. What I can say is that he was shot from behind at very close range, I understand that the pistol was on the floor next to the accused and it had her finger print on the trigger and that there were no other finger prints on the weapon.'

The firearms officer confirmed that the bullet removed from the brain of the deceased had been fired from the gun lying on the hotel room floor.

The finger print expert confirmed what his colleague had said, that the only prints on the pistol were those of

Lizaveta Feldman. He added that the fingerprints of the deceased had been found on the door knob on the inside of the door. Again it was Frau Berman who had a question, 'So it appears the he had tried to open the door?' The reply was that on some occasion the deceased had handled the door knob but whether this was at the time he was shot or on another visit to the room the expert was unable to say.

Next was the statement made by the doctor at the *Kantonsspital* who had dealt with the accused when she was admitted that morning under police guard. He had been unable to establish the cause of her loss of consciousness. He hazarded an opinion that it might have been due to shock but then admitted that he would have expected her to come to much more quickly - it had been several hours before she had done so. In his opinion the accused had been a very fit woman apart from signs of a very mild rheumatic condition. *Advokat* Brunner had asked for the doctor to be called to answer questions. The President warned him of his obligation to answer honestly and then the defence *Advokat* began her questioning.

'Doktor Schmidt, how many years have you practised as a medical doctor?'

'For twenty two years, all of it here in Basel.'

'And have you had many other cases where someone was unconscious for so long and for no apparent cause?'

'Possibly one or two but I wouldn't like to swear to the number.'

'It's unusual?'

'Very, without some substantial brain damage or due to drugs.'

'What did you do in the case of Fräulein Feldman? What tests did you carry out?'

'The full range of tests - blood and urine - then later that day we did an MRS scan of her brain, as clearly she had fallen and struck her head a heavy blow, but there were no abnormalities whatsoever.'

'If you had been asked to say what was wrong when you first saw your patient what would you have said?'

'I would have guessed that she was suffering from an overdose of drugs as well as the blow to her head. But I must emphasise that that was merely a first opinion, a working hypothesis which was later disproved by the path-lab tests.'

'Are you sure that she wasn't faking her unconsciousness?'

'On that I can reply unequivocally. She was, without any doubt whatsoever, unconscious.'

A thought struck *Advokat* Brunner, or so it seemed to those in Court. In truth this was something she had agonised over for some time. She had suspected from the beginning that her client had been doped and Sam's tapes had made it practically certain. Normally she would have dealt with the matter as one of pre-trial fact-finding but she had had a hunch that a request for clarification from the white-heat of the trial itself would be more effective in concentrating minds and getting to the truth. It was just the sort of matter that she would have discussed with her father but she no longer had the benefit of his counsel. It had been a difficult decision and she had taken it alone.

'Would you please tell the court about the arrangements for taking samples for analysis by the path lab.'

'Samples of blood or urine are taken by a nurse, labelled and then taken down to the lab with a note of the tests required.'

'And when were these particular samples taken, Dr Schmidt?'

He paused, 'I would have liked the blood test to be taken right away and that is what I told the nurse to do but it was a busy morning - *Fasnacht* with more than the normal number of accident cases and other emergencies - and it wasn't done until the afternoon. When I saw Fräulein Feldman at 2 o'clock that afternoon her records showed that the blood sample had not been taken and so I ordered it to be done. She had come to by then and the urine sample was taken at the same time. We got the first results by the evening and they indicated nothing of note. Later I was notified of the signs of very mild rheumatism that was all. The cause of unconsciousness was and remains a mystery.'

'And one which annoys you I think?'

'Yes, we like to think that we can diagnose what is wrong with a patient pretty accurately these days. In the case of Fräulein Feldman we were unable to do so.'

'You didn't detect that she was in the tenth week of pregnancy?'

He paused, 'No, if the tests had shown such a condition it would have been included in my report.'

'You are surprised, Dr Schmidt.'

'I am indeed.'

'You would have expected it to show up on the tests?'

'If she had been pregnant it would have shown up.'

'Herr President if I might have a word with my client.'

'But of course, *Fräulein Verteidiger*. Do you wish to withdraw from the *Gerichtsaal*?'

'No, I think it will be satisfactory to remain here.' She turned to Elizabeth and spoke quietly, 'When did you know that you were pregnant, Elizabeth?'

'Early in January. My general practitioner in

Hampstead gave me the results of the test.' Sylvia already knew the answer but she had wished to give the impression that it was news to her.

'Good girl Elizabeth, we're on our way! It was a good thing that you had those tests in London.' She addressed the President, 'I have spoken with my client. May I resume my questions to Dr Schmidt, please?'

'Of course.'

There was a silence that could be felt as the court waited for her to resume the questioning. Peter Lewis was sweating and sat fidgeting.

'My client, Dr Schmidt, tells me that her general practitioner in London informed her that she was pregnant. He did that some weeks ... ' she looked at Elizabeth, ' ... six weeks before she was taken into your hospital. Now supposing that what Fräulein Feldman says is true, and it will be for the court to decide whether they require evidence from London to corroborate her statement, if pregnancy tests six weeks earlier were positive – and the child was in fact born on 1st August - what conclusion do you draw about the accuracy of the tests carried out for you at the *Kantonsspital*?'

Dr Schmidt was silent gazing down at the table in front of him. He looked up at the President, 'I am puzzled, Sir. Puzzled and unhappy.'

Something else occurred to *Advokat* Brunner, she was about to ask to produce Elizabeth's child as an 'exhibit' but a look in Frau Berman's direction changed her mind. That lady's views on law and order and high morality suggested that to do so could well be counterproductive.

Advokat Brunner addressed the President, 'I am led to wonder whether the hospital tests do not leave us with grounds for doubting their accuracy, Herr President. I am sure that *Herr Staatsanwalt* is also puzzled. Tomorrow the court will not be sitting and I wish to request that he and I use the time to interview together all those involved in taking, transporting and testing the samples of which Dr Schmidt has spoken today.'

'*Herr Staatsanwald*, do you have a view on the matter?'

He was an old hand at the job. This was one of his more straightforward cases when it was stripped of its foreign elements, and the Federal Prosecutor had been pretty strong in laying down that the Russian element should be played down as much as possible. He looked at the President, 'I have no strong view, though I'm not sure of the relevance of the matter. But if the court wishes to approve *Fräulein Verteidiger's* plans for how she and I are to spend tomorrow morning together I have no objection - none at all.' He smiled in her direction and raised an eyebrow a millimetre or two in the President's direction. The President took the message, Herr Guillaume had the reputation in legal circles of being something of a goat - people wondered, sometimes to one another, whether he would one day end up in the *Strafgericht* on a rape charge prosecuted by one of his colleagues.

The President addressed a few quiet words to his colleagues and then turned to *Advokat* Brunner, 'Yes, we too are puzzled and will be more than interested to hear the outcome of your enquiries. It will be helpful, indeed necessary for this to be clarified. Do you have any more questions for Dr Schmidt?'

'Not today Herr President but it is quite possible that, after we have seen him and his hospital colleagues tomorrow, there may be matters to put to him here in court.'

'You understand that Dr Schmidt? You may be wanted

back here to continue giving evidence and answer questions. You are to do all in your power to ensure that all those who were involved with the samples are available tomorrow morning at 8.15 a.m. to meet the two *Advokaten*. I ask that you do no more than tell those concerned what is the problem, that they must attend and that questions will be asked and must be answered honestly and completely about the samples concerned.'

'Yes, sir.'

'And you, *Herr Staatsanwalt*, do you have any questions for Dr Schmidt at this juncture? No?'

The Prosecutor shook his head.

'Good. The court will adjourn until 2.30 p.m.'

***

The English reporter turned to her Swiss colleague, 'Well, what do you think? Have the defence found something or is it just for show?'

'There's probably something in it ... Sylvia Brunner knows what she's doing, she's very astute. Dr Schmidt certainly didn't look a very happy witness at the end did he?'

***

'I almost asked for young Olga to be brought up into the court as part of the evidence for your pregnancy at the material time but I refrained. It would have been a bit too theatrical.'

Elizabeth was feeding the child who seemed to have a very healthy appetite, 'You're probably right Sylvia. It's not exactly a baby show up there though it's not nearly so bad as I feared. They're a civilised lot, or so it seems.'

She looked down at the child at her breast and smiled, 'Sylvia's going to get us out of here, Olga, we won't be jail birds much longer.'

'Sylvia will do her level best and a bit more besides for you both.'

***

'Your girl's lawyer is onto something, Peter. Always good to take the initiative early on like that, to make a tidy open and shut case appear more complicated.'

'My girl? Not really, though the child Olga is ours, Jakob. I didn't know that she was pregnant until we celebrated Russian Christmas early in January. I thought at the time that the celebration was just a joke, but now I can understand where the idea came from. I've got little Olga's photo here.' He fumbled in the inside pocket of his jacket, produced his wallet and withdrew a photograph of a dark haired baby. 'Well Jakob, I've got one of each sex, one boy and one girl - one from each of the women in my life. But I wonder how much I will be seeing of little Olga as the years progress.'

***

Monday 10th November 1997 – Afternoon

The afternoon had none of the morning's revelations. The report of the psychiatrist appointed by the court was read. She had found that Lizaveta Feldman exhibited no mental abnormalities, was well balanced and definitely exhibited no signs of having a psychopathic personality. Fräulein Feldman appeared to be suffering from amnesia concerning events around the killing. On whether this was genuine or contrived she was unable to give a definitive verdict though on balance she inclined to the view that it was genuine. She highlighted the help the accused had given to her fellow prisoners in the *Untersuchungsgefängnis* and also her deep remorse for the death of the man known as Eugene.

The President began his questioning of the accused, 'Fräulein Feldman, I need to put some questions to you about your visit to this city and the events of Sunday 16th February 1997.'

'Yes, Sir.'

'After the American journalist, Mr Sam Charles, had departed for Hamburg what happened?'

'I returned to my room in the hotel and sat listening to music on the radio and relishing the day I had spent in the mountains. I spoke to my partner Peter Lewis on the telephone. Then I remember Vladimir coming to my room. We had a general discussion but then things begin to become blurred ... ' She paused and made an effort to recollect but was no more successful than she had been in the months since the killing. 'I'm sorry, Sir, I really am but I cannot bring the events into focus, It's all blurred.' She wiped her eyes with a tissue. 'I'm sorry, Sir, I'm not much help, there's a gap between Vladimir coming into my room and finding myself in the *Kantonsspital.* I had already been told of the evidence long before this hearing began, I have heard it in detail today, I cannot dispute it. I had no intention to kill Vladimir, I have never had any intention to do so. Everything points to me having killed him and so I have pleaded guilty to manslaughter.'

'Fräulein Feldman, you are absolutely sure that you are unable to remember the final events of that Sunday night?'

'Absolutely certain, Sir, which is something I deeply regret.'

The President looked towards Herr Guillaume, '*Herr Staatsanwald*, you no doubt have some questions to put to Fräulein Feldman.'

Guillaume, who had just muttered to his assistant, 'A suitable case for the thumbscrew!' began his questioning.

'Fräulein Feldman, your amnesia is a matter of some concern. The psychiatrist appointed by the Court has reported that she is, on balance, satisfied that it is genuine. But I put it to you that, from your point of view, it is rather convenient to be unable to recollect the events that have brought before this Court.'

'Sir, I have just told the President that I deeply regret this situation – that the most significant event in my life should be a smudge, a blur on my memory isn't something I welcome. I have cooperated fully with the Court's psychiatrist but all to no avail.'

'Fräulein Feldman, I put it to you that you are, or perhaps were, a member of a foreign security service.'

'Yes, I admit I was.'

'But no longer?'

'I suppose not, only they haven't written to tell me that I'm out of work.' She and Sylvia immediately wished that she hadn't resorted to levity. At once she turned to the President, 'Sir, I apologise for that flippant response. I appreciate the seriousness of these proceedings, but the tension was getting to me.'

'Fräulein, the Court accepts your apology. But please refrain from any levity. *Herr Staatsanwald*, please continue.'

'It is reasonable to assume that you were well trained for your rôle as an agent of that service.'

'Yes.'

'The training was long and arduous?'

'Yes.'

'How long?'

'I decline to answer that question.'

'Your refusal is noted. But it was arduous?'

'Very.'

'And it would be realistic to assume that you are well versed in interrogation techniques and in *resisting* such techniques, of being skilled in the art of denial, even when under pressure.'

'It would be foolish to deny that I received such training, and while that makes it more likely that my amnesia is faked it doesn't make it certain. All I can say is that I would give much to know what happened that evening, I have lost a significant episode in my life.'

'Fräulein Feldman, I put it to you that your amnesia is contrived and not genuine.'

She looked towards the President, 'Sir, I appreciate that the Court may think it improbable, given my employment by a security service, but I can only assert that my amnesia is genuine, something that annoys and frustrates me as much as I am sure it does the Court.'

'The Court hears your assertion, Fräulein Feldman. *Herr Staatsanwald*, you wish to proceed?'

'One more question, please. Fräulein Feldman, you appear to have or have had more than one employer – were you also involved in the activities of any other organisation, for example one involved in illegal international activities?

'Certainly not, *Herr Staatsanwald*.'

'That Sir, that concludes my questions.' Swiss Security had warned him off quizzing her on her London and Basel security activities.

'*Fräulein Verteidiger*.'

'Fräulein Feldman, what was your intention when you came to Basel on Friday 14th February, what was the purpose of your visit?'

'I came with Peter Lewis, my partner and the director of a scientific glassware company. We were making a delivery of glassware to a laboratory here in Basel. Mr Lewis was also making a social call with his family on a director of the laboratory.'

'You worked for Mr Lewis' company?'

'Yes, I was his secretary.'

'But you also had another employer?'

'Yes, a security service.'

'A State security service.'

'Yes. But I'm unable to identify the State for now.'

'Other members of that security service were also present in Basel?'

'Yes.'

'The deceased, Eugene Preston, otherwise known as Vladimir, was a member of the same service.?'

'Yes.'

'Did you have an active part in whatever the foreign service was doing in this city?'

'No, I was told to keep out of the way and amuse myself while what they planned took place.'

'What do you remember of the fatal Sunday when Vladimir was killed?'

'A day that was almost wholly delight and ends with me speaking to Vladimir and then a fog, a total blur ... .'

'The blur is genuine and not contrived?'

'Completely genuine. I have contrived nothing. I have already said how frustrating it is.'

'You brought the weapon with you from England/'

'It had been issued to me, I brought my equipment.'

'Had it ever been your intention to use it on your

colleague Vladimir?

'Never, not that day nor at any other time.'

'Herr President that concludes my questioning.'

***

Various other technical matters were dealt with and the court adjourned early at 4.30 to the relief of the British journalist who was able to file her report and see something of the city of Basel.

Chapter 29

Tuesday 11th November 1997

By 8 o'clock the next morning all the personnel of the *Kantonsspital* who had been involved in taking, handling and testing Elizabeth's samples had assembled in a conference room at the hospital. They were ill at ease as they sat around a large table waiting for the lawyers' arrival. At 8.10 Sylvia Brunner arrived and, once she had been introduced to the others, she and Dr Schmidt stood by the window and turned to discussing the play currently on at the Basel Theatre. It was a few minutes after 8.15 before Herr Guillaume hurried into the room. His attire, with his tie somewhat awry, and his demeanour suggested that he had overslept after a binge the previous night. It occurred to Sylvia that he wouldn't have risked appearing like that in court and she hoped that he would be content to let her make the running in questioning the hospital staff. She was determined to play it low key, avoiding harsh inquisitorial techniques. Sylvia and Herr Guillaume were seated on one side of the long table and Dr Schmidt sat in the middle of the hospital staff facing them. She was pleased when Guillaume said, 'OK *Advokat* Brunner go ahead, you wanted this session - make the most of it but don't be too long over it.'

She turned to Dr Schmidt, 'Doktor, I wonder if you would introduce your colleagues to us once again and let them say what was their rôle in dealing with Elizabeth Fielder and the samples back in February.'

'Certainly *Advokat* Brunner.'

'I'd be happier if you called me Fräulein Brunner, we're in your hospital now and not in court.' She wanted to have as few barriers as possible between herself and the medical staff, it would help if they found it easy to talk and they knew that they weren't being blamed if something had gone wrong in their procedures. And she felt sure in her own mind that something had gone wrong. It had to be made as easy as possible for someone to admit to the fact. She needed to keep Herr Guillaume out of the questioning as far as possible.

Dr Schmidt made the introductions and she turned to the others in the room and continued, 'So can we go back to *Fasnacht* in February, to the first day of the carnival. It's probably helpful that the matters that concern us happened then, somehow it's easier to pinpoint things when you remember what else was happening at the same time. Dr Schmidt will have explained what the Court President said, that he was to tell you to attend here this morning and to answer fully and honestly any questions that I and my colleague Herr Guillaume put to you. It may be that there has been some mistake with the samples and their testing and if so it has to be cleared up so that justice is done. The court needs to have all the facts and to be sure that they are accurate. Now back to you *Doktor*.' She had refrained from referring to Guillaume as *Herr Staatsanwalt*, the Public Prosecutor, that sounded too threatening, too unfriendly. She wanted them to be relaxed and comfortable.

'Fräulein Fielder, that was the name under which she was admitted to the hospital and which was used in the hospital records and, if I may, it would be easier to stay with that name ... '

'Yes do call her by that name - we know who you mean.'

'Fräulein Fielder was brought into the *Kantonsspital* at around 8 o'clock on the morning of Monday 17th February. She was unconscious, though there were no indications of any injury apart from bruising to her head which she appeared to have struck in falling, and she gave no sign of being in any danger. Her breathing and blood pressure were normal, for instance. She was accompanied by two policemen and a woman police officer who told me that there had been a shooting and that the Fräulein might be involved. She remained under police guard until they took her to the *Waaghof*, the prison, the following afternoon. I gave instructions to Nurse Anders for a blood sample to be drawn at once and sent to the path lab for testing. I also told her to take a urine sample as soon as the Fräulein regained consciousness, also for immediate testing. It must have been around 8.45 a.m. early on the Monday morning, that is when I gave the instructions to Nurse Anders. Unfortunately Nurse Anders is no longer here, she set off on a long tour of the Far East a couple of months ago.'

'I don't think that's a problem, Dr Schmidt, our concern is with the taking of the samples and what followed rather than with why they weren't taken earlier.'

'Good, I'm glad that's not a problem. As it happens she was a reliable nurse and there were good reasons for the delay, that morning we were very busy and at almost the same time as Fräulein Fielder was brought in we had two admissions with cardiac arrest.' He couldn't resist adding, 'Fräulein Fielder's police arrest was less trouble to us than the cardiac variety!' Sylvia joined in the laughter. Good the atmosphere was relaxing, people were beginning to feel more at ease. 'At about 2 o'clock on the Monday afternoon I saw Fräulein Fielder again - I had come from dealing with a man who had burned himself on the gas jets lighting his *clique's Fasnacht* lantern, burns to the arms and chest that is - and when I checked her papers I discovered that neither of the samples had been taken. She was by then conscious and displayed no serious after effects from whatever had caused her loss of consciousness. A brain scan that afternoon showed nothing untoward. But to get back to the blood and urine samples. The Fräulein consented to giving them and they were taken by Nurse Larat who is present today.'

'No world tour for you Nurse Larat?'

'Not this year, Fräulein Brunner, my boy friend wouldn't approve of me going off for months on end.'

Sylvia sensed Guillaume's annoyance at the banter. He might dislike it, not the sort of thing that appealed to Public Prosecutors when they were involved in interrogation, but it suited her.

'You'll have to take him with you some other year then. But getting back to the samples, perhaps you would tell us how they were taken and what you did with them. Go into all the detail, we lawyers are not too experienced at drawing blood despite what people say of us!' More laughter, this time not at all forced, and again she was conscious of Guillaume's restless disapproving personage beside her. An aloof individual except when he was trying to get a woman into bed with him: then he over compensated and became nauseatingly familiar, or so she had been told.

Nurse Larat gave a detailed account of how the samples were taken. The tubes had been labelled and she had personally taken them to the path-lab.

Then it was the turn of Frau Schneider, the head of the path-lab. The samples had been booked into the register and taken by her assistants for analysis. Reports had been prepared and sent to Dr Schmidt. Nothing untoward had been found save for the indication of very mild rheumatism. She paused for a moment and continued, 'Yesterday afternoon Dr Schmidt told me that your questions in court had given him cause to worry about the accuracy of our tests. May I assure you Fräulein Brunner that I too was concerned, very concerned. It is the job of the path-lab to give a speedy and accurate service to the hospital. Our disciplines and procedures are all directed to those ends.'

So they are all denying responsibility for any errors, was Sylvia's reaction.

But Frau Schneider continued, 'I was concerned and so I have spent the time from yesterday afternoon until 6 o'clock this morning making some checks on the off chance that I might be able to find an explanation. I believe that I have one. I asked myself the question, "If samples had been mixed up and then a report supplied for the wrong patient what would be the result?" We drew a blank with Fräulein Fielder's samples when the likely explanation for her condition was an overdose of drugs and when her pregnancy should have been apparent. Well, was there someone whose results indicated such conditions? I worked through the register and the reports for samples received that day and found nothing amiss. So I went back to the samples received the previous day and at 5.30 this morning I came across a report on tests on samples from Frau X - I hope you will respect medical confidentiality and allow me to identify her in that way.'

'I don't think that will be a problem, Frau Schneider.'

'The results for Frau X showed, firstly, that she had taken Flunitrazepam which is also known as Rohypnol – which is a bit easier to say - a sedative that's also known more familiarly as the 'date rape drug' and, secondly, that she was pregnant. After some persuasion I was able to see the medical records for Frau X. Dr Elling. one of Dr Schmidt's colleagues, had written "Nonsense" against the pregnancy finding - I am paraphrasing, his language was rather more colourful.' She laughed and the others with her, they all knew Dr Elling and guessed how he would have expressed himself. 'You see, the lady concerned was in her 70's and had had a hysterectomy some years ago. She was also suffering from a touch of rheumatism. While I cannot prove that the results were switched, inadvertently I must emphasise, the overwhelming probability is that they were and that Fräulein Fielder had taken a dose of Rohypnol, enough to render her unconscious for eight hours or more. The pregnancy result tallies of course with what Dr Schmidt tells me was said in court. Mix ups like this should never happen. On this occasion it has happened and I am very sorry for the problems caused.'

Her distress at the lapse by her laboratory was beginning to show and Sylvia stepped in quickly, 'Frau Schneider, we are very grateful to you for being so open with us. It's not easy to be as open as you have been today. You must carry out thousands of tests in your laboratory every year so I personally am not surprised that one has got mixed up in this way, though I can well understand and respect your concern about the matter as a professional. Even more we are grateful for your labours through the night to find what certainly seem to be the real results of the tests on Fräulein Fielder.' She turned to Herr Guillaume, it was time to get him on board. '*Herr Staatsanwald,* I wonder if you would be happy for Frau Schneider to work with me on a statement setting out what she has just told us. We could discuss it this afternoon at your office and then, assuming that you were happy with it, she could sign it later this afternoon and we could present it to the court tomorrow.'

He was helping himself to a cup of black coffee from a vacuum flask that had just been brought in. 'By all means,

I have a number of important matters to attend to this morning. The pressure on lawyers in the public service never seems to relent - it must be pleasant to be in private practice Fräulein Brunner, pleasant and profitable!'

'Satisfying, hard work and sometimes profitable, *Herr Staatsanwalt*. Don't forget that I too give service to the public and where someone needs help but cannot pay I don't turn them away.'

Sylvia turned to Dr Schmidt and his colleagues, 'You have our thanks and the thanks of the court for your assistance this morning. I hope that it will be clear in due time that you have helped to ensure that justice is done. We have been here on behalf of the court and it is therefore proper that you should not discuss what has been said in this room, either with colleagues or friends. Is it convenient for us to work on your statement now, Frau Schneider? Good, when the others have gone we will get to work on it.' She turned to Guillaume, 'I will call this afternoon at 2.15 if that is convenient.'

'I could manage lunch if you like the idea.'

'Sadly I don't. At 2.15 then.'

***

That afternoon Sylvia called at the Public Prosecutor's Office with Frau Schneider's statement. Herr Guillaume still showed signs of suffering from his over-indulgence the previous night and was happy to agree the statement as it stood. 'And where does it get you?' he asked.

'The presence of Rohypnol is clearly significant from the Defence's point of view.'

'So she took a sleeping potion? What difference does that make?'

'Or it was administered to her by someone else when she did not want it. You did hear the other name they used for the drug this morning?'

'What other name?'

' "The date rape drug", was what they said.'

'So the defence is going to be that she shot him when he tried to rape her? First of all she is Sleeping Beauty and now she's Red Riding Hood.'

'She's what, Herr Guillaume?'

'Red Riding Hood. Some English version that a much too clever writer's done, one of my kids likes it. Before the wolf can eat Red Riding Hood she whips a pistol from her *knickers* - that really appeals to my son - and shoots the beast. So ... your Little Red Spy shot her rapist wolf! You'll need much more evidence than traces of a drug commonly known as the "date rape drug". I'm sure that tons of it are consumed every year and that only the merest fraction of 1% is used to further the purposes of rapists. A man must be very inadequate to have to resort to such means, Fräulein Brunner. Don't you think so?'

'There seems to be no shortage of inadequate men in the world, Herr Guillaume, though most don't seem to realise their inadequacy.'

'You'll need far more evidence than that to get the murder charge dismissed, Fräulein Brunner. Rape? I think it's pure speculation on your part. I don't think the court will be over-impressed, she showed no sign of sexual assault. You need more than a botched path-lab report to make your case, much more.' He smiled contentedly, it would be good to have another murder conviction under his belt. It really would be pleasant to be a Court President. There were another 25 lawyers like him in the Public Prosecutor's Office, if he were a Court President that would give him more status in the social circles in which he moved. 'Find some more evidence, Fräulein Brunner! More evidence!'

'Perhaps I will, *Herr Staatsanwalt*, perhaps I will!'

***

The remand prison, the *Untersuchungsgefängnis* or *Waaghof* as it was also known, was in the same building as the Public Prosecutor's Office so Sylvia made her way to the prison to see her client.

'So, Elizabeth, we now have pretty good evidence that you were drugged. Have you ever taken Rohypnol? Ever had it prescribed or been given it to take by anybody/'

'Never. In fact I've never heard of it until now.'

'Good. Your London GP can testify to that? OK we really are on our way. Things are coming together very nicely, very nicely indeed. We've got strong evidence that you had Rohypnol in your system, by the way they call it the "date rape drug" and that tallies with what is on the tapes that your friend and rabbi Sam Kagan has available. He's ready to appear in court whenever his evidence is needed. I'm not sure how the Public Prosecutor will react to the appearance of a witness at this late stage but I can handle it. Sam's looked after that. First of all he signed me up as his lawyer, tying my hands with client confidentiality, and then he made sure that he didn't hand over the tapes but kept them under his control. So it's been in the court's interest that I've said nothing so far about him and his evidence. But now I can introduce Sam to the proceedings, he's given his consent. You know what the consequences are likely to be?'

'Yes, you've told me that the Swiss come down heavy on people who bug rooms and telephones and do the dirty work of foreign governments on their soil. To the extent that his evidence of events on that Sunday evening is effective on my behalf it will damn him in Swiss eyes.'

'*Gerade richtig*, Elizabeth! Quite right! But seemingly your friend is able to look after himself, or so he says, though he wouldn't enlighten me further on the subject.'

'And when do I see him, Sylvia. You say he's seen me arriving at court and I must have seen him, though without knowing who he was.' There was excitement in her voice.

'Not until he appears in court to give evidence, I'm afraid. It would lessen the value of his evidence if he had had contact with you beforehand. Sufficient time once they've released you.'

'And what about him, Sylvia. You don't think he'll end up on the inside with me free, do you?'

'He's sharp, very sharp. He knew just how to tie my hands and I wouldn't be surprised in the least if he did the same with the Swiss Police as well as Swiss Security. I have a gut feeling that it's going to work out for both of you.' As she said it she wondered what her feelings would have been if Sam hadn't been able to heal the breach with his brother David and recruit him to de-programme her after her disastrous experience of another therapy. David, her therapist and much, much more than that. She found herself crying.

"What's wrong, Sylvia?' There was a look of concern mixed with fear on Elizabeth's face.

'Wrong? Nothing's wrong, Elizabeth. I'm suddenly sure that it's all coming right - for you and Sam, for David and myself. It's been like a jigsaw and now we've reached the last few pieces and soon the picture will be complete. I've already said that the case is coming together, I'm intellectually convinced of that, but there's something more - call it instinct or gut feeling or whatever you like - a deep, deep feeling that it's all going to be all right for all of us. I've never felt anything like it and I've certainly never told a client anything like it. But how's little Olga today? Missing the attention she gets from the police at the court?'

'She's fine. It's as well she doesn't know the significance of where we live! But I'd like a word with you about Sonja, the girl who's in on a drugs charge. She's going down hill fast and you probably have some ideas on what we can do to get her some help.'

'The others here will miss you when you're out, Elizabeth.'

'After my experience here I've decided that I'll find a job working with prisoners, in jail or after they've come out. Most have never had a chance, I never realised that until I came here.'

'And the remainder, Elizabeth.'

'Some are fools, some are evil. But most have never really had a chance or any relationship worthy of the name.'

'So no experience is wasted?'

'None, Sylvia! None at all!' And she said it with genuine conviction.

Chapter 30

Tuesday 11th November 1997 – later in the afternoon

Later Sylvia and the Public Prosecutor provided the Court President with copies of Frau Schneider's statement. When he had read it he asked, 'And do we need to call Frau Schneider to testify in person?'

'Probably not,' was Sylvia's response as she had no wish to expose the lady to publicity over the mistake.

The Prosecutor was not so sure, 'We might need clarification from her. After all she says she is "almost certain" that the samples were switched. And it would, be helpful to have that clarified.'

The President fixed him with a stare, 'You need to know whether she is 95% certain or only 90% certain, I suppose?'

He didn't reply and Sylvia took her cue, 'Perhaps if we have her available on the premises but only call her if it's essential, Sir.'

'That seems sensible, you don't object to that *Herr Staatsanwalt*, do you?'

Herr Guillaume agreed.

The President continued, 'Now that it appears to be "almost certain" that there was this drug – Rohypnol – in the accused's system we will need testimony from an expert on its effects, a pharmacologist I presume. I believe it's made locally. *Fräulein Vertidiger* I suspect you have done some research on the matter.'

'On-line, Sir. Nothing that would carry weight with the Court. The makers are indeed local, Roche.'

'That's convenient, I know one of their Directors. I'll call him and see whether he can find a pharmacologist to testify to the Court. You are both happy with that? If we can have him with us first thing tomorrow morning that will be most convenient.'

Both signified their agreement and the meeting was about to adjourn when Sylvia dropped her bombshell.

'I have here a sworn statement from a late witness, Samuel Kagan. I believe it is of the highest importance. Would you be prepared to read it?'

The President agreed and the Prosecutor didn't dissent.

They read it in separate rooms in the Administrative Block of the court and then all three met together at 4.15 to consider the situation. They sat in the President's office, both the lawyers facing him across his desk.

'Well *Herr Staatsanwalt*, what is your view of this development. How do you suggest that we should proceed?'

'It's highly irregular, Herr President. This is the second time that *Verteidiger* Brunner has upset the smooth running of this hearing. We had our excursion to the *Kantonsspital* over the tests this morning ... '

The President interrupted him, 'And with good cause. *Advokat* Brunner had spotted a lacuna in the medical evidence and the "excursion to the *Kantonsspital*", as you have put it, was necessary to establish the truth of the situation and correct the evidence which was given in all good faith by Dr Schmidt but which, if uncorrected, would have misled the Court. We are grateful to you *Advokat* Brunner for your perceptiveness.'

'Thank you for saying so, Herr President. I believe that the evidence that Mr Kagan is prepared to give will also enable the Court to come nearer to the truth and come to the proper verdict in this case.'

The President looked at her over his glasses, 'But *Advokat* Brunner, it is very unusual for a witness to bargain with the Court in this way. He could have come forward, contacted *Herr Staatsanwald* many weeks, perhaps months, ago and given him an account of the events of the evening of Sunday 16th February. That would have been a more regular way in which to proceed.'

'But Mr Kagan's evidence was obtained by him in ways that are ... somewhat irregular. He is of the opinion, and I have advised him that he is not mistaken, that *Herr Staatsanwald's* Office or his colleagues in Bern will be more than a little interested in what he is volunteering to tell the Court. He does not wish to come here if his evidence is not going to be given consideration so far as the trial of my client, Lizaveta Feldman is concerned. He sees no point in hazarding himself if in doing so there will be no benefit to my client. For that reason he is not at the moment in Switzerland but waiting nearby for me to call him to let him know the Court's decision on whether it will hear him.'

The Court President had been making a note on a pad. He looked up, 'It seems to me *Advokat* Brunner that you are involved in a clash of loyalties. You appear to be representing two clients whose interests do not coincide but which are at odds with one another. Should you not, in the light if your responsibilities to Fräulein Feldman, have declined to act for Mr Kagan. It is difficult to see how you could possibly look after both their interests at once.'

Herr Guillaume was anxious to turn the knife, 'One has to exercise the greatest care in such matters. You could find yourself facing disciplinary proceedings.'

She smiled to herself. Her reply was well rehearsed, 'As soon as I found that there was a link between my two clients I realised that I was in a difficult position. But then, as now, Mr Kagan organised matters so as to tie my hands completely. He told me, as his lawyer, of the events in which he had been involved and I advised him accordingly. It was only then that he revealed that he had evidence relating to Fräulein Feldman's case. As his lawyer my lips were sealed about his bugging and surveillance activities and additionally he made sure that the original tapes would not be available unless and until he was able to testify before the Court in Fräulein Feldman's case. He was fully aware of the clash of interests but would not discharge me as his lawyer. From the point of view of the client that I am currently defending it was essential that I should do nothing to risk losing Mr Kagan who was the only witness to the killing, not that he saw it, rather he heard it and has it recorded on tape and available for the Court to hear ... that is if the Court is willing to admit him as a witness.'

'Blackmail is one way of describing it.' Guillaume was not in the best of moods. 'My Office has not been able to interrogate him and he wants to stroll into Court, testify, stroll out again and no doubt set off into the sunset. All this makes nonsense of the President's *Beweisliste* (evidence list).' He was losing his temper, his straightforward murder case was showing signs of falling apart in his hands and he was not pleased.

His lapse into the facetious did not please the Court President. '*Herr Staatsanwald*, perhaps you would tell me what sort of court this is?'

'A court of law, a criminal court, Herr President.'

"Yes, a court of law but more importantly a court of justice. And justice requires the best evidence available. All this might be rather untidy, and I would not be happy if it happened every week or even every other week, but it is exceptional and it is pertinent to the proceedings.'

'Fräulein Brunner we will hear your witness, Mr

Samuel Kagan. By the way do you know where he comes from? Are you able to tell me that?'

'From Brooklyn, Sir. Though I believe that he probably comes from a number of other places as well. He seems to have led a somewhat nomadic existence.'

'And his profession, if he has one?'

'He is a rabbi, Sir.'

'Eavesdropping on young women and their late night visitors seems to be an odd activity for a rabbi, Fräulein, but no doubt all will become clear with his telling of the tale. I will speak to my fellow *Richter*. The court will resume at 8.15 tomorrow morning and you may tell your witness that we will require him at about 10.30. *Herr Staatsanwalt*, have you any further observations.'

'No, Sir.'

'Fräulein Brunner?'

'No, Sir. I am most grateful and so is my client.'

The Court President again looked over his glasses, 'Which client, I wonder? Which client would you be referring to Fräulein?'

'Primarily to Fräulein Feldman, Herr President, but Mr Kagan will also be grateful, very grateful.' She held his gaze and smiled. Another hurdle cleared in the defence of Lizaveta Feldman.

As she left the administration building she breathed a prayer of thanksgiving for Sam and David Kagan - without their help she would still be the victim of her false memories. That help had liberated her. Never had she felt more able, more in command of her job as an *Advokat*. This was a complex and difficult case but she was fully up to the task. She was happy in herself and she was happy in her work.

Chapter 31

Wednesday 12th November 1997

The Court President referred to the previous day's evidence by Dr Schmidt and to the visit to the *Kantonsspital* by the *Advokaten* and then read Frau Schneider's sworn statement

'And so it appears that a mistake was made by the hospital path-lab over some of the samples and those originally thought to be Fräulein Feldman's were from another patient. And it is almost certain that if there had not been this error, it would have been clear that Fräulein Feldman was suffering from the effects of a drug by the name of Flunitrazepam or Rohypnol. I don't know whether Dr Schmidt wishes to qualify yesterday's evidence as a result of this revelation?'

'It is sufficient to say, Sir, that this information explains the condition of Fräulein Feldman on admission to the hospital. I believe that a pharmacologist is to give evidence and if you wish to call me after he has testified I will, of course, be pleased to assist. May I say now that the hospital apologises for the error that was made on a busy *Fasnacht* morning.'

'Thank you Dr Schmidt, although it was unfortunate that an error was made such things are inevitable from time to time. Now Dr Dieter Briner, who is a pharmacologist who has worked in the pharmaceutical industry and in academia at the University of Basel has come at very short notice to inform the Court on the drug and its effects, perhaps it will be easier if we refer to it as Rohypnol rather than by its more complicated name. Dr Briner, we look forward to your testimony.'

Dr Briner looked the part of the academic with a mop

of white hair and metal spectacle frames and he was clearly at home before an audience.

'Thank you Herr President. I will follow your suggestion and refer throughout to Rohypnol rather than Flunitrazepam. It was developed by Hoffmann-La Roche in 1963. It is also known somewhat emotively as the "date rape drug" and although it has been used in that way it has been used more often in drug facilitated robbery. I take it, Sir, that the Court is seeking a general overview of the drug and its effects rather than the sort of discourse I would give in the Lecture Room?'

The President confirmed that this was so.

'Rohypnol is highly potent and causes loss of consciousness and strong amnesia which are two reasons for its more emotive name. It has a long half-life of 18 to 26 hours, if it is given at night the effects persist through the next day. It creates an inability to remember events experienced while under its influence, so when given as a prelude to rape the victim may be unable to recall the assault clearly, the identity of the assailant or the events surrounding the assault. It can result in speech becoming slurred as well as in loss of balance.

'Rohypnol is available in many countries although the form in which it is supplied varies. As a disincentive to its use as a prelude to rape or robbery it is often hard-pressed to make it difficult to dissolve in a drink and also coloured to make its presence known. But on the other hand it is also available in some countries in a white, easily dissolved, tablet form and in solution in ampoule form. Either of these could be readily used to spike a drink without detection.

'It has just been given in evidence in Frau Schneider's submission that the concentration in Fräulein Feldman's blood was 30 micrograms per litre which is indicative of a substantial dose which would have resulted in considerable impairment. That's a general overview, Sir. I will of course be more than happy to answer questions.'

The President consulted the other Judges who shook their heads. 'Perhaps the *Advokaten* have questions? Does the *Staatsanwald* require further elucidation?'

'Only on the scale of the use of Rohypnol as the "date rape drug" - does it happen very frequently?'

'Less so than for robbery but it does happen.'

The President turned to Sylvia, '*Fräulein Verteidiger*, do you have a question?'

'Only one, Sir. Can Dr Briner tell us what is the effect of alcohol on the potency of Rohypnol?'

'If alcohol has been consumed it synergises the effect of the drug – that is the effect is more one of multiplication rather than the simple addition of the individual effects. The effect of the Rohypnol is considerably enhanced.'

'No other questions? Then thank you Dr Briner for helping us at such short notice. Perhaps you would wait until we break for coffee in case anything else emerges. Again thank you for your help. Now Dr Schmidt, perhaps you would care to come forward again. Thank you. Now in the light of Dr Briner's testimony and of your medical experience would you like to comment further on the condition of Fräulein Feldman or Elizabeth Fielder as she was known on admission to the *Kantonsspital* on that first morning of *Fasnacht*.'

'Thank you Sir. Knowing that the strong probability is that the Fräulein had been dosed with or had taken Rohypnol fully explains her dazed condition and the time it took for her to come round completely. The Court's procedures have solved what to me was a mystery and for that I am grateful.'

'And to you we are grateful, Dr Schmidt. Does anyone

have further questions? No? Then we will take a long coffee break and reconvene at 10.30 to hear the testimony of Mr Samuel Kagan.' And he led the Judges out of the Court. It was 9.35.

***

People did not want to go far and were anxious not to lose their seats in the public area. Elizabeth tried to concentrate on feeding her daughter and Sylvia, walking to and fro, was uncharacteristically edgy. At 10.20 she opened the file with her notes of the questions for Sam and tried to read through them but nothing went in, though that really didn't matter as she knew them by heart. She had asked one of the police officers to let her know when Sam arrived. He had promised to be there at 10.15 and the absence of a message was getting to her - what if he didn't turn up? It wouldn't be her fault but it would look bad for her and wouldn't improve her reputation with the Judges. More importantly it would be bad for Elizabeth, worse for her than if Sam had never been mentioned as a potential witness. Sylvia wished it were the same time the next day, with all this over and behind her. Elizabeth had been watching her, 'You're worried aren't you, Sylvia? You're beginning to wonder if Sam's going to turn up.'

'I'll be a lot happier when I know he's here, Elizabeth. But I trust him - in the months I've known him he's never given me any reason to think that he's less than 100% reliable.'

'Good. From my 24 hours of knowing him, a lifetime away in February, I came to the same conclusion. He'll be here come hell or high water.'

A police officer called them to return to the Court and

they made their way upstairs after Elizabeth had put the baby back into its cot under the friendly eye of a woman officer from the prison.

In Court there was the stillness of expectation. Word had somehow got around that the surprise witness had yet to arrive and people were wondering whether he had decided at the last minute not to appear. The *Staatsanwalt* sat trying to hide the smirk that was beginning to build up. OK she had been right about the medical evidence but now she stood a good chance of looking a fool in this very public place. He could well understand Kagan having second thoughts about coming here to incriminate himself. He hoped that he had taken off for the safety of Brooklyn or wherever he had more recently made his home.

The Judges entered, took their seats and the President looked towards Sylvia. '*Fräulein Verteidiger,* it appears that your special witness has not arrived. Have you received any message of explanation from him?'

'I have heard nothing Herr President. I apologise for this happening but from what both I and my client know of Mr Kagan we are sure that he must have been unavoidably delayed. I can only ask that the Court be prepared to wait a little longer for his arrival. I do have a mobile telephone number and if I may be permitted to do so I will try to make contact.'

'What do you have to say *Herr Staatsanwalt*? Do you have an opinion on the matter?'

He took his time, looking and sounding suitably solemn, 'Herr President. You will know that I raised no strong objection to the somewhat irregular turn of events which added Mr Kagan to the list of witnesses, as

Fräulein Verteidiger's deus ex machina. This is after all a Court of justice and additional evidence was offered. It would have been improper and unbecoming for me to have opposed the request but now that Mr Kagan has chosen not to appear perhaps the Court would see it right to proceed to hearing argument from Fräulein Brunner and myself on the matters of culpability and sentence.'

The President consulted his colleagues. 'We will remain on the premises until the lunch adjournment at 12.30 and if Mr Kagan is not here by 2.30 we will resume and deal with the matters to which *Herr Staatsanwalt* has just alluded.' He was in the process of rising from his chair when a police office entered the Court and passed a piece of paper to the President. He took his spectacles from his breast pocket and read the note. 'It appears that Mr Kagan has arrived but requires a few minutes to prepare for his appearance here. The Court will adjourn for ten minutes.'

Elizabeth and Sylvia exchanged looks of relief. 'Thank God we were right about him, Elizabeth.'

'Perhaps it should be, thank God he's lived up to our expectations. I'll be glad when today's over, I really will!'

The *Staatsanwalt* could not disguise his annoyance at Sam's arrival and muttered to a colleague, 'We could have done without the time wasting. Never mind, let our friends from Bern know that Kagan's arrived, they're sure to be pleased that they can have a word or two with him.'

***

The Judges had taken their seats and the President nodded to the police officer at the door. Sam Kagan was shown to a seat facing the President. To the horror of Elizabeth and Sylvia he was a mess, his suit covered in dirt. He stood before the President in a medium gray suit, the jacket and trousers stained with mud. There were blood marks on the collar of his white shirt and on the pale blue tie. His hair and beard though had been combed and he wore a scull cap. He looked more like someone who slept rough than the vital witness they were expecting. Neither of the women had ever seen him looking other than immaculate, whether formally or casually dressed he had always looked just right.

'You are Mr Samuel Kagan of Crown Heights, Brooklyn?'

'Yes, Sir.'

'And your occupation?'

'I'm a rabbi, Sir.'

A thrill of excitement could be sensed in the Court, it wasn't everyday that a tattered American rabbi came into a Basel court to testify in a murder case. This would make good copy for the newspapers and the German magazines.

He continued. 'May I first apologise to the Court for any seeming discourtesy due to my late arrival and my appearance. On my way here I was involved in a road accident and so was unable to attend at the proper time. Once again I offer my sincere apologies to the Court.'

'Mr Kagan. I can assure you that your apologies are accepted. Are you sure that you are in a fit state to give evidence. If necessary the Court could adjourn to this afternoon to give you time to recover from your experiences of this morning.'

'Thank you, Sir, but that won't be necessary. I'm ready to testify to the Court.'

'*Herr Staatsanwalt*, you wish to make an observation?'

'Yes, Herr President. I too trust that Mr Kagan is in a fit state to give his evidence to the Court. One other matter, please?'

'Yes, *Herr Staatsanwalt*?'

'I wish to ask that Mr Kagan be put on oath before he begins to give evidence.'

'*Fräulein Verteidiger*, what do you say to that request.'

'The defence is happy for the Court to proceed in whatever manner it considers appropriate.'

'And you Mr Kagan, what do you think about the matter?'

'I am more than willing to give oath if the Court considers it appropriate that I should do so. Whether on oath or otherwise I will be telling the whole unvarnished truth, subject only to this caveat - that there are likely to be some questions that I will not be at liberty to answer, they concern my own activities and are not directly relevant to the matters before the Court. To such questions I will have to decline to reply, in the USA I would be invoking the Fifth Amendment and I assume that you have some similar provision in Swiss law.'

'On oath then Mr Kagan. We understand what you say regarding self incrimination - your position in Swiss law is broadly similar to that in the USA. You have told us that you are a rabbi and so you would wish to swear on ... '

'On the Tanach, the Hebrew Bible ... the Old Testament as you would probably call it, Sir.' The Court's *Gerichtschreiber* (Secretary) was ready for the request and took the book to Sam. He rose from his seat, took the book reverently in his right hand and repeated the words of the oath from the card that the *Gerichtschreiber* held before him. He handed the book back and there was total silence. Many of those there had the distinct impression that as Sam had taken the book and begun to speak he had grown in physical stature before their eyes. The deep voice, rich and melodious, in which he took the oath was partly responsible for the impression he created. Sam had concentrated on the words of the oath but at the same time there was in his mind the memory of the relief panel on the Warsaw Ghetto Rising Memorial. *There* the rabbi had held the Torah scrolls, accompanied by his flock, prominent among whom had been a pregnant woman. *Here* he, Sam Kagan, held the Tanach and his flock of one, no longer pregnant but recently delivered of her daughter, sat behind him. His evidence was likely to be crucial in deciding the question of her liberty or imprisonment.

The President seemed unwilling to break the silence but eventually he got matters on the move with the comment, 'Now, Mr Kagan, I wish to take you through a sworn statement that you have provided for the Court. Incidentally how would you prefer to be addressed, as Rabbi Kagan or as Mr Kagan?'

'Mr Kagan will be fine, Sir'

'Then, Mr Kagan, I will read through the whole of your statement to the Court and afterwards put some questions to you, probably after we have heard the tapes. My colleagues may also wish to put questions and of course the prosecution and defence will also wish to do so. One preliminary point though - do you have with you the audio tapes to which you refer in the statement?'

'Yes, Sir, they are in my briefcase.' He opened it and placed them on the desk before him.

'There are three tapes, Mr Kagan?'

'Yes, three, Sir. Do you wish to have them now?'

The President looked towards a technician who had been sitting to one side of the Court. 'Perhaps you would take the tapes Herr Weiss and when the time comes play them to the Court. They fit the equipment that you have brought?'

The technician checked the tapes. 'Standard audio tapes, Sir. There shouldn't be any problem and they are numbered one to three. They should be fine.' He put the first into the player and sat down.

Sam removed some papers from his briefcase, 'I have transcripts of the tapes for you and your colleagues and for the Prosecutor together with a translation into German. They should save you having to make notes.' The *Gerichtschreiber* took the transcripts and handed them round.

The *Staatsanwalt* couldn't resist the chance for a dig, 'And *Fräulein Verteidiger* has had access to her copy for weeks or, perhaps, months.'

'And you have your copy now Herr Guillaume. The Court will ensure that you have enough time to master the material. We all know that you are very quick to master *quite* complicated facts.' The Prosecutor had caught the inflection in the President's voice but didn't let his annoyance show. The President had been a little nettled by his intervention, Herr Guillaume didn't seem to know when to keep his mouth shut. And on the previous day the President had first heard from a colleague of Herr Guillaume's presumption - he saw himself as a Court President!

The President began to read:

"I am Rabbi Samuel Kagan of Eastern Parkway, Brooklyn, New York, USA and I state on oath that this is a true statement of events as I recollect them.

"During 1996 and 1997 I was concerned with others in an operation which involved surveillance by electronic and other means of the accused - Elizabeth Fielder, known to the Court as Lizaveta Feldman - and the deceased - Eugene Preston but also known as Vladimir. For almost all of this period the surveillance of these two persons was carried out in London, England. Electronic listening devices - "bugs" as they are commonly known - were placed in the premises occupied by them and their telephones. In February they came to Basel, Switzerland and I came as well. Their hotel rooms and telephones were fitted by a colleague with electronic listening devices whose output was received and recorded.

"I have in my possession some of the taped recordings of what was picked up by the listening equipment and received by myself and my colleagues both in England and here in Switzerland."

The President paused and looked at Sam, 'Mr Kagan, you referred earlier to avoiding incriminating yourself by what you said in this Court. Have you received legal advice on this statement. That is independent legal advice from someone unconnected with the defendant? By that, of course, I mean to show no disrespect to the ethics of *Advokat* Brunner but I wish to be sure that you fully understand the danger in which this statement may place you.'

'I have been fully and independently advised, Sir. I am well aware of the problems that I may be creating for myself and quite prepared to accept the personal consequences of making this statement and appearing in this Court. I am here to assist in seeing that justice is done. The personal consequences are another matter. I am grateful to you for showing concern in the way you have just done.'

'Thank you Mr Kagan. I would simply remark that the circumstances of your testimony are unusual, indeed unique in my experience and also for my colleagues I expect.' He looked to the left and right and they responded in the affirmative with a vigorous nodding of heads.

'So to continue from your sworn statement:

"The three tapes that I am making available to the Court are marked "Samuel Kagan Exhibits 1 to 3". They are the original recordings and not copies and they have not been edited or doctored in any way whatsoever. They have been in my personal custody or under lock and key throughout the period from their being made until now.

"The Court will find of particular interest recordings of the events that took place in the accused's room at the Hotel International on the evening of Sunday 16 February 1997. The first tape includes a telephone conversation between Fräulein Fielder and Peter Lewis her friend and employer. It is included by way of contrast with the second tape to convey to the Court something of her mood, if that is the appropriate word, earlier that evening. The second recording includes a conversation between the accused, known to me as Elizabeth Fielder and Eugene Preston, also known as Vladimir, and culminates with the shooting of the deceased.

"The recording on the evening of 16 February 1997 is, I believe, evidence that the deceased attempted to rape Elizabeth after administering a drug to her. I believe that the shooting was a direct result of those criminal acts by the deceased but that is for Elizabeth Fielder's defender to bring out in her argument before the Court.

"There is also tape 3, a recording of a telephone call after events in England some months earlier when Eugene Preston attempted to rape the defendant, but on that occasion without the benefit of drugs. You will hear that on that occasion she was more than able to defend herself and send a rather painful Eugene Preston back to his London apartment. Once again it will be for *Advokat* Brunner to draw out for you the significance of that event.

"I have referred to the accused as Elizabeth Fielder

because that was how I knew her both throughout long months of surveillance and personally over a period of a little more than 24 hours."

The President looked up from the statement on the desk before him. He looked first at Sam and then at Elizabeth, cleared his throat and continued:

"That 24 hour period began on Saturday 15 February when we shared a table for dinner at the Hotel International. The restaurant was extremely busy, no doubt with visitors who were in Basel for the *Fasnacht* carnival on the Monday, and I had the audacity, indeed the impertinence, to suggest to a waiter that he ask the Fräulein if I could share the table with her. He did so and to my satisfaction she agreed. When, for nearly a whole year, you have watched someone from the distance and listened to their conversations, the music they play and the TV programmes they watch, there comes an almost irresistible urge to make their acquaintance. The atmosphere of pre-carnival Basel simply encouraged the venture.

"The meal proved to be a very enjoyable and stimulating occasion and we agreed to take the train to the Berner Oberland the next day, that is on the Sunday morning. We spent the day in glorious weather on the Rigi and returned to Basel and had dinner at *Die Drei Könige*. We parted in the bar of the Hotel International and later that evening I heard, by means of the electronic listening equipment, the events that are the immediate concern of this Court. I was deeply shocked by the turn of events.

"In concluding I wish to clarify a number of issues:

1. The relationship between Elizabeth Fielder and myself was from my point of view, and I can only speak for myself, one of friendship. We were not and we never

have been lovers. She has a child but I am not the father of that child.

2. The activities in which I have been involved here in Switzerland and in England have in no way been directed at undermining the security or commercial interests of Switzerland or England. They targeted the security agency of another power entirely.

3. I am no longer in the employment of the organisation I served when the recordings were made. I am not here on their account or on behalf of anyone else. Neither am I funded by them. I am here in a purely personal capacity, drawn by my friendship for Elizabeth Fielder and my concern that the Court should be in possession of all the facts of the case so that justice should be done to her and her baby daughter."

The President looked up, 'It is signed by Mr Kagan and sworn before a notary here in Basel Stadt. Perhaps you would confirm that this is your signature Mr Kagan?'

Sam stood and walked to the President's desk. Taking the statement he looked and nodded, 'Yes this is my signature and all that you have read to the Court is the truth, Sir.' He returned to his seat and waited for the President to proceed.

'Well it's perhaps a good time for the Court to adjourn for lunch. When we reassemble at 2.30 we will hear the tapes and then I will begin the questioning of Mr Kagan. If the *Gerichtschreiber* would take charge of the tapes we will adjourn.'

As they were about to rise a police inspector had a word with the President who called the Court back into session. 'It came as a surprise to me, as I am sure it must have done to all of you when Mr Kagan arrived in such a tattered state. He explained to you that he had been involved in a road accident. Inspector Sturmer has just told me something of what happened and I have asked him to address the Court so that the matter may be on record. Inspector, perhaps you would like to speak from where the *Staatsanwalt* normally addresses the Court.

The Inspector walked to the Prosecutor's desk, faced the President and began, 'At 9.50 this morning I was called to an accident in the *Marktplatz*, opposite the *Rathaus*. A young woman had been hit by a tram as she had tried to cross the road and, despite the tram's equipment - I don't know the technical term but a "cow catcher" is what they would call it in the USA - to prevent her being run over by the wheels, she had been badly injured. Beside the young woman there was a man under the tram, Mr Kagan who is sitting over there. I was told that he had been passing the scene and had immediately dived under the tram to help. He was there for about half an hour while heavy lifting gear was brought in to free the young woman. He stayed with her and was able to stem her bleeding from a most dangerous wound. The ambulance crew told me afterwards that if he hadn't gone straight to her she would not have survived more than a couple of minutes. As it is she is expected to recover. Not only was Mr Kagan fully competent in the first aid he gave, but he stayed with her and helped the ambulance crew to administer a pain killing injection. Once the young woman had been removed to the *Kantonsspital* I spoke to Mr Kagan and he told me he was due here at 10.30. So I drove him to Court and have stayed as I felt I should be able to explain his lateness and commend him to you, Sir.'

The newspaper reporters had been writing furiously, here was a story within a story, they'd been lucky to be assigned to this one!

'Mr Kagan, we have heard the Inspector's account

with admiration, not just for your bravery and sense of public duty but also for your competence in dealing with the young woman's potentially lethal wounds. We recognise that you are a minister of religion, it is good to see that your religion is practical and not merely a matter of words, important as words are to law and religion. May I ask you where you acquired your medical skills?'

'Thank you, Sir, but I would really have preferred this not to have been publicised in this way. There was an accident and I did what I could. To have saved a life is its own reward, "He who saves one life saves, as it were, the whole world", as Jewish sages have taught. My medical skills were gained in the forces.'

'Well the US forces trained you well.'

Sam paused a moment, 'Not the US forces Sir - the IDF, the Israel Defence Forces. I served in the Golani Brigade.' And there came back to him, with the vividness of yesterday, an experience in the Lebanon when the armoured personnel carrier he commanded had been destroyed by a Hezbollah bomb at the roadside and he had saved his sergeant's life, staunching his profuse bleeding while they lay alongside the wrecked vehicle sheltering from hostile small arms fire and praying that another bomb was not about to be detonated. Giving aid beneath a Basel tram was almost a picnic by comparison.

'Then, Rabbi Kagan, the Golani Brigade and your seminary - *yeshiva*, is it? - equipped you well. What you did has been entered on the Court record and I hope that you will receive acknowledgement from the proper authorities. May I warn any reporters present that, however much you might wish to speak with Mr Kagan and however much your editors might wish it, you must on no account do so: he is a vital witness and you are forbidden to contact him. Neither is he to be photographed. If these instructions are infringed there will be the most serious consequences for those concerned. The Court will rise.'

The Judges filed out and Sam turned to make his way from the Court. They had found him a room in the administrative block for the break and he would eat there on his own. His eyes met Elizabeth's with a look of recognition and they smiled at one another. Something within each of them confirmed that what they had felt for one another way back in February had not been a passing emotion: they knew they were kindred souls. They could not meet now, it would not be right for accused and witness to meet. But it could not be long before they were together. Each wondered about the circumstances in which the meeting would take place.

Sylvia guided Elizabeth from the Court and they went downstairs accompanied by two of the police officers. Elizabeth had been unable to speak and when they were in the room by the cells her tears began to flow. 'Thanks for getting my rabbi here, Sylvia. He's everything I remembered and much, much more besides ... '

The *Staatsanwalt's* colleague looked up from tidying his papers, 'Quite a morning Herr Guillaume! That rabbi's an interesting fellow.'

'Too damn interesting. He's got them eating out of his hand. I'm going to have to be very careful how I question the *Hero of the Marktplatz*! It should have been easy, very easy to discredit him. A spy or some sort of snooper who's broken a list of laws as long as your arm and who ought to be behind bars - the sort of shady foreigner who should attract neither sympathy nor credence in this Court. Instead they'll trust him and his evidence. Still I won't give up without a fight!'

'You're going to play the Russian *Mafiya* card, then?'

'It might just work, not with the President but it might swing the Vice-President. Frau Berman's strong on law and order. If we can sell the idea of the Russian *Mafiya* fighting it out in our city she might give us a satisfactory verdict.'

'And the rabbi, what's his future?'

'You know that's in the hands of our colleagues in Bern. They'll be having a word with the fellow very soon.'

***

At a little after 2.30 the President asked Herr Weiss to play the first of the tapes. Sylvia had made sure that Jakob Gold was looking after Peter Lewis and keeping him well away from the Court and the distress that hearing the tapes would have caused him. There was an intent silence as Herr Weiss took them from the *Gerichtschreiber* and placed the first into the player. The President looked at Sam, 'Would you please tell the Court what they are about to hear.'

'The first tape is of a telephone call made from her room at the Hotel Continental by Elizabeth Fielder to her partner with whom she lived in London, Peter Lewis who was also her employer – he was staying elsewhere in Basel for the duration of their visit. The date is Sunday 16 February 1997 and the time 10.35 p.m. As I told the Court this morning, I am the person who had dinner with Fräulein Fielder on the Saturday evening and spent the Sunday with her. In the second recording she refers to me as Sam Charles as that, I am afraid, is how I introduced myself to her.'

The technician switched on the player.

The sound of light classical music could be heard with occasional movements in the room. Then came the sound of a number being dialled on the telephone and there followed a light-hearted conversation between the two. The woman spoke of the day she had spent in the Alps, enthused about the air and the scenery. She was clearly relaxed and happy, at ease with herself and the world. The man was a little less so and the call ended with them confirming an arrangement to meet the next evening and assurances of their love for one another. The tape continued with light classical music after the telephone call.

When Sam and Sylvia had played and discussed the tapes they had wondered whether to include this one among those to be produced to the Court. David Kagan had been asked for his opinion and he had had no doubts: the tape portrayed a lively young woman in a relaxed and happy mood. It would contrast strongly with the dark turn of events only a little later that evening and indicate that something very serious must have taken place during Vladimir's visit to force such a drastic and sudden change.

Sam addressed the President, 'The remainder of this tape is just like you are hearing at the moment. Unless the Court wishes to continue with it I would suggest that we move on to the second tape.'

The technician had stopped the tape and the President consulted his fellow judges and then the lawyers, 'We agree - if *Herr Staatsanwalt* wishes to listen to the remainder of the tape after the Court has risen he is at liberty to do so. I have to say that the quality of the sound is first rate Mr Kagan, though that does not make the bugging and recording any less reprehensible! And now Mr Kagan perhaps you would introduce the second tape?'

'It begins at 10.55 p.m. on the evening of Sunday 16 February 1997. We will hear Eugene Preston – as he is called throughout the conversation apart from the defendant's final words after the shooting - arrive in the room, their conversation and the events leading up to the killing. I am afraid that Mr Preston wasn't the only one to appear under a false name that evening! The President and a couple of the other judges smiled.'

The technician had removed the first tape and inserted the second.

After about two minutes of light music there was a knock on the door:

A woman's voice, 'Who's there?'

The door was unlocked and opened.

The woman again, 'Well, good evening Eugene.'

No response but the sounds of the door closing and of movement in the room

A man's voice, 'Pleasant enough but not up to the quality of your work.'

'Standard sort of thing for an international hotel. The workmanship is good but the choice of fabrics and paper lacks imagination, I feel. I'm pleased that you agree - too much gold in evidence, I think'. A pause, 'Like a drink?'

'You haven't a Calvados, I suppose?'

'As a matter of fact I do.' Movement and the sound of a drawer being opened. 'I brought some with me knowing that you liked it.'

'Well done Elizabeth, you do know how to look after a fellow ... in some ways.'

The sounds of a glass being placed on a surface and more movement in the room

'Thanks, can I get *you* something?'

'An orange juice would do fine, please.'

The sounds of a refrigerated drinks cabinet being opened and of a drink being poured.

The man's voice with a hint of anger, 'Where have you been all day?'

The woman's quiet response, 'I might ask the same question of you about yesterday evening and this morning, but I won't.'

His angry response, 'You might, but you bloody well won't. I'm in charge and I *would* like to know where you have been all day.'

'That's easy, I met Sam Charles, a rather personable American newspaper reporter at dinner last night and we spent today in the Alps. We came back to this hotel, changed in our own rooms, had dinner at the *Drei Könige* and said goodnight in the bar here, at which point we went to our respective rooms. It was all very chaste and, for that reason, very pleasant. He's gone to Hamburg on the night sleeper and that's that. And as for not letting you know that I was going out for the day, the fact is that I couldn't make contact with you before I went out after breakfast, no more than I was able to find you last night - when you were probably amusing yourself.'

His angry response, 'Don't be so dammed impertinent. This morning I was meeting another member of our team, a technical expert, and for the rest of the time I was following up a lead.'

'Not chasing a bitch in heat?'

'A bitch in heat is better than a frigid bitch! ... Sorry that was uncalled for ... but unlike you I've had a very difficult day, but I won't bore you with all the details.'

There was a lull in the conversation, someone left the room presumably for the bathroom and then returned.

'Just what do you think you were doing by going off for the day without a word, you might have been involved in an accident and anyway who was the fellow who picked you up?'

She responded angrily, 'Picked me up? I don't like the expression, I'm not a tart looking for customers. Let me tell you again what happened! At dinner last night I met an American to whom I took an immediate liking, no nothing sexual, he was clearly good company and when he offered to go with me to the Alps, by train I would stress - not in his car - I was pleased to accept. I had no wish to spend the day here just waiting for the action to begin tomorrow - whatever it might be that you've planned. As it turned out I was right in my assessment of him ... we had a splendid day out and the weather was simply glorious ... and he made no attempt to get me into bed with him. He was attractive and at the same time a complete gentleman, someone who respects women and doesn't take them for playthings!'

'He might have been from Swiss Security or the CIA!'

There was a slight muttering in the Court as people's suspicions were confirmed.

She responded with a cutting retort, 'And pigs might fly - he wasn't one of *your* sort, I've told you that he was a *gentleman*!'

A pause.

'You *are* sure that you know what to do tomorrow?'

'Really, Eugene I'm not a novice and neither am I stupid. We've been through it all often enough. I'm to be available if needed but otherwise keep out of the way. I'll have the mobile 'phones in my handbag so I'll always be in touch if you need me. You've chosen to keep me out of your plans and I am very happy with that. Ask once more and I'll take the first 'plane to London and leave you to

your own devices!'

A pause in the conversation.

She changed the subject, 'How old are your children, Eugene?'

'Evgeny is twelve and Sera ten.' Another pause while he evidently located some photographs. 'These are some recent shots of them.'

A sympathetic response from the woman, 'They're fine kids ... you should be proud of them ... and you're not keen to go back home, I don't understand it.'

'The kids are fine, it's my wife who's the problem, you should know that, I've told you often enough! We just don't get on together any more and the kids, fine as they are, take her side. Besides, it isn't fair on them to make them take my side – they're on her side already and I'm not wanting to bring conflict into their lives.'

'They need a father!'

'I'm fully aware of that but I would bring more problems than benefits you know!'

There was a silence, the man seemed to be playing for time.

He spoke, 'I'll just make a visit to your bathroom.'

So Elizabeth had been the first to go there some minutes earlier. Then the sound of his return and the resumption of the conversation.

'Besides I'd rather be away from Moscow - life in the West is to my taste, especially when I can feel that I'm exploiting it for the benefit of our Motherland. It's the only job for which I've been trained. It's good to feel that you can enjoy life and at the same time be of service to your country.'

'You'll have to go back home for good one day!'

A momentary pause and then an angry, 'I was given instructions today that we are *both* to return to Moscow immediately this operation is completed.'

Another momentary silence and then a calm response from Elizabeth, 'I don't know what they'll have for me to do next. What about you? Will they have another ... job in the West that's to your liking or will they have ... a desk job waiting in Moscow?' Though calm her speech had slowed and was becoming slurred.

Sam broke in, 'It would be of help, Sir, if we could listen to Fräulein Fielder's response once again and hear how she is beginning to slur her words.' The President nodded to the technician who stopped the tape, rewound it a short way and restarted it.

'I don't know what they'll have for me to do next. What about you? Will they have another ... job in the West that's to your liking or will they have ... a desk job waiting in Moscow?' There could be no doubt about what Sam had just pointed out.

A short pause and then a loud man's voice full of tension and pent up anger, 'Please, Elizabeth, I want you in bed ... I want you now, remember the good times we had',

Elizabeth's response, even more slurred than before, 'Just a moment ... ' clearly she was struggling to put words together, 'I must get ... my lipstick.' Then her voice suddenly took on a note of clarity and determination, 'You're not having me! You've doped my drink! You want to rape me! You want to abduct me!'

'No, Elizabeth don't!'

The sound of a scuffle, an attempt to turn a door handle, then the muffled sound of what must have been a firearm – strange that something so deadly should make so little noise!

Her cry, 'Oh, Vladimir why?'

A slight bump, followed by another as something

struck a wardrobe or another piece of furniture.

Apart from a Strauss waltz playing quietly on the radio, there was silence.

The President caught Sam's eye. He nodded and the technician was told to stop the tape. The Court was totally and utterly silent. Silent apart from Elizabeth's quiet sobbing.

Sylvia rose, 'Herr President, my client has not heard this recording of what took place that February night until now. One does not have to guess at the emotional effect it has had on her ... '

The President stopped her, 'I fully understand *Advokat* Brunner. The Court will adjourn for half an hour or longer if that is required . Does your client need to have the services of a doctor?'

'I had anticipated Lizaveta's reaction and have waiting outside a friend of mine who specialises in traumatic problems. If you are agreeable to him attending to her ... '

'Yes that sounds entirely reasonable and appropriate.'

'There is one thing however, Herr President and if I did not mention it now I would be rightly accused of misleading the Court, the consultant in question is Mr David Kagan, who is the brother of Mr Samuel Kagan. He is not a witness in the trial.'

'*Herr Staatsanwalt*. Do you have any representations to make on the matter?' Somehow the President managed to convey with a look in the Prosecutor's direction that an objection would not be well received.'

'If the Court deems it appropriate I do not object.

'The Court does indeed deem it appropriate and will rise for half an hour. When we return, and provided that Fräulein Feldman is in a suitable state, we will hear the third tape. Mr David Kagan should be asked to sit with the Fräulein for the remainder of the trial, that is if he is available to do so.'

***

The Court resumed with Elizabeth sitting between David and Sylvia. The last recording was not likely to be so traumatic for Elizabeth though it would disturb her. Again Sam was asked by the Court President to introduce the recording.

'It is of events in the Spring of 1996, on Wednesday 10 April to be precise. The recording is of a telephone conversation between Elizabeth Fielder, or Lizaveta Feldman as this court knows her, and Vladimir, the deceased then known as Eugene Preston, at her apartment in West Hampstead, London, England. There had evidently been an encounter earlier that evening. If we could hear the tape, please.

There was the sound of a telephone ringing. There was evidently no hurry to take the call and it was left to ring for a full half minute. When the woman did reply all she said was, 'Yes.'

'It's me. I'm back home. I'm sorry about what happened earlier, I promise it won't happen again.' His voice had a plaintive ring about it.

Elizabeth took her time before replying, 'Well you asked for it, didn't you?' She paused, a note of concern creeping into her voice, 'You are all right Eugene, aren't you?'

'Just about. I had to crawl into my apartment and lie on the floor for twenty minutes after the driver helped me in ... he wanted to take me to the hospital, you know. My shoulder and other parts ache but generally I'm in working order. I'm OK now and about to hit the hay. ... I just wanted to say sorry before I did so.'

'Thanks for the apology. I hope that there's no permanent damage to your more tender parts. But do remember that if you attempt to rape me again I will defend myself as vigorously as I did tonight. I know that we had a good time together in California, I'll treasure the memories - you know that - but it's in the past. I don't want a relationship that is going nowhere. If I have another relationship I want it to last and to be official. You can't offer that with your wife and kids. That's the end of the matter. Our relationship from now on is purely that of colleagues and ... I hope ... friends.'

'Good night then.'

'Goodnight, Eugene. And take care in future.'

She put the receiver down and it was just possible for the Court to hear her postscript to the conversation, 'Georgian bastard!'

'That's all, Sir. We've heard all the tapes now.'

'Thank you Mr Kagan. Now I have some questions to put to you and so, I expect, have my colleagues as well as the *Staatsanwalt* and the *Verteidiger*.'

'I had expected that, Sir, though it is likely that I will be unable to reply to some of the more obvious ones.'

'Let's try anyway, Mr Kagan. Can you tell me the identity of your employers? From the sophistication of your surveillance of Fräulein Feldman and her colleague it is clear that you weren't concerned in some amateur action but in a highly organised and professional operation. Were you working for a security service?'

There was a momentary pause before Sam replied, 'I was, Sir.'

'And can you divulge its identity?'

'No Sir. I'm not free to do that.'

'But one might hazard a guess - say the CIA or Mossad.'

'But I wouldn't be free to comment. I must repeat however what I said at the beginning of my testimony: that my activities here in Switzerland and in England have in no way been directed at undermining the security or commercial interests of Switzerland or England. They targeted the security agency of another power entirely. I am aware that I may have infringed the Swiss legal code and I am ready to face the consequences.'

'Very well Mr Kagan, the question and your reply are now on record.'

'Yes, sir.'

'In your sworn statement you have given an address in Brooklyn. Is that your current address.'

'It is one of my current addresses, Sir. I travel a good deal and my other main address is at a kibbutz in Israel, I am happy to give you the address in confidence but would prefer, for security reasons - that is for reasons of the personal safety of myself and my colleagues who work there in completely ordinary occupations - I would prefer not to have to give the address in open court.'

The President consulted his colleagues. 'If you would let me have the address in writing, Mr Kagan.'

Sam wrote on a piece of paper, rose from his seat and handed it to the President who nodded and Sam returned to his seat.

'Thank you, Mr Kagan. Perhaps we could turn our attention to the period of twenty four hours when your acquaintance with Fräulein Feldman was personal and direct rather than mediated electronically. How would you describe her manner, her demeanour, during that time?'

'Miss Feldman was throughout that time calm and relaxed. She was very good company, indeed she was the best of company, enjoying whatever she was doing - whether it was having dinner in the restaurants of the Hotel International and *Die Drei Könige* or finding wonder in the beauty of the panorama of the Alps from the summit of the Rigi. It was for me a memorable time when my own enjoyment was immeasurably enhanced by her delight at everything.' He paused, 'Miss Feldman radiated joy and happiness though there were moments when there was a short lived change of mood, like a cloud casting a momentary shadow over a landscape. She was a woman with a great delight in life but with concerns that pierced the surface now and then.' David had suggested to him that he should underline this - it would present a more realistic picture that the judges were likely to accept and give the lead in for Sylvia to speak of Elizabeth's pregnancy and the disintegrating relationship with Peter Lewis.

'Was there anything about the Fräulein's manner that suggested a woman planning murder?'

'Nothing whatsoever. When I heard the events of that Sunday evening from the tape I was absolutely astounded. It was like being hit by a thunderbolt. We had stood looking out from the Rigi, we had thrown snowballs at one another, we had enjoyed a fine dinner with equally fine wine - my companion drinking no more than a glass, that was all the alcohol she consumed while I was with her that day - it was staggering to discover that she had shot and killed the man known as Vladimir. No, there was nothing to presage the tragic events of that evening.'

'And your recollection, Mr Kagan, is it in any way coloured by the personal, the emotional impression that the lady had made on you. Would you admit to having been conquered by her?'

'There are two questions, Sir. One - I believe I am giving a true, fair and unvarnished account of Miss Feldman's demeanour. Two - I am not ashamed to admit that the personal impression made on me was, and remains, a profound one. I have been trained to make dispassionate analyses and I believe that if aspect two has distorted aspect one it is only so to the very smallest degree.'

'Mr Kagan, why have you come back to Basel to appear as a witness in this case. I take it that the business that brought you here in February - the business of some sort of action by some security service against another such service which you assure us was neither Swiss nor British - I take it that the action was completed and that you went home, either to Brooklyn or to Israel.'

'Yes, the action was completed.'

'Satisfactorily from your point of view?'

'From my masters' point of view.'

'But not from yours?'

'I would prefer not to answer that question, Sir.'

'Your preference is noted and you will not be surprised if I assume that you were unhappy about the outcome.'

'I'm sorry but I cannot comment on that, Sir. And to come to the second question I did indeed go home afterwards.'

'And you are here on your own account, not as an employee of anything like the CIA or Mossad?'

'On my own account, in a purely private capacity, Sir.'

'Are you being paid for coming here or have you been given any inducement or promise to encourage you to come here?'

'I have come without any payment, inducement or promise, Sir. I came because I believed that I must do so.'

'In reply to a question which I put to you during the reading of your sworn statement you acknowledged that you were aware of the legal danger in which you might find yourself as a result of the evidence you are now giving to this Court. You confirmed that you had received independent legal advice on the matter. What were your reasons for coming forward to appear as a witness before this Court.'

'There are two reasons. Firstly I wish to see justice done to Miss Feldman. Secondly, and I will not try to hide it, that of our friendship, albeit that we had less than twenty four hours together - the night was, after all spent in separate bedrooms, indeed we never saw one another's rooms.' His reply brought the odd laugh, quickly suppressed, from the public area at the rear of the Court. He added, not entirely sure that he knew why he was doing so, 'When I was in Poland a few months ago, investigating my family roots I came to the conclusion that I must appear here, no matter what the personal consequences.' He paused, this wasn't something he had intended to say and he certainly hadn't cleared raising the matter with Sylvia. Still he felt he must continue, though an account of a night-time encounter with a Warsaw memorial would be out of place. 'Perhaps it was that, faced with the reality of the utter injustice and lawlessness that had swept away so many of my people and family, I found it easier to respond to the summons of conscience and make sure that this Court had before it all the evidence needed for it to administer justice with mercy.' There was silence and a sense of a slight uneasiness. The Holocaust was a difficult subject for the Swiss. A subject made no easier by a critical world which enjoyed the advantage of hindsight and the pleasure of passing moral judgements on others. Sam wondered whether he hadn't made a big mistake in raising the issue.

The President broke the silence, 'Mr Kagan, I too have been to Auschwitz ... and like you I have wept at the reminder there of human evil and malice. I can well understand how, faced with memories that for you had the added force of being direct and personal, you saw the course of duty with compelling clarity. Thank you for what you have said. The Court will bear it in mind in assessing your integrity as a witness.'

Elizabeth squeezed Sylvia's hand and David placed his hand on her arm. Sam looked uncomfortable and in doing so did himself no harm as a witness. The *Staatsanwalt* muttered something to his assistant.

The President turned again to his colleagues, 'Are there any questions that you wish to address to Mr Kagan?' The shaking of heads indicated that no one wished to do so and he turned to Sylvia, '*Fräulein Verteidiger* I expect there are some questions you wish to address to Mr Kagan.'

'Yes, Herr President. But there are only two of them as his evidence and that of his tapes has, I feel, been very clear.' Sam had turned to face her and she addressed him, 'Mr Kagan, in answer to a question put to you by the President you spoke of my client's demeanour during the twenty four hours in February. To paraphrase it was like a sunny landscape but with the occasional cloud passing across it.'

'I didn't put it quite so poetically, Fräulein, but that expresses it better than I did in my reply to the President.'

'Those occasional clouds might have been caused by Fräulein Feldman worrying over a crime she planned to carry out, by fear at the prospect of what she was intending to do on the Sunday evening or whenever it might be that she would next meet the man known as Vladimir. Does that seem possible to you?' It seemed a strange question from the defence but she had decided to put it to forestall Herr Guillaume.

Sam took his time before replying, '*Fräulein Verteidiger*' - his use of her title emphasised the strangeness of her question - 'As a soldier and in other rôles I have seen men and women who have been about to set out on a mission where it was likely that they would have to kill - in defence of their own lives, their unit or their own country - apart from two or three pathological killers, not one of those men and women was even remotely as relaxed and at peace as Fräulein Feldman during those twenty four hours.'

Sylvia couldn't resist asking, 'And the pathological killer types?'

'Cold, unfeeling and dangerous. There was ice about them and their personalities. I can assure you that there was nothing of that about Fräulein Feldman.' There was a low rumble of laughter around the Court and the President smiled. Sam continued, 'I didn't have much experience of the pathological killer type as I had them removed from the unit as soon as I had detected that defect in their make up but I did find that afterwards, when I checked their records, my assessment was invariably correct.'

'At the time you met Fräulein Feldman she had recently discovered that she was pregnant and that her relationship with her lover was crumbling. Would that in your experience account for the occasional cloud passing across the otherwise sunny landscape?'

'From several years looking after students in a pastoral capacity I would say that your explanation fits very well indeed. Some women would have allowed themselves to be devastated by such experiences, others - and I believe the Fräulein is among them - feel as deeply, and sometimes for far longer, but they do not wear their hearts on their sleeves. Such people are not insensitive but they get on with living their lives; that is how I would assess the Fräulein.'

Sylvia looked at the President, 'That completes my questioning of the witness, Herr President.'

He looked in the direction of the Prosecutor, '*Herr Staatsanwalt,* you no doubt wish to question Mr Kagan. Perhaps you would do so now.'

The Prosecutor walked to his desk, paused for effect and then addressed Sam, 'Mr Kagan you have provided the Court with a good deal of *opinion* rather than evidence.' He paused again, 'Perhaps you would be so good as to tell the Court something of your background so that they can decide what weight can be given to your *opinions*.'

'Perhaps you could be more specific, *Herr Staatsanwalt*. The bulk of my evidence concerned the three audio tapes which were played to the Court and the twenty four hours during the greater part of which I was with Fräulein Feldman when I spoke of her demeanour.'

'You gave your *opinion* on her demeanour.'

'No, *Herr Staatsanwalt*, I told the Court about her demeanour as I perceived it - that was fact and not opinion.'

'But you were prepared to say that you did not think she was contemplating murder and to agree with *Fräulein Verteidiger* that the pregnancy of the accused and her crumbling love affair with an *Englishman*' - he seemed to think that the word *Engländer* gave added colour to his question, that affairs with the *English* were the last word in decadence - 'were adequate reason for her occasional mood swings. Those were opinions and the Court ought to know what is your experience that enables you to speak authoritatively on these subjects.' He smiled, satisfied with himself.

Sylvia had warned Sam to expect this and he turned to the President, 'I have no objection to giving a reply to that question, Sir. But I am not happy to have to do so in open Court. Would you be satisfied if I provided the answer in writing for yourself, your fellow judges and for the two *Advokaten*?'

The President, Vice-President and the *Gerichtschreiber* went into a huddle and after a few minutes of muttering together, followed by a consultation with the other Judges, the President turned to the Prosecutor, '*Herr Staatsanwalt* what are your views on this, please?'

'It's highly unusual, Herr President, but I place the matter in your hands.'

'Yes it's highly unusual but we have considered the issue and we will accept Mr Kagan's offer.'

Sam lifted his briefcase onto the desk and removed a number of sheets of paper which he gave to the *Gerichtschreiber* to distribute. As this was being done Sam addressed the President, 'I thought it likely that this information would be required and so I typed it out in advance rather than mystify the Court with my handwriting.' The President nodded in acknowledgement.

The note read:

'1. Three years in the Israel Defence Forces, leaving with the rank of Lieutenant. This included combat service in the Occupied Zone of the Lebanon.

'2. Four years in Theological Studies

'3. Three years as a teacher and with pastoral

responsibilities at the Hebrew University of Jerusalem

'4. Subsequent employment with a Security Service until my retirement earlier this year.'

As they read the note Sam added, 'That, Herr President, is as far as I can go in reply to the question put to me by the *Staatsanwalt*.'

'That, *Herr Staatsanwalt*, does seem to indicate that Mr Kagan speaks from a wealth of relevant experience.'

The Prosecutor felt the need to have the last word on the subject, 'And are you enjoying a decent pension from activity No 4, Mr Kagan?'

'My employers were fair rather than bountiful, *Herr Staatsanwalt*, beyond that I will not go. I hope it doesn't become a relevant matter for the Swiss tax authorities, in other words I am not seeking to become resident here.' Several of the judges smiled.

There wasn't much mileage there for the *Staatsanwalt* so he turned his attention to what he hoped would muddy the waters and carry weight with the Judges, 'Mr Kagan, you have American and Israeli links, the accused is Russian - though she posed as a Canadian when she entered Switzerland. You have told the Court that you were working for an undisclosed Security Service and the same sort of thing has been alleged in respect of Fräulein Feldman, though hers is said to have been a rival organisation to yours. How are we to know that you weren't in fact working for rival *Mafiya* groups and that the shooting of the man known as Vladimir wasn't a gangland execution.'

By training Sylvia was always attentive to the Judges' reactions to events in Court. She caught a look of recognition on the face of the Vice-President as the question went home. Sylvia had always known that she would be the most difficult of the Judges to convince and that she had been re-elected to office on a hard line law and order ticket, not that she had dirtied her hands campaigning - well placed friends had done it for her. And the next election of Judges was only six months away.

'*Herr Staatsanwalt*, I might show you my pension book but it isn't something I carry round the world. All I can do is to look you in the eye and say that I have never worked for or had any dealings with the *Mafiya* in any of its forms. Neither, to the best of my knowledge has Fräulein Feldman.'

Sylvia had kept her eyes on the Vice-President: she didn't look convinced. It occurred to Sylvia that she had been looking for an excuse to come down hard on her client and the law and order issue would provide a pretext. The vision of the Russian *Mafiya* fighting it out on the streets, or at any rate in the hotels, of Basel was suitably scary. But how influential would she be with her colleagues? She probably carried little weight with the President but Sylvia wasn't sure about the others.

'We will just have to take your word for it then, Mr Kagan.'

'As you say, *Herr Staatsanwalt*, as you say.'

'That will be all Herr President.'

'Thank you *Herr Staatsanwalt. Fräulein Verteidiger*, do you wish to ask anything more?'

'No, Herr President. Thank you.' She did not want to labour the issue, Sam had denied the suggestion for himself and for Elizabeth, that was enough. She had an idea on how to deal with the Vice-President's concerns.

'Before the Court rises for the day there is one other matter. I have given some thought to the situation of Mr Kagan. Although it appears that he has completed his testimony it is not impossible that he will be needed again by the Court before we have finished. *Herr Staatsanwalt*, it may be that your colleague in Born is interested in making Mr Kagan's acquaintance and speaking with him. That is right but it is not to happen until after this Court has reached its decision on the case before them. Mr Kagan you are to surrender your passport to the *Gerichtschreiber*, the Court Secretary, but you are free to go your way so long as you do not stray outside the boundaries of Basel-Stadt. And if it is objected that a man of various names and from a security service might, just conceivably, have more than one passport I would remark that Rabbi Kagan's testimony would lose much of its weight should he abscond, something I am satisfied he has no intention whatsoever of doing. And I must remind the Press and indeed the public that they are not to approach Mr Kagan or his brother or to photograph them. If this warning is ignored the consequences for the offender will be very severe. The Court will rise.'

Once more Sam and Elizabeth's eyes met. Each wondered how long it would before they were together: there were many possibilities, some too awful to contemplate.

Sylvia had a few telephone calls to make. She thought she could see a way of putting pressure on the Vice-President. The nearness of the impending election of *Richter* would help.

Chapter 32

Thursday 13th November 1997

The next morning those arriving at the *Strafgericht* Basel-Stadt had to make their way through a large crowd of women with banners. They weren't menacing but did have a determined look about them. The previous evening there had been many meetings and telephone calls resulting in an excellent turn out, probably the largest ever of *Frauen gegen Notzucht* - Women Against Rape. It was unusual for there to be a demonstration outside a Basel court and one on this scale was unprecedented. Inevitably it became the subject of discussion for everyone there that morning, as much for the Judges as for court officials and the public. The journalists were particularly pleased as it gave something striking and pictorial to accompany their written or spoken reports.

In the Judges' room Frau Berman, the Vice-President, was waiting for the President, Dr Bruno Schreiber, to arrive. No sooner was he through the door when she accosted him, 'What are we going to do about the mob surrounding the Court, Dr Schreiber? It is wrong, totally wrong that we should be threatened in this way.'

'Threatened, Frau Berman? I don't follow you. They look good natured to me. Determined, yes, but also good natured. I didn't feel threatened.'

'But who do they represent? Probably made up of University radicals and the like.'

'Really? I expect some of them are but your niece was among them, I doubt if you would rank her among the radicals! As for who they represent I suppose the answer is at least half the population of Basel. There can't be many women in the city who are in favour of rape, Frau Berman. So perhaps the answer is that they represent at least half our *constituency* - probably much more because I suspect that the vast majority of my gender are also opposed to rape.' He hoped he hadn't over done things with his stress on the word "constituency" but from her face he could see that she took his point.

'Well I hope we aren't subjected to this sort of thing regularly, Dr Schreiber!'

'So do I, but this is an unusual case and I can well understand that when those women out there heard about yesterday's evidence and the circumstances in which the shooting took place they wanted to make a statement. Ah look, it's 8.16. We need to get started. Today will see the end of the hearing and then we will have to turn our minds to the verdict and possibly sentence.' He led the way out of the room, greeting the duty policeman on the way.

The Court quietened immediately the Judges appeared. There was a sense of excitement and expectancy. So far there had been the presentation and probing of the evidence. Sam Kagan's dramatic appearance had shed fresh light on the events of that February night. Now they were about to hear what the lawyers made of it all ... and ultimately they would all be back in Court to hear what the Judges had decided. And there was the demonstration going on outside the Court.

'*Herr Staatsanwalt*, perhaps you would give us the benefit of your representations on the matters of the guilt of Fräulein Feldman and the sentence you consider appropriate?'

'Thank you, Herr President. Before that, however, I need to refer to what is happening around this Court building in which we find ourselves. To come here this morning was a most intimidating experience, getting through the crowd of demonstrators was somewhat unnerving and there are members of Women Against Rape in the public area of the Court.'

'Herr Guillaume. I am surprised that you felt threatened. A demonstration there is, but it appears to me to be a thoroughly peaceful one. I hope that all those present in this Court today are men and women against rape. If you need help on the way home I am sure that one of our police officers would be prepared to hold your hand and help you through, but I'm sure that you won't find it necessary.' Dr Schreiber told himself that he had better watch his temper in relation to the Prosecutor, it wouldn't do to give any grounds for impugning the integrity of the Court's decision in the event of an appeal. He added, 'Of course the police will keep their eye on events to ensure that the demonstration remains a peaceful one and that there is no intimidation. No one in this Court should feel that the demonstration now taking place is in any way coercing them as to what they say or as to what they decide. It is however a salutary reminder that rape is regarded by our fellow citizens and by all decent people as a particularly abhorrent offence. Now *Herr Staatsanwalt*, my fellow Judges and I look forward to your assistance as we come to the time when we have to make important decisions.'

'Thank you, Herr President. Firstly, I ask the Court to hold that Fräulein Feldman is guilty of murder under Article 112 of the Penal Code.' Protests could be heard from the public area.

The President stopped the Prosecutor. 'It is essential that there should be no recurrence of that interruption. Members of the public are here to observe what takes place and not, I repeat not, to participate in the proceedings of the Court. Anyone interrupting again will be removed by the police and may be held by them in the cells downstairs until the Court has time to deal with them. Is that understood?' There was a silence, it was unlikely that anyone would jump up and say, 'Yes Sir.'

'Herr Staatsanwalt.'

'There are several factors pointing to the inevitability of a murder verdict and I will detail them to the Court:

'1. Fräulein Feldman came to Switzerland with the weapon with which she killed the man known as Vladimir. It carries the fingerprints of the Fräulein and of no one else. In particular it has not been alleged that it was Vladimir's weapon and there were none of his fingerprints on it. Why carry a weapon if you do not plan to use it?

'2. The victim was shot in the back of the head as he was fleeing from the Fräulein's hotel room. Does this suggest that she was defending herself? I do not think so. *If*, as it has been suggested, and I wonder if there really is any evidence for that suggestion to which the Court ought to give credence - but I will turn to the evidence of Rabbi Kagan in due course - *if* there had been an attempt to rape the Fräulein, that danger was over by the time the terrified victim managed to reach the door in his attempt to flee the Fury who was threatening death within the room.'

Elizabeth and Sylvia exchanged a few words and David Kagan patted Elizabeth's arm.

Guillaume watched them and paused, it would be good for the Judges to study the Fräulein's reactions to his address. He knew from experience how difficult it was to keep a straight and serious face when under stress - it was all too easy to betray oneself with an inappropriate expression and that sometimes said more to the Judges than a torrent of forensic argument from the Prosecutor. He continued:

'3. There were no marks on the person of the accused or signs of disturbance to her apparel indicative of an attempt by the deceased to force his attentions on her. The bruising to her head had clearly been caused by her fall against some piece of furniture.

'4. It has been suggested that the victim drugged the accused. I suggest that there is no evidence whatsoever for that. It is just as likely that the drug, Flunitrazepam, or as it is commonly known Rohypnol, was taken by the accused of her own volition as a sedative. Do not be swayed by the fact that in the USA Rohypnol is known as the "Date Rape Drug": Millions take it as a sedative, very few have it administered to them as a prelude to rape. It has been stated that this drug has never been prescribed for the accused but it is not difficult to obtain it without a prescription. May I remind you of Dr Schmidt's words that, "she had been dosed with *or had taken* Rohypnol".'

'These I suggest are weighty reasons for doubting the claim of the accused that the man known as Vladimir died as a result of her defence from his attempts to rape her.

'I must now address the subject of the evidence presented to the Court by Rabbi Kagan. At an earlier stage in this trial I registered a protest at the appearance of Rabbi Kagan so late in the proceedings, produced like a *deus ex machina* by *Fräulein Verteidiger.* He swept onto the scene without the Public Prosecutor's Office being able to interview him in the proper way ... '

'The President broke in, 'As you have said, Herr Guillaume, this was raised earlier on. It was dealt with then and should not be raised again. This Court decided to admit the evidence of Mr Kagan. The circumstances were most unusual but we considered that to refuse to hear his evidence would not have been in the interests of justice. And, Herr Guillaume, *justice* is what these proceedings are about. Please continue.'

Sylvia restrained a smile and busied herself making notes, writing for Elizabeth to see, 'One yellow card for Herr Guillaume!'

The Prosecutor looked down at his notes and with a pencil struck through a section before continuing, 'Rabbi Kagan has presented his evidence to the Court most persuasively, I would suggest too persuasively. He is in fact a mystery man: he gives addresses in the USA and in Israel, claims to have served in the Israel Defence Forces, to have trained and served as a rabbi and then to have worked for an unidentified foreign security service, refusing to answer when the CIA and Mossad were put to him as possibilities. It is an extraordinary *mélange* of activities. It's not the sort of *curriculum vitae* that you meet very often. Rabbi Kagan presented a sworn statement to the Court and of course three audio tapes. *If* the tapes are genuine, and we only have it on his say so that they are genuine, then they were made in flagrant contravention of Swiss law. But *are* they genuine? Could it not be the case that far from being players for opposing teams, as has been claimed, Rabbi Kagan and Fräulein Feldman are on the same side, either working for the same organisation or for illegal organisations which are happy to co-operate with one another. That is not an impossible situation. Start with that as a given and move on to the certainty of the organisation or organisations wanting Fräulein Feldman out of custody, perhaps for her own good or perhaps wishing to question her about the violent death of one of her colleagues before, maybe, taking appropriate measures.' He paused, paint it black so that they were convinced of her culpability and at the same time glad that they had kept her out of the cellars of the Lubyanka, giving her the safety of a decent, clean, progressive Swiss prison!

'The audio tapes were very clear, indeed when they were played you remarked about that very point, Herr President. I suggest to the Court that that very fact should ring alarm signals. Was the making of these tapes contemporaneous with the events of which they are purported to be the record? Or were they, perhaps, concocted in a recording studio some time later with the aim of leading the Court to believe that on that night in February the accused, Fräulein Feldman, was defending herself from a violent rapist. You only have the word of Rabbi Kagan for the authenticity of these tapes. I am prepared to admit that Rabbi Kagan has presented his evidence with conviction but that in itself is no proof of truth. An actor can carry conviction and make his audience suspend their disbelieve when they know that it's really no more than play acting. Rabbi Kagan claims that he was an officer of a foreign security service. If we admit that claim for the moment it becomes highly likely that he would have little difficulty in giving the most far fetched story every appearance of verisimilitude. The agents of organisations such as the CIA and Mossad are well trained in the ways of deceit and in giving away nothing under interrogation - even heavy handed interrogation techniques verging on torture that this Court would never permit a mere *Staatsanwalt* to use.' There was some laughter, not so much at the humour of his speech but more from the very idea of Herr Guillaume as some sort of Grand Inquisitor. Guillaume, however, thought his humour was being appreciated and smiled broadly. He debated with himself whether to play the *Mafiya* card and decided to do so.

'Although the Court has been led to believe that Rabbi Kagan and Fräulein Feldman were the operatives of foreign security services I would like to suggest the possibility that they were instead involved in some kind of *Mafiya* activities here in Basel and that the murder of the man known as Vladimir was the result of gang warfare or a reprisal of some kind.' His eye rested on Frau Berman. Sylvia, who had been watching the general reaction of the Judges also turned her attention to the Vice-President. An ambiguous response flickered across Frau Berman's face, she betrayed to neither *Advokat* what she thought of the Prosecutor's suggestion. It was clear that the Prosecutor, knowing the President's assessment of Sam Kagan as a witness, was nevertheless hoping to raise doubts in the minds of the Vice-President and the other Judges.

'And so I ask the Court to treat the evidence of Rabbi Kagan with considerable suspicion and to reach a verdict of murder: Fräulein Feldman brought the weapon into Switzerland, she shot the victim in the back of the head, she could easily have taken the drug Rohypnol as a sedative to help her sleep that night and finally there were no marks of struggle on her person or clothing.

'As to the appropriate sentence this of course will be life, meaning in practice between 10 and 25 years. The evidence presented to the Court has been of a well balanced young woman with no mental abnormalities, certainly nothing that would mitigate or excuse in any way the violent taking of the life of the person known as Vladimir. That concludes my submission to the Court.'

He returned to his chair and sat down. Elizabeth had gasped at the mention of the sentence. Of course she already knew what it could be but to hear it demanded by the Prosecutor came as a powerful shock. She had a baby daughter and could only keep the child in prison with her for less than another three years. She could almost hear the prison gate clang behind her. She dug her nails into her palms and gritted her teeth, she would not show her distress, least of all to that swine the Prosecutor who sat there looking pleased with himself. Sylvia put her arm round Elizabeth. She herself was profoundly moved. She whispered, 'Don't worry, Elizabeth. I can do much better than that. He thinks he's done well, but it's a measure of his ineptitude that he's so badly mistaken.

The Judges consulted and the President spoke, 'We will take our coffee break now and afterwards if *Fräulein Verteidiger* would address us we would be grateful.' There was an old fashioned courtesy about his manner. The Judges left the Court. David rose from beside Elizabeth, stood behind the two women and put a hand on the shoulder of each of them, 'Time for coffee and afterwards Sylvia's going to turn that self-opinionated slob into mincemeat. I've seen her notes, Elizabeth, you have nothing to fear.' At the moment both women needed encouragement and he was convinced that the weight of the argument was in Elizabeth's favour. But he also knew that Courts were capable of making mistakes. Despite his secular philosophy he found himself praying for Elizabeth's acquittal, 'Master of the Universe let her go free.' As a psychiatrist he was amused at himself, but there was more to it than that and he was slightly troubled. Was his reaction the result of his upbringing, something genetic or some sort of folk memory? Faced with existential predicaments how many remained pure rationalists? Only a few and he knew that he was not among them. He led the women to the door where their friendly policemen waited to take them below.

***

'My address to the Court will not take very long, Herr President. I intend to put the case for my client to you in as succinct a way as I can and not labour the points that I have to make.

'When she speaks to you shortly my client, Fräulein Feldman, will express her regrets at the death of Vladimir. She does not deny killing him, she admits that she did so. But my submission to the Court is that her action did not amount to murder, that it did not come anywhere near to being Murder within Article 112 of the Penal Code. Neither did it amount to Wilful Homicide within Article 111. It is my contention that if Fräulein Feldman is guilty of an offence, it is that of Manslaughter under Article 113 - as when a wife kills her husband while he is battering her. If the Court wishes me to review those cases where manslaughter verdicts have been given I will, of course, be most willing to do so, though I am sure that the Judges are fully conversant with them.

'Firstly I must address the points put to the Court by the *Staatsanwalt* when he contended that my client was guilty of the offence of murder:

'1. That the weapon was brought into Switzerland by the accused. Why, he asked, was she carrying the weapon if she did not intend to use it? Thousands of our fellow Swiss carry weapons as part of their military equipment, they keep them at home in readiness should they ever be called to defend our land. Apart from their regular visits to firing ranges they do not use those weapons. They are there for use in the remote eventuality that the day might come when the invader has to be driven back from our borders.

'Fräulein Feldman was issued with the weapon as part of her equipment as an officer of the Russian SVR, the successor of the First Chief Directorate of the KGB.'

What had previously been hinted at was now explicit and the faces of the Judges were an interesting study as they took it in. Members of the public began talking to one another and the President called the Court to order.

Sylvia continued, 'You may wonder why this has not been said earlier. The answer is that I have refrained from doing so on the instructions of our National Security Service who are concerned about the task of ensuring the safety of my client in the event of any attempted reprisal by her former masters. This was known to the Court President and the *Staatsanwalt*.

'The Federal Prosecutor in Bern has advised me that, having heard the tapes yesterday evening, he will not be bringing charges against my client in respect of her activities on behalf of the SVR. The Court will not need to be reminded that my client is before it charged with murder and not with being a member of the SVR or working for it in our country. Fräulein Feldman came to Basel with her British employer on a bona fide business visit, making a delivery of scientific glassware to a laboratory here. National Security have accepted the evidence from the audio tape of the events of that February night in Fräulein Feldman's room at the Hotel International, the second tape that the Court heard and of which the Judges and the *Staatsanwalt* have transcripts. You will remember that when they discussed the planned events of the following day, the Monday - the first day of Fasnacht - my client said:

"I'm to be available if needed but otherwise keep out of the way."

National Security have decided that the evidence of

intention is too weak to proceed with any charges.' She did not add that Elizabeth's assistance to Swiss and British Security had also been a factor, there was no point in further increasing the risk of Russian retaliation. And in indicating that Security had accepted the tapes as evidence Sylvia had enhanced their status in the eyes of the Court and sunk the prosecutor's attempts to sideline them or label them as fabrications.

'2. The deceased was shot in the back of the head, that is not denied. But let me take the Court back to the situation in which my client found herself in her hotel room on that fateful night. She was locked in with a man who had previously attempted to rape her. She had been dosed by him with a knock out drug and she could feel it taking effect rapidly - do not forget that she had drunk wine – albeit a solitary glass - with her dinner that night, so the effect of the Rohypnol would have been enhanced: evidence to that effect was given by the pharmacologist, Dr Briner, who testified before the Court. You will remember that the word he used for the interaction of Rohypnol and alcohol was *synergic* – a multiplying together rather than a simple addition of their separate effects. Fräulein Feldman was pregnant by her British lover, not as the result of some casual liaison but of a long term relationship which was sadly beginning to unravel. She knew that Vladimir was promiscuous, very promiscuous indeed, and she feared for the health of the child within her.' Sylvia paused for the merest moment but it added force to her next words. 'Post mortem tests on the deceased showed him to be HIV positive.'

The Prosecutor was on his feet, 'Where did you … '

Sylvia addressed the President, 'Sir, that information is in the appendix to the pathologist's report. I'm sure the *Staatsanwald* has a copy.' She looked in his direction but he had sat down quickly and didn't venture to continue his interruption.

She paused again, her gaze searching the eyes of the Judges, particularly those of Frau Berman. 'Fräulein Feldman's daughter Olga was born fourteen weeks ago, a healthy, lively child. Things might have been very different for both the child and her mother if the deceased had succeeded with his attempted rape.' Sylvia took a sip of water from the glass on the desk keeping her eye on Frau Berman, the point seemed to have been taken by her.

'A final comment is necessary on the assertion that the deceased was fleeing at the time he was killed. This objection by the *Staatsanwalt* implies that once the deceased had left the room my client would have been safe. But that is simply not true, it is clearly a completely mistaken reading of the situation. You have heard the tape recording and the evidence of how Fräulein Feldman was found on the floor near the door of her room supports the impression that the tape left: within moments of firing the gun my client had lost consciousness due to the Rohypnol that Vladimir had administered. I submit that there is every reason to believe that had he not been killed he would have returned to the room and, depraved as it may seem to the Court, carried out the planned rape. In the circumstances it appears that she took the only action possible to defend her person and the child she was carrying. Add to that the hazy view she must have had on what was going on around her and you might even feel that her action was heroic. I must tell the Court that is how I see her action. But it is not how Lizaveta Feldman sees it and she will tell you so herself shortly. I ask myself and I ask every woman in this Court how they would have responded to the situation in which my client found herself, I have little doubt that most of us would have responded exactly as she did or at the very least wished that they had the courage to do so.' She took another sip of water. For a moment, but no more, she had held Frau Berman's gaze as she came to the end of this part of her address. Things felt right, the Court seemed to be with her. But she was not so arrogant as to think the verdict was in her pocket, she was a very different personality from the Prosecutor. She glanced at him: he was looking unhappy. Good.

'I continue with the points raised by the Staatsanwalt:

'3. That there were no marks on her person of my client or disturbance of her clothing. It is agreed that the substantial blow that my client suffered to her head that night came not from the deceased but from her falling, due to the Rohypnol, and striking her head against a bedroom cabinet. My client was fully aware of what Vladimir was capable. You have heard an audio tape which clearly records an attempted rape some months earlier in England which my client was able to prevent by the use of less fatal tactics. To be drugged and then told by the person who has done it that he wants you in bed can mean only one thing: that he intends to rape you. There is no room there for consensual sex, none at all. That he had not fought with her is irrelevant, by drugging my client the deceased knew that he had no need to force himself on her, shortly she would have been, by reason of her loss of consciousness, unable to resist. In such circumstances could anyone really expect to find the signs of struggle on the person or clothing of the rapist's intended *victim*.' She knew it was good to get the message to the Court that if her client hadn't defended herself *she* would have been the victim of Vladimir's criminal intentions.

'4. I move on to the last of the *Staatsanwalt's* points: That there is no proof that the drug Rohypnol was administered to my client by Vladimir. The Court has received a sworn statement by Mr Peter Lewis, who was my client's partner and who is the father of their child. In it he stated that he had never known her to have any sleeping problems and that he had never known her to take sleeping tablets of any kind. There was also a sworn statement from Fräulein Feldman's medical practitioner in London saying that he had never prescribed any sleeping tablets for her, indeed he said that apart from a course of antibiotics and the contraceptive pill he had never prescribed any drug for her. The Court has heard the audio recording where my client's speech, previously very crisp and clear, becomes slurred and she says to the deceased:

'You're not having me! You've doped my drink! You want to rape me! You want to abduct me!'

'I submit that what you heard her say was the truth and that she had no reason whatsoever to lie when she said that. The drug was not self administered but used by the deceased to spike my client's drink and prevent her from resisting him.

'Those were the *Staatsanwalt's* four points in favour of a conviction for murder and I believe that I have answered them more than adequately. There are some other matters to be dealt with.

'The first is the matter of the organisations for which Fräulein Feldman and Mr Samuel Kagan were working at the time of the events that are the concern of this Court. I have already told you that my client was an officer of the SVR, Russian Overseas Intelligence. She will shortly confirm this when she addresses the Court. If the Court is unable to accept this I ask that an officer of the National Security Service should be called to testify. Mr Kagan is not prepared to name his former employers but he has testified that they are not the *Mafiya* or any such organisation. Further he has testified that he has in no way harmed the State or commercial interests of Switzerland or its people. I ask that you accept his sworn word on this.

'It is one of the vital tasks of the Court to weigh up the witnesses who come before it and to decide whether they are to be believed or not. In this the members of the Court must call on all their experience of people, both those they have met within the legal framework and the people they meet in their private daily life. So, confronted by Mr Kagan, how should he be assessed and what weight should the Court give to his evidence? I wish to make three points:

'1. There was nothing to force Mr Kagan to come to this Court and testify. There was every reason for him to stay away. No one apart from him and his colleagues knew about the bugging of Fräulein Fielder's telephones and accommodation. In coming here and giving evidence he has laid himself open to legal action. He has received notice that the Federal Prosecutor in Bern wishes to question him. He faces charges which, if upheld, could result in him spending up to eight years in prison.' She heard a quiet gasp from Elizabeth. She had already been told this but hearing it said in Court, like her own possible sentence, made it more real and threatening. 'That there is a romantic element in his motivation I will not deny. The memory of twenty four hours direct acquaintance with my client has proved indelible. He knows that there is no certainty as to the outcome of things between himself and Fräulein Feldman. I do not think that this romantic element detracts from his testimony, but that is for the Court to consider. Mr Kagan has come here and testified to the Court without receiving payment or any inducement or promise whatsoever.

'2. What impression has Mr Kagan made in his appearance before the Court? I believe he has shown himself to be a man of integrity and principle. His appearance on his first arrival in Court came as a shock to all of us. He told us he had been involved in a road accident and it was not until the end of the morning that Inspector Sturmer told us what had in fact taken place, the saving of a young woman's life, a situation to which he applied his medical expertise with great effectiveness and selfless devotion. I have here a letter from the young woman and her family thanking Mr Kagan for his prompt and effective action which without a doubt saved her life.'

The Prosecutor muttered to his colleague, 'We lost the case at that point. She's a lucky bitch, they're both lucky bitches.'

'Despite his other activities Mr Kagan was and remains a rabbi, a man of the cloth. The Court will give that whatever weight they think appropriate, but let me say this: the presumption must be that a man whose calling is to teach the Word is exceedingly unlikely to regard his oath taken on the Sacred Scriptures as other than binding in the most solemn way. You have seen and heard Mr Kagan. You have heard his sworn statement and you have seen him respond to questioning. I do not need to labour the point further, just let me say that in my eyes he is a man of total integrity.

3. The *Staatsanwalt* suggests that the tapes could have been manufactured in order to mislead this Court. The short answer to that, and an answer of which the *Staatsanwalt* should be well aware, is that the Federal

Prosecutor has been prepared on the strength of the evidence presented by those very tapes to decide not to proceed against my client in respect of SVR activities on Swiss soil. Clearly the Federal Prosecutor is satisfied that the tapes are kosher ... that they are genuine.' She hadn't meant to say it that way but there it was.

'In conclusion, a verdict of murder under Article 112 will only be open to the Court if you are satisfied beyond all reasonable doubt that it was my client's intention to kill Vladimir, that she was waiting for him in that room with malicious intent determined to take his life. That is completely contrary to the evidence before the Court. From the audio tape it is clear that she was calm and doing her best to keep the deceased calm that night. My client defended herself and her unborn child from the rape which this man intended: *he* was the one who planned evil that night! Let me leave the Court with this thought: if Vladimir had succeeded in what he had planned he would be alive today but carrying in his body that harbinger of an early death, the HIV virus. And it is likely that Lizaveta Feldman and her innocent daughter Olga would be similarly infected, carrying in their bodies that agent of a slow demise, making their situation not so very different from the long term residents of Death Row in Mississippi or some other American State with that penalty.

'Neither is she guilty of Intentional Homicide under Article 111. Fräulein Feldman has pleaded guilty to Manslaughter under Article 113 and as to the sentence she casts herself on the Court's mercy.'

There was a long silence which the President seemed unwilling to break. Then he turned to the Prosecutor, '*Herr Staatsanwalt*, do you wish to make any response to

Fräulein Verteidiger's address?'

The Prosecutor looked down at the note his colleague had passed him. The message was clear enough:

"Keep your mouth shut!"

'No, Sir, I have nothing further to add.'

'Good. Then if Fräulein Feldman wishes to address the Court we will be able to complete business for today. Fräulein Feldman the Court interpreter will translate as you proceed, so if you would pause regularly he will be able to convey to us as accurately as possible what you have said'

Elizabeth stood and faced the President. She was wearing a charcoal gray suit with a dark blue blouse. Her sombre dress underlined her serious manner but there was also a quiet confidence about her. The Court was gripped by a sense of expectation as she began, 'Herr President it will not be necessary for the Court interpreter to be involved as I will speak in German. It is a language I learnt some years ago and whose acquaintance I have renewed during my time in the *Waaghof*. I have been appreciative of the translation that has been provided of the Court proceedings as it has enabled me to catch subtleties of language which would have escaped me had it been necessary to rely on my partial knowledge of German. I have written out what I am going to say and discussed the translation with my *Advokat* but what I have to say is *my* statement, prepared by *myself* and changed in no material respect. It is what I feel I must say to the Court and it concerns how I regard the events of that awful February night earlier this year.

'The Court has shown great patience and consideration in the way it has dealt with hearing the charges against me and for that I am deeply grateful. My

Vertidiger, Fräulein Sylvia Brunner, has been a tower of strength throughout the entire time she has been my *Advokat.* And I am immensely grateful to Mr Samuel Kagan for coming forward to give evidence before the Court and by doing so clarifying events that were a blur in my memory.

'More important, for the purposes of the present proceedings, is the one essential thing that I must say about the killing of Vladimir. It is this, however much I may be persuaded in my mind by my own reasoning and the arguments of Fräulein Brunner that I had no alternative but to defend myself and my unborn child in the way I did, I am unable in my heart and my emotions to feel anything other than the deepest sorrow and regret for my action and its consequence. For a number of years Vladimir was my friend and colleague. We had worked together well and amicably but our relationship, from a while before our arrival in London, had turned sour due to his attempts to force himself on me sexually. But nevertheless he could be charming and the best of company - and that is the Vladimir I shall try to remember. I deeply regret the circumstances that gave rise to his death, the death of a friend however strained the relationship had become. As an officer of the Russian External Security Service I had been trained in the use of firearms, I do not deny it. This, the only occasion on which I have ever used one to serious purpose, is something that will be with me for the rest of my life whatever the decision of this Court might be. My future is in your hands and the hands of your colleagues, Herr President. I am glad that this is a Swiss Court: were I am before a Moscow Court I would not be so confident of a just outcome to the proceedings.' She took her seat and waited. David whispered, 'You said that well' and Sylvia put her arm round Elizabeth's shoulders.

'Thank you, Fräulein Feldman. That concludes matters for the moment. My colleagues hope that we will be able to return to this Court to give our verdict and sentence, if that is appropriate, in five days time - that is on next Tuesday morning the 18th November at 8.15. If we find that more time is required for our deliberations, and I hope that it will not be so, we will ensure that all concerned are warned in good time.' He rose and the Judges followed him from the Court.

'Elizabeth it's going to be a long five days for you. Time will go slowly for all of us. But my sense of things is we've got the right message through to the Judges. The best indication is Herr Guillaume's reaction. He's not a happy *Staatsanwalt* at the moment, I'm sure of that!' They looked across to the side of the Court as the Prosecutor gathered his papers together and muttered savage things to his assistant. Sylvia smiled in his direction but he was avoiding eye contact with anybody. As they left the Court she told Elizabeth and David, 'It's rumoured that he's got aspirations of becoming a Court President but I don't think he's happy about his latest performance.'

***

Elizabeth was returned to the prison and rested on her bed before supper and the intense questioning of the other women. She refused to allow her spirits to rise too high, the next few days were going to be very difficult. Thank God for little Olga, she would be needing a substantial amount of love and care from her. And there were two or three of the women who needed help and advice. The next few days would be tense but there would be plenty other things to occupy her time.

***

Sylvia spent the afternoon in her office tidying up her file from Elizabeth's case and getting other urgent matters out of the way. She was glad she had trained her assistant well and given him confidence to take responsibility when she was away or tied up with an important case. He had kept her work in order while she had devoted herself to preparing for the trial and appearing in court. He would also keep things going for the next few days, indeed he had insisted that she go away for a long weekend and stay out of the office until the Monday afternoon, the day before the verdict was expected. David collected her a little before six and they set off for a few days in the Ticino on the southern side of the Alps, hoping for a little sunshine. On the way she called in at the *Waaghof* to give Elizabeth a few words of encouragement.

Chapter 33

Tuesday 18th November 1997 – Judgement Day

The morning had begun early for Elizabeth who had been up since 5.30 to feed Olga and to prepare herself for the final day in court, the day of fateful decision. After a breakfast of cereal and toast washed down with coffee she returned to get Olga ready in her babygrow and one of the little dresses that Ruth had sent.

'Well Olga, today we'll know what's to become of us. Whatever I've done *you* don't deserve to be locked up in prison.'

She kissed the little head and a tear ran down onto the child's cheek. The little one looked up, vulnerable, totally dependent and uncomprehending.

'No Olga, I must pull myself together. None of this in court, I'm not going to make that Prosecutor happy!'

***

When Elizabeth arrived at the familiar location below the court both Sylvia and David were waiting. For Sylvia it was a strange feeling. This case had been more personal than any she had handled: it had brought her into contact with the Kagan twins and she knew what the consequences were likely to be for Elizabeth and Sam. She had done her level best in presenting Elizabeth's case, now she could do nothing but wait for the verdict and the sentence. More than any previous case the tension was getting to her. They had run out of conversation: Elizabeth was holding Olga in her arms and Sylvia and David stood hand in hand watching her. A policeman called out that it was time to go upstairs and they were on their way but not before Elizabeth had kissed Olga and placed her gently in her carrycot.

***

The English journalist was chatting with her Basel opposite number when Elizabeth and her companions arrived in court. She had been fortunate to retain her seat with its partial view of Elizabeth. She was pleased to have persuaded her Editor to permit her to spend a few days in Switzerland and write a travel piece, so she would be seeing the mountains after all. She noted down that Elizabeth was dressed as she had been for her last appearance there, in a charcoal gray suit though with a lighter blue blouse. Elizabeth's facial expression told her nothing of the butterflies she knew the young woman must be experiencing.

The Judges filed in and the President called the court to order.

'Will Fräulein Feldman please stand while the *Gerichtschreiber* reads the verdict of the court.'

Elizabeth felt flat emotionally as she stood to face the Court Secretary. The waiting was over and in a minute or so she would know her fate and that of Olga. It was a moment that Sylvia hated: memories of the hearing crowded in and there were always things that you might have put better or left unsaid.

The *Gerichtschreiber* had also risen. He picked up his notes and put on the spectacles that moments before he had been polishing assiduously.

'Fräulein Lizaveta Feldman, the Court has found you not guilty of the murder of Eugene Preston, also known as Vladimir, but it has found you guilty of the lesser charge of Manslaughter under Article 113. The sentence which the Court imposes is a custodial sentence of 275 days in prison. Would you please sit while the President of the Court explains the decision of the Court.'

From the back of the court there was applause from some members of Women Against Rape, but this was quickly stopped by a look in their direction from the President.

Elizabeth remained on her feet looking at the *Gerichtschreiber*: she had heard that she was not guilty of murder but had taken in nothing else. Her head had begun to swim. She felt Sylvia tugging her sleeve and responded to her signal to sit down. She pushed a glass of water in Elizabeth's direction and whispered in her ear, 'They accept that you didn't murder him and you're free – 275 days is exactly the time you've already spent in custody.'

Elizabeth looked at her, 'Honestly?'

'Yes, honestly.'

Elizabeth began to cry quietly and David passed her a box of tissues.

The President looked at Sylvia who indicated that he should go ahead.

'We will wait a moment before proceeding and I insist that the Court remain quiet. These are serious matters and not to be trivialised.'

He waited until Elizabeth had composed herself, wiped her eyes and managed a kind of smile before he began:

'I am always glad that the procedure of the Court is to spell out its decisions right at the very beginning and then to follow with an account of the reasoning behind the verdict and sentence. It is not the most dramatic way to proceed but it is the most appropriate way: it is not the purpose of courts of justice to provide contrived drama.

'This has not been an easy case to decide, but then it is only very rarely that a case fails to exhibit complexities which the Court must consider and to which it must give appropriate weight. Here in this Court we are dealing with people and with the way that people behave. We see much of the dark side of humanity and we encounter, on occasion, actions that remind us that all is not unbroken gloom. Of that I will say more later.

'First of all there is the verdict of the Court. We hold that Fräulein Feldman is not guilty of Murder under Article 112 or of Intentional Homicide under Article 111 but we have made a finding of her guilt of the crime of Manslaughter under Article 113. It was not disputed by her *Vertidiger* that she had brought the weapon with her into Switzerland but we do not consider that, at any time prior to the shooting, she intended to use it on Eugene Preston. Certainly no such intention was evident from the circumstances of her ownership of the weapon and there is no evidence of any intent on her part to take the life of Mr Preston. We consider that it was not until she found herself drugged and in grave danger of being raped that she determined to save herself from what Mr Preston was intending to do.

'We considered what *Fräulein Vertidiger* said in her *Plädoyer* (pleading). She depicted the situation of Fräulein Feldman, trapped in her hotel room, rapidly losing consciousness due to a drug with which the deceased had spiked her drink, knowing from past experience and from his present actions that he intended to rape her. She knew that he was a promiscuous man and, in our modern world, that means that the risk to both the Fräulein and to her unborn child was very real. *Fräulein Vertidiger* asked every woman in Court to face the question of how they would have responded in such a situation. I and the other men on the panel also addressed that question. All of us, irrespective of gender, came to the same conclusion: that Fräulein Feldman was fully justified in using all the means available to her to prevent the rape that threatened her and her unborn child. Whether she could have used the weapon in a way that would not have resulted in the death of Mr Preston is a matter that took much of our thought and time. We concluded that given all the circumstances, particularly the fact that Fräulein Feldman was rapidly losing consciousness and the ability to defend herself, a verdict of Manslaughter under Article 113 of the Penal Code was appropriate. The *Staatsanwald* was unable to satisfy us beyond all reasonable doubt that it was the intention of the accused to kill Mr Preston, that she was waiting for him in that hotel room with malicious intent determined to take his life. Accordingly we decisively reject the charges of Murder and Intentional Homicide. In coming to the finding that Fräulein Feldman was guilty of Manslaughter we followed the suggestion of *Fräulein Vertidiger* that the situation was analogous to that of a battered wife killing her tormentor.

'I now turn to the sentence of the Court. It is good that on occasion we should remind ourselves of precisely what is the intent behind the imposition of a judicial sentence. Classically there are three elements: the punishment of the offender, deterrence – both of the offender from repeating their action and of others from similar activity – and, thirdly, the reform of the offender. These considerations are proper not only to the realm of academic jurisprudence but also to the daily work of the courts in this and other countries. Rarely will we achieve the perfect balance in considering these three aspects but that is not to say that we should not always venture to do so.

'It is perhaps an old fashioned view of the matter that gives priority to the punishment of the offender, but that is not to say that this view is mistaken. There are many who would argue that to give punishment priority suggests a vengeful society. I believe that they are wrong and that it is seeing it as punishment that gives moral weight to a sentence and acts as a safeguard against well intentioned but nevertheless potentially oppressive sentencing. The criminal act itself, the circumstances and intentions of the perpetrator of the act, when put into the balance together, enable the Court to reach a right decision on what is an appropriate sentence. Those who have attended some of the English Circle's musical productions may recognise the phrase about "making the punishment fit the crime". It may sound a hackneyed expression but underlying it is the salutary reminder that a proper sentence is an appropriate one and the prime measure of that appropriateness is its rôle as a punishment.

'There are times, and I believe this is one, when to receive punishment is a healthy corrective to an excessive sense of remorse and to one's inability to forgive oneself. Strangely, for some, punishment received can be a healing thing as it enables them to draw a line under what has happened and to move on.

'Deterrence of re-offending and of others committing similar offences comes next. Society must be protected. The combination of the likelihood that the police will catch you and that a court will impose an unpleasant sentence reaches parts of society that conscience and consideration for others do not. This Court has seen the demeanour of Fräulein Feldman and heard her statement to us with its expression of remorse. We are fully satisfied that she is in no danger of re-offending. To others similarly situated the fact that we have imposed a custodial sentence and the reminder that its length, in this instance as in any other, turns on the particular facts of the case should be sufficient warning.

'The third and final aspect is the reform of the offender. I have already alluded to Fräulein Feldman's remorse, expressed openly and patently obvious to us from her demeanour in Court. We have also heard the report submitted by the psychiatrist appointed by the Court to assess her and report back to us. That report dealt not merely with her state of mind at the time of the killing and subsequently, it also gave us a picture of her life in custody in the *Waaghof*. It was very clear to us that Fräulein Feldman had spent a substantial part of her time while in prison helping her fellow prisoners, giving them sound advice and emotional support. Clearly, in respect of the Fräulein, there is no further place for prison as an agency of reform. If reform were ever needed it has already taken place.

'Accordingly, in the light of these factors, we consider that a sentence of 275 days imprisonment, precisely the time that Fräulein Feldman has spent in the *Waaghof*, is appropriate. Therefore, Fräulein, when the Court rises you will be able to walk out of this building a free woman. We have no doubt that you will wish to return to the *Waaghof* to collect your belongings and also, I suspect, to say farewell to those who have been your companions there.

'Before we rise, however, there are some other remarks that I must make:

'Firstly regarding Rabbi Samuel Kagan and his evidence. Had he not come forward it is possible, indeed likely, that the Court would have come to a different conclusion. Rabbi Kagan had evidence that threw light on the events of that February night. He was not afraid to come forward, at considerable risk to his liberty, to testify before this Court. That risk is a real one in the light of what he had to disclose of his own activities in this city. I have kept the Federal Prosecutor at bay since Rabbi Kagan first appeared in this Court and I can do so now for only a very little longer, and to that I will allude in a moment.

'I ask that the Federal Prosecutor and any Court concerned should give full weight to the fact that Rabbi Kagan came forward completely of his own volition, compelled by conscience and not by any employer or agency. His life-saving action in the Marktplatz has already been commended by this Court and I am sure that any other Court will also regard it as a substantial factor in Rabbi Kagan's favour.

'The Court expresses its thanks to the *Advokaten*, The *Staatsanwald*, Herr Guillaume, has given the Court the benefit of his experience and we thank him.'

The Prosecutor didn't lift his eyes from the note he was writing. 'Damn me with faint praise, then,' he muttered to himself.

'But particular thanks are due to the *Verteidiger*, Fräulein Brunner for her persistence in ferreting out relevant evidence and for her presentation of the case. She has made a laudable contribution to the cause of justice.

'I referred earlier to temporarily keeping the Federal Prosecutor at bay. I have been able to extend this for another hour but no more. It occurred to us that Rabbi Kagan and Fräulein Feldman might well wish to continue their conversation that was terminated by the Rabbi's journey to Hamburg on the eve of Fasnacht.' Those who got the joke laughed and the President smiled. 'They will have an hour together by themselves in my office before the Federal Prosecutor makes his call.'

'Once again no photographs are to be taken of Fräulein Feldman, Rabbi Kagan or Dr David Kagan, neither are they to be approached. The Court will rise.'

As the judges filed out there was noisy discussion in Court. The journalists got into a huddle and a group from Women Against Rape, in the absence of the judges, began to clap with some others joining them.

'Come on Elizabeth, lets get down below to Olga and give her the good news. Then you can take her to meet Sam.' Sylvia turned to find David waiting to give her a warm embrace, 'I think that my *Verteidiger's* done rather well today!' All of them had moist eyes.

Sam who had waited to one side asked Elizabeth, 'If you could spare an hour ... ' Her face expressed her unambiguous reply and he set off for the door that the judges had taken.

In the Judges Retiring Room they stood relaxing, a difficult case over. 'Well Bruno, I think we got it right, don't you?'

'Yes, Trudi, I believe that justice has been done but that is why we were here. And I think that Fräulein Brunner will one day make a very good Court President, don't you?'

Jakob Gold led Peter out of the Court, 'Well Peter, it couldn't be better. She's free and so is your daughter. I know it will be hard but we'll be seeing them later. Where they will end up I do not know but it will not be behind bars.'

***

The press conference took place later that afternoon in Sylvia Brunner's office. It didn't last long as Elizabeth had decided to make a short statement and to decline to answer any questions.

Sylvia introduced her client and Elizabeth began, 'What I am going to say will be brief. I wish to touch on two or three aspects of the events that have taken place in this city. I will not be answering any questions and neither will my *Advokat*, Sylvia Brunner. I am sorry about that but I can assure you that I will not be selling my story to anyone either, so you needn't feel cheated.

'First I must thank *Advokat* Brunner for all that she has done for my defence, for her hard work, for keeping my spirits up when I felt low, for being a friend as well as my lawyer.

'Then I have to thank Sam Kagan for having the courage to put his liberty in jeopardy in order that the true facts of what happened on that sad night in February could be presented to the court. On the strength of having known me for less than 24 hours Sam has proved a faithful friend. Through the kindness of the Court President we were able to meet and speak after the end of the trial. You may not know that subsequently while still on the Court premises Sam was arrested by the Basel police and taken into custody. Once all this has been dealt with, whenever that might be, it is our intention to resume our friendship and to see where it leads.

'The demonstration by *Frauen gegen Notzucht* - Women Against Rape - was something which drew the world's attention to the trial: I am grateful to the women who took part and also to the men who stood with them - particularly the men. It was right that a public statement should have been made that rape is totally unacceptable in this or any other society. Some might wish to dismiss such actions but peaceful demonstrations of that kind have their effect on the public awareness of the issue concerned.

'Finally I must say something about the killing of which I have been found guilty. As you know the verdict of the court was that I was guilty of manslaughter and not of murder. I fully accept the verdict, there will be no appeal either against the verdict or the sentence, and I am grateful to the Court for the mercy they have shown. The events of that evening in February remain blurred in my mind but I wish to say - and I wish you to make sure that your papers print this if they print nothing else of what I have said - that I do not ever expect to lose the feeling of remorse and grief over what happened. Vladimir who died at my hand was a colleague of long standing, a man who had been my friend. His behaviour justified my resistance and self defence but that I had to go so far as to kill him is a matter of abiding sadness. Between leaving the court and coming to this office I have been to Vladimir's grave and laid flowers there - the tears that I wept there for a man I once loved were real.' She fought back her tears and took Sylvia's hand.

'I am relieved at the outcome of the trial but I am not in a celebratory mood. You may take photographs of Sylvia Brunner but *not* of myself but then we ask that you should leave - we will not be answering any questions either now or at a later date. Neither will I be writing about my experiences My daughter is not here and I ask that you leave the two of us in peace and that you do not intrude on our return to a normal life.' She paused, 'One final thing, and with this I really will end! My time in the *Untersuchungsgefängnis*, the remand prison for those of you who don't speak German, has been an education. I gladly testify to its progressive and humane regime. But what has impressed itself indelibly on me is that the great majority of the women who were in prison with me had never had a genuine chance in life, had never, even as children, had a relationship that was real and lasting. It is my hope that, wherever I end up living, I will have the opportunity to be of help to such women whether in jail or after they have been released. I believe that no experience in life should ever be wasted, I pray that what I have learned from my time in Basel Prison will be put to good use in the years to come. Thank you.'

The photographers did their work then they all filed out and once they were gone the women were joined by David. The press hadn't been told that all three had visited the cemetery earlier that afternoon. While Elizabeth had stood alone at Vladimir's grave Sylvia and David had gone to Sylvia's father's grave where she had placed a bunch of white lilies and, after standing for a few moments with bowed head, had turned to David, embracing him warmly and telling him, 'David, I can never thank you enough for ridding me of all those false memories so that I can enjoy the real ones which are so very good and for which I am thankful to the bottom of my heart.'

The next arrival at the office was Peter Lewis in the company of Jakob Gold who left him with Elizabeth and took coffee with Sylvia and David. He kissed her on the cheek, 'I think I'm allowed that much familiarity Elizabeth.'

She smiled and returned the greeting, 'You are Peter, we're not exactly strangers are we?'

There was a knock on the door and one of the typists brought in little Olga. Elizabeth indicated that she should be handed to Peter. 'You're free Olga, free to live a normal life, thank God.' He felt the warmth of the little head against his cheek, 'We made her Elizabeth, that's something that will link us for good. And don't forget I've got to set up a trust fund for Olga but first we need to know where you're going to live.'

First a string of nots: not England, USA or Canada I don't want the attentions of their Security people ... Oh sorry Peter!' She had not wanted to remind him of his grilling back in the apartment in West Hampstead.

He shook his head, managed a wan smile and said, 'They haven't been back, they've kept away and left me alone.'

'The Swiss have indicated that they'll let me stay for a short while. It all depends on how things pan out with Sam. You know that Swiss Security have arrested him? Well, they did as soon as our hour together was up. So he's behind bars but he's assured me that he has plans for shortening his time in Swiss hands. He wouldn't say how but he seemed pretty certain. Assuming that he's right and assuming that we do make a go of it ... our home is likely to be in Israel. And Peter, Sam has insisted that I should say this, you will always be welcome to visit us and your daughter. But please tell me how things are between Ruth and yourself and how young Michael's getting on ... '

'And Elizabeth there's a lonely Steinway grand piano sitting in an apartment in West Hampstead wondering where it's going next. What should I do with it?'

'Peter I would love to keep it to take it to Israel, or wherever I'm going, to teach Olga to play and to have it as a reminder of a very happy time and of ... ' she had difficulty with the words, 'a lovely, very kind, English gentleman ... ' They were both moved to tears.

Chapter 34

Tuesday 18th November 1997 , 12.45 p.m.

Sam Kagan knew that they would be waiting for him. And they were very civilised about it all. Elizabeth had just left and there was a knock on the door, 'Excuse me, Mr Kagan.' It was one of the police officers who had been observing the day's proceedings in the court. 'I'm Klaus Schoen from the Basel Police.' He shook Sam warmly by the hand. 'I'm afraid that one of my colleagues would like a word with you as soon as it's convenient.'

'Which means?'

'Now, I'm afraid. He said that I was to wait until you had spoken to Fräulein Feldman before I approached you. He also said that you could speak to *Advokat* Brunner - we assume that she will be looking after your interests.'

'Thank you. No, it will be Ernst Weber one of the partners in Sylvia Brunner's firm. We had anticipated that my evidence would be of interest to you and your colleagues. I assume that your colleague is the Public Prosecutor.'

'Just so, but not from Basel. Lieutenant Blum is from Bern, from the Federal Prosecutor's Office. Though he'll see you here in Basel. Here we deal with common criminals, in Bern they deal with uncommon ones, if you don't mind my putting it that way. To be frank you have caused quite a stir with your evidence. And, though I'm sure you won't quote me on it, Sir, we hope they're not too severe on you. It was chivalrous of you to put yourself at risk as you have. She's an attractive young woman - it certainly made the front pages of the newspapers. After your bravery in coming forward it seems a shame to have to take you into custody, Mr Kagan.'

'Well, if it's all about bravery and chivalry, being arrested seems a necessary part of the action. There'd be no bravery if I could just walk away and go home. Be encouraged, Officer, it's your arresting me *now* that makes what went before it brave! But as far as the newspapers are concerned I would prefer to keep my face off their pages.'

'We had assumed that, Sir. We have a van available, one without windows that will give no opportunity to the photographers or the TV cameras - it's amazing how quickly they gather when something unusual is happening. I know that the President warned off the photographers but there are plenty of them out there who are willing to risk his wrath to get a shot of you, the German magazines would pay them good money. And even if there were no photographers out there, Sir, we would still have to be very careful in case someone wished to use you for target practice! If you would come with me we will go to the van now.'

'I need first to telephone *Advokat* Weber before we leave, he's anticipating a call from me.' The Officer indicated the public telephone and Sam made the call, checking with Schoen the address where he was to meet Lieutenant Blum.

'No handcuffs, Officer?'

'Certainly not, Mr Kagan. That would be totally unnecessary and inappropriate for the likes of you, a minister of religion!'

'You only have my word for it.'

'Your word has carried quite a lot of weight in the last few days and, in any case, you can be sure that Lieutenant Blum will have checked you out in the public records and the not so public ones. He's got the reputation of being very thorough in everything he handles.'

The van halted for the gate to open and then pulled into the yard behind the Public Prosecutor's Office which faced onto the *Binningerstrasse*. On the other side of the yard was the *Waaghof*, the remand prison where Elizabeth had spent the last nine months and where she would shortly be collecting her belongings and saying farewell to her former companions. Sam wondered whether he would be moving into it shortly, not to take her place exactly - they were unlikely to have mixed wings!

They took the lift to the third floor and were shown into a conference room with both a large and a small table. Windows ran the length of one side giving a view of the road and the viaduct crossing it. Sam and the officer stood at the window watching a tram clatter past and chatting generally.

'Good afternoon, Mr Kagan. I'm delighted to have the pleasure of meeting you.' Sam had heard the door open but Blum had crossed the room more quickly than he had expected. He was a restless man, over six foot tall and smartly dressed. Sam took in the dark jacket, navy chinos and dark brown shoes. The man had taste and was clearly concerned with his appearance, he probably shopped over the border in Italy. Only his tie was somewhat awry, as if asserting itself in protest at the good order of the remainder of his clothing. Certainly he was far smarter in appearance than any policeman in civvies that Sam had encountered. Blum indicated to Schoen with a movement of the head that he could go his way.

Sam and Blum exchanged inconsequential pleasantries and Blum showed him to a seat at a small table at the end of the room, 'More friendly if we use the small table, Mr Kagan. It's hard to relax when a handful of us are seated around the big conference table. Coffee?'

Sam smiled, 'And a relaxed meeting is a productive meeting - one at which secrets and confidences are willingly exchanged? Yes, black and without sugar, please.'

'A relaxed meeting is a civilised meeting, Mr Kagan. *Advokat* Weber will be with us in around ten minutes and he has told me to restrain myself and leave off questioning you until he joins us. So it's up to you, Mr Kagan, what we discuss until he comes, though if you can tell me about the archeology of Masada ... I've read Yigael Yadin's account of it and it fascinates me, though I'm ashamed to admit that I've yet to visit your country. Do you think that the Zealots really took their own lives rather than falling into Roman hands or could it be ... '

'That Josephus was an effective public relations man for the Romans and covered up the fact that their soldiers butchered the defenders, man, woman and child?'

'Yes, that's what puzzles me.'

'On the basis that if you challenged the security of the Roman Empire you were likely to be butchered or crucified by them wholesale - something they were more than happy that people should know - then I tend to believe that old Josephus was reporting actual events and not doing a cover up job for his new masters.'

'And the defenders ... they were a mixture of armed Zealots and religious folk from Qumran, the Dead Sea Scroll people?'

They were deep in discussion when *Advokat* Weber arrived and found himself drinking coffee while Sam and Blum finished their discussion on Masada.

'Our apologies *Advokat* Weber but we were involved in

deciding whether certain deaths in CE 73 were murder or assisted suicide. A considerable time ago I agree and the Federal Prosecutor's Office in Bern generally gets quicker results than that. But your client has persuaded me that it was a mixture of assisted suicide and actual suicide so I can close my murder file - unless assisted suicide amounts to some form of homicide! I've also got an invitation to visit the scene of the crime but that, of course, is not the reason for our being here this afternoon. Sadly we must turn to business and first of all we have to deal with certain activities to which Mr Kagan owned up in the Basel Court last week. I have to remind you that our meeting will be tape recorded.' He indicated a microphone, the recording equipment and technician were evidently in another room.

Weber took a legal pad from his briefcase and produced a fountain pen. Blum wondered to himself why some lawyers wrote with such old fashioned devices and decided that it was to slow down the progress of the questioning. 'Right Lieutenant, you wish to put some questions to Mr Kagan. You have already said that they arise from his evidence in the *Strafgericht* and neither of us is surprised at that. You will caution him, of course.'

Blum gave the caution and added, 'But Rabbi Kagan you have already incriminated yourself very publicly in the Court here in Basel! I assume that you don't intend to retract your testimony?'

'No, Lieutenant it was given on oath. I won't be retracting anything.'

'Mr Kagan's activities in this city last February included bugging hotel rooms, tapping telephones and carrying on the business of a foreign power on Swiss soil. Just how many of our laws he has broken I do not know - it may well be that what has been revealed in court is merely the tip of the iceberg and that Mr Kagan has much more to confess.'

'And why should my client bring forward further offences - assuming, that is, that there *are* any further transgressions for him to confess to you?'

'There were events which took place around *Fasnacht* that are inexplicable and it may be that Mr Kagan can shed some light on them. There is also the involvement of the Russian SVR, Fräulein Feldman's former employers - I am assuming that she has either resigned from their service or been dismissed from it? I ... we would feel happier and perhaps more secure if we could find some adequate explanation for the events in question. If Mr Kagan could assist in these matters it might well affect how the Court would view his very serious transgressions of our criminal law.'

'You are proposing to cut some sort of deal?'

'Perhaps, Herr Weber, perhaps. Now Mr Kagan, I take it that you stand by what you said in Court - that you bugged the lady's room and her telephone and that in doing so you were working for a foreign power.'

'As I've already said I testified under oath, I admit to it now and I will have to do so if you bring me to Court, Lieutenant.'

'And there is the question of the identity of your former employers. There seem to be only two possibilities, either the CIA or Mossad and my colleagues are putting their bets on Mossad. So which is it Mr Kagan?'

'No comment, I'm afraid. Lieutenant.'

'I didn't really expect any admission but I had to ask. A Court might not be so happy with that response. They might feel that you were being somewhat unco-operative and, as you heard during your friend's trial, they might begin to wonder whether you weren't part of some

Mafiya-like operation.'

'They might think that, whatever I said about the CIA or Mossad, mightn't they, Lieutenant? But you shouldn't forget that the Court appeared to accept that Fräulein Feldman worked for the Russian SVR: whoever tangles with them is more likely to be from a security service than from the *Mafiya*. And, from what you have just said, you clearly believe it too.'

'Yes, perhaps ... but it could influence the attitude of the Prosecutor - for instance in the charges brought against you and the penalty he seeks from the Court.'

'But that's not the main thing you want cleared up. You spoke of other events at *Fasnacht* that remain a mystery to you. Perhaps you could be more specific. If it is possible for me to help without a breach of trust then I will do so.'

'Good. I can say that the more assistance you give me, the better Court and Prosecutor will like it. Well, the events are those of the afternoon of the first day of the *Fasnacht* Carnival - the Monday. They took place at the time when Fräulein Feldman was recovering in hospital from her experiences of the Sunday evening and when you, under your alias of Sam Charles, should have been many kilometres away in Hamburg. You clearly didn't go to Hamburg that night, did you?'

'No, Lieutenant, I remained in Basel for nearly another day.'

'Good. That is interesting. But to proceed. The events have to do with three persons connected with your Russian lady friend - with Ruth Lewis, the wife of Fräulein Feldman's lover, the Lewis son Michael and a Swiss friend of the Lewis family, Frau Paula Gold. You know the people to whom I am referring?'

'I know who you mean.'

'During the afternoon carnival procession Frau Gold collapsed, or rather she was rendered unconscious by a knock-out injection. A fake ambulance was used to kidnap the three of them and take them to a disused warehouse but then they were rescued. Michael, the Lewis' son, described it as like the outbreak of World War III. However, more importantly, he took a video film of most of what went on and we also have statements from the three of them about these events. What we don't know is the reason for the kidnap or, for that matter, for the rescue. Neither do we know the identity of the combatants. Perhaps you would enjoy seeing the film that the youngster made - I'm sure you would enjoy it, Mr Kagan. You might even enjoy reliving those stirring events!'

Advokat Weber broke in, 'Mr Kagan do you really think that you ought to comment on these matters?'

'Thanks for warning me Herr Weber but I am perfectly happy to assist the Lieutenant so far as I can, he's only asking me to see a video film. Lieutenant, please go ahead - I'm very interested to see what happened that afternoon.'

Blum indicated a television set in the corner and, using a remote control which he produced from the drawer of the table, switched it on and set the video running. At first there were rather shaky views of the Basel streets and then commandos coming over a wall in what appeared to be the yard of a warehouse, ambulance doors being thrown open by more commandos and people being made to get out of the ambulance in response to orders from men with American accents. After that the tape ran out.

Sam was glad that it stopped when it did and that he personally hadn't featured in it. He turned to Blum, 'And that's it? I trust no one was badly hurt.'

'That's all we have, I fear and, as for casualties, that's something I would like to hear you tell me about, Mr Kagan.'

Again Herr Weber advised caution and again Sam thanked him for his advice.

'Tell me more Lieutenant.'

'You saw the commando, party? Well they rescued the three who had been kidnapped. Of course the women were grateful for their rescue and reported that their rescuers had American accents - the one who took them to the *Kantonsspital* after everyone else had left apparently had a pleasant sense of humour and wished them a "Nice day" when he departed. It couldn't have been you, of course, Mr Kagan as he didn't have a beard!'

'Well that's a relief, Lieutenant. I just thought for a moment you might be accusing me of rescuing some kidnap victims!' Sam smiled and Blum smiled back, unbelief written on his face.

'And what can you tell us to steady Swiss nerves, Mr Kagan?'

'I will have to ponder this, Lieutenant, and see whether I can be of assistance to you. I'm sure you'll be asking about it again.'

'If you can bring yourself to remember Mr Kagan it would be well received by my masters. I will most certainly come back to you on this. I think that for the moment that will complete my questioning. Is there anything you would like to add to the proceedings?'

'Just this, Lieutenant. In the next day or so Ben Friedman, a friend of mine, will contact you to arrange a meeting. He has some material that may interest you, some papers and another video tape. It's not a trap of any kind but he will not be able to meet you on Swiss territory, you have laws that could place him in a difficult position, so he will suggest a meeting in France - he enjoys a glass or two of wine and he's enjoying a stay in Alsace at the moment and that's likely to be where he will want to see you, Lieutenant. As I say it's not a trap, harming you would not improve my prospects in Swiss hands would it? I assume that shortly you will be accommodating me securely across the way in the *Untersuchungsgefängnis*, though not in the cell vacated by Elizabeth today.'

'Yes, I'm afraid it will be necessary to deprive you of your liberty, Mr Kagan. I greatly regret the necessity. Incidentally, your friend Mr Friedman, he's not another rabbi, is he?'

'No Lieutenant, he's a night club singer and entertainer and you'll like him.'

'And how will he identify himself, has he a code word or something of that sort?'

'He has indeed, he will tell you he wishes to discuss the Basel Exodus. I suspect no one has asked to do that before.'

'You are quite right, Mr Kagan. I will be most interested to hear from him. In the next day or so, you say?'

'In the next day or so.'

'And Rabbi, with a password like that am I to see the Rhein divided for you to cross over?'

'Probably not, Lieutenant though strange things can happen.'

'And now I'm afraid that I must confirm that you are under arrest on suspicion of offences which include the bugging of a hotel room and its telephones and may also extend to other actions in this city in and around last February. A colleague will be here shortly to take you across to the *Waaghof*. I am sure that you will be comfortable there - they are aware of your dietary requirements and I suspect that, with your varied interests, you will be able to occupy your mind during your stay there more fully than most of the others accommodated with you. If you're short of reading matter let me know and I'll see that it's put right. Thank you for your assistance Mr Kagan and thank you for being here to look after your client's interests, Herr Weber.' They shook hands and Blum left, no doubt to collect the tape after he had checked its quality.

Weber looked at Sam, 'And what am I to do now, Mr Kagan?'

'Just stay tuned and await events. The Lieutenant's trip across the border to Alsace will add a new dimension to the proceedings, I promise.'

'One beneficial to your case, I trust?'

'Of course, what else?' Sam was interested that Blum had not mentioned the other events of that Monday in February, those at the Bahnhof SBB - the main railway station. He either thought it was nothing to do with what had happened earlier that day or he was keeping it as a topic for a later meeting. Well Blum would soon be hearing of that happening as well.

Chapter 35

Friday 21st November 1997

Lieutenant Blum of the Bern Federal Prosecutor's Office parked his Volvo outside the *Musée Français du Chemin de Fer* - the French National Railway Museum - in Mulhouse. Half an hour before he had been in Switzerland and a quick journey down the *Autoroute* had brought him over the border into France and to an industrial estate in this corner of Alsace. It was a cold dull day and light rain was falling. It was an odd place to meet anyone on official business but then this was a very odd case. He strolled to the entrance and bought a ticket, a copy of a railway paper and the museum guide book at the kiosk. It was a quarter of an hour before the start of his encounter with "Mr Friedman". He would kill time wandering around the main hall and locate the place for the meeting - the message had said "next to the brown Nord de Glehn-du Bosquet compound Atlantic locomotive, number 2.670". It was like some game and Lieutenant Blum didn't enjoy playing games. A colleague from Bern was somewhere in the museum filming the locomotives with a video camera and planning to get some shots of Blum with Friedman when they met.

The museum wasn't busy apart from a group of British visitors who were taking their time over photographing anything and everything that could be photographed. Funny how these Brits seemed to wander the world looking for railways - he'd seen them all over Switzerland especially if steam trains were involved - you'd think they'd invented the railway! It was cold in the museum and he wished he hadn't left his overcoat in the car. He was dressed in navy trousers and a dark blue sports coat, a tall thin figure with a restless, hungry look and dark thinning hair. He determined to walk around at a fair pace in order to keep warm but then decided that this would make him conspicuous: museums were for inspecting the exhibits, not racing past them. He slowed down and hoped the meeting would be a short one. He'd already located the meeting place, the brown locomotive was near the entrance and the board next to it confirmed its identity. He'd wondered whether he was being sent on a wild goose chase - it might still turn out to be that. He returned to the locomotive, it was a couple of minutes before four o'clock but a man was standing there, seemingly engrossed in inspecting it. Perhaps he really was interested in the thing! He wore a light fawn belted raincoat and was about a head shorter than Blum. He had dark hair, cut in a style that suggested the military to Blum, and to the Swiss he looked slightly overweight. Blum wandered up and stood nearby. The man carried a copy of *La Vie du Rail* and Blum placed his own copy of the paper on top of the guide book and turned to the stranger. He wanted to ask, 'What sort of fools play games like this?' but instead he said, 'A fine piece of machinery isn't it?'

The stranger glanced at the journal Blum held and was direct with his reply, 'Blum? Good, I'm Friedman we have business to do and the Basel Exodus to discuss.' There was no mistaking Friedman's American accent. They shook hands and Friedman continued, 'I'm rather shy of cameras. Perhaps you'd like to call your friend over, take his video camera from him and give me the tape. I'd be much happier if you did that. Indeed without your co-operation in this respect I will be very unhappy.'

Blum looked over his shoulder and indicated with a movement of his head that his colleague should come over. The fellow had been supposed to keep in the background, instead he had attracted attention right away. He took the camera, removed the tape and handed it to Friedman who pocketed it, 'OK keep the camera, put it into its case and send him away - he'll only catch a chill in here.' Blum did as he was bid and dispatched his colleague.

Friedman began, 'Now to do business, Lieutenant. You are here to look after the interests of the Swiss government. I'm here on behalf of Sam Kagan who is at the moment in the custody of that government in prison and wishes to be on his way as soon as possible.'

Blum smiled, 'Of course, Mr Friedman. But first of all he has to face a few charges and an appearance in court before he does so. And it is rather more than likely that we will wish to entertain him in secure accommodation for some time afterwards. He may not find that too unpleasant, after all he seems reasonably happy with the present arrangements, he's busy with the study of some heavy theology. We've had to find him some books that weren't in the prison library - Maimonides' *Guide for the Perplexed* and Karl Barth's *Church Dogmatics* - so a spell in custody would give him plenty of time to get to grips with that sort of thing without too many interruptions. Several years inside, that's what seems to be in prospect. Quality thinking time!'

This was greeted with a smile in return, 'That is the way my friend Sam Kagan understood you and your colleagues to be thinking. He would prefer alternative arrangements and has asked me to discuss them with you, Lieutenant.'

Blum nodded, 'I'm sure he has his preferences but I don't think we can entertain them. Why should we? OK he's a sort of public hero in Basel, putting his neck in the noose to save the lady from jail. He's also the Hero of the *Marktplatz*. But he's a Mossad operative or at any rate he was one until a few months ago - now he's a Mossad pensioner I suppose! You surely don't think that you can come to Switzerland, bug rooms, tap telephones, get up to I don't know what other offences on behalf of Mossad, admit to it in court and then wave us goodbye, do you Mr Friedman? Besides, your people have been giving the Swiss rather a hard time recently, blackening the good name of Swiss banking and I don't think we owe you any favours.' He was warming to his task even though the museum was freezing.

'I expected that you would be keen to keep him in your care but there are a few factors that your people might wish to consider before coming to a final decision, Lieutenant. Let me acquaint you with some of them.' Blum nodded, he was curious about what they had as bargaining points, there would have been no reason for this meeting unless they had something to offer. Friedman continued, 'I expect you remember the visit of the Russian ambassador to the office of the Basel Central Police Station on the evening of the first day of *Fasnacht* this year.'

Blum tried to look blank but without much success. He managed a guarded response, 'Well as a working hypothesis let's assume that the gentleman made such a visit on that particular evening.'

'And it wasn't to discuss the delights of the carnival.'

'As a hypothesis that's reasonable.'

'He was retrieving a member of his staff, a certain Second Secretary, who had been found with some incriminating material earlier that evening at the Bahnhof SBB?'

'Let's continue with this fascinating hypothesis, Mr

Friedman.' Blum was very interested in what he was being told and wondered where it was going to lead. Kagan was from Mossad, or that was the conclusion Blum's colleagues had reached, the CIA was another possibility though an outside one, but what was the Russian connection this time?

'I can be specific about the material, Lieutenant. There were a number of bank statements for members of the Swiss Council of Ministers - not exactly the sort of information that your rather anonymous rulers like to have in the wrong hands?'

For Blum they were on holy ground, discussing such sensitive matters, and he found himself looking around to be sure that there were no eavesdroppers listening in to their conversation. Perhaps the locomotive was bugged - these Israelis, or whoever they were, seemed good in that area. 'Mr Friedman I would prefer to make a tour of this splendid museum. Wonderful though this locomotive is, perhaps we should see what else is on display and besides I'm getting very cold standing here.' The locomotive might be bugged but as he spoke he remembered that it was more likely that Friedman himself was wired for sound. Never mind, he would take care what he said but he would be glad to move around.

'Of course, Lieutenant, and yes it's a wonderful locomotive. Do you know that even the Brits thought so and bought three of them! There's much for us to see, if we don't finish it today - and I expect you will have to report back to your masters and then meet me again - we can continue on our next visit.'

'Perhaps and perhaps not. Supposing my masters, as you call them, supposing they wish to continue this interesting discussion it's possible they might send someone other than myself.'

'I think that they might prefer to keep these matters within the smallest circle possible, Lieutenant. I will expect to see you again. But let us make what progress we can today.' They were standing by a fence facing a large dark blue steam locomotive whose wheels began to rotate as it emitted recorded sounds. 'Your toys seem to work, Mr Friedman.'

'Yes 232 U1 is quite a splendid locomotive, although my favourite is the one you've torn me away from. But they're even better when they're working properly ... like my friend Sam, he would prefer to be out in the real world rather than being looked after with the infinite care you lavish on the guests of the Swiss Confederation. He has no wish to remain a museum piece. My task is to help your masters to see it the same way.'

'So we return to our discussion of certain events and documents.'

'Documents like this one. It's only a sample of what I have elsewhere, Lieutenant.' He produced a bank statement and handed it over.

Blum looked at the sheet with barely concealed excitement. Before he could stop himself he'd said, 'There's a lot of money in that account.'

'Your Council of Ministers isn't exactly poor is it, Lieutenant? What I have to offer is to hand over all the copies of the bank statements in return for Sam getting out of Switzerland. If they weren't handed over they *might*, I say no more than that, they *might* end up in the wrong hands and though it's certain that your Ministers would have no difficulty in explaining how they came by their money there can be little doubt that they would prefer not to have the indignity of doing so'

'And I may take this sample of your wares with me?'

'By all means. Take it back to your masters in Bern, let

them see and decide.' Blum took out his wallet, folded the bank statement and placed it carefully inside, if he lost this he would be out of a job. Friedman produced a video cassette from his pocket and handed it to Blum. 'And there's one more thing. When the Russian ambassador called on your colleagues in Basel that evening he was recorded on the security cameras as he went into the building and as he came out with his Second Secretary. This is a copy of the video tape of those events. Not only do you get the bank statements in return for my friend but you get the only other copy of the tape that exists outside of Switzerland - indeed outside of the hands of the Swiss police. If this were to get into the hands of the German press they would have some fun at the expense of Russia and Switzerland - and just think about it, should it ever come out that the bank records of even the Swiss Council of Ministers are not secure, there might be some reluctance on the part of wealthy Russians and others to bank with you. People don't have to read John Grisham to know that there are plenty of bankers in the Cayman Islands ready to do business and ask a minimum of questions.'

'Blackmail!'

'No certainly not! I'm just providing cogent arguments for the release of Sam Kagan!'

'There is one aspect Mr Friedman that needs clarification. *If* my masters were to accept your proposal and take the interesting material you have on offer in return for the speedy departure of Mr Kagan from Swiss soil, they would have no guarantee that you wouldn't circulate other copies to unfriendly German magazines or to anyone else. You would get Mr Kagan and we would still get a whole load of trouble!'

'I'll put a question to you, Lieutenant. How does your

banking system work?'

'What exactly do you mean, Mr Friedman? Which aspects of banking do you have in mind?'

'Let me put it like this, if I were a potential foreign customer of one of your banks then what would be the features of Swiss banking that would be likely to appeal to me?'

'That's easy. Confidentiality, trustworthiness and security.'

'Good, Lieutenant. That is what we can offer as our part of the deal - confidentiality, trustworthiness and security. We have no quarrel with Switzerland. OK, and this is of course purely hypothetical, the Israeli government and a variety of Jewish organisations have a few bones to pick with you and your banks but my friend and I have no problems with you apart from the fact that you are impeding his departure from your country. Let me ask you a few questions. First, are you satisfied that Sam Kagan wasn't working against Swiss interests either security or commercial ones?'

Blum had smiled at the introduction of the hypothetical. Relations between the two men were thawing. Blum was now satisfied that he could do business with this man. There was a pause. 'Apart from your possession of these documents I can accept that he was only working against Russian interests. And I am prepared to accept that these bank statements came to him via those Russians.'

'Good. Second, are you satisfied that Sam knows how to keep his mouth shut?'

'No problem there considering his former employment.'

'Excellent. Finally how do you rate his character and trustworthiness?'

"Of the very highest in every way. He has earned great respect with the Court and, I must add, my colleagues. He has risked his freedom for someone else - and if there is a romantic element in the story that adds to his stature for many of us - and though I did refer in jest to the Hero of the *Marktplatz* that action has not gone without notice.'

'If you were assessing him as a banker with whom you might do business, Lieutenant?'

'Mere Lieutenants in the Public Prosecutor's Office do not have wealth requiring sophisticated banking - or if they do they are ripe for investigation themselves.' They both laughed heartily and Blum continued, 'OK I'd trust him to handle my business with integrity.'

'Fine. What we promise we can and will deliver, you and your masters can be completely satisfied on that. And that takes us about as far as we can go at the moment. You have one of the bank statements to take back to Bern. You also have a copy of the security video of the Russian ambassador. I promise you that there is only one set of the bank statements and one other copy of the video tape in our possession or, and of course this is entirely hypothetical, in Israeli possession. If you oblige by releasing Sam Kagan and letting him leave Switzerland, then both Sam and I promise that no further copies of the bank statements or video will be made. We will give you all we have.'

'When do we meet again, Mr Friedman, and where?'

'How long are your masters likely to need to ponder the matter?'

'Three days, four at most.'

'Then I'll call you by telephone on Wednesday morning, say at about 10 o'clock. We can make arrangements then, that's if you have anything to offer in the matter of the Basel Exodus.'

'Mr Friedman would you like to join me for a cup of coffee in the cafeteria? I certainly need a warm drink of some kind - *Kafi Fertig* would be better but I never drink alcohol on duty.'

'Delighted, Lieutenant. The cafeteria's upstairs near the exit, I think.'

But at the stairway to the cafeteria was a notice: *"Cafeteria fermée pour les vacances des personnels."*

'The French! They're impossible. Mr Friedman, it would never happen in Switzerland It is no wonder that the Baslers make fun of the Alsatian peasants in their *Fasnacht* carnival by depicting them as *Weggis* - ridiculous characters with long yellow hair! To close the refreshment facilities because the staff decide to go on holiday, it is laughable - that is unless you are frozen to the bone and in dire need of a drink!'

Friedman smiled, 'This of course is entirely hypothetical, Lieutenant, but such things are far from unknown occurrences in Israel.' They smiled, shook hands and went their way - Blum back to his office in Bern, Friedman to his hotel in Colmar from where he would telephone Sam's *Advokat*. Both were satisfied with the way things had gone, both were in need of a good cup of coffee or something stronger.

Chapter 36

Monday 24th November 1997

He had reached Moscow late that afternoon on a train from Kiev. "Hard class", the timetable had called it, and the plastic seats had lived up to that description. The fourteen and a half hours since his departure from Kiev at 2 o'clock that morning had seemed far longer. This visit to Russia and what had once been constituent parts of the USSR had lasted nearly three weeks. His stock of tinned food was almost exhausted and he was longing for home, his family and his colleagues. It was a job for a younger man, perhaps time for him to begin to think of handing over. But he knew that he wouldn't, at any rate not for some time to come. The work, for all its discomforts, still drew him. After a few days at home he would be planning his next journey eastwards as an emissary.

His supply of clean ironed shirts had been used up long ago and the one he was wearing, though clean, hadn't seen an iron for a while. The Metro train clattered on and he observed his fellow passengers. Like him they showed signs of weariness, a day at the office or factory followed by the travails of commuting homewards. The doors closed on *Filevsky Park:* three more stations and he would be at his destination. The train halted for signals and stood waiting to move on. The silence felt unnatural until a motor or pump of some kind whirred into action. Apart from two men at the far end of the carriage deep in conversation the passengers were inhabiting their own private worlds longing to be home with their families or at any rate behind their own front doors.

He thought back over the last few days and smiled to himself. Four days had been spent trying to get a non-observant Jew to give his former wife a *get*, the Jewish divorce document. They had had a civil divorce in Kiev. The man had stayed there and remarried. The woman had gone to Brooklyn to join her sister. Because she didn't have a religious divorce she couldn't remarry in the synagogue and she didn't wish to marry elsewhere. Her ex-husband, out of a mixture of malice and greed, had refused to sign the *get*. Argument and pleading with the man had achieved nothing and just when it had seemed hopeless - with four days wasted - the man's new wife had come into the room. They hadn't heard her enter the apartment but she had been there for the previous hour and heard nearly the whole of their conversation. In five minutes she had told her husband that he was going to sign the *get* and that if he didn't he would have another divorce on his hands. Whether she was moved by a sense of fair play or whether it was that she didn't want him remaining married to another woman in Jewish eyes wasn't clear. What was certain was that she meant business. He had signed promptly and another task had been accomplished.

The train started again and he looked at his watch - 6.35 p.m. - he hoped he would be able to eat before he left his destination for the journey back to the centre of Moscow and then outwards to more nondescript suburbs on the other side of the city where he would spend the night.

At last the train arrived and as he picked up his suitcase a chest muscle gave him a twinge of pain. He had pulled the muscle getting his case down from the luggage rack in a train two weeks before. Then the case had been heavy with tinned food. Not much of it left now, in fact only enough for one more meal. That didn't matter, he would be with friends for tomorrow's meals. He joined the crowd getting out at *Molodezhnaya* He had memorised the map, it didn't do to look as if you were a stranger. You had to be street-wise in these parts to stay out of harm's way. In some respects his work was safer since the fall of Communism but in other ways it was more dangerous: he was more at risk from random violence on the streets, whether as a direct target or merely as an accidental victim caught unwittingly in the middle of violence. It took him five minutes to reach the street, *Marshala Timoshenko*, and locate the apartment block. It was the sort of place he knew well. 'Khrushchev flats' they called them. Jerry built and run down with untidy courtyards and uncut grass. Lifts were to be avoided. He remembered only too clearly an encounter with a drunken thug in a lift in a similar block in Leningrad, as it had then been. So he climbed the stairs to the sixth floor and found Flat 658. He paused, prayed and rang the bell. No response. He rang again and thought he could hear movement within. He continued his prayer.

Someone came to the door, 'Who are you and what do you want at this time of the day?' It was surprising how often his conversations began in this sort of way.

'Mrs Feldman I have a message for you from your daughter, Lizaveta.'

'And why would she want to send you with a message, there's a postal system as well as the telephone.'

'I suppose she just wanted to make sure it got to you and didn't get lost on the way.'

The door opened a little on a chain and the face of a frightened woman looked out, 'Move back into the light will you, I want to see you.'

He did as she asked and waited. 'You don't look like one of them. If you have a letter from her you can let me have it.'

He walked to the door and passed the letter through the narrow opening. 'I can talk to you about her when you've read it. I hope you feel able to trust me.' The letter was taken from his hand and the door closed. He waited, hoping that none of the neighbours would appear and want to know his business. It was cold and he was tired. A dog barked down in the courtyard. The sound always brought back to him thoughts of the camps - the German *Konzentrationslager* and the Russian *Gulag*, there wasn't much to choose between them - totalitarian regimes had always had an unpleasant way with dissidents. Orwell's vision of the military boot crashing down onto the human face was a powerful depiction of what life had held for dissidents under such regimes - and it still was so in some parts of the world. He was tired but not too tired to pray. He wanted to get this business done and get back across the city to his friends and his bed for the night. He knew it was likely that he'd have to come back to this apartment again the next day. On the stairway people were talking, he hoped they weren't coming to this floor. Their footsteps continued on upwards. The door opened, but still on the chain, and the woman spoke quietly, 'Thank you for bringing it. I haven't heard from her for a year now. You aren't Russian are you?'

He was close to the door and his reply was also in a low voice, 'American, Mrs Feldman and I'm here to help.'

He saw the woman cross herself and then the chain was undone and the door opened. He stepped into the apartment. Obstacle number one had been overcome. He did not forget a prayer of thanks. She closed and chained the door, then she bolted it. They looked at one another. Both were short and dark. The woman was in her 60's and was the heavier of the two. She wore an old black dress with her gray hair pulled back into a bun. Her face showed anxiety verging on fear. The man showed his tiredness in his face but not in his posture - he had a presence about him, he stood upright with his shoulders back. He was in his late thirties or early forties and a good head of black hair showed from under his hat. He had a full beard.

'Your coat Mr ....'

'Avraham Shazar, Madam.'

'You're tired. You have come a long way?'

'From Kiev today. But I have been travelling for nearly three weeks since I set out from Brooklyn, New York.'

'And you have come here. Don't you know it's dangerous here?'

'I know that Russia is dangerous, I've been in your country many times before.'

'That was not what I meant. It's dangerous for you to be here in my apartment. Only yesterday they were here trying to get information about Lizaveta. As if *I* knew what she was doing! But I don't and they won't believe it. They tap my telephone and read my mail, though there's little enough of that.'

'Who are *they*?'

'The KGB, who else? The lot she used to work for. When they offered her the job I thought she was made for life but it took her away from here and from me - we've almost lost contact. I'm here on my own in this place on a pittance of a pension that doesn't increase and buys less and less. We've always had them and we probably always will. Some organisation to spy on people and terrorise them! And now we've got the *Mafiya* as well.'

'I believe they're the SVR nowadays.'

'Okhrana, Cheka, NKVD, KGB or SVR - what does it matter?'

'A sad fact of Russian life, Mrs Feldman.'

'And of American life too?'

'I won't say that our security people haven't intruded, it's not unknown even today, but it's much rarer.'

'Excuse my discourtesy Mr Shazar. You need something to drink. Lemon tea perhaps? Good. Then if you would like to have a seat I will make some. Your hat, I should have taken it from you.'

'If it doesn't offend you I would prefer to keep my head covered.'

'You're a Jew then?'

'Yes I travel on the business of a Jewish group called the Lubavitchers. We're based in Brooklyn but we originated in central Russia as part of a larger movement. Our founder around 250 years ago was Rabbi Schneur Zalman of Liady. We feel a strong call to assist Russian Jews facing persecution or wanting to get out of the country. And that's part of the reason for my visits.' He wondered whether he ought to be telling her this but he had sensed that she was sympathetic. 'I wonder if you would be willing to leave me to myself in this room to pray while you get the tea.'

'You can pray all you like, Mr Shazar. There's a lot of praying done in this room.' She indicated a table in the corner with three icons, 'That's where I pray where the holy icons are. Let me know when you have finished. What about food? What can I get you?'

'At the risk of seeming rude, would you mind if I ate some food that I have brought with me it's ... '

'Kosher? Of course you can. You have your rules and I have mine, some of them from the same Source!'

He opened the case and removed his last tin. As he did so her eye caught sight of something familiar. She pointed to it, 'My father used to wear *tefillin* when he prayed. I haven't seen them in years.'

'Your father was Jewish then?'

'And my mother too, though I've gone another way. It's strange to have a rabbi in my home. Strange but not unpleasant - my childhood memories are happy ones. My mother lighting the Shabbat candles ... ' Her voice tailed off, there had been a lot of life since then, a lot of very hard life. And it wasn't a pleasant prospect, having to face what was left of life on your own, having lost parents, two husbands and now your daughter. The memory of her own childhood threw into stark relief her present situation. She took control of herself again, 'Let me know when you are ready Rabbi and I will have your tea and food.' She closed the door on him and went to the kitchen. She had many questions to ask him about Lizaveta. A feeling of hope welled up within her, perhaps she would see her daughter again.

Avraham Shazar looked around the room. It was strange to be praying in the company of Christian icons. He turned his back on them and began his prayers. There was much to give thanks for, much praise to offer and requests to make. He remembered his daughter's school examination the next day, he was fortunate to have a loving family who supported him in his calling. Being away from home so often was hard for him, but he knew that in many ways it was harder for his wife and daughters, waiting and praying for his safe return. And he gave special thanks for his discovery of his host's Jewishness - this had removed most of the reservations he had had about complying with Sam Kagan's request for him to contact Mrs Feldman.

They sat facing one another across the table. He felt refreshed after the tea and his meal. There was much talking. He told her that the news was both good and bad.

Lizaveta wanted to see her but had been in a Swiss jail charged with murder. The murder of an SVR colleague at that - no wonder *they* were spending so much time and effort on tapping her telephone, messing round with her post and trying to intimidate her. Word of the verdict had just reached him and he was able to tell Mrs Feldman that Lizaveta was free. Then he added:

'Lizaveta has recently given birth to a daughter.'

'So I'm a grandmother?'

'Sounds likely to me that you are!'

'And the father? Her husband? Is he Russian?'

'English I believe and I'm afraid he isn't her husband.'

This didn't seem to perturb her, 'A grandmother! You are the bearer of good news Mr Shazar.'

But immediately her mood changed. 'Where will she and her baby go?' she asked, her words heavy with concern. He replied that Lizaveta was still in Switzerland but that Israel was a possible destination. It worried him that Sam had put himself at risk to provide the evidence to clear her of murder. But he knew that he, Avraham Shazar, was a risk taker too. He regularly took risks for those in danger as he was doing now - and not just for Jews. He had come to this apartment thinking that he was going to meet a Gentile: instead he had discovered the she was Jewish, though a Russian Orthodox Christian. Did that put her on the edge or nearer the centre of his world? He wasn't sure. He felt that he ought to have been more certain but he wasn't. He empathised with Sam and his situation. He felt for this lonely, fearful woman and he was aware that he had already made up his mind what to do.

'Mrs Feldman it seems to me that if you want to see your daughter again there's only one way for you to do so.'

'I've come to the same conclusion.'

'You will have to leave Russia. And if you do I don't think they will let you back. It won't be easy for you if you take that way. You've known nowhere else and it won't be easy to settle in a foreign country.'

'But you've got people out of Russia and they've settled down where they've gone?'

'Yes, that's true. And some have been much older than you are. I'm thinking of a Pole I know who fought with the Russians in the Great Patriotic War and lived in Russia until around 1990. Then we brought him to Brooklyn when he was in his 80's and placed him in one of our homes. He's settled in well enough, part of our community and cared for by us.'

'But who would have me? Could I go to Brooklyn? If not, where? I can't wander round as a displaced person at my age!'

'You *are* Jewish, Mrs Feldman. Perhaps you can settle in Israel under the Law of Return. It's odd for me to be telling you this, but there's a strong Russian Orthodox presence in Jerusalem. You'd find a community there. You could put down your Christian roots there as well as your Jewish ones.' If he was wrong about the law applying to Mrs Feldman he felt sure that Sam would be able to manage something, that is *if* he regained his liberty.

'Right I'll go. But to see my daughter first. I must see Lizaveta. It must be Switzerland first of all. Can you help me?' She had begun assertively but ended on a plaintive note. Without help she would never get out of the clutches of Mother Russia.

'When, Mrs Feldman? How long do you need to get ready?'

He wasn't prepared for her reply, 'Half an hour, an

hour at most. There's little here for me to pack and the sooner I'm gone the less chance of another call from the KGB.' He didn't bother to update her designation of the foe. But he was used to dealing with things as they developed. His friends near the University would be able to accommodate her and they were adept at finding a way out of the country for those at risk.

He smiled, 'Then you had better pack and we'll get your travel arrangements organised. I agree that the sooner you're away from here the better. Bring what papers you have. My friends may have to manufacture some more to get you out safely. That's not my area and I would rather keep out of it. Any illegality on my part and I would be barred from entering Russia again - and they might lock me up before throwing me out!'

While he sat and read she went to her bedroom to pack. One case would do. It was strange how little she was intending to take. Sixty years in Russia, leaving for good and one case would suffice! A couple of black dresses, a couple of bright summer ones, underwear, nightwear, towels, soap and toiletries. She went into the sitting room and collected the holy icons, her Bible and her Prayer Book, From another table she took a photograph of a young girl. She took them to the bedroom and wrapped them carefully, kissing the icons and the photograph before she did so. She made her way to the kitchen and looked around. Two hours ago she would have been looking forward to spending the rest of her life here and now she was saying goodbye to it for ever. She was surprised how little it moved her. But she was consumed with excitement at what lay ahead. She knew that there were risks, big risks if she tried to get out on forged papers. But then there was enough risk if she stayed here and continued to be favoured with the attentions of the KGB. She placed the case next to the front door of the apartment, returned to the bedroom, closed the door and prayed.

'Ready, Mr Shazar. I'm on my way to Israel or somewhere outside Russia.' A schoolgirlish excitement had taken hold of her, she hadn't felt like this for years.'

'I cannot guarantee success in this venture, Mrs Feldman but I can promise my best endeavours and my prayers.'

'That's sufficient for me, Mr Shazar. I somehow think your prayers are pretty good! Let's be on our way. After all I have a granddaughter to meet!'

Chapter 37

Thursday 27th November 1997

By the Thursday afternoon the weather had improved and Blum enjoyed the journey to Mulhouse. But this time his destination was another of its transport museums. Seemingly Friedman wanted a change from railways.

'I'm glad not to be walking around with a copy of *La Vie du Rail* this time, Mr Friedman. On Monday it was too much like a parody of what I do for a living for me to feel comfortable.'

'No need this time, we each know who the other is and you don't seem to have had any difficulty in finding me. Incidentally the name's Ben.'

'And mine's Erik.' They were relaxed together, professionals who respected one another and, more than that, they found one another interesting. Indeed they were coming to like one another.

'So we have a deal in the making, Erik?'

'Yes, I hope we can agree most of it today and then fine tune it later if necessary. Afterwards you will want to tell me why you chose this car museum for our meeting. What are we looking at?'

'The place majors in Bugattis and this is the greatest of them all, a Bugatti *Royale*. Look at the length of it! One thing's certain you or I wouldn't find it very easy to steer - we'd need a driver with the arm muscles of a lorry driver who could manage without power steering. But let's talk business first before we talk cars.'

'Fine. The first thing is that, while Bern are keen to send your friend on his way, they won't bypass the Courts. Your friend's evidence in the Lizaveta Feldman case was very public. Everyone world-wide knows the sort of things he was doing in Basel in February, they've heard from his own mouth. Those were not the kind of activities that visitors to our country can indulge in with impunity. Don't worry Ben, things are better than that might suggest. Bern don't intend to bring all the charges that they might and they will accept a plea of mitigation as to sentence - indeed they will tell the Court that Mr Kagan has co-operated fully and given considerable help to Swiss intelligence. We'll need to talk about that assistance in a moment.'

'And the sentence?'

'A substantial fine and immediate deportation.'

'As you know Sam is on a pension, he's not a wealthy man.'

'In Bern we too are on modest salaries and face the prospect of even more modest pensions. My masters are sympathetic to your friend's financial position. We have funds to pay the fine, nothing that will be traced of course. If you give me the details of an overseas bank account, say in Israel or the USA, then it will be funded appropriately. After all we will be giving Mr Kagan the cash simply to take it back through the Court, it will cost the Swiss government nothing except the cost of moving the cash around. Honour and Swiss law will be satisfied and Sam Kagan will be free to go on his way.'

'That sounds very reasonable, Erik. There are just two points. The first will strike you as odd, I know. It's this, Sam does not wish to be deported and barred from entry to your country. Believe it or not he likes your country and has enjoyed his stay in Basel this year. No, it's not that he wants to settle in Switzerland. Rather it's that, as you can probably guess, there are romantic and emotional associations for him here. If he were barred from ever coming back he would feel that he had lost a part of himself. I know it sounds strange but he loves your country.'

'I'll see what I can do on that, Ben. It might just be music in my masters' ears to hear of a Jew who loves Switzerland!'

'And the co-operation that Sam is to give to you boys?'

'Boys and girls, please! Equal opportunities for all in Switzerland. Women can now vote in all Cantons. Our half-canton of Appenzell Innerrhoden gave way on local elections as long ago as 1990! Switzerland is a veritable paradise on earth!'

'Is it really?'

'No! The women get in the way and foul up promotions but you mustn't say so! You're not wired for sound are you - I'm more scared of our Personnel Section than my Line Managers!'

'I've a recorder on me but I'll only use it when we've agreed terms. Then, if you're agreeable we can read them into the machine.'

'We'll think about that later, Ben. You have this other point on co-operation?'

'Yes. Just what are you wanting from Sam? Reverting to the world of hypotheses, he wouldn't be willing to tell you about the workings of Mossad or any other security agency he *might* have worked for.'

'We don't expect him to do that. Of course we have asked him the all relevant questions and he has declined to answer. It would be nice to have the answers but we're not at all surprised that he doesn't want to satisfy our curiosity. And in Switzerland we're too civilized to apply electrodes to sensitive parts of the body to encourage co-operation! No, what interests Bern is an incident in Basel on the afternoon of the first day of *Fasnacht*, the Monday afternoon. Two women, one Swiss and the other English, and a boy in his teens were kidnapped while they watched the carnival procession. One of the women was knocked out by a drug which someone in the crowd injected and they were taken in a bogus ambulance to a warehouse from which they were rescued almost immediately by an armed force! It's the sort of event that makes Swiss hair stand on end. To give you some more detail, the women were friends of Lizaveta Feldman - No, that's not quite right: one of them was the wife of a friend of her employer, the other was her employer's wife and the employer was Lizaveta's lover. I don't know what that makes his wife.'

'Angry I expect!' They laughed - men who had no such problematic relationships, for the moment at any rate.

'I expect you're right, Ben. Well the boy had a video camera and left it running while he was in the ambulance. It ran long enough to record the military force in action and it seems probable that one of the leaders of the rescuers was your friend, Sam. We're not wanting to bring any charges in respect of those events - they're not public knowledge and we want to keep it that way. Once again it seems possible that your friend was the White Knight riding to the rescue. What we want to do is to put the file to rest. To know more or less what was going on rather than having it as an unsolved riddle that gives my bosses sleepless nights. So will Mr Kagan be prepared to tell us something helpful about what the boy described as the beginning of World War III and calm the shattered nerves of my colleagues in Bern?'

'On that I'll need to check, Erik, but my guess is that he will be able to help in the way you want. One other very important thing - when do your people intend to get Sam into Court to punish him for his disregard for Swiss law?'

'They will move fast. Three weeks or four at the outside.'

'And can they get the verdict they are offering? What if the Court wants to do its own thing?'

'We have a panel of judges lined up that we can trust. Just whisper *security* and they will do what we ask. We could say that your friend was *continuing* to give us valuable assistance. Yes, that's a good idea. Besides the Court President is after early retirement and his co-operation might improve his pension and other benefits. So if the national interests and his personal interests coincide ... '

'You can deliver?'

'We can, Ben. That's for sure.'

'Good. I'm seeing Sam's *Advokat* for dinner this evening. He'll pass on the information to Sam and let me know his response. You can meet me on Tuesday? Good. Let's give the educational visits a miss. How about lunch at 12.30 at *Der Storch* in Colmar? Don't you drive, bring a driver and sign off from duty when we start lunch. Then you can enjoy good Alsatian food and wine and break none of your rules!'

'OK. And why this museum today, why the French National Car Museum?'

'Easy, Erik. Just a reminder of the benefits of Swiss banking. You know whose cars these once were? The Brothers Schlumpf! Ring any bells? I thought so. Well it was whistle blowing by their workers rather than bell ringing! The workers' action brought the brothers' hidden car collection to light while the business went bankrupt – buying the cars had drained it dry of funds. The brothers fled to Basel, to a penthouse suite at *Die Drei Könige*, something you couldn't do without funds. Swiss banks are always helpful! The French courts seized the collection after the workers had opened it to the public and later it was turned into the museum we've enjoyed today. Coffee? Perhaps we'll be more successful this time! I don't think we need to record our agreement, after all each of us understands the other well enough.'

'One other thing Ben. Why does the French National Car Museum major on Italian cars?'

'Because they're not Italian but French - they made them at Molsheim just west of Strasbourg. They were the local car builders and the racing cars are in French racing blue.'

'You are well informed, Ben.'

'Information is, after all, our business, Erik.'

Chapter 38

Thursday 27th November 1997

A gray November afternoon at Yasenovo in the south-western suburbs of Moscow: outside it was cold and raw, the winter was closing in. Problems with the building's antiquated heating system ensured that the inside temperature was not what it should have been. It was just another reminder to the personnel in this outpost of the SVR that things were not as they had once been back in those golden days when being in the First Chief Directorate of the KGB had struck fear into others' hearts and enabled you to carry your head high. An ailing leader and the resulting lack of direction in government was something Russia had experienced before. In the days of the USSR they had had Leonid Brezhnev and Yuri Andropov to contend with. There had been times of chaos and then things had been brought under control again. But the Yeltsin regime seemed to stagger on from day to day, week to week, year to year with assurances about the President's health followed quickly by evidence that flatly contradicted the official version. Nothing new there but things were much more public now. And the contenders for the crown were much more public and open about their ambitions. Which was fine as long as they weren't too high profile in opposing corruption and racketeering - Members of the Duma who took that line and displeased the mobsters were in dire danger of the gun. But there weren't too many Members motivated by a crusading spirit, they were much more interested in factional infighting, the struggle to get rid of Yeltsin, and in feathering their own nests.

Evgeny had got through a morning of shifting paper -

even in the computer age there was no end to the stuff and there were some things which were better committed to paper than too readily accessible to others on the computer screen. This afternoon he would be discussing his report on the Basel trial with his Section Head. The Basel operation had not done much good for Evgeny's career. Now he bitterly regretted pushing it so hard at meetings when others had wanted to bring it to an early conclusion. It had turned out to be an expensive project that had brought nothing by way of result. Indeed it had brought only trouble - trouble for those directly involved and trouble for those who had planned and organised it. First there were the obvious casualties, Vladimir shot by Lizaveta while attempting to rape her, if the woman's Court evidence were to be believed. Then Dr Gordeyev their technical expert should never have been sent abroad, terminally ill and in no fit state to travel he had just made it back to Moscow before dying. Like the others he had spent some days held captive somewhere in Switzerland by a gang of ruffians from another security service who had then released them.

The interrogation of the team on their return to Moscow had been rigorous, so much so that there had been several fatalities. None of the team would admit to having divulged anything to their foreign captors but there had been suspicion that something must have been leaked then and much earlier, which was far worse, and so the interrogation had been very thorough indeed. To Evgeny it all seemed to be a return to the ways of the past and he wondered whether there wasn't some sort of *Mafiya* involvement in the interrogation. Perhaps they had been after the drug for their own illicit trade and believed that the Basel team had sold it to someone.

Worse still, Evgeny had discovered that he himself

was under suspicion. They must have suspected him of being in league with the CIA or whoever it was that had frustrated the operation back in February. He had been questioned at length, though not with the ferocity that the others had faced. For some months he had been followed everywhere - presumably they had been looking for links with a foreign espionage service. On one level that had presented no problem as he had no such links. But it had been wearisome to suffer the constant invasion of his privacy and for a while it had cost him the affection of his new mistress, a school teacher who did not like the attention to which she was subjected and who feared for her job. Fortunately his masters had soon tired of keeping him under surveillance. Either that or they had satisfied themselves that he was clean. The relationship with the young woman had resumed, although he noticed that she was often on the lookout for someone following them. He didn't blame her, it had had the same effect on himself. They had found nothing to prove his disloyalty but he had quickly become the person blamed for the fiasco, the man who carried the can and who would probably continue to be associated with the failed venture for the remainder of his career, however long or short that might be. Now he badly needed to be associated with some successful operation and was working hard at reviewing commercial intelligence from Western Europe to pick some winners. Even one success would do - if it paid off well enough.

Once the SVR had known of Lizaveta Feldman's arrest on the charge of killing Vladimir she had been the subject of much thought and many plans had been proposed to deal with the situation. The first suggestion had been to do away with her, either in prison or on one of her monthly visits to the Court. Some had favoured placing someone in the jail to poison her, others had favoured shooting her as she left the police van at the court - she was known to spend a short time enjoying the fresh air before going into the Court building. This speculation had been ended by an interview between a Swiss ministry official and the Russian ambassador to Bern. It had been made clear that Russia would be held responsible if anything untoward happened to Lizaveta and that Russian commercial and banking relations with Switzerland would undoubtedly suffer. Swiss banking services were valued by the makers of big money in the new Russia and the Swiss message had been heeded.

One of the SVR people who worked under journalistic cover had kept them informed on the progress of her trial. The SVR's involvement had come out in open court but nothing of the purpose of the operation. They wondered, however, what she had told the Swiss security service. But the appearance of Sam Kagan had given the SVR something substantial to work on in their efforts to identify the organisation that had thwarted their plans for the Basel operation. His appearance had surprised them as much as it had the Swiss. Most of Evgeny's colleagues had decided that Mossad had been involved and not the CIA, but there were some who still suspected the CIA or some sort of joint operation.

Evgeny looked at his copy of the report and wondered whether it would be the last on the failed operation. If he had his way it would. The sooner he could put it behind him and move onto something productive the better. The door opened and Oleg came in. Exuding confidence, in his early thirties - ten years younger than Evgeny - and with abundant energy, his swift progress within the SVR was resented by the older man. He took the chair and faced Evgeny across the desk.

'I've read your report on the trial and your conclusions,

Evgeny. You'll be pleased to hear that I'm broadly in agreement with those conclusions. What's come out in court is minimal. We've got something to go on if we want to follow up Sam Kagan and find out who his employers really are. We could, if we want, keep an eye on his activities in Brooklyn and we could use some of the pork eating Jews we've been able to export to Israel to watch out for him there. Though what good it would do us I don't know. In the past there would have been no problem in liquidating him - and the woman if she's with him. But now we seem to have lost the stomach for that sort of thing. We'll keep it under review but with our present financial situation it's never likely to be high on our list of priorities, Evgeny.'

'So we review it in ... '

'In a couple of years, no earlier. Prepare a review slip and I'll sign it, Evgeny. I don't suppose you'll be sorry to see the back of it, will you?'

'Not in the least, Oleg. But when I think of all the effort and persuasion that went into keeping it going, making sure that funds and personnel were available ... and then it turns out to be a complete fiasco ... '

'Put it down to experience, that's all we can do. Now about that operation we discussed yesterday, the one at that electronics company just north of London. You said the Chinese were interested in the development going on there ... '

***

Evgeny put on his coat and fur hat. Well they had now drawn a line under the Basel operation. He hadn't had to fight to have it put to sleep. That was a relief. The papers would be off his desk for the next two years unless anything blew up. He telephoned home and left a message for his wife on the machine, 'Another urgent meeting, probably home before midnight and don't worry about food, they'll have some at the meeting. No need to wait up for me.' Evgeny wondered to himself why he got the machine so often when he 'phoned home. He suspected that he knew the answer. He looked around the room, all was tidy - the way he liked to see it when he left of an evening. Perhaps it wasn't such a bad job, not what it had once been in the days of the KGB certainly, but in the chaos of modern post-communist Russia it really wasn't at all bad. And it gave him the opportunity for evening meetings which, for reasons of security, had to remain mysterious so far as his wife was concerned. The clock showed 7.00 p.m. as he left the building. He would be with his young teacher in half an hour and she would have finished preparing the next day's lessons, ready for his "evening class" as she called it! The evening of bliss that lay ahead occupied his mind as he set off for the Metro Station.

Suddenly he found himself between two men of very heavy build who had come up unnoticed behind him.

'Evgeny Komiakov?'

It was chilling to hear his name in such circumstances. These were men who wanted him and not his money. He felt something pressing into the small of his back and guessed it was a hand gun.

'Yes that's my name. What do you want with me.' He was surprised that he had been able to manage a coherent reply.

'Just keep quiet and give no trouble. See that car ahead, you're coming with us in it. So just walk naturally and don't do anything stupid. Co-operate with us and you won't get hurt.' And he knew that, though the Basel file might have gone from his desk, the consequences of the operation were still very much with him. He had no doubt that these thugs were from the *Mafiya* and that they were probably the same lot who had interrogated the Basel team on their return. It had always seemed likely to him that there were to have been private enterprise beneficiaries from the Basel operation. He shuddered and passed out. Each of his companions took an arm and walked him to the car. The meeting they had scheduled for him that evening would definitely not be one of bliss. He would survive, provided that he told them all he knew and he satisfied their boss that he had not been part of a double-cross. The way they had treated the members of the Basel team had caused considerable trouble with their contacts in the security service and they would not be repeating it with this fellow if it could be avoided. They had needed to wait until the SVR's own people had given up following him. What to him had seemed a threat had in fact been keeping him safe for a while. But now he was on his own ...

***

Meanwhile Evgeny's wife was locking the door as she left their apartment. She had listened with satisfaction to his telephone message as he had dictated it to the machine. His late meetings were frequently on Tuesday evenings and if *he* could be out late with such regularity so could *she*. Her destination was the next door apartment block for dinner with one of Evgeny's colleagues. They had met when she worked in the registry of the KGB's First Chief Directorate some years before. Their evening was to prove considerably more pleasant than Evgeny's, for not only was Josef an excellent cook but also ...

Chapter 39

Wednesday 17th December 1997 – Sam's Judgement Day

Sam's appearance in the Bern Federal Court had little of the excitement of Elizabeth's trial in Basel. Matters were very technical and substantial parts of the hearing were held *in camera* on security grounds. There was considerable press interest but little action to make good copy.

The Judges filed into the hushed Court and took their seats. The Court President glanced down at his papers, then he looked at Sam Kagan and asked him to stand while the *Gerichtshreiber* – the Court Secretary – read the judgement:

'Mr Samuel Kagan, this Court has found you guilty on charges, under Article 179 of the Penal Code, of electronic eavesdropping on the occupants of a room at the Hotel International in Basel and of tapping telephones in that Hotel and elsewhere in the same city and, under Article 271, of unlawful activities on behalf of a foreign state. This court fines you the sum of 500,000 Swiss Francs, to be paid within 30 days. The Court President will now explain the verdict and the sentence. Please sit while he does so.'

The President waited until Sam had taken his seat and began:

'I do not need to tell you that the offences of which you have been found guilty by this Court are regarded by us in this country as very serious indeed. Ours is a country where people are still entitled to their privacy, to conduct their lives and business without the intrusion of prying eyes and ears. And that right to privacy applies equally to foreign visitors and to our own people - everyone in the Swiss Confederation is entitled to their privacy and the Courts are determined to protect that right. We feel particularly aggrieved when the perpetrator of such an offence is a visitor to our country. Ours is an agreeable country, as you have no doubt found. We welcome the many visitors who come to us on holiday or to do business. We feel let down and disappointed when our hospitality is abused by those from outside our borders.

'Were there no redeeming features in your case it would have been the duty of this Court to impose a custodial sentence. However it has been argued before us, both by your *Verteidiger*, Herr Weber, and by the *Staatsanwalt*, that there are reasons for the Court to take a more lenient view of your conduct than would otherwise have been the case. As you know part of the hearing was held *in camera* for reasons of State security and it was during that time that the *Verteidiger* and certain witnesses from the State Security Service made strong pleas for clemency on your behalf - I am alluding to this now as the Press were, of course, absent from those proceedings and an explanation of sentence is due to them and, indeed, to the people of Switzerland. I was assured by the State Security Service that your activities had in no way endangered the interests of the Swiss Confederation, no damage was done by you to either State security or to the commercial interests of the State or our people. Further, the Security Service have testified to your continuing assistance in providing information which is of considerable value to them.

'I turn now to your *Verteidiger's* plea that you only came to the notice of the authorities because you were willing to give evidence in another trial, that of Fräulein

Feldman in Basel on a charge of murder. He pointed out that your intervention resulted in that charge being reduced to one of manslaughter. Had you not appeared as a witness, he said, justice would not have been done and the Fräulein would have faced a long sentence that she did not deserve. Your conduct in saving the life of a young woman injured by a tram in the Basel *Marktplatz* was also something that was brought to our attention. That action rightly received national publicity at the time but it was right that it should have been brought to the notice of this Court and placed on the record.

'It has been an unusual experience for this Court to have the *Staatsanwalt* and the *Verteidiger* testifying unitedly to the uprightness and good character of the accused. Against this we have had to set the interests of the State, the right of visitors as well as Swiss nationals to privacy and the need to deter others from the sort of activities in which you were involved. It has not been an easy matter to arrive at a sentence that balances these factors adequately but we believe that on balance we have got it right. Mr Kagan, this court fines you the sum of 500,000 Swiss Francs, to be paid within 30 days. In default of payment you will go back to prison and this court will reconvene to consider the custodial sentence to be imposed. In the mean time your passport will be retained by the Federal Prosecutor's Office but you will be free to leave the remand prison. It is my hope and the hope of my colleagues, Mr Kagan, that it will not be necessary for us to reconvene - in other words we trust that you will make payment of the penalty in full and in good time. You are now free to leave as soon as this Court rises.

'I must now address some remarks to the Press. If any attempt is made to contact or photograph Mr Kagan or anyone connected with this case those responsible will be in contempt of Court and the same will apply to any editor who prints anything beyond what has been said in open court. You may, of course, comment on the case and the Court's sentence but you are not to go searching for further information on the persons or events concerned. In the case of Fräulein Feldman a similar order was made by the *Strafgericht* of Basel-Stadt and should be observed meticulously. I trust that I have been fully understood and that there is no dubiety about the matter. Anyone who ignores this warning can be sure of a custodial sentence.

'Finally, before the Court rises, I have to announce that this is the last case I will hear as a President of the *Strafgericht* Bern. I have decided that the time is right for me to retire from an office in which it has been an honour to serve for the last twelve years. I wish to thank my fellow *Richter* with whom I have worked over these years, the *Gerichtschreiber* who have assisted and advised and, of course, the many *Advokaten* who have given us the benefit of their learning and wisdom. Also there are the many Court officials who work together to ensure that the task of dispensing justice is carried out efficiently and with dignity - to them also I extent my thanks. The Court will rise.'

He had got his early retirement package and it had been a very generous one. That evening he was due to have dinner with an old friend who was a director of a Zurich bank and the brother of a senior official in the State Security Service. The draft contract in his pocket for two days a week as an adviser to the bank was very acceptable. Less than 40% of his present hours and a bigger income! He was pleased that Sam Kagan's case had come his way, it had been an interesting one - a good way to bow out! How satisfactory that his personal interests and those of State Security should have coincided! And, after all, there didn't seem to be any real injustice about the verdict and sentence. Everyone had got what they wanted and that didn't happen too often in Court!

***

Avraham Shazar stood near the car park at Zurich Airport and put away his mobile 'phone. He had spoken to Sylvia's office: the Judges were out and were expected back at any time to deliver their verdict and sentence on Sam. He made his way to the Arrivals area. Mrs Feldman was due in a few minutes on a flight from Warsaw. She was safely out of Russia, having taken the night train from Moskva Byelorussia to Minsk and then on into Poland. She would be tired after her journey, perhaps she would prefer to rest and then meet Lizaveta that evening or the next day. The board indicated that the LOT flight had arrived a little early and as he stood and looked over the barrier he saw her. She strode purposefully towards him, pushing the trolley with her solitary case. It struck him that there were not many people he knew who could travel so lightly in the fullest sense of the word. She had left the land where she had lived for the whole of her 60 years and this was all that she had brought out with her. The little woman exuded confidence.

They met and she took him in her arms and hugged him. 'Well I made it Mr Shazar. They couldn't keep me in!'

'You've made it all right!'

'My papers worked very well. There was some jumped up official at the border who queried something. I told him, "My daughter works for the SVR, so you'll have them to deal with if you give any trouble." He didn't need telling twice, he just waved me on! And you see, Mr Shazar, I got the title right, though I *almost* said KGB to him.'

They laughed together. 'So this is the West, show me more Mr Shazar and take me to Lizaveta and Olga.' She was clearly on a high.

He took out the mobile 'phone, 'You ought to speak to Lizaveta and let her know you're here.' She nodded so he dialed the hotel number, asked to be put through to her room and handed the 'phone to her. He moved away to give her privacy but heard her initial confusion and then a fervent, 'Lizaveta!' Good, her arrival at the hotel would be less of a shock now.

He led the way to the hire car and, as they set off for Bern, explained that she would be entering into a somewhat chaotic situation as the verdict on Sam was awaited. Much would depend on what that verdict was. It wasn't the day he would have chosen for reuniting mother and daughter but that was the way things had turned out.

He pulled into a lay-by and called Sylvia's office again. Their message was brief, 'Verdict: Guilty. Penalty: A substantial fine.' He told her the message and put the 'phone away. He was shaking. 'Mrs Feldman would you mind if I prayed?'

'You don't have to ask permission, Mr Shazar. It's not an unnatural activity and I suspect you've got more to pray about than most people. The verdict is more or less what I've been praying for myself!'

***

Elizabeth hadn't been in court that afternoon or indeed present for any of the hearing. She had been unable to face the tension and she had taken Sylvia's advice that it would be wiser not to attract the attention of the Press. She and Sylvia had taken up residence in a hotel a couple of blocks away from the Bern Court for the duration of Sam's trial. They had a suite with two bedrooms, a lounge and a small kitchen. The kitchen had been particularly useful when Elizabeth had been up during the night to feed Olga.

A secretary telephoned from the Court to let them know that the Judges were expected to return in under half an hour. They sat trying to read the magazines that Sylvia had bought from the kiosk in the hotel foyer after lunch. Not that they had eaten in the restaurant, instead they asked for light salads that had been sent up to their room. But they had merely picked at their food, more in an exercise of occupying time than anything else. An almost empty bottle of Sion Fendant stood on the coffee table. Neither of them would be driving a car that day and they had felt free to indulge.

Olga stirred and began to cry. 'She's hungry again Elizabeth, your daughter has a good appetite.'

'And good lungs, Sylvia. She makes sure I get the message.'

Elizabeth lifted the baby from the cot and kissed her. She handed her to Sylvia, 'Hold her while I get ready to satisfy her. I hope I'm not going to feed her any of the wine I've just had. She shouldn't start on that at her tender age!' She pulled up her sweater and made ready to feed the child. 'OK, Sylvia, I'm ready. Glad to have something to occupy my time I just can't concentrate to read at the moment. How long till they're back?'

"Fifteen minutes since the telephone call, sixteen at the most. I've no idea how long it will take.'

They were quiet as the baby settled down comfortably at Elizabeth's breast. Warm and content and oblivious of the tension in the room.

'What's it like being a mother, Elizabeth?'

'Very strange, Sylvia. But then the circumstances of Olga's conception and my pregnancy have been extremely strange.'

'How does Peter feel about her? You saw him at the weekend, didn't you?'

'Yes. He and Ruth were over visiting Jakob and his wife, though the real reason was for Peter to see Olga and discuss his involvement in her future. He wants to keep in touch and see her regularly and there's no problem about Olga's upkeep, he's more than generous there and it's with Ruth's blessing and encouragement. She's really a remarkable woman - I like her a lot. We get on surprisingly well. But then she knows that Peter's back for good. Poor old Peter, he's not completely over the hurt of it all yet but he's certainly a lot better. Michael's fine, of course, and that makes a great difference. I didn't take Peter from Ruth, when I came along they'd been separated for a while. It was the affect of their splitting up on Michael that turned it into such a traumatic business.'

'So he's back with Ruth and you're left holding his baby?'

'No, I don't see it like that. Peter behaved honourably. If he hadn't been such a gentleman he wouldn't have suffered the way he has. It's not as if Olga hasn't a father - I somehow feel that she's going to have two fathers in due course. She won't go short of love, I'm certain of that!'

The telephone rang and Sylvia leapt up to take the call. Elizabeth watched her, trying to read her face. To her surprise Sylvia looked confused, surely Sam wasn't going to jail. She couldn't face that. Elizabeth turned and held the handset towards her, 'It's a woman speaking in a foreign tongue and I've no idea what it's all about.'

Elizabeth took the telephone, making sure as she did so that Olga was secure at her breast, 'Hello, Elizabeth Fielder speaking.'

It was Sylvia's turn to study the other woman's face which was showing total astonishment. There was a pause as Elizabeth listened to the caller, then she began to speak quickly, fluently and emotionally in a language Sylvia guessed to be Russian. Elizabeth replaced the telephone handset and burst into tears.

'Whatever is it, Elizabeth?'

'My mother, she's here!'

'She's where?'

'At Zurich Airport. She's just flown in and she's on her way here to Bern!'

The telephone rang again and each woman looked at the other. Sylvia took the call, listened for a moment, 'Thanks. That's very good.' She replaced the handset and smiled at Elizabeth, 'Sam's been fined. They're not going to lock him up. He's free and David's bringing him here in a few minutes. What an afternoon! But tell me about your mother, didn't you know she was coming?'

'You remember the message you passed on from Sam to say he was trying to get in touch. Well I hadn't heard anything more and I assumed she was unable to get out. I'm absolutely shattered, Sylvia. Absolutely shattered.' She looked down at Olga, smiled as she moved her to the other breast, and whispered, 'Olga dearest, your grandmother is on her way.' Tears ran down her cheeks and she wiped them away with the back of her hand. 'I wasn't really sure how I felt about my mother, now I know, Sylvia. It's the most wonderful thing that she's coming here. And Sam, he's free! Why do we cry when we're happy?'

Sylvia took her hand and there were tears in her eyes as she said, 'Elizabeth it's all come right. It's come right for all of us at last!'

***

Sylvia and David were waiting for Avraham Shazar and Mrs Feldman in the lobby of the hotel. Sylvia glowed with happiness. The two trials were over and the results were far better than she could have reasonably hoped for. Her hand seemed weighed down by the engagement ring that David had given her that afternoon. She made a call from reception to let Elizabeth and Sam know that they were on their way and then showed them up to the suite on the first floor. She knocked and opened the door. Elizabeth and Sam were standing on the far side of the room. Mrs Feldman halted in the doorway, suddenly overcome. There was a moment's silence and then:

'Lizaveta!'

'*Mamochka*!'

They met in the middle of the room and threw their arms around one another. The quietness was broken by a child's cry.

'Lizaveta! You have made me a grandmother!'

David indicated with a nod of his head to Sam that they ought to leave Olga, Lizaveta and her mother together for a while. With reluctance Sam complied, introductions could come later. In books everything was neatly organised: real life was different and untidy! Besides he had still to congratulate Sylvia and David and he needed to thank Avraham for the part he had played.

Avraham was intent on speaking to Sam in any case, 'I have a surprise for you Sam Kagan.'

'What sort of surprise. Pleasant?'

'I definitely think so. Lizaveta's maternal grandmother was Jewish - and her husband too for that matter. Which of course makes Lizaveta ... '

'Jewish.' It was David who had replied, Sam had been too surprised to speak. David continued, 'So it won't be too difficult for you to be both a good *Cohen* and a good human being, Sam!'

Avraham smiled, knowing the different outlooks of the twin brothers he could guess what lay behind those comments. Things still weren't entirely tidy from the *halakhic* point of view but they could have been far worse. If Sam married Lizaveta their children would be Jewish: continuity was all important, it was one way of asserting a personal triumph over their would-be exterminators in this and earlier centuries. And how many centuries of persecution, pogrom and *Shoah* there had been! The descendants of Amalek had never ceased to be active in their malice.

David took charge, 'Coffee now, Champagne later! We'll have to treat this as though it were Purim!' His thoughts too had been turning to the continuity of his people - though he would want to assert personally that having a Jewish *father* was sufficient. The annual remembrance of deliverance through Mordechai and Queen Esther was a festival that had always appealed to him. For children it was a time of dressing up and fun: for adults the injunction of the sages to drink until you were tipsy was a good one, on occasion! And it amused him that the story was recorded in a Biblical book that made no reference whatsoever to the Deity.

Chapter 40

Saturday 7th February 1998 (being the 11th Sh'vat 5758), Basel

Sam and Elizabeth/Lizaveta had spent the two months since Sam's release in a quiet courtship. They had begun believing that their affection was strong enough to sustain a good marriage. After a few weeks they had no doubts on the matter whatsoever. It had been a chaste affair as they had needed to be sure that the attraction wasn't simply physical, though they knew full well that it was certainly that: they had been concerned to be sure that they were suited to one another in a way that would endure. After that first month they had begun organising their wedding.

***

The civil ceremony had taken place in Basel a few days before and now it was time for what they regarded as the real wedding, the religious celebrations.

A light breeze had sprung up overnight clearing the sky of low cloud so Saturday dawned as a day of spring promise, blue skies and warm sunshine. David was to collect Elizabeth and Sylvia and take them to the prison before going on to the Basel Synagogue. It was the accepted tradition for the bride not to be at the synagogue on the Sabbath before her wedding. Properly, Elizabeth was supposed to be at home with her friends but she would be spending the morning at the *Untersuchungsgefängnis*, the remand prison, or *Waaghof* as it was also known. For so much of the last year it had been her "home". Some of the women she had been with had asked that she visit them that morning with little Olga who was now over six months old and not so very little. Sam, Jakob Gold and Avraham Shazar would walk from Allschwil to the synagogue. Paula Gold was given the task of taking Mrs Feldman to the synagogue by car.

In one way Mrs Feldman found being in the synagogue gallery, separated from the men below, a strange experience. But as she was used to Orthodox Church services where the clergy were for a large part of the service out of sight in the sanctuary behind the screen - the *ikonostasis* - the separation of the participants in a place of worship did not seem so very peculiar. She had abandoned her black dresses for a smart navy and cream two piece outfit that she and Elizabeth had chosen a few days earlier in Globus. It was accompanied by a navy blue broad brimmed straw hat, she looked and felt every inch the mother of the bride. She felt it a pity that Lizaveta – she had no wish to change her daughter's name from the one she had always used - wasn't there to be seen by the other women. The Hebrew language was not the problem she had expected as her memories from childhood were reviving. The melodies chanted by the Cantor were not that different from those of Russian Orthodoxy, so she let the sound, with its feel of another place and another time, drift with the ancient words into her sub-conscious. She was surprised to find herself more at home with the service than the sermon in German, where she picked up a word here and there, as she had with the prayer for the Swiss President.

The Synagogue Warden called up Samuel ben Ya'akov and David ben Ya'akov to the Torah reading. To Sam's amusement David found himself being asked to which charities he would make contributions. Sam prompted him and he found that he was contributing to a rabbis' pension fund and a fund for poor brides! They would have to send the money by post, they weren't allowed to pay it there and then on the Sabbath and no one was allowed to break the Sabbath by making a written record of the promise.

Avraham had met with the synagogue's Rabbi a few days before and persuaded him to follow a mediaeval Ashkenazi custom of having a portion from the Prophet Isaiah chanted as the *haftarah* portion in honour of the groom:

> "I will greatly rejoice in the Lord, my soul shall be joyful in my God; for He hath clothed me with the garments of salvation, He hath covered me with the robe of righteousness, as a bridegroom decketh as a priest and as a bride adorneth herself with her jewels.
> "For as the earth bringeth forth her bud, and as the garden causeth the things that are sown in it to spring forth; so the Lord God will cause righteousness and praise to spring forth before all the nations."

The reference to a priestly bridegroom was very appropriate for the marriage of a *Cohen* and that argument carried the day with the synagogue's rabbi.

Paula Gold had found the passage for Mrs Feldman in her Russian Bible so she would feel even more of a participant. She also enjoyed her involvement with the other women in pelting Sam from the gallery with nuts and raisins as symbols of prosperity. The things these Jews did! And then she remembered that she was one, smiled to herself and threw the nuts and raisins with renewed energy.

It had not escaped Sam that a few verses earlier in the Prophecy were the words:

> " .... to proclaim liberty to the captives and the opening of the prison to them that are bound."

He now knew from personal experience what it was to suffer captivity and imprisonment, though it had not lasted for very long, and he rejoiced in his liberty. He also rejoiced that Elizabeth had gone to the *Untersuchungsgefängnis* that morning to be with women who had been her prison companions. He knew that for her imprisonment had been a defining experience. She had learnt a lot about herself while she had been there and discovered gold in the lives of women for whom she would once would have had little time. Learning about their circumstances and backgrounds had opened her eyes. She had told him that wherever they settled down she would want to have the opportunity of working with women prisoners. He was glad that she felt called in this way - she was warm hearted and hard headed, a combination that would make her useful and effective in such a rôle.

After the service they met for a simple *kiddush*, the sharing of wine and a cake, to which the congregation was invited, before making their separate ways back to the Golds' house in Allschwil. Strangers came up to Mrs Feldman and congratulated her. In faltering German and managing to hold back tears of happiness she thanked them in return.

***

David had to wait for a while at the *Waaghof* before

Elizabeth and Sylvia, together with Olga in her carry-cot, appeared at the entrance. The *Direktor* was with them. He knew Sylvia as a regular visitor to his charges and was introduced to David as her fiancé. He thanked Elizabeth and asked, 'May I kiss the bride?'

Sylvia was quick with her reply, 'Only in the presence of her *Advokat, Herr Direktor!'*

Elizabeth got her kiss, as did Sylvia, and they left with David. Laughter had driven away the tears that Elizabeth had been fighting back. It had been an emotional visit. She had been able to speak with one of her former companions who had once been in danger of suicide but was now much improved. The girls had given her a number of small wedding presents including a painting that one of them had done of a rural scene with an orchard in blossom and mountains in the background. Another of the girls, a drug addict, had framed it beautifully. It wasn't easy being able to walk out of the door and know that they remained behind bars. But she knew it was necessary to hold them there, her concern was that they should be properly helped and turned round while they were inside and stay out once they had served time.

***

Back in Allschwil at the Golds' home an elaborate *kiddush* was ready. Paula Gold and the other women had been busy preparing it the previous day. There was a sense of thankfulness and celebration as Jakob said the benediction over the wine:

> 'Blessed are You O Lord, King of the Universe, Creator of the fruit of the vine.'

A while later the telephone rang and David took the call. He reported back, 'It's Peter and Ruth Lewis. They're free to come to the wedding tomorrow after all.'

Elizabeth and Sam exchanged looks. She nodded and Sam replied, 'Tell them that we are delighted and honoured. We'll find somewhere for them to stay, that's no problem. Ask them how long they'll be over here, David.' It was good that they were coming, it was part of the healing process.

***

Sunday 8th February 1998 (being the 12th of Sh'vat 5758) at Frutigen in the Berner Oberland

Sunday's weather was as warm as it had been the previous day. David had taken charge of the arrangements and persuaded Sam and Elizabeth that a small synagogue near the mountains would be better for them than the Basel Synagogue. It was about two hours away and Elizabeth and her mother had been taken by Sylvia and David to a nearby hotel late the previous afternoon. A friend of Sylvia had gone as well to look after Olga. David was in charge of all the paperwork and had collected from Elizabeth the certificate from her visit to the *mikvah* - the ritual bath - at the Basel Synagogue on the Thursday evening. He'd checked that it was all in order and been assured that this was fine, it was not more than four days before the wedding.

Elizabeth's dress in a light gold satin fabric had been made by Paula Gold's dressmaker. When she first saw it tears had come into Mrs Feldman's eyes, 'Lizaveta, I thought I would never see you again, let alone see you as a bride adorned for her wedding. You have made me a grandmother and the mother of the bride - perhaps not the best order for those events but that in no way diminishes my joy and my pride in you.' At the hotel Sylvia took charge of making sure that Elizabeth and her mother would be ready for the ceremony in good time. She had got them back from the hair salon by ten and by eleven they were dressed and ready to go. Fine, the car would be there in fifteen minutes. She had been careful not to have them killing time for too long. As they sat in the car waiting to leave the hotel Elizabeth whispered to her mother, '*Mamochka*, do make sure you don't cross yourself in the synagogue!'

'My child, for today at any rate, I'll let my Jewishness predominate. Don't forget I'm the proud Jewish mother of a lovely Jewish bride. I know *exactly* how to behave.' They laughed and relaxed. They were closer now than they had ever been before.

At the synagogue they were led into a small vestry where Sam was waiting. Here the witnesses would sign the *Ketubah*, the marriage contract. David, who was an accomplished calligrapher had taken considerable interest in the history of such contracts and had prepared it as his contribution to the proceedings.

He had discovered during his research that in marriage contracts of the Sephardic (or Mediterranean Jews) the word 'virgin', used by the Ashkenazi, (or Eastern European Jews), was replaced by the expression "beautiful, graceful gazelle". This, he decided, dealt rather nicely with what seemed to be the one remaining problem area for his brother as a *Cohen*. Besides the phrase was a pleasantly poetic addition to a document which, despite its calligraphy and decoration, was rather prosaic. He had referred the point to Sylvia as his legal expert and she had approved, while declining to take responsibility for the forensic soundness of the document in Jewish Law.

Sam left Elizabeth in the room and was escorted by the officiating rabbi, David and the other guests into the synagogue to await his bride under the *chuppah*, the bridal canopy. Elizabeth then joined him there. Accompanied by her mother and Paula Gold, taking the place of Sam's deceased mother, as well as by Sylvia. She walked three times around Sam and then took her place on his right side. Her escorts, *Unterfeurerin*, as well as Sam's had carried lighted candles. David was best man for all practical purposes but he kept in the background making sure that all was in order. Ben, known once again as Noam, assisted.

Sam took the gold ring from his pocket and turned to address Elizabeth, 'Behold you are consecrated unto me with this ring in accord with the law of Moses and Israel.' He repeated the words in English and in rather faltering Russian for the benefit of Mrs Feldman. Elizabeth smiled and he placed the ring on the index finger of her right hand.

The officiating rabbi pronounced the blessing over a cup of wine:

'Blessed are You O Lord, King of the Universe, Creator of the fruit of the vine.'

Sam translated it into English and Russian and then he and Elizabeth drank from the cup.

The rabbi continued with another blessing.

The marriage contract was handed by David to Rabbi Avraham Shazar, as a guest of honour, and read by him to the assembly. When he had finished he handed the document to Lizaveta – for that was how she was shown in the contract - who passed it, temporarily, to her mother.

The benediction was said over another cup of wine and a further six benedictions were recited by various guests, concluding with Avraham's richly musical declamation of the final benediction:

> 'Blessed are you O Lord, King of the Universe, Who has created rejoicing and happiness, groom and bride, joy and song, delight and pleasure, love and brotherhood, peace and companionship. Soon, O Lord our God, may there be heard in the cities of Judah and in the streets of Jerusalem the voice of joy and happiness, the voice of groom and bride, the voice of grooms' and brides' jubilation from their *chuppah* and youths from the feast of their singing; blessed are You O Lord, who makes happy a groom with a bride and a bride with a groom.'

He had made one or two additions, giving thanks for the bride's joy as well as the joy of the groom.

Sam smashed a wine glass wrapped in a napkin under his foot. He broke it in remembrance of the ancient destruction of Jerusalem and the Temple; the world beyond was still violent and vengeful. Joy was often a frail and transitory thing in the face of the unexpected events of life. "If I forget you, O Jerusalem ... ." Friends had sought to persuade Sam that Jerusalem was where the wedding should have taken place. He had wondered but finally come to accept the rightness of Switzerland, to be wed in this place with the mountains nearby somehow sanctified all that had happened to him and Elizabeth since they had first come to the country in the February of the previous year.

Cries of *'Mazel tov!'* - 'Good luck!' - marked the termination of the service, Mrs Feldman being the most vocal of the company. Photographs outside the synagogue followed, the officiating Rabbi having been persuaded by Avraham Shazar to face a camera for the first time in his life. And then it was back to the hotel for the wedding breakfast with Noam in the rôle of singer and entertainer.

***

'Well, Mrs Feldman, you've heard a lot of Hebrew in the last two days!'

'It has brought back memories and created new ones. The events of the last few months will never leave me Mr Shazar. Your coming to my apartment was a miracle. I wonder what the KGB thought about me disappearing. I expect some of them were glad, it can't be much pleasure to have to keep going and upsetting an old woman as part of your job. I was afraid of them, I won't deny that, but at the same time I felt a little sorry for them - not the sort of work for a grown man, is it?'

'But there have always been those willing to do it. My information is that they've given up on your daughter and yourself and found others to trouble. And where next for you?'

'Israel with Lizaveta and Sam, though it won't be under the Law of Return - I'm a Christian and I'm not prepared to change. But Sam has some way of getting me in and letting me stay there and I'm happy with that.'

***

'So it's back to Israel with your new bride is it, Sam?'

'Yes, Ruth. Once there we've got to decide on what I - or I should say we - will do for a living. I'd like to do something that actively involved Elizabeth. She's not the sort of woman to be forever sitting at home looking after children, though she'll enjoy that some of the time, of course. Have you seen her with Olga? Sorry, perhaps I shouldn't have mentioned the little one.'

'Why ever not, Sam? I'm adult enough to live with that and, from the evidence of today's events, so are you. I've told Peter that he must continue to take an active interest in Olga both financially and in person but he didn't really need telling. I hope that won't cause you difficulty, Sam. The ties of paternity are not to be discarded lightly.'

'Elizabeth and I have thought about it, Ruth, and we agree with you. We agree with you wholeheartedly. It is good and right that Peter should both undertake his responsibilities for Olga and enjoy the privileges of being her father. Olga will be told who Peter is, we've no wish to hide the truth from her or take his fatherhood from him. I've always had a liking for Peter, he's what I would call your decent, honourable Englishman. I'm sorry for all he's gone through. How's he now?'

'Much improved, Sam. Pretty well completely back to normal and running the business with real energy. Though sometimes I catch him with a look on his face that's, how can I describe it? ... Wistful perhaps. It's as though he was standing at a station having just missed the last train and watching it roll out of the platform. I remember Elizabeth and know what he is missing. But then he shows real affection towards me and Michael. He knows there is no other course for him. So he's, perhaps, 95% happy and 5% sad - and that, in all truth, isn't a bad balance, is it?'

'I'm glad, Ruth, really glad for you all. And how about you?'

'I've had to think seriously about what I did to contribute to all that happened. I believe I'm a better wife and mother now. No lesson ought to be wasted and I don't think this one has been wasted on any of us. But let me congratulate you on your lovely bride. Elizabeth looked ravishing today. She always looks wonderful but today - well she was simply radiant. And it was lovely to see her mother. Mrs Feldman's certainly had some surprises lately and she's got some adapting to do. Still now she's found her daughter again she's got a lot to look forward to. She's pure delight when she's with little Olga!'

'She's forgiven Elizabeth everything on account of Olga. I've never seen anyone so taken with being a grandmother.'

'I wonder if a suggestion about your future would be in order, Sam? I don't want to intrude but something came to me the other day.'

'I'd be delighted to hear what you are thinking, Ruth.'

'You have an interesting mix of qualifications and experience, Sam. You're a computer whiz and you've lived on a kibbutz and still have links with it?'

'Indeed, if my roots are anywhere now it's there in the Upper Galilee. It's the place of my childhood. It's there that my mother and father are buried. A place of many memories, the majority good with a few sad ones - the deaths of my parents, a gentle death for my mother but a violent one for my father. You don't know the story but he was killed by a *Hezbollah* rocket attack from over the border in the Lebanon. Perhaps it should have put me off the Northern Galilee and made me want to move somewhere safer but then nowhere is 100% safe whether in Israel or anywhere else for that matter. So if you ask me where's home I have to say *Kibbutz Kfar Jakob.*'

'And that's no great distance from the Golan Heights?'

'None. The Golan runs along the eastern side of the Galilee.'

'What do you know of its vineyards and winery?'

'I know they exist and they have a good reputation in Israel. How do you rate them?'

'I have to be honest and say that until recently Israeli wine was, in general, pretty awful stuff. Sweet and lacking in any sort of character. OK for ceremonial, no disrespect intended, but not for drinking with any real enjoyment. But now all of a sudden things have improved radically. The Golan Winery is producing wine that's a pleasure to drink - I handle some of it and there's a respectable market in England. Jewish customers, of course, some of whom who will buy anything from Israel, but there are also discerning wine drinkers who recognise a good vintage when they meet one and have no links with Israel. On the Golan they use decent grape types and the most modern wine making methods, rather like the Californian wineries. You could do worse than think about growing grapes and turning them into wine. I've some surplus funds I'd be willing to invest, so if, when you've been back in the Galilee for a while and you've both had time to reflect on it, you want to take the idea further get in touch. After all Peter will be wanting to visit Olga and I could always fly out with him and look at the Galilee and the Golan Heights and talk it through.'

'We'll take it on board, Ruth. Thanks for the idea. It certainly won't be dismissed out of hand. In fact I was discussing that very idea on my last visit to the kibbutz.'

'And, by the way Sam, it does a wine dealer good to hear the Almighty being blessed so frequently for the fruit of the vine!'

***

'And how are you Peter. I really want to know. I'm sorry for all the hurt.'

'Well nigh recovered from the experience, Lizaveta.'

'Why not Elizabeth?'

'Because it underlines the situation as it is. It was as Lizaveta that you married. In a sense Elizabeth died with your marriage and so far as I am concerned that's as it should be. Though when I see Olga I'll always think of Elizabeth. That way I'll tread on no one's toes!'

'You promise you'll come to see Olga regularly? You must! Sam and I have talked this over and we both want you to stay in touch with her and with us. Olga will not be kept in the dark about who her father really is and we want you to enjoy her and for her to enjoy you.'

'That's very generous, Eliza ... veta. Though I don't want to get in the way and cause embarrassment for anyone ... '

'Don't be silly Peter you won't do that.'

And the piano? Where's that to go?'

'We're going to live in the Upper Galilee, up on the northern edge of Israel. If you could arrange for it to be shipped out there ... we'll pay for the transport, of course.'

'Fine, Elizabeth – I think I'm going to stick with your original name, well original to me that is – but *I'll* be paying the freight. The piano itself was a gift just over a year ago and sending it to your new home will be our wedding present from Ruth and myself. It will be good to have you and Olga playing it.'

'Thank you Peter for being your kind, generous self as ever. Now come and meet my mother. She's the leader of Olga's fan club – your daughter's fan club!'

***

She lay awake. She could just make out the wedding gown draped over the sofa on the other side of the bedroom. Sam had placed it there when her had unzipped her from it at the end of the evening. Beside it lay the lingerie that she had slipped off so hurriedly and the night gown she hadn't needed. All was quiet, her mother had insisted on looking after Olga on the wedding night. She had told Elizabeth, 'You will need your rest after a strenuous day.' But both had known that Mrs Feldman had meant something totally different.

She was happy and totally relaxed. She felt deeply grateful. Sam lay next to her breathing quietly. She was so glad they had decided on a chaste courtship. Waiting had increased the delight of their intimacy. Her thoughts went back to that February Sunday they had spent together in the Alps almost a year ago - how that memory had sustained her, even over the months when there had seemed to be no hope of ever seeing Sam again. Yet they had been months when Sam's mind had been continually exercised by the problem of how to get her out of custody. He had been there in Basel all the time watching over her like some unseen guardian angel.

Her guardian angel stirred, 'Lie still Elizabeth, let the seed do its work. I'm longing for you to have my child - our child.'

'A girl or a boy?'

'A child, I'm not worried which.'

'And you said that the Sages and King Solomon himself approve of our delight in each other?'

'Indeed, Elizabeth, the Song of Songs delights in the physical aspects of lovemaking.' And he began his recitation:

' "Let him kiss me with the kisses of his mouth: for thy love is better than wine."

"Until the day break, and the shadows flee away, turn my beloved, be like a gazelle." '

'And that's what the marriage contract calls me Sam. "a beautiful graceful gazelle," *your* gazelle!'

' "Thy two breasts are like two young roes that are twins, that feed among the lilies." '

Elizabeth laughed, 'I don't know about that - I'll have to think about it!'

He continued his recitation:

' "Many waters cannot quench love, neither can the floods drown it." '

'I like that Sam, we've come through so much to bliss and tranquility. If only time would stand still.'

'You can be sure it won't, we must always move on. Even experiences like these would become stale in time, we have to change and grow together. And that we will do! Part of the secret lies with something else from King Solomon, the bride says:

"This is my beloved and this is my friend."

Friendship between lovers keeps them lovers, Elizabeth - at any rate if they cease to be friends they're likely to cease to be lovers.'

'We'll never cease to be friends and lovers, Sam! We won't! Our courtship has put us on the right track.'

'When you've finished in the bathroom, Elizabeth, put on the night gown I bought you. I don't think we have energy left for anything other than sleep tonight. No husband could be more delighted and satisfied, deeply, deeply satisfied, than Sam Kagan.'

'And no bride could have experienced greater delight than Elizabeth Kagan has shared tonight with Sam Kagan. I love you Sam, I love you with all my being.'

***

They strolled around the hotel garden. The sun had yet to break through the clouds but the morning carried with it the promise of a fine day. The mountain air was crisp and they felt the wonder and excitement of life. Elizabeth had just been to her mother's room to see little Olga. Mrs Feldman was greatly enjoying her rôle as grandmother, doubly so as she could feel that she was helping and not taking Olga away from Lizaveta.

'You've brought me into a whole new world, Sam. Tradition isn't something I've come into contact with before. It reminds you of your roots - us of *our* roots - doesn't it?'

'Strange, you see the virtues and I see the dangers. I fear an empty repetition that is elevated into something essential. Nevertheless it's true, there's a reminder of our roots, a sense of being anchored to something that has lasted and will continue. Sometimes what I try to do is to see what lies behind a practice and apply the principle. In that way the old rule is filled with new life.'

'How about an example of what you mean, Sam. Your pupil needs some help in seeing what you're after!'

'That's no problem. There's a tradition that a bride or groom whose parent has died goes to their grave before the wedding to "*invite*" them to the wedding. Now I visit my parents' graves when I'm in Israel, it's the pious act of a grateful son. And that's the kernel of the pre-wedding practice - gratitude. I'm always profoundly grateful to my parents, for the people they were and for all that they taught me and did for me. My memories are very rich and happy ones. Not that we were ever very rich if you measure it in terms of dollars or *shekelim*, but you can be rich that way and poor emotionally and relationally. The whole of my childhood, whether we were in Brooklyn or the Galilee was a rich, enduring experience. So how did I invite them to our wedding, Elizabeth? Well, they have been in my mind these last few days and that's made me vow that, as a husband and parent I will follow the example they set. So not only were my parents invited to our wedding they were also invited to continue to give direction to life, not in a restrictive way but by giving the principles and showing me how to live a richly satisfying life. Sorry, end of sermon!'

'No need to be sorry Sam. I'm going to enjoy learning from you. I think we're going to have quite a few seminars before I'm properly instructed. Tell me what are your earliest memories of family life?'

'Of my mother lighting the Sabbath candles and of *Pesah* - Passover - probably because it was something done in the home with regularity, the one weekly and the other annually. *Pesah* tells the dramatic story of our people's escape from Egypt in the Exodus, our escape from captivity. For Israel it was a defining event.'

'And for us Sam, we've both emerged from captivity,

We've had our own Exodus. What shall I call it? How about the Basel Exodus?'

'As long as that doesn't involve the Basel *Staatsanwalt* pursuing us in his chariots to the banks of the Rhein! And do you know, Elizabeth, that was the password - *The Basel Exodus* - that Ben used when he negotiated my sentence with Erik Blum!'

'Was it indeed. But going back to the traditions, Sam. You must teach me the prayers for lighting the Shabbat candles. In fact you'll have to teach me Hebrew.'

'What sort of Hebrew, Elizabeth. Modern or Biblical Hebrew?'

'All sorts, Sam. I'm going have to be able to speak to people when we settle down in Israel and I want to be able to understand Judaism and share your life and beliefs to the full. By the way, talking of life in Israel, you mentioned that Ruth Lewis had an idea - something about vineyards and the Golan Heights. Tell me more and tell me what you think of the idea. And don't forget I want to find time to help rehabilitate prisoners.'

'To start with Elizabeth, it won't be just my decision. We'll decide together what we will be doing. You've already said that you're keen to go to Israel and I'm delighted with that. Now Ruth was saying ... '

Chapter 41

Monday 2nd March 1998

Sylvia Brunner reviewed her appointments for the week. It had every appearance of being a very ordinary one with no court hearings but a variety of meetings with familiar clients dealing with ongoing and non-contentious matters. Fritz Ellinger was due in at 10 o'clock which meant that her stocks of *Karlovarska Becherovka* - which had been severely depleted by Sam - would be replenished.

It had been a good weekend away at the chalet in Grindelwald with David. Being out in the snows had been invigorating and had brought added enjoyment to the warmth and hubbub of restaurants where they had warmed up with *Gulaschsuppe* and *Glühwein*. She remembered her time in the chalet with Sam in the summer and his patient work to ween her off the fictitious memories that were then consuming her. In a way it had felt strange, but in no way unpleasant, to have the other twin as her companion and as a rather more intimate one.

The weekend had been a celebration of all that had happened to them both in the past year and in particular of David's appointment to an academic post at the University of Basel. Alternating weekends between Basel and Paris had been fun but it would be good to be together all the time. She still wondered about David's encounter with a young post-graduate student at the Psychology Faculty who had appeared to recognise him, made some remark about lingerie and then made off in a hurry to cover her embarrassment with a comment that she thought he'd shaved off his beard. What, she wondered, had Sam Kagan been up to at the University?

She glanced up at the notice board with a couple of

postcards on display. One from Sam and Elizabeth, had a view of Mount Hermon clad in snow, the other, from Mrs Feldman had a view of Jerusalem from the Mount of Olives. Evidently they were all settling into their new homes.

There was a knock on the door and her secretary came in. 'There was a call about half an hour ago from Herr Guillaume, I've got the details here for you.' She handed the note to Sylvia.

'I didn't expect to hear from him of all people, Anna. It's surely not an invitation to lunch or dinner'

'Read it - he needs to see you urgently at the Public Prosecutor's Office.'

Sylvia began to read and stopped amazed, 'On a rape charge! They've arrested him! Accused of attempting to rape an off duty police woman. I know his reputation but surely he's not that stupid.'

'Seems that he is.'

Suddenly she laughed, 'So the wolf picked on another Red Riding Hood with a pistol in her knickers. Stupid wolf!'

'Wolf? Red Riding Hood? Whatever do you mean Fräulein Sylvia?'

'Ask me tomorrow and I'll tell you, I've got to get ready for Dr Ellinger at ten.' She thought for a moment, 'Should I take it? Should I defend *him*? Herr Guillaume, a man with a reputation like his and definitely not my favourite Prosecutor. I wonder, though, whether someone set him up - a police woman seems too much of a coincidence. OK even people like him deserve justice, I'll take it. Anna would you call my apartment and keep ringing until David replies. Then tell him to get to the airport himself and wait for me there at 2.30. Tell him that I've got to see a

Prosecutor who's been transferred from the staff of the *Kriminal Kommissariat* to residence in the *Waaghof* on the other side of the building. Oh yes, but first of all call Guillaume's old employers, tell them I'm representing him and make sure that he's being kept on his own. It could be unpleasant if someone he'd put inside before got too near to him!'

She took Dr Ellinger's file from the cabinet and placed it on the desk unopened. For a moment she sat there looking through the window at the bare winter trees. Three weeks, then she and David would be in Eilat for a lazy week in the sun. No more therapy, he had done the trick and she had never felt so good, so satisfied with life, so fulfilled. Their plans to marry in Basel in two months time had more than a little to do with her contentment. And she enjoyed her work, no lack of interesting cases. She knew she had done a good job defending Elizabeth and others would have taken note. More work would come in as a result and it was likely to be interesting work. The defence of the Wolf from the *Kriminal Kommissariat* was guaranteed to attract attention! Though what Women Against Rape would think was another matter!

She picked up the telephone and spoke to Anna. 'Get Guillaume's wife if you can. I need a word with her. The poor woman's probably scared out of her wits.' And she added to herself, 'Or relieved that they've got him behind bars at last!'

Life certainly had its ups and downs and she was grateful that the downs were behind her and she prayed that things would continue like that.

***

And in West Hampstead, London, a Steinway grand piano was beginning its long journey to Israel's Upper Galilee.

Glossary

These are not authoritative definitions but a guide to the meaning of various terms.

A. Swiss Legal Terms

Advokat – lawyer appearing in court for the prosecution or defence, English equivalent term is counsel.

Gerichtsaal – courtroom.

Gerichtschreiber – court secretary, clerk of the court.

Hoftrichter – remand judge.

Richter – judge or magistrate.

Strafgericht - criminal court.

Staatsanwald – public prosecutor.

Statthalter - Court Vice-President.

Untersuchungsgefängsnis Basel-Stadt – Basel remand prison, also known as the *Waaghof*.

Verteidiger – defence lawyer.

B. Jewish Terms

Aliyah – immigration of Jews into the land of Israel.

Cabalistic – a mystical understanding of the Jewish scriptures.

Chabad-Lubavitch – One of the most dynamic Chassidic groups with headquarters in Brooklyn, New York. Founded 250 years ago it was based for many years in a Russian town which gave it the name Lubavitch, "the city of brotherly love". Its last Rebbe died in 1994 and there has been no successor though the group continues to be very active.

Chassidism – a Jewish religious movement, divided into numerous separate groups There are at least 30 larger groups. It was founded in 18th-century Eastern Europe by Rabbi Israel Baal Shem Tov as a reaction against what was perceived by some as excessively legalistic Judaism. It may be said to emphasise a felt faith rather than just a cerebral one.

Cohen - (or *Kohen*), the Hebrew word for priest, required to be of direct patrilineal descent from Aaron, the name has a vast number of variants. Being a Cohen brings privileges and responsibilities. Problematic for Sam is the prohibition of a Cohen from marrying a woman who has had intercourse with a non-Jew. That Elizabeth/Lizaveta is Jewish does not remove every problem!

Halakha – Jewish law.

Haredi - literally one who trembles" at the word of God. The word connotes an awe-inspired fear and anxiety to perform the will of God. It is used to describe staunchly Orthodox Jews in place of the term "ultra-Orthodox", which some view as inaccurate or offensive, it being seen as a derogatory term suggesting extremism. Suggested alternatives include "fervently Orthodox" and "strictly Orthodox".

Kaddish – the Jewish mourner's prayer which praises, magnifies and sanctifies the name of God.

Kibbutz - an economically and socially independent society founded on principles of communal ownership of property, social justice, and equality, often (though not always) agricultural.

Kippah – Jewish scullcap, also known as a *yarmulka.*

Mitzvah – one of the 613 commandments in the Torah and also having a secondary meaning of a moral deed performed as a religious duty, an act of human kindness.

Rebbe – the leader of a Chassidic group, a sort of super-rabbi.

Shabbat – Sabbath, the Jewish day of rest and worship.

Shalom – Hebrew for peace, harmony, wholeness, prosperity, welfare and tranquility. Commonly used to say both hello and goodbye.

Shabbat shalom – the Sabbath greeting.

Shoah – (the catastrophe), the preferred Jewish term for the *Holocaust*.

Shtetl – a small Jewish town or village in Eastern Europe.

Shulchan Aruch – the code of Jewish law, written in 1563 by Yosef Karo at Safed in the Upper Galilee and published in 1565 in Venice.

Torah – the first five books (books of Moses) of the *Tanakh (*Hebrew Bible).

C. Other Terms

Frauenspital – women's hospital

Kantonsspital – Canton's Hospital (approximately County Hospital and since June 2004 the *Universitätsspital* – Basel's University Hospital).

The Institute - "The Institute for Intelligence and Special Operations" or Mossad is Israel's national intelligence agency.

And what next?

And so Sam and Elizabeth return to the Upper Galilee to begin life together on Kibbutz Kfar Jakob. Sam's Mossad career is behind him ... that is until a message comes from Captain Erik Blum in Bern warning Mossad that transactions through a private bank in Basel indicate an impending terrorist attack on Israel and Blum will only deal with Sam Kagan.

The story continues in The Basel Account, the third part of The Basel Trilogy, due out in late 2016.

About the Author

Born 21 August 1939, Plymouth, Devon, UK. Secondary education at Plymouth College.

Working life with HM Customs and Excise (on purchase tax in north and west London and at a distillery in Dagenham) and then with the Inland Revenue, including five years at the Special Investigations Section, dealing with tax avoidance and also tax evasion cases, followed by spells as a Senior Inspector in charge of tax offices in Willesden (north-west London), Dalston (north-east London) and finally Paignton, Devon.

From 1960 to 1962 did National Service in the RAF, servicing V-bomber navigation and bombing radar equipment, mainly at Marham, Norfolk.

Married to Jennifer with a son (in Australia) and a daughter (in the UK) and five very sporty grandsons.

Interests: politics, music, history, theology (Christian and Jewish), travel, railways and photography (which two often combine).

Published in 2015 *The Basel Formula (Part 1 of The Basel Trilogy) and in 2016 The Basel Exodus (Part 2).* Both are available from Amazon on Kindle and in Paperback.

Due for publication later in 2016: Part 3, *The Basel Account.*

Also in the pipeline, an unconnected novel: *O Château, O*

Seasons!

Apart from Moscow he has visited all the locations featured in these novels.

His book of railway photographs, *Plymouth Steam 1954 to 1963* was published in 1984 and he has contributed photographs to several railway magazines.

55314252R00280

Made in the USA
Charleston, SC
25 April 2016